THE COLLECTED WORKS OF W. B. YEATS
Richard J. Finneran and George Mills Harper
General Editors

VOLUME I: *The Poems,*
ed. Richard J. Finneran

VOLUME II: *The Plays,*
ed. David R. Clark

VOLUME III: *Autobiographies,*
ed. Douglas Archibald, J. Fraser Cocks III, and Gretchen L. Schwenker

VOLUME IV: *Early Essays,*
ed. Warwick Gould

VOLUME V: *Later Essays,*
ed. William H. O'Donnell and Elizabeth Bergmann Loizeaux

VOLUME VI: *Prefaces and Introductions,*
ed. William H. O'Donnell

VOLUME VII: *Letters to the New Island,*
ed. George Bornstein and Hugh Witemeyer

VOLUME VIII: *The Irish Dramatic Movement,*
ed. Mary FitzGerald

VOLUME IX: *Early Articles and Reviews,*
ed. John P. Frayne

VOLUME X: *Later Articles and Reviews,*
ed. Colton Johnson

VOLUME XI: *The Celtic Twilight* and *The Secret Rose,*
ed. Warwick Gould, Phillip L. Marcus,
and Michael Sidnell

VOLUME XII: *John Sherman and Dhoya,*
ed. Richard J. Finneran

VOLUME XIII: *A Vision* (1925),
ed. Connie K. Hood and Walter Kelly Hood

VOLUME XIV: *A Vision* (1937),
ed. Connie K. Hood and Walter Kelly Hood

The Collected Works of W. B. Yeats

Volume VI

W. B. YEATS

Prefaces and Introductions

UNCOLLECTED PREFACES AND
INTRODUCTIONS BY YEATS
TO WORKS BY OTHER AUTHORS
AND TO ANTHOLOGIES
EDITED BY YEATS

EDITED BY
William H. O'Donnell

Macmillan Publishing Company

NEW YORK

Macmillan Publishing Company
866 Third Avenue, New York, NY 10022

Library of Congress Cataloging-in-Publication Data
Yeats, W. B. (William Butler), 1865–1939.
Prefaces and introductions: uncollected prefaces and
introductions by Yeats to works by other authors and to anthologies
edited by Yeats / W. B. Yeats: edited by William H. O'Donnell.
p.   cm.—(The collected works of W. B. Yeats; v. 6)
Bibliography: p.
ISBN 0–02–592551–2
1. Prefaces.   2. Ireland—Intellectual life.   3. Literature—
History and criticism.   4. English poetry—Irish authors—History
and criticism.   I. O'Donnell, William H., 1940–   .   II. Title.
III. Series: Yeats, W. B. (William Butler), 1865–1939.   Works.   1989.   v. 6
PR5900.A2F56   vol. 6
[PR5902]
821.8 s—dc19
[809]   88–37045   CIP

Macmillan books are available at special
discounts for bulk purchases for sales
promotions, premiums, fund-raising, or
educational use. For details contact:

Special Sales Director
Macmillan Publishing Company
866 Third Avenue
New York, NY 10022

10   9   8   7   6   5   4   3   2   1

Printed in the People's Republic of China

CONTENTS

EDITOR'S PREFACE

The prefaces and introductions that Yeats wrote for works by other writers and for anthologies that he edited have special interest because they reflect a broad range of his literary and cultural interests during nearly the full length of his career. Other volumes in *The Collected Edition of the Works of W. B. Yeats* give the prefaces and introductions that Yeats chose finally to include in collections of his essays; *Prefaces and Introductions* makes available the other thirty-two prefaces and introductions that were published in separate books.

The contents of *Preface and Introductions* are arranged according to dates of first publication. For each introduction the copy-text is the last version that Yeats revised; in three instances the copy-texts are typescripts that he submitted in 1937 to Charles Scribner's Sons, New York, for the never-published 'Dublin' collected edition. The textual history of each introduction and the evidence for the selection of each copy-text are discussed in the individual textual introductions, which are printed near the end of the volume.

I have examined the manuscripts, typescripts and printed versions of each text. Because of Yeats's acknowledged willingness to accept the editorial decisions of Mrs Yeats and of Thomas Mark at Macmillan, London, I have also studied the revisions made for Macmillan editions after his death. Documentary evidence of Yeats's regard for their judgement is available in two signed replies by him to editor's queries on Macmillan proofs, date-stamped 30 September 1931, for a prose volume in the never-published collected 'Edition de Luxe'. When asked whether to regularise the format for quoted passages, Yeats answered, 'I leave this to Macmillan's reader. I have accepted his suggestions, wherever he has made the correction but I am a babe in such things' (corrected page proofs of *Mythologies*, vol. II of the 'Edition de Luxe', volume half-title page, NLI MS. 30,030; SUNY-SB 12.9.246). And a few pages later in the same set of proofs, when the editor asked whether to change 'Knock-na-gur', in *The Celtic Twilight*, to one word without hyphens, 'like Knocknarea [and] Knockfefin in Vol. I', Yeats replied,

Yes. W. B. Y. It is difficult to decide on a uniform usage. The familiar words above are always written without hyphens. On the other hand the names of woods in Vol I 167 seem to require hyphens to help pronunciation and to mark the words they are compounded from. I would be glad if Macmillan's reader would decide for me. W. B. Y. (p. 8 [NLI MS. 30,030; SUNY-SB 12.9.251]; for 'Knocknagur', see *Myth* 9; for 'Knocknarea' and 'Knockfefin', see *P* 22, 55, 81, 280, 384)

In 1939, a few months after Yeats's death, the introductions to *The Midnight Court* (1926), to *Coinage of Saorstát Éireann* (1928) and to *Selections from the Poems of Dorothy Wellesley* (1936) were typeset for Macmillan's never-published collected 'Edition de Luxe'/'Coole Edition', volume XI, to be titled *Essays and Introductions*. Mrs Yeats corrected the page proofs, date-stamped 19 July 1939, of the introduction to *Coinage of Saorstát Éireann* (BL Add. MS. 55895), but the extant proofs lack a group of pages (pp. 305–20) that contained the introductions to *The Midnight Court* and *Selections from the Poems of Dorothy Wellesley*. A copy-edited typescript of the latter is extant (BL Add. MS. 55895). In 1962 the introductions to *Cuchulain of Muirthemne* and *Gods and Fighting Men* and to *The Midnight Court* were reprinted, with extensive copy-editing, in *Explorations*. That Macmillan volume was prepared largely by Thomas Mark, despite the title-page's statement that the works were selected by Mrs Yeats. I have described those changes, in the individual textual introductions, even though the posthumous copy-editing made to the introductions to *Coinage of Saorstát Éireann* and *The Midnight Court* has, at best, only problematical authority. Whenever I have made an emendation that follows one of those posthumous copy-editing emendations I have mentioned it as a supplemental authority, within square brackets. I have disregarded the *Explorations* version of the combined introduction to *Cuchulain of Muirthemne* and *Gods and Fighting Men* because it mistakenly overlooked the extensive revisions that Yeats had made in 1908, and therefore lacks textual authority.

Yeats's own notes to his introductions are printed among the explanatory annotation, prefixed with the notation '[Yeats's note:]'. His notes outside his introductions, to works that he anthologised, are given in textual appendixes. I have included any notes whose authorship is uncertain, but I have excluded any notes, not written by him, that were already in the texts that he anthologised. See pp. 318–19, 320 and 321 for listings of additional exclusions of notes to material that was not written by Yeats.

Other textual appendixes give any sections that had once been published in an introduction but that Yeats later dropped from the copy-text version. For example, a textual appendix to 'Thoughts on Lady Gregory's Translations' (1902) gives the opening two sections of his introduction to *Cuchulain of Muirthemne* that Yeats retained in his collected works in December 1908, but which he excluded in 1912 from the copy-text version.

Explanatory annotation is provided for all quotations, direct references and allusions that occur in the introductions, in Yeats's notes to the introductions, or in the textual appendixes. However, Yeats's notes to material other than his introductions have explanatory annotation only when needed to identify the work to which a note refers. Explanatory notes are marked in the text by superscript numerals and are printed towards the end of the volume, following the textual appendixes. The numbering of notes restarts in a new series for each preface or introduction or appendix. Notes to Yeats's notes included in the numbered explanatory notes are signalled by the number of the note plus a letter (e.g. 35a) and are printed immediately following the note to which they relate.

Emendations to the copy-texts are marked with a dagger (†), which refers to a list of emendations at the end of the volume. That list gives the page and line number of the emendation, its copy-text reading, and any specific authority for the emendation. For emendations of spelling or capitalisation, the list of emendations gives the copy-text word without appended punctuation, if any. (In those cases the dagger immediately follows the emended word and precedes any appended punctuation.) These dagger notations are provided even for emendation of word-division or hyphenation and for standardisation of the spelling of proper names.

The emendation principles and their carefully limited extent can be illustrated with the following examples. The two largest emendations in the volume consist, respectively, of the substitution of a comma for 'and', and then, two paragraphs later, of 'and' for a comma. Where the copy-text of *Representative Irish Tales* confusingly conflates the titles of two novels, *Frank* and *Rosamond*, in the midst of a series of titles, as '*Frank and Rosamond*', I have emended to '*Frank,†* *Rosamond*' (p. 38, l. 37); and later I have joined the wrongly separated parts of another novel's title as '*Harry and†* *Lucy*' (p. 40, l. 8).

The copy-text of *Representative Irish Tales* once misnames the *Dublin University Magazine* as the *Dublin University Review* (p. 55, l. 21), but then, only a few lines later, twice uses the correct name of the journal; all nine other instances of the name, in two other introductions, are also correct. I have emended the single instance of '*Dublin University Review*' to '*Dublin University Magazine†*'.

In the case of an introduction that had first been published in 1898 and then, when it was collected in 1908, was incorrectly dated '1899', I have supplied the correct date, with a dagger: '1898†' (p. 112, l. 35). Yeats's factual errors that might simply be his poor spelling or a printer's misreading of Yeats's handwriting are emended and marked with a dagger. Examples are Yeats's statements that Maria Edgeworth was born at 'Hare Hack' (p. 37, l. 31) rather than 'Hare Hatch', and that William Allingham lived at 'Whitby' (p. 69, l. 18) rather than 'Witley'.

Spelling emendation has been avoided except for proper names and the titles of works. Thus, in the introduction to *Fairy and Folk Tales of the Irish Peasantry* I have retained the copy-text's random mixture of six instances of 'among' and five instances of 'amongst'. In the introduction to *Representative Irish Tales* I have retained the copy-text's American spellings, such as 'gayety' and 'neighborhood'. Similarly, I have retained minor eccentricities of capitalisation. Hyphens and ellipses in the text are authorial. The spelling of Tír-na-nÓg has been standardised, and is marked with a dagger when the copy-text has been emended; however, in *Fairy and Folk Tales of the Irish Peasantry* I have retained the widely differing spellings that Yeats adopted from his several authorities: one of Yeats's notes has one instance each of three spellings (Thierna-na-noge, Tir-na-hóige, Tir-na-n-óg), and his text has two instances each of two other spellings (Tír-na-n-Og, T'yeer-na-n-Oge).

The following typographical and format conventions are silently adopted in each prose volume of *The Collected Edition of the Works of W. B. Yeats*:

1 The presentation of headings is standardised. In this volume, the main headings are set in full capitals (capitals and small capitals for subtitles), and include brief details of date and source (for fuller information see the textual introductions and list of copy-texts). Where the item includes several pieces, the main heading names each in turn or gives a general description where there are several pieces of the same type (e.g. 'headnotes'). In all such composite items, the text of the first piece follows the main heading, without a separate heading of its own, if entitled simply 'Introduction' or 'Preface'; otherwise, each piece is headed by its title in full capitals (capitals and small capitals for subtitles). Section numbers are in roman capitals. All headings are centred and have no concluding full point.

2 The opening line of each paragraph is indented, except following a displayed heading or section break.

3 All sentences open with a capital letter followed by lower-case letters.

4 British single quotation mark conventions are used.

5 A colon that introduces a quotation does not have a dash following the colon.

6 Quotations that are set off from the text and indented are not placed within quotation marks.

7 Except in headings, the titles of stories and poems are placed within quotation marks; titles of books, plays, long poems, periodicals, operas, paintings, statues and drawings are set in italics.

8 Contractions (abbreviations, such as 'Mr', 'Mrs', 'Messrs' and 'St', that end with the last letter of the word abbreviated), are not followed by a full point.

9 Abbreviations such as 'i.e.' are set in roman type.

10 A dash – regardless of its length in the copy-text – is set as a spaced en rule when used as punctuation. When a dash indicates an omission, as in 'the village of B——', a two-em rule is used.

11 Ampersands are expanded to 'and'.

12 Each signature of the author is indented from the left margin, set in upper- and lower-case letters, and ends without punctuation; when present, the place and date are indented from the left margin, set in italics in upper- and lower-case letters, and end without punctuation.

I am pleased to acknowledge the generous assistance of Paul C. Bonila, Temple University; George Bornstein, University of Michigan; Nicola Gordon Bowe, National College of Art and Design, Dublin; W. Patrick Bridgewater, University of Durham; F. J. Byrne, University College, Dublin; Stephen Calloway, Victoria and Albert Museum; David R. Clark, University of Massachusetts; Robert Cook, Newcomb College, Tulane University; Catherine de Courcy, National Gallery of Ireland; Marilyn Dekker and Patrick E. Dempsey, Library of Congress; Paul Delany, London; Rupin W. Desai, University of Delhi; Alan R. Eager, Royal Dublin Society Library; Richard J. Finneran, Newcomb College, Tulane University; Mary M. Fitzgerald, University of New Orleans; Warwick Gould, Royal Holloway and Bedford New College, University of London; George M. Harper, Florida State University; Toshimitsu Hasegawa, Kyoto University; Barbara Hayley, St Patrick's College, Maynooth; Narayan Hegde, State University of New York, Stony Brook; John Kelly, St John's College, Oxford; Mary M. Lago, University of Missouri; Patience-Anne W. Lenk, Colby College; Phillip L. Marcus,

Cornell University; William M. Murphy, Union College; C. D. Narasimhaiah, Mysore, India; Peter Nicolaisen, Pädagogische Hochscule, Flensburg; Edward O'Shea, State University of New York College at Oswego; Yukio Oura, Kyoto University and Notre Dame Women's College, Kyoto; Lee Sayrs and W. Ronald Schuchard, Emory University; Michael J. Sidnell, Trinity College, University of Toronto; Shalini Sikka, Jesus and Mary College, New Delhi; Colin Smythe, Gerrards Cross, Buckinghamshire; Barry and Joan Stahl, Enoch Pratt Library, Baltimore; Ann Stewart, National Gallery of Ireland Library; James Tyler, Cornell University; and Hugh Witemeyer, University of New Mexico. At the Pennsylvania State University I wish to thank Samuel P. Bayard, Ronald E. Buckalew, Michael H. Begnal, Kathryn M. Grossman, Amelia S. Harding, Wendell V. Harris, Paul B. Harvey, Jr, John T. Harwood, Nicholas A. Joukovsky, Michael T. Kiernan, the late Susan Lieberman, Charles W. Mann, Jr, Noelene P. Martin, Grace Perez, Ruth Senior, E. Jean Smith, Evelyn Smith, Sandra K. Stelts, and Daniel A. Zager. I am particularly grateful to the library staffs at the British Library; Cornell University; Emory University; the Library Company of Philadelphia; the University of Maryland; the National Gallery of Ireland; the National Library of Ireland; the Henry W. and Albert A. Berg Collection, New York Public Library; the Peabody Institute, Baltimore; the University of Pennsylvania; the Pennsylvania College of Optometry; Pennsylvania State University; the Philadelphia Free Library; Princeton University; the State University of New York, Stony Brook; the Harry Ransom Humanities Research Center, University of Texas, Austin; and Villanova University. I wish to thank Graham Eyre and Valery Rose for helpful copy-editing, and also Gloria and Clare O'Donnell for help with careful proof-reading. Research travel for this volume was supported, in part, by Pennsylvania State University's Institute for the Arts and Humanistic Studies, Department of English, and the College of the Liberal Arts Fund for Research; by the National Endowment for the Humanities; and by my parents, to whom this volume is dedicated, along with the late Liam Miller who would have been pleased by this volume that begins to answer his call, some twenty years ago, for an annotated, accurate edition of Yeats's prose.

Memphis, Tennessee   **W. H. O.**

LIST OF ABBREVIATIONS

The following abbreviations are used in the editorial apparatus; additional abbreviations that are confined to the list of emendations to the copy-texts are explained at the head of that list.

PUBLISHED WORKS

Au	W. B. Yeats, *Autobiographies* (London: Macmillan, 1955)
BIV	*A Book of Irish Verse Selected from Modern Writers*, ed. W. B. Yeats (London: Methuen, 1895; 2nd edn London: Methuen, 1900). [When the reference is to only one of the editions the date of that edition is mentioned]
CL1	*The Collected Letters of W. B. Yeats*, vol. I, ed. John Kelly, associate ed. Eric Domville (Oxford: Clarendon Press; New York: Oxford University Press, 1986)
E&I	W. B. Yeats, *Essays and Introductions* (London and New York: Macmillan, 1961)
Ex	W. B. Yeats, *Explorations*, sel. Mrs W. B. Yeats (London: Macmillan, 1962; New York: Macmillan, 1963)
FFT	*Fairy and Folk Tales of the Irish Peasantry*, ed. W. B. Yeats, Camelot Classics series, no. 32 (London: Scott, 1888)
L	*The Letters of W. B. Yeats*, ed. Allan Wade (London: Hart-Davis, 1954; New York: Macmillan, 1955)
LMR	*Ah, Sweet Dancer: W. B. Yeats – Margot Ruddock, A*

	Correspondence, ed. Roger McHugh (London and New York: Macmillan, 1970)
LTWBY	*Letters to W. B. Yeats*, ed. Richard J. Finneran, George Mills Harper and William M. Murphy (London: Macmillan; New York: Columbia University Press, 1977)
Mem	W. B. Yeats, *Memoirs*, ed. Denis Donoghue (London: Macmillan, 1972; New York: Macmillan, 1973)
Myth	W. B. Yeats, *Mythologies* (London and New York: Macmillan, 1959)
OBMV	*The Oxford Book of Modern Verse, 1892–1935*, chosen by W. B. Yeats (Oxford: Clarendon Press, 1936)
P	W. B. Yeats, *The Poems, a New Edition*, ed. Richard J. Finneran (New York: Macmillan, 1983; London: Macmillan, 1984)
PWB	*Poems of William Blake*, ed. W. B. Yeats, The Muses' Library, 2nd edn (London: Routledge; New York: Dutton, 1905)
PWB (1893)	*The Poems of William Blake*, ed. W. B. Yeats, The Muses' Library (London: Lawrence and Bullen; New York: Scribner's, 1893)
SB	W. B. Yeats, *The Speckled Bird, with Variant Versions*, ed. William H. O'Donnell (Toronto: McClelland and Stewart, 1977)
SR	*The Secret Rose, Stories by W. B. Yeats: A Variorum Edition*, ed. Phillip L. Marcus, Warwick Gould and Michael J. Sidnell (Ithaca, NY, and New York: Cornell University Press, 1981)
SS	*The Senate Speeches of W. B. Yeats*, ed. Donald R. Pearce (Bloomington: Indiana University Press, 1960; London: Faber, 1961)
TB	*Theatre Business: The Correspondence of the First Abbey Theatre Directors: William Butler Yeats, Lady Gregory, and J. M. Synge*, ed. Ann Saddlemyer (Gerrards Cross, Bucks: Smythe; University Park: Pennsylvania State University Press, 1982)

UP1	*Uncollected Prose by W. B. Yeats*, vol. 1, ed. John P. Frayne (New York: Columbia University Press; London: Macmillan, 1970)
UP2	*Uncollected Prose by W. B. Yeats*, vol. 2, ed. John P. Frayne and Colton Johnson (London: Macmillan, 1975; New York: Columbia University Press, 1976)
V(A)	W. B. Yeats, *A Vision* (London: Werner Laurie, 1925 [Jan 1926])
V(B)	W. B. Yeats, *A Vision*, 2nd edn (London: Macmillan, 1937)
VP	*The Variorum Edition of the Poems of W. B. Yeats*, ed. Peter Allt and Russell K. Alspach (New York: Macmillan, 1957). [Cited from the corrected third printing (1966) or later printings]
VP1	*The Variorum Edition of the Plays of W. B. Yeats*, ed. Russell K. Alspach (London and New York: Macmillan, 1966). [Cited from the corrected second printing (1966) or later printings]
Wade	Allan Wade, *A Bibliography of the Writings of W. B. Yeats*, 3rd edn, rev. Russell K. Alspach (London: Hart-Davis, 1968)
WWB	*The Works of William Blake: Poetic, Symbolic, and Critical*, ed. Edwin J. Ellis and W. B. Yeats, 3 vols (London: Quaritch, 1893)

OTHER SOURCES

Berg, NYPL	Henry W. and Albert A. Berg Collection, New York Public Library
BL	British Library
HRC	Harry Ransom Humanities Research Center, University of Texas at Austin
NLI	National Library of Ireland
SUNY-SB	Yeats Archive, Frank Melville, Jr, Memorial Library, State University of New York at Stony Brook. [References are to material on microfilm, identified by reel, volume and page numbers]

LIST OF PLATES

1. Jacynth Parsons, 'The Little Black Boy', water-colour illustration (1926) to William Blake's poem. See pp. 165 and 295, n.5. Source: William Blake, *Songs of Innocence*, illus. Jacynth Parsons (London: Medici Society, 1927), facing p. 10.

2. Some of the photographs supplied to the artists by the Committee on Coinage Design. See pp. 166 and 296, n.1. Source: *Coinage of Saorstát Éireann 1928* (Dublin: Stationery Office, 1928), plate XI.

3. Coin designs by Carl Milles. See pp. 168–70; 297, n.7; and 298, n.17. Source: *Coinage of Saorstát Éireann 1928*, plate V.

4. Coin design by Ivan Meštrović. See pp. 168 and 297, nn.7 and 10. Source: *Coinage of Saorstát Éireann 1928*, plate IX.

5. Coin designs by Percy Metcalfe (as submitted by the artist). See pp. 169–71 and 298, nn.15 and 22. Source: *Coinage of Saorstát Eireann 1928*, plate IV.

6. Coin designs by Percy Metcalfe (revised, as minted). See pp. 170–1 and 298, n.22. Source: *Coinage of Saorstát Éireann 1928*, plate I.

PREFACES AND INTRODUCTIONS

Introduction and headnotes to
Fairy and Folk Tales of the Irish Peasantry,
ed. W. B. Yeats (1888)

Dr Corbett, Bishop of Oxford and Norwich, lamented long ago
the departure of the English fairies. 'In Queen Mary's time' he
wrote –

> When Tom came home from labour,
>   Or Cis to milking rose,
> Then merrily, merrily went their tabor,
>   And merrily went their toes.

But now, in the times of James, they had all gone, for 'they were
of the old profession', and 'their songs were Ave Maries'.[1] In
Ireland they are still extant, giving gifts to the kindly, and
plaguing the surly. 'Have you ever seen a fairy or such like?' I
asked an old man in County Sligo. 'Amn't I annoyed with
them,' was the answer. 'Do the fishermen along here know
anything of the mermaids?' I asked a woman of a village in
County Dublin. 'Indeed, they don't like to see them at all,' she
answered, 'for they always bring bad weather.' 'Here is a man
who believes in ghosts,' said a foreign sea-captain, pointing to a
pilot of my acquaintance. 'In every house over there,' said the
pilot, pointing to his native village of Rosses,[2] 'there are
several.' Certainly that now old and much respected dogmatist,
the Spirit of the Age,[3] has in no manner made his voice heard
down there. In a little while, for he has gotten a consumptive
appearance of late, he will be covered over decently in his
grave, and another will grow, old and much respected, in his
place, and never be heard of down there, and after him another
and another and another. Indeed, it is a question whether any
of these personages will ever be heard of outside the newspaper
offices and lecture-rooms and drawing-rooms and eel-pie

houses of the cities, or if the Spirit of the Age is at any time more than a froth. At any rate, whole troops of their like will not change the Celt much. Giraldus Cambrensis found the people of the western islands a trifle paganish.[4] 'How many gods are there?' asked a priest, a little while ago, of a man from the Island of Innistor.[5] 'There is one on Innistor; but this seems a big place,' said the man, and the priest held up his hands in horror, as Giraldus had, just seven centuries before. Remember, I am not blaming the man; it is very much better to believe in a number of gods than in none at all, or to think there is only one, but that he is a little sentimental and impracticable, and not constructed for the nineteenth century. The Celt, and his cromlechs, and his pillar-stones,[6] these will not change much – indeed, it is doubtful if anybody at all changes at any time. In spite of hosts of deniers, and asserters, and wise-men, and professors, the majority still are averse to sitting down to dine thirteen at table, or being helped to salt, or walking under a ladder, or seeing a single magpie flirting his chequered tail. There are, of course, children of light who have set their faces against all this, though even a newspaper man, if you entice him into a cemetery at midnight, will believe in phantoms, for every one is a visionary, if you scratch him deep enough. But the Celt is a visionary without scratching.

Yet, be it noticed, if you are a stranger, you will not readily get ghost and fairy legends, even in a western village. You must go adroitly to work, and make friends with the children, and the old men, with those who have not felt the pressure of mere daylight existence, and those with whom it is growing less, and will have altogether taken itself off one of these days. The old women are most learned, but will not so readily be got to talk, for the fairies are very secretive, and much resent being talked of; and are there not many stories of old women who were nearly pinched into their graves or numbed with fairy blasts?

At sea, when the nets are out and the pipes are lit, then will some ancient hoarder of tales become loquacious, telling his histories to the tune of the creaking of the boats. Holy-eve night,[7] too, is a great time, and in old days many tales were to be heard at wakes. But the priests have set faces against wakes.

In the *Parochial Survey of Ireland* it is recorded how the story-tellers used to gather together of an evening, and if any

had a different version from the others, they would all recite
theirs and vote, and the man who had varied would have to
abide by their verdict. In this way stories have been handed
down with such accuracy, that the long tale of Deirdre† was,
in the earlier decades of this century, told almost word for word,
as in the very ancient MSS in the Royal Dublin Society. In one
case only it varied, and then the MS. was obviously wrong – a
passage had been forgotten by the copyist.[8] But this accuracy is
rather in the folk and bardic tales than in the fairy legends, for
these vary widely, being usually adapted to some neighbouring
village or local fairy-seeing celebrity. Each county has usually
some family, or personage, supposed to have been favoured or
plagued, especially by the phantoms, as the Hackets of Castle
Hacket, Galway, who had for their ancestor a fairy,[9] or
John-o'-Daly of Lisadell, Sligo, who wrote 'Eilleen Aroon', the
song the Scotch have stolen and called 'Robin Adair',[10] and
which Handel[11] would sooner have written than all his
oratorios,[12] and the 'O'Donahue of Kerry'.[13] Round these men
stories tended to group themselves, sometimes deserting more
ancient heroes for the purpose. Round poets have they gathered
especially, for poetry in Ireland has always been mysteriously
connected with magic.

These folk-tales are full of simplicity and musical
occurrences, for they are the literature of a class for whom every
incident in the old rut of birth, love, pain, and death has
cropped up unchanged for centuries: who have steeped
everything in the heart: to whom everything is a symbol. They
have the spade over which man has leant from the beginning.
The people of the cities have the machine, which is prose and a
parvenu. They have few events. They can turn over the incidents
of a long life as they sit by the fire. With us nothing has time to
gather meaning, and too many things are occurring for even a
big heart to hold. It is said the most eloquent people in the
world are the Arabs, who have only the bare earth of the desert
and a sky swept bare by the sun. 'Wisdom has alighted upon
three things,' goes their proverb; 'the hand of the Chinese, the
brain of the Frank, and the tongue of the Arab.' This, I take it,
is the meaning of that simplicity sought for so much in these
days by all the poets, and not to be had at any price.

The most notable and typical story-teller of my acquaintance is one Paddy Flynn, a little, bright-eyed, old man, living in a leaky one-roomed cottage of the village of B——, 'The most gentle – i.e., fairy – place in the whole of the County Sligo,' he says, though others claim that honour for Drumahair or for Drumcliff.[14] A very pious old man, too! You may have some time to inspect his strange figure and ragged hair, if he happen to be in a devout humour, before he comes to the doings of the gentry. A strange devotion! Old tales of Columkill, and what he said to his mother. 'How are you to-day, mother?' 'Worse!' 'May you be worse to-morrow;' and on the next day, 'How are you to-day, mother?' 'Worse!' 'May you be worse to-morrow;' and on the next, 'How are you to-day, mother?' 'Better, thank God.' 'May you be better to-morrow.'[15] In which undutiful manner he will tell you Columkill inculcated cheerfulness. Then most likely he will wander off into his favourite theme – how the Judge smiles alike in rewarding the good and condemning the lost to unceasing flames. Very consoling does it appear to Paddy Flynn, this melancholy and apocalyptic cheerfulness of the Judge. Nor seems his own cheerfulness quite earthly – though a very palpable cheerfulness. The first time I saw him he was cooking mushrooms for himself; the next time he was asleep under a hedge, smiling in his sleep. Assuredly some joy not quite of this steadfast earth lightens in those eyes – swift as the eyes of a rabbit – among so many wrinkles, for Paddy Flynn is very old. A melancholy there is in the midst of their cheerfulness – a melancholy that is almost a portion of their joy, the visionary melancholy of purely instinctive natures and of all animals. In the triple solitude of age and eccentricity and partial deafness he goes about much pestered by children.

As to the reality of his fairy and spirit-seeing powers, not all are agreed. One day we were talking of the Banshee.[16] 'I have seen it,' he said, 'down there by the water "batting" the river with its hands.' He it was who said the fairies annoyed him.

Not that the Sceptic is entirely afar even from these western villages. I found him one morning as he bound his corn in a merest pocket-handkerchief of a field. Very different from Paddy Flynn – Scepticism in every wrinkle of his face, and a travelled man, too! – a foot-long Mohawk Indian tatooed on one of his arms to evidence the matter. 'They who travel,' says a neighbouring priest, shaking his head over him, and quoting

Thomas à Kempis†, 'seldom come home holy.'[17] I had mentioned ghosts to this Sceptic. 'Ghosts,' said he; 'there are no such things at all, at all, but the gentry, they stand to reason; for the devil, when he fell out of heaven, took the weak-minded ones with him, and they were put into the waste places. And that's what the gentry are. But they are getting scarce now, because their time's over, ye see, and they're going back. But ghosts, no! And I'll tell ye something more I don't believe in – the fire of hell;' then, in a low voice, 'that's only invented to give the priests and the parsons something to do.' Thereupon this man, so full of enlightenment, returned to his corn-binding.

The various collectors of Irish folk-lore have, from our point of view, one great merit, and from the point of view of others, one great fault. They have made their work literature rather than science, and told us of the Irish peasantry rather than of the primitive religion of mankind, or whatever else the folk-lorists are on the gad after. To be considered scientists they should have tabulated all their tales in forms like grocers' bills – item the fairy king, item the queen. Instead of this they have caught the very voice of the people, the very pulse of life, each giving what was most noticed in his day. Croker and Lover,[18] full of the ideas of harum-scarum Irish gentility, saw everything humorised. The impulse of the Irish literature of their time came from a class that did not – mainly for political reasons – take the populace seriously, and imagined the country as a humorist's Arcadia; its passion, its gloom, its tragedy, they knew nothing of. What they did was not wholly false; they merely magnified an irresponsible type, found oftenest among boatmen, carmen, and gentlemen's servants, into the type of a whole nation, and created the stage Irishman. The writers of 'Forty-eight, and the famine[19] combined, burst their bubble. Their work had the dash as well as the shallowness of an ascendant and idle class, and in Croker is touched everywhere with beauty – a gentle Arcadian beauty. Carleton, a peasant born, has in many of his stories – I have been only able to give a few of the slightest – more especially in his ghost stories, a much more serious way with him, for all his humour.[20] Kennedy, an old bookseller in Dublin, who seems to have had a something of genuine belief in the fairies, came next in time. He has far less literary faculty, but is wonderfully accurate, giving often the very words the stories were told in. But the best book since Croker is Lady Wilde's *Ancient Legends*.[21] The humour has all given way to pathos and tenderness. We have here the innermost heart of the Celt in the moments he has grown to love through years of persecution, when, cushioning himself about with dreams, and hearing fairy-songs in the twilight, he ponders on the soul and on the dead. Here is the Celt, only it is the Celt dreaming.

Besides these are two writers of importance, who have published, so far, nothing in book shape – Miss Letitia Maclintock and Mr Douglas Hyde. Miss Maclintock writes accurately and beautifully the half Scotch dialect of Ulster; and Mr Douglas Hyde is now preparing a volume of folk tales in Gaelic, having taken them down, for the most part, word for word among the Gaelic speakers of Roscommon and Galway.[22] He is, perhaps, most to be trusted of all. He knows the people thoroughly. Others see a phase of Irish life; he understands all its elements. His work is neither humorous nor mournful; it is simply life. I hope he may put some of his gatherings into ballads, for he is the last of our ballad-writers of the school of Walsh and Callanan – men whose work seems fragrant with turf smoke.[23] And this brings to mind the chap-books. They are to be found brown with turf smoke on cottage shelves, and are, or were, sold on every hand by the pedlars, but cannot be found in any library of this city of the Sassanach.[24] *The Royal Fairy Tales*, *The Hibernian Tales*, and *The Legends of the Fairies* are the fairy literature of the people.[25]

Several specimens of our fairy poetry are given. It is more like the fairy poetry of Scotland than of England. The personages of English fairy literature are merely, in most cases, mortals beautifully masquerading. Nobody ever believed in such fairies. They are romantic bubbles from Provence. Nobody ever laid new milk on their doorstep for them.

As to my own part in this book, I have tried to make it representative, as far as so few pages would allow, of every kind of Irish folk-faith. The reader will perhaps wonder that in all my notes I have not rationalised a single hobgoblin. I seek for shelter to the words of Socrates.[26]

'*Phaedrus.* I should like to know, Socrates, whether the place is not somewhere here at which Boreas is said to have carried off Orithyia[27] from the banks of the Ilissus?

'*Socrates*. That is the tradition.

'*Phaedrus*. And is this the exact spot? The little stream is delightfully clear and bright; I can fancy that there might be maidens playing near.

'*Socrates*. I believe the spot is not exactly here, but about a quarter-of-a-mile lower down, where you cross to the temple of Artemis, and I think that there is some sort of an altar of Boreas at the place.

'*Phaedrus*. I do not recollect; but I beseech you to tell me, Socrates, do you believe this tale?

'*Socrates*. The wise are doubtful, and I should not be singular if, like them, I also doubted. I might have a rational explanation that Orithyia was playing with Pharmacia, when a northern gust carried her over the neighbouring rocks; and this being the manner of her death, she was said to have been carried away by Boreas. There is a discrepancy, however, about the locality. According to another version of the story, she was taken from the Areopagus, and not from this place.[28] Now I quite acknowledge that these allegories are very nice, but he is not to be envied who has to invent them; much labour and ingenuity will be required of him; and when he has once begun, he must go on and rehabilitate centaurs and chimeras dire. Gorgons and winged steeds flow in apace, and numberless other inconceivable and portentous monsters. And if he is sceptical about them, and would fain reduce them one after another to the rules of probability, this sort of crude philosophy will take up all his time. Now, I have certainly not time for such inquiries. Shall I tell you why? I must first know myself, as the Delphian inscription[29] says; to be curious about that which is not my business, while I am still in ignorance of my own self, would be ridiculous. And, therefore, I say farewell to all this; the common opinion is enough for me. For, as I was saying, I want to know not about this, but about myself. Am I, indeed, a wonder more complicated and swollen with passion than the serpent Typho,[30] or a creature of gentler and simpler sort, to whom nature has given a diviner and lowlier destiny?'[31]

I have to thank Messrs Macmillan, and the editors of *Belgravia*, *All the Year Round*, and *Monthly Packet*, for leave to quote from Patrick Kennedy's *Legendary Fictions of the Irish Celts*, and Miss Maclintock's articles respectively; Lady Wilde, for leave to give what I would from her *Ancient Legends of Ireland* (Ward and Downey); and Mr Douglas Hyde, for his three unpublished stories, and for valuable and valued assistance in several ways; and also Mr Allingham, and other copyright holders, for their poems. Mr Allingham's poems are from *Irish Songs and Poems* (Reeves and Turner); Ferguson's†, from Sealey, Bryers, and Walker's shilling reprint; my own and Miss O'Leary's from *Ballads and Poems of Young Ireland*, 1888, a little anthology published by Gill and Sons, Dublin.[32]

W. B. Yeats

THE TROOPING FAIRIES

The Irish word for fairy is *sheehogue* [*sidheóg*]†, a diminutive of 'shee' in *banshee*. Fairies are *deenee shee* [*daoine sidhe*]† (fairy people).

Who are they? 'Fallen angels who were not good enough to be saved, nor bad enough to be lost,' says the peasantry. 'The gods of the earth,' says the Book of Armagh.[33] 'The gods of pagan Ireland,' say the Irish antiquarians, 'the *Tuatha De Danān*, who, when no longer worshipped and fed with offerings, dwindled away in the popular imagination, and now are only a few spans high.'[34]

And they will tell you, in proof, that the names of fairy chiefs are the names of old *Danān* heroes, and the places where they especially gather together, *Danān* burying-places, and that the *Tuatha De Danān*† used also to be called the *slooa-shee* [*sheagh sidhe*]† (the fairy host), or *Marcra shee* (the fairy cavalcade).

On the other hand, there is much evidence to prove them fallen angels. Witness the nature of the creatures, their caprice, their way of being good to the good and evil to the evil, having every charm but conscience-consistency†. Beings so quickly offended that you must not speak much about them at all, and never call them anything but the 'gentry', or else *daoine maithe*,

which in English means good people, yet so easily pleased, they
will do their best to keep misfortune away from you, if you leave
a little milk for them on the window-sill over night. On the
whole, the popular belief tells us most about them, telling us
how they fell, and yet were not lost, because their evil was
wholly without malice.

Are they 'the gods of the earth'?[35] Perhaps! Many poets, and
all mystic and occult writers, in all ages and countries, have
declared that behind the visible are chains on chains of
conscious beings, who are not of heaven but of the earth, who
have no inherent form but change according to their whim, or
the mind that sees them. You cannot lift your hand without
influencing and being influenced by hordes†. The visible world
is merely their skin. In dreams we go amongst them, and play
with them, and combat with them. They are, perhaps, human
souls in the crucible – these creatures of whim.

Do not think the fairies are always little. Everything is
capricious about them, even their size. They seem to take what
size or shape pleases them. Their chief occupations are feasting,
fighting, and making love, and playing the most beautiful
music. They have only one industrious person amongst them,
the *lepra-caun* – the shoemaker. Perhaps they wear their shoes
out with dancing. Near the village of Ballisodare is a little
woman who lived amongst them seven years. When she came
home she had no toes – she had danced them off.

They have three great festivals in the year – May Eve,
Midsummer Eve, November Eve. On May Eve, every seventh
year, they fight all round, but mostly on the 'Plain-a-Bawn'
(wherever that is), for the harvest, for the best ears of grain
belong to them. An old man told me he saw them fight once;
they tore the thatch off a house in the midst of it all. Had anyone
else been near they would merely have seen a great wind
whirling everything into the air as it passed. When the wind
makes the straws and leaves whirl as it passes, that is the fairies,
and the peasantry take off their hats and say, 'God bless them.'

On Midsummer Eve, when the bonfires are lighted on every
hill in honour of St John, the fairies are at their gayest, and
sometime steal away beautiful mortals to be their brides.

On November Eve they are at their gloomiest, for, according
to the old Gaelic reckoning, this is the first night of winter. This

night they dance with the ghosts, and the *pooka* is abroad, and witches make their spells, and girls set a table with food in the name of the devil, that the fetch[36] of their future lover may come through the window and eat of the food. After November Eve the blackberries are no longer wholesome, for the *pooka* has spoiled them.

When they are angry they paralyse men and cattle with their fairy darts.

When they are gay they sing. Many a poor girl has heard them, and pined away and died, for love of that singing. Plenty of the old beautiful tunes of Ireland are only their music, caught up by eavesdroppers. No wise peasant would hum 'The Pretty Girl Milking† the Cow' near a fairy rath, for they are jealous, and do not like to hear their songs on clumsy mortal lips. Carolan, the last of the Irish bards, slept on a rath, and ever after the fairy tunes ran in his head, and made him the great man he was.[37]

Do they die? Blake saw a fairy's funeral;[38] but in Ireland we say they are immortal.

THE TROOPING FAIRIES: CHANGELINGS

Sometimes the fairies fancy mortals, and carry them away into their own country, leaving instead some sickly fairy child, or a log of wood so bewitched that it seems to be a mortal pining away, and dying, and being buried. Most commonly they steal children. If you 'over look a child', that is look on it with envy, the fairies have it in their power. Many things can be done to find out in a child a changeling, but there is one infallible thing – lay it on the fire with this formula, 'Burn, burn, burn – if of the devil, burn; but if of God and the saints, be safe from harm' (given by Lady Wilde).[39] Then if it be a changeling it will rush up the chimney with a cry, for, according to Giraldus Cambrensis, 'fire is the greatest of enemies to every sort of phantom, in so much that those who have seen apparitions fall into a swoon as soon as they are sensible of the brightness of fire.'[40]

Sometimes the creature is got rid of in a more gentle way. It is on record that once when a mother was leaning over a wizened changeling the latch lifted and a fairy came in, carrying home again the wholesome stolen baby. 'It was the others,' she said, 'who stole it.' As for her, she wanted her own child.

Those who are carried away are happy, according to some accounts, having plenty of good living and music and mirth. Others say, however, that they are continually longing for their earthly friends. Lady Wilde gives a gloomy tradition that there are two kinds of fairies – one kind merry and gentle, the other evil, and sacrificing every year a life to Satan, for which purpose they steal mortals.[41] No other Irish writer gives this tradition – if such fairies there be, they must be among the solitary spirits – Pookas, Fir Darrigs, and the like.

THE TROOPING FAIRIES: The Merrow

The *Merrow*, or if you write it in the Irish, *Moruadh* or *Murrúghach*, from *muir*, sea, and *oigh*, a maid, is not uncommon, they say, on the wilder coasts. The fishermen do not like to see them, for it always means coming gales. The male *Merrows* (if you can use such a phrase – I have never heard the masculine of *Merrow*) have green teeth, green hair, pig's eyes, and red noses; but their women are beautiful, for all their fish tails and the little duck-like scale between their fingers. Sometimes they prefer, small blame to them, good-looking fishermen to their sea lovers. Near Bantry, in the last century, there is said to have been a woman covered all over with scales like a fish, who was descended from such a marriage.[42] Sometimes they come out of the sea, and wander about the shore in the shape of little hornless cows. They have, when in their own shape, a red cap, called a *cohullen druith*, usually covered with feathers. If this is stolen, they cannot again go down under the waves.

Red is the colour of magic in every country, and has been so from the very earliest times. The caps of fairies and magicians are well-nigh always red.

THE SOLITARY FAIRIES: Lepracaun.
Cluricaun. Far Darrig[43]

'The name *Lepracaun*', Mr Douglas Hyde writes to me, 'is from the Irish *leith brog* – i.e., the One-shoemaker, since he is generally seen working at a single shoe. It is spelt in Irish *leith bhrogan*, or *leith phrogan*, and is in some places pronounced Luchryman, as O'Kearney writes it in that very rare book, the *Feis Tigh Chonain*.'[44]

The *Lepracaun*, *Cluricaun*, and *Far Darrig*. Are these one spirit in different moods and shapes? Hardly two Irish writers are agreed. In many things these three fairies, if three, resemble each other. They are withered, old, and solitary, in every way unlike the sociable spirits of the first sections. They dress with all unfairy homeliness, and are, indeed, most sluttish, slouching, jeering, mischievous phantoms. They are the great practical jokers among the good people.

The *Lepracaun* makes shoes continually, and has grown very rich. Many treasure-crocks, buried of old in war-time, has he now for his own. In the early part of this century, according to Croker, in a newspaper office in Tipperary, they used to show a little shoe forgotten by a Lepracaun.[45]

The *Cluricaun* (*Clobhair-ceann*, in O'Kearney)[46] makes himself drunk in gentlemen's cellars. Some suppose he is merely the Lepracaun on a spree. He is almost unknown in Connaught and the north.

The *Far Darrig* (*fear dearg*), which means the Red Man, for he wears a red cap and coat, busies himself with practical joking, especially with gruesome joking. This he does, and nothing else.

The *Fear-Gorta* (Man of Hunger) is an emaciated phantom that goes through the land in famine time, begging an alms and bringing good luck to the giver.

There are other solitary fairies, such as the House-spirit and the *Water-sheerie*, own brother to the English Jack-o'-Lantern; the *Pooka* and the *Banshee* – concerning these presently; the *Dullahan*†, or headless phantom – one used to stand in a Sligo street on dark nights till lately; the Black Dog, a form, perhaps, of the *Pooka*. The ships at the Sligo quays are haunted sometimes by this spirit, who announces his presence by a sound like the flinging of all 'the tin porringers in the world' down into the hold. He even follows them to sea.

The *Leanhaun Shee* (fairy mistress), seeks the love of mortals. If they refuse, she must be their slave; if they consent, they are hers, and can only escape by finding another to take their place.

The fairy lives on their life, and they waste away. Death is no escape from her. She is the Gaelic muse, for she gives inspiration to those she persecutes. The Gaelic poets die young, for she is restless, and will not let them remain long on earth – this malignant phantom.

Besides these are divers monsters – the *Augh-iska*, the Water-horse, the Payshtha (*píast = bestia*), the Lake-dragon, and such like; but whether these be animals, fairies, or spirits, I know not.

THE SOLITARY FAIRIES: THE POOKA

The Pooka, *rectè* Púca, seems essentially an animal spirit. Some derive his name from *poc*, a he-goat; and speculative persons consider him the forefather of Shakespeare's† 'Puck'. On solitary mountains and among old ruins he lives, 'grown monstrous with much solitude', and is of the race of the nightmare. 'In the MS story, called "Mac-na-Michomhairle", of uncertain authorship,' writes me Mr Douglas Hyde, 'we read that "out of a certain hill in Leinster, there used to emerge as far as his middle, a plump, sleek, terrible steed, and speak in human voice to each person about November-day, and he was accustomed to give intelligent and proper answers to such as consulted him concerning all that would befall them until the November of next year. And the people used to leave gifts and presents at the hill until the coming of Patrick and the holy clergy." This tradition appears to be a cognate one with that of the Púca.' Yes! unless it were merely an *augh-ishka* [*each-uisgé*]†, or Water-horse. For these, we are told, were common once, and used to come out of the water to gallop on the sands and in the fields, and people would often go between them and the marge and bridle them, and they would make the finest of horses if only you could keep them away from sight of the water; but if once they saw a glimpse of the water, they would plunge in with their rider, and tear him to pieces at the bottom. It being a November spirit, however, tells in favour of the Pooka, for November-day is sacred to the Pooka. It is hard to realise that wild, staring phantom grown sleek and civil.

He has many shapes – is now a horse, now an ass, now a bull, now a goat, now an eagle. Like all spirits, he is only half in the world of form.

THE SOLITARY FAIRIES: THE BANSHEE

[†The *banshee* (from *ban* [*bean*], a woman, and *shee* [*sidhe*], a fairy) is an attendant fairy that follows the old families, and none but them, and wails before a death. Many have seen her as she goes wailing and clapping her hands. The keen (*caoine*), the funeral cry of the peasantry, is said to be an imitation of her cry. When more than one banshee is present, and they wail and sing in chorus, it is for the death of some holy or great one. An omen that sometimes accompanies the banshee is the *coach-a-bower* (*cóiste-bodhar*) – an immense black coach, mounted by a coffin, and drawn by headless horses driven by a *Dullahan*. It will go rumbling to your door, and if you open it, according to Croker, a basin of blood will be thrown in your face.[47] These headless phantoms are found elsewhere than in Ireland. In 1807 two of the sentries stationed outside St James's Park died of fright.[48] A headless woman, the upper part of her body naked, used to pass at midnight and scale the railings. After a time the sentries were stationed no longer at the haunted spot. In Norway the heads of corpses were cut off to make their ghosts feeble. Thus came into existence the *Dullahans*, perhaps; unless, indeed, they are descended from that Irish giant who swam across the Channel with his head in his teeth. – Ed.][49]

GHOSTS

Ghosts, or as they are called in Irish, *Thevshi* or *Tash* (*taidhbhse*, *tais*), live in a state intermediary between this life and the next. They are held there by some earthly longing or affection, or some duty unfulfilled, or anger against the living. 'I will haunt you,' is a common threat; and one hears such phrases as, 'She will haunt him, if she has any good in her.' If one is sorrowing greatly after a dead friend, a neighbour will say, 'Be quiet now, you are keeping him from his rest'; or, in the Western Isles, according to Lady Wilde, they will tell you, 'You are waking the dog that watches to devour the souls of the dead.'[50] Those who die suddenly, more commonly than others, are believed to become haunting Ghosts. They go about moving the furniture, and in every way trying to attract attention.

When the soul has left the body, it is drawn away, sometimes, by the fairies. I have a story of a peasant who once saw, sitting in a fairy rath, all who had died for years in his village. Such souls are considered lost. If a soul eludes the fairies, it may be snapped up by the evil spirits. The weak souls of young children are in especial danger. When a very young child dies, the western peasantry sprinkle the threshold with the blood of a chicken, that the spirits may be drawn away to the blood. A Ghost is compelled to obey the commands of the living. 'The stable-boy up at Mrs G——'s there,' said an old countryman, 'met the master going round the yards after he had been two days dead, and told him to be away with him to the lighthouse, and haunt that; and there he is far out to sea still, sir. Mrs G—— was quite wild about it, and dismissed the boy.' A very desolate lighthouse poor devil of a Ghost! Lady Wilde considers it is only the spirits who are too bad for heaven, and too good for hell, who are thus plagued. They are compelled to obey some one they have wronged.[51]

The souls of the dead sometimes take the shapes of animals. There is a garden at Sligo where the gardener sees a previous owner in the shape of a rabbit. They will sometimes take the forms of insects, especially of butterflies. If you see one fluttering near a corpse, that is the soul, and is a sign of its having entered upon immortal happiness. The author of the *Parochial Survey of Ireland*, 1814, heard a woman say to a child who was chasing a butterfly, 'How do you know it is not the soul of your grandfather.'[52] On November eve the dead are abroad, and dance with the fairies.

As in Scotland, the fetch is commonly believed in. If you see the double, or fetch, of a friend in the morning, no ill follows; if at night, he is about to die.

WITCHES, FAIRY DOCTORS

Witches and fairy doctors receive their power from opposite

dynasties; the witch from evil spirits and her own malignant will; the fairy doctor from the fairies, and a something – a temperament – that is born with him or her. The first is always feared and hated.[53] The second is gone to for advice, and is never worse than mischievous. The most celebrated fairy doctors are sometimes people the fairies loved and carried away, and kept with them for seven years; not that those the fairies† love are always carried off – they may merely grow silent and strange, and take to lonely wanderings in the 'gentle' places. Such will, in after-times, be great poets or musicians, or fairy doctors; they must not be confused with those who have a *Lianhaun shee* [*leannán-sidhe*]†, for the *Lianhaun shee* lives upon the vitals of its chosen, and they waste and die. She is of the dreadful solitary fairies. To her have belonged the greatest of the Irish poets, from Oisin down to the last century.

Those we speak of have for their friends the trooping fairies – the gay and sociable populace of raths and caves. Great is their knowledge of herbs and spells. These doctors, when the butter will not come on the milk, or the milk will not come from the cow, will be sent for to find out if the cause be in the course of common nature or if there has been witchcraft. Perhaps some old hag in the shape of a hare has been milking the cattle. Perhaps some user of 'the dead hand' has drawn away the butter to her own churn. Whatever it be, there is the counter-charm. They will give advice, too, in cases of suspected changelings, and prescribe for the 'fairy blast' (when the fairy strikes any one a tumour rises, or they become paralysed. This is called a 'fairy blast' or a 'fairy stroke'). The fairies are, of course, visible to them, and many a new-built house have they bid the owner pull down because it lay on the fairies' road. Lady Wilde thus describes one who lived in Innis Sark: 'He never touched beer, spirits, or meat in all his life, but has lived entirely on bread, fruit, and vegetables. A man who knew him thus describes him – "Winter and summer his dress is the same – merely a flannel shirt and coat. He will pay his share at a feast, but neither eats nor drinks of the food and drink set before him. He speaks no English, and never could be made to learn the English tongue, though he says it might be used with great effect to curse one's enemy. He holds a burial-ground sacred, and would not carry away so much as a leaf of ivy from a grave.

And he maintains that the people are right to keep to their ancient usages, such as never to dig a grave on a Monday, and to carry the coffin three times round the grave, following the course of the sun, for then the dead rest in peace. Like the people, also, he holds suicides as accursed; for they believe that all its dead turn over on their faces if a suicide is laid amongst them.

' "Though well off, he never, even in his youth, thought of taking a wife; nor was he ever known to love a woman. He stands quite apart from life, and by this means holds his power over the mysteries. No money will tempt him to impart his knowledge† to another, for if he did he would be struck dead – so he believes. He would not touch a hazel stick, but carries an ash wand, which he holds in his hand when he prays, laid across his knees; and the whole of his life is devoted to works of grace and charity, and though now an old man, he has never had a day's sickness. No one has ever seen him in a rage, nor heard an angry word from his lips but once, and then being under great irritation, he recited the Lord's Prayer backwards as an imprecation on his enemy. Before his death he will reveal the mystery of his power, but not till the hand of death is on him for certain." '[54] When he does reveal it, we may be sure it will be to one person only – his successor. There are several such doctors in County Sligo, really well up in herbal medicine by all accounts, and my friends find them in their own counties. All these things go on merrily. The spirit of the age laughs in vain, and is itself only a ripple to pass, or already passing, away.

The spells of the witch are altogether different; they smell of the grave. One of the most powerful is the charm of the dead hand. With a hand cut from a corpse they, muttering words of power, will stir a well and skim from its surface a neighbour's butter.

A candle held between the fingers of the dead hand can never be blown out. This is useful to robbers, but they appeal for the suffrage of the lovers likewise, for they can make love-potions by drying and grinding into powder the liver of a black cat. Mixed with tea, and poured from a black teapot, it is infallible. There are many stories of its success in quite recent years, but, unhappily, the spell must be continually renewed, or all the love may turn into hate. But the central notion of witchcraft everywhere is the power to change into some fictitious form, usually in Ireland a hare or a cat. Long ago a wolf was the favourite. Before Giraldus Cambrensis came to Ireland, a monk wandering in a forest at night came upon two wolves, one of whom was dying. The other entreated him to give the dying wolf the last sacrament. He said the mass, and paused when he came to the viaticum. The other, on seeing this, tore the skin from the breast of the dying wolf, laying bare the form of an old woman. Thereon the monk gave the sacrament. Years afterwards he confessed the matter, and when Giraldus visited the country, was being tried by the synod of the bishops. To give the sacrament to an animal was a great sin. Was it a human being or an animal? On the advice of Giraldus they sent the monk, with papers describing the matter, to the Pope for his decision. The result is not stated.

Giraldus himself was of opinion that the wolf-form was an illusion, for, as he argued, only God can change the form.[55] His opinion coincides with tradition, Irish and otherwise.

It is the notion of many who have written about these things that magic is mainly the making of such illusions. Patrick Kennedy tells a story of a girl who, having in her hand a sod of grass containing, unknown to herself, a four-leaved shamrock, watched a conjurer at a fair. Now, the four-leaved shamrock guards its owner from all *pishogues* (spells), and when the others were staring at a cock carrying along the roof of a shed a huge beam in its bill, she asked them what they found to wonder at in a cock with a straw. The conjurer begged from her the sod of grass, to give to his horse, he said. Immediately she cried out in terror that the beam would fall and kill somebody.[56]

This, then, is to be remembered – the form of an enchanted thing is a fiction and a caprice.

T'YEER-NA-N-OGE[57]

[†There is a country called Tír-na-n-Og, which means the Country of the Young, for age and death have not found it; neither tears nor loud laughter have gone near it. The shadiest boskage covers it perpetually. One man has gone there and returned. The bard, Oisin†, who wandered away on a white horse, moving on the surface of the foam with his fairy Niamh, lived there three hundred years, and then returned looking for his comrades. The moment his foot touched the earth his three hundred years fell on him, and he was bowed double, and his beard swept the ground. He described his sojourn in the Land of Youth to Patrick before he died. Since then many have seen it in many places; some in the depths of lakes, and have heard rising therefrom a vague sound of bells; more have seen it far off on the horizon, as they peered out from the western cliffs. Not three years ago a fisherman imagined that he saw it. It never appears unless to announce some national trouble.

There are many kindred beliefs. A Dutch pilot, settled in Dublin, told M. de la Boullaye le Gouz†, who travelled in Ireland in 1614, that round the poles were many islands; some hard to be approached because of the witches who inhabit them and destroy by storms those who seek to land. He had once, off the coast of Greenland, in sixty-one degrees of latitude, seen and approached such an island only to see it vanish. Sailing in an opposite direction, they met with the same island, and sailing near, were almost destroyed by a furious tempest.[58]

According to many stories, Tír-na-n-Og is the favourite dwelling of the fairies. Some say it is triple – the island of the living, the island of victories, and an underwater land.]

SAINTS, PRIESTS

Everywhere in Ireland are the holy wells. People as they pray by them make little piles of stones, that will be counted at the last day and the prayers reckoned up. Sometimes they tell stories. These following are their stories. They deal with the old times, whereof King Alfred of Northumberland wrote:

> I found in Innisfail the fair,
> In Ireland, while in exile there,
> Women of worth, both grave and gay men,
> Many clericks and many laymen.
>
> Gold and silver I found, and money,
> Plenty of wheat, and plenty of honey;

I found God's people rich in pity,
Found many a feast, and many a city.[59]

There are no martyrs in the stories. That ancient chronicler
Giraldus taunted the Archbishop of Cashel because no one in
Ireland had received the crown of martyrdom. 'Our people
may be barbarous,' the prelate answered, 'but they have never
lifted their hands against God's saints; but now that a people
have come amongst us who know how to make them (it was just
after the English invasion), we shall have martyrs plentifully.'[60]

The bodies of saints are fastidious things. At a place called
Four-mile-Water, in Wexford, there is an old graveyard full of
saints. Once it was on the other side of the river, but they buried
a rogue there, and the whole graveyard moved across in the
night, leaving the rogue-corpse in solitude. It would have been
easier to move merely the rogue-corpse, but they were saints,
and had to do things in style.

GIANTS

When the pagan gods of Ireland – the *Tuatha De Danān*† –
robbed of worship and offerings, grew smaller and smaller in
the popular imagination, until they turned into the fairies, the
pagan heroes grew bigger and bigger, until they turned into the
giants.

'William Carleton',
in *Stories from Carleton*,
ed. W. B. Yeats (1889)

At the end of the last century there lived in the townland of Prillisk, in the parish of Clogher, in the county of Tyrone,[1] a farmer named Carleton. Among his neighbours he was noted for his great memory. A pious Catholic, he could repeat almost the whole of the Old and New Testament, and no man ever heard tell of Gaelic charm, rann,[2] poem, prophecy, miracle, tale of blessed priest or friar, revelation of ghost or fairy, that did not already lie on this man's tongue.

His wife, Mary, was even better known. Hers was the sweetest voice within the range of many baronies. When she went to sing at wake or wedding the neighbours for miles round would flock in to hear, as city folk do for some famous *prima donna*. She had a great store of old Gaelic songs and tunes. Many an air, sung once under all Irish roof-trees, has gone into the grave with her. The words she sang were Gaelic. Once they asked her to sing the air, 'The Red-haired Man's Wife', to English words. 'I will sing for you,' she answered, 'but the English words and the air are like a quarrelling man and wife. The Irish melts into the tune: the English does not.'[3] She could repeat many poems, some handed down for numberless years, others written by her own grandfather and uncle, who were noted peasant poets in their day. She was a famous keener likewise. No one could load the wild funeral song with so deep sorrow. Often and often when she caught up the cry the other keeners would become silent in admiration.

On Shrove-Tuesday, in the year 1798, when pitch-caps were well in fashion, was born to these two a son, whom they called William Carleton.[4] He was the youngest of fourteen children.

Before long his mind was brimful of his father's stories and his mother's songs. In after days he recorded how many times, when his mother sat by her spinning-wheel, singing '*Shule agra*' or the '*Trougha*', or some other 'song of sorrow', he would go over with tears in his eyes, and whisper, 'Mother dear, don't sing that song; it makes me sorrowful.'[5] Fifty years later his mind was still full of old songs that had died on all other lips than his.[6]

At this time Ireland was plentifully stored with hedge schoolmasters. Government had done its best to crush out education, and only succeeded in doing what like policy had done for the priestcraft – surrounding it with a halo. Ditchers and plough-boys developed the strangest enthusiasm for Greek and Latin. The worst of it was, the men who set up schools behind the hedges were often sheer impostors. Among them, however, were a few worthy of fame, like Andrew Magrath, the Munster poet, who sang his allegiance to the fairy, 'Don of the Ocean Vats'.[7]

The boy Carleton sat under three hedge schoolmasters in succession – Pat Frayne†, called Mat Kavanagh in the stories; O'Beirne of Findramore; and another, the master in 'The Poor Scholar', whose name Carleton never recorded, as he had nothing but evil to say of him.[8] They were great tyrants. Pat Frayne† caused the death of a niece of Carleton's by plucking her ear with such violence that some of the internal tendons were broken, and inflammation set in.

When Carleton was about fourteen, the unnamed schoolmaster was groaned out of the barony; and his pupil, after six months' dutiful attendance at all wakes, weddings, and dances, resolved to make his first foray into the world. He set out as 'a poor scholar', meaning to travel away into Munster in search of education. He did not go beyond Granard,[9] however, for there he dreamed that he was chased by a mad bull, and, taking it as an evil omen, returned home. His mother was delighted to have her youngest once more. She had often repeated, while he was away, 'Why did I let my boy go? Maybe I will never see him again.'[10]

He now returned to his dances, fairs, and merry-making with a light heart. None came near him at jig or hornpipe. He was great, too, with his big peasant's body, at all kinds of athletic contests, could swing a shillelah with any man, and leap twenty-one feet on a level. But in his own family he was most admired for his supposed learning, and showed a great taste, as he tells, for long words. Hence it was decided that he should become a priest.

When about nineteen he made his second foray into the world. His father often told him of St Patrick's Purgatory on an island in Lough Derg – how St Patrick killed the great serpent and left his bones changed into stone, visible to all men for ever, and of the blessing that falls upon all pilgrims thither. To the mind of the would-be priest, and tale-weaver that was to be, the place seemed full of endless romance. He set out, one of the long line of pilgrims who have gone thither these twelve hundred years to murmur their rosaries. In a short time a description of this pilgrimage was to start him in literature.[11]

On his return he gave up all idea of the priesthood, and changed his religious opinions a good deal. He began drifting slowly into Protestantism. This Lough Derg pilgrimage seems to have set him thinking on many matters – not thinking deeply, perhaps. It was not an age of deep thinking. The air was full of mere debater's notions. In course of time, however, he grew into one of the most deeply religious minds of his day – a profound mystical nature, with melancholy at its root. And his heart, anyway, soon returned to the religion of his fathers; and in him the Established Church proselytisers found their most fierce satirist.

One day Carleton came on a translation of *Gil Blas*,[12] and was filled at once with a great longing to see the world. Accordingly, he left his native village and went on his third foray, this time not to return. He found his way to the parish of Killanny, in Louth,[13] and stayed for a while with the priest, who was a relation of the one in his native parish. At the end of a fortnight, however, he moved to a farmer's house, where he became tutor to the farmer's children. A quarter of a mile from the priest's house was Wildgoose Lodge, where, six months before, a family of eight persons had been burnt to ashes by a Ribbon Society. The ringleader still swung on a gibbet opposite his mother's door, and as she came in and out it was her custom to look up and say, 'God have mercy on the sowl of my poor martyr.' The peasants when they passed by would often look up too, and murmur, 'Poor Paddy'.[14] The whole matter made a deep impression on the mind of Carleton, and again and again in his books he returns to the subject of the secret societies and their corruption of the popular conscience. He discusses their origin in book after book, and warns the people against them.

Presently he found that he was not seeing the world in this parish of Killanny, and finding, beside, that life in the farmer's household was very dull, he started for Dublin, and arrived with two shillings and ninepence in his pocket. For some time he had a hard struggle, trying even to get work as a bird-stuffer, though he knew absolutely nothing of the trade. He wrote a letter in Latin to the colonel of a regiment, asking his advice about enlisting. The colonel seems to have made out the Latin, and dissuaded him.

In those days there lived in Dublin a lean controversialist, Caesar Otway. A favourite joke about him was, 'Where was Otway in the shower yesterday?' 'Up a gun-barrel at Rigby's.'[15] He also had been to Lough Derg. When he had looked down upon it from the mountains he had felt no reverence for the grey island consecrated by the verse of Calderón†[16] and the feet of twelve centuries of pilgrims. His stout Protestant heart had merely filled with wrath at so much 'superstition'.

Carleton and Otway came across each other somehow. The lean controversialist was infinitely delighted with this peasant convert, and seems to have befriended him to good purpose. By his recommendation, 'The Lough Derg Pilgrim' was written. A few years later, Carleton cleared away many passages. Caesar Otway would hardly approve its present form.[17] As we have it now, the tale is a most wonderful piece of work. The dim chapel at night, the praying peasants, the fear of a supernatural madness if they sleep, the fall of the young man from the gallery – no one who has read it forgets these things.

From this on, there is little to be recorded but the dates of his books. He married, and for a time eked out his income by teaching. When about thirty he published the *Traits and Stories*,[18] and with them began modern Irish literature. Before long there were several magazines in Dublin, and many pens busy. Then came *Fardorougha†, the Miser*,[19] the miser himself being perhaps the greatest of all his creations. In 1846 was published *Valentine M'Clutchy*:[20] his pronouncement on the Irish

Land Question, and on the Protestant–Catholic Controversy. The novel is full of wonderful dialogues, but continually the intensity of the purpose lowers the art into caricature. Most of the prophecies he made about the land question have been fulfilled. He foretold that the people would wake up some day and appeal to first principles. They are doing so with a vengeance. Many of the improvements also that he recommended have been carried out.

Young Ireland and its literature were now in full swing. The 'National Library', founded by Davis, was elbowing the chap-books out of the pedlars' packs. As *Traits and Stories* had started the prose literature of Ireland, Ferguson's articles on Hardiman's minstrelsy, with their translations from the Gaelic, had sown a harvest of song and ballad.[21] Young Ireland was crusading in verse and prose against the sins of Old Ireland. Carleton felt bound to do his part, and wrote a series of short stories for the 'National Library' – 'Art Maguire', a temperance tale; 'Paddy Go-Easy'†, finished in nine days to fill a gap left by the death of Davis, and attacking the bad farming and slovenly housekeeping of so many peasants; and *Rody the Rover*, on his old theme – the secret societies.[22] Rody is an *agent provocateur* – a creature common enough in Ireland, God knows. At the tale's end, with mingling of political despair and Celtic fatalism, evil is left triumphant and good crushed out.

A few years later, on the death of John Banim, an attempt was made to have his pension transferred to Carleton. It might have saved him from the break-up of his genius through hack-work. But some official discovered that this author of a notable temperance tale drank more than was desirable. 'The Red Well', 'The Dream of a Broken Heart',[23] and all his beautiful and noble creations counted for nothing. Government, that did not mind a drunken magistrate, more or less, was shocked, and the pension refused.

The rest of his life was an Iliad of decadence, his genius gradually flickering out. Many a bright, heavenward spark on the way, though! At last, nothing left but the smoking wick, he died at Woodville, Sandford, near Dublin, on the 30th of January 1869, aged seventy, and was buried at Mount Jerome. A short time before his death he received the pension refused years before, but seems to have known much poverty.

William Carleton was a great Irish historian. The history of a nation is not in parliaments and battle-fields, but in what the people say to each other on fair-days and high days, and in how they farm, and quarrel, and go on pilgrimage. These things has Carleton recorded.

He is the great novelist of Ireland, by right of the most Celtic eyes that ever gazed from under the brows of story-teller. His equals in gloomy and tragic power, Michael and John Banim, had nothing of his Celtic humour. One man alone stands near him there – Charles Kickham, of Tipperary. The scene of the pig-driving peelers in *For the Old Land*,[24] is almost equal to the best of the *Traits and Stories*. But, then, he had not Carleton's intensity. Between him and the life he told of lay years in prison, a long Fenian agitation, and partial blindness. On all things flowed a faint idealising haze. His very humour was full of wistfulness.

There is no wistfulness in the works of Carleton. I find there, especially in his longer novels, a kind of clay-cold melancholy. One is not surprised to hear, great humorist though he was, that his conversation was more mournful than humorous. He seems, like the animals in Milton, half emerged only from the earth and its brooding. When I read any portion of the *Black Prophet*, or the scenes with Raymond the Madman in *Valentine M'Clutchy*,[25] I seem to be looking out at the wild, torn storm-clouds that lie in heaps at sundown along the western seas of Ireland; all nature, and not merely man's nature, seems to pour out for me its inbred fatalism.

W. B. Yeats

Introduction and headnotes (1890) to
Representative Irish Tales,
ed. W. B. Yeats (1891)

Chance and Destiny have between them woven two thirds of all history, and of the history of Ireland wellnigh the whole. The literature of a nation, on the other hand, is spun out of its heart. If you would know Ireland – body and soul – you must read its poems and stories. They came into existence to please nobody but the people of Ireland. Government did not make them on the one hand, nor bad seasons on the other. They are Ireland talking to herself. In these two little volumes I give specimens of a small part of this literature – the prose tales of modern Irish life. I have made the selection in such a way as to illustrate as far as possible the kind of witness they bear to Irish character. In this introduction I intend to explain the fashion I read them in, the class limitations I allow for, the personal bias that seems to me to have directed this novelist or that other. These limitations themselves, this bias even, will show themselves to be moods characteristic of the country.

I notice very distinctly in all Irish literature two different accents – the accent of the gentry, and the less polished accent of the peasantry and those near them; a division roughly into the voice of those who lived lightly and gayly, and those who took man and his fortunes with much seriousness and even at times mournfully. The one has found its most typical embodiment in the tales and novels of Croker, Lover, and Lever, and the other in the ruder but deeper work of Carleton, Kickham, and the two Banims.[1]

There is perhaps no other country in the world the style and nature of whose writers have been so completely governed by their birth and social standing. Lever and Lover, and those like them, show constantly the ideals of a class that held its acres once at the sword's point, and a little later were pleased by the tinsel villany of the Hell Fire Club – a class whose existence has, on the whole, been a pleasant thing enough for the world.[2] It introduced a new wit – a humor whose essence was dare-devilry and good-comradeship, half real, half assumed. For Ireland, on the other hand, it has been almost entirely an evil, and not the least of its sins against her has been the creation in the narrow circle of its dependants of the pattern used later on for that strange being called sometimes 'the stage Irishman'. They had found the serious passions and convictions of the true peasant troublesome, and longed for a servant who would make them laugh, a tenant who would always appear merry in his checkered rags. The result was that there grew up round about the big houses a queer mixture of buffoonery and chicanery tempered by plentiful gleams of better things – hearts, grown crooked, where laughter was no less mercenary than the knavery. The true peasant remained always in disfavor as 'plotter', 'rebel', or man in some way unfaithful to his landlord. The knave type flourished till the decay of the gentry themselves, and is now extant in the boatmen, guides, and mendicant hordes that gather round tourists, while they are careful to trouble at no time any one belonging to the neighborhood with their century-old jokes. The tourist has read of the Irish peasant in the only novels of Irish life he knows, those written by and for an alien gentry. He has expectations to be fulfilled. The mendicants follow him for fear he might be disappointed. He thinks they are types of Irish poor people. He does not know that they are merely a portion of the velvet of aristocracy now fallen in the dust.

Samuel Lover, confined by the traditions of his class, and having its dependants about him, took pleasure in celebrating the only peasant-life he knew. His stories, with seldom more than the allowable exaggerations of the humorist, describe the buffoon Irishman with the greatest vigor and humor. 'Barny† O'Reirdon'[3] is an incomparable chronicle. The error is with those who have taken from his novels their notion of all Irishmen. *Handy Andy*[4] has been the cause of much misconception, and yet, like all he wrote, is full of truthful pages and poetic feeling. Samuel Lover had a deal more poetry in him than Lever. It gives repose and atmosphere to his stories and crops up charmingly in his songs. 'The Whistling Thief', for instance, is no less pretty than humorous.[5] But at all times it is the kind of poetry that shines round ways of life other than our own. It is the glamour of distance, and is the same feeling that in a previous age crowded the boards of theatres with peasant girls in high-heeled shoes, and shepherds carrying crooks fluttering with ribbons. At the same time it has a real and quite lawful charm.

Crofton Croker, the historian of the fairies and an accomplished master of this kind of poetry, was much more palpably injured than was Lover by his narrow conception of Irish life. He had to deal with materials dug out of the very soul of the populace. You feel the falsity at once. The people take the fairies and spirits much more seriously. Under his hands the great kingdom of the *sidhe*[6] lost its nobility and splendor. 'The gods of the earth' dwindled to dancing mannikins – buffoons of the darkness. The slighter matters of other-world life – the humor, the pathos – fared better. 'The Priest's Supper' and 'Daniel O'Rourke' deserve to be immortal.[7] I was unfortunately prevented by the plan of these volumes – a plan that does not allow me to stray from Irish human nature to Irish fairy nature – from including either, but I have substituted a fine conversation with an Irish 'fairy doctor', or village seer.[8]

Charles Lever, unlike Lover and Croker, wrote mainly for his own class. His books are quite sufficiently truthful, but more than any other Irish writer has he caught the ear of the world and come to stand for the entire nation. The vices and virtues of his characters are alike those of the gentry – a gentry such as Ireland has had, with no more sense of responsibility, as a class, than have the *dullahans*, *thivishes*, *sowlths*, *bowas*, and *water sheries* of the spirit-ridden peasantry.[9] His characters, however, are in no way lacking in the qualities of their defects – having at most times a hospitable, genial, good soldier-like disposition.

Croker and Lover and Lever were, as humorists go, great fellows. They must always leave some kind of recollection; but, to my mind, there is one thing lacking among them. I miss the deep earth song of the peasant's laughter. Maginn went nearer to attain it than they did. In 'Father Tom and the Pope' he put himself perfectly into the shoes of an old peasant hedge schoolmaster†, and added to the wild humor of the people one

crowning perfection – irresponsibility.[10] In matters where
irresponsibleness is a hindrance the Irish gentry have done
little. They have never had a poet. Poetry needs a God, a cause,
or a country. But witty have they been beyond question. If one
excepts *Traits and Stories*†,[11] all the most laughable Irish books
have been by them.

The one serious novelist coming from the upper classes in
Ireland, and the most finished and famous produced by any
class there, is undoubtedly Miss Edgeworth. Her first novel,
Castle Rackrent,[12] is one of the most inspired chronicles written
in English. One finds no undue love for the buffoon, rich or
poor, no trace of class feeling, unless, indeed, it be that the old
peasant who tells the story is a little decorative, like a peasant
figure in the background of an old-fashioned autumn landscape
painting. An unreal light of poetry shines round him, a too
tender lustre of faithfulness and innocence. The virtues, also,
that she gives him are those a poor man may show his superior,
not those of poor man dealing with poor man. She has made
him supremely poetical, however, because in her love for him
there was nothing of the half contemptuous affection that
Croker and Lover felt for their personages. On the other hand,
he has not the reality of Carleton's men and women. He stands
in the charming twilight of illusion and half-knowledge. When
writing of people of her own class she saw every thing about
them as it really was. She constantly satirized their
recklessness, their love for all things English, their oppression
of and contempt for their own country. The Irish ladies in *The
Absentee*[13] who seek laboriously after an English accent, might
have lived to-day. Her novels give, indeed, systematically the
mean and vulgar side of all that gay life celebrated by Lever.

About 1820, twenty years after the publication of *Castle
Rackrent*, a new power began in literary Ireland. Carleton
commenced writing for the *Christian Examiner*.[14] He had gone to
Dublin from his father's farm in Tyrone, turned Protestant,
and begun vehemently asserting his new notion of things in
controversial tales and sketches. The Dublin *dilettanti*, and
there were quite a number in those days, were delighted. Here
was a passion, a violence, new to their polite existence. They
could not foresee that some day this stormy satire would be
turned against themselves, their church, and, above all, this

proselytizing it now sought to spread. The true peasant was at last speaking, stammeringly, illogically, bitterly, but none the less with the deep and mournful accent of the people. Ireland had produced her second great novelist. Beside Miss Edgeworth's well-finished four-square house of the intelligence, Carleton raised his rough clay 'rath'[15] of humor and passion. Miss Edgeworth has outdone writers like Lover and Lever because of her fine judgement, her serene culture, her well-balanced mind. Carleton, on the other hand, with no conscious art at all, and living a half-blind, groping sort of life, drinking and borrowing, has, I believe, outdone not only them but her also by the sheer force of his powerful nature. It was not for nothing that his ancestors had dug the ground. His great body, that could leap twenty-one feet on a level, was full of violent emotions and brooding melancholy.

Carleton soon tired of controversy, and wrote his famous *Traits and Stories*. Peasant though he was, he could not wholly escape the convention of his time. There was as yet no national cultivated public, and he was forced to write for a class who wished to laugh a great deal, and who did not mind weeping a little, provided he allowed them always to keep their sense of superiority. In the more early tales, peasant life is used mainly as material for the easier kinds of mirth and pathos. He put himself sometimes in the position of his readers and looked at the life of the people from without. The true peasant had been admitted into the drawing-room of the big house and asked to tell a story, but the lights and the strange faces bewildered him, and he could not quite talk as he would by his own fireside. He at first exaggerated, in deference to his audience, the fighting, and the dancing, and the merriment, and made the life of his class seem more exuberant and buoyant than it was. What did these ladies and gentlemen, he thought, with their foreign tastes, care for the tragic life of the fields?

As time went on, his work grew deeper in nature, and in the second series he gave all his heart to 'The Poor Scholar', 'Tubber Derg', and 'Wildgoose Lodge'.[16] The humorist found his conscience, and, without throwing away laughter, became the historian of his class. It was not, however, until a true national public had arisen with Ferguson and Thomas Davis and the 'Young Ireland' people,[17] that Carleton ventured the creation of a great single character and wrote *Fardorougha the Miser*.[18] In *Fardorougha* and the two or three novels that followed he was at his finest. Then came decadence – ruinous, complete.

It seems to be a pretty absolute law that the rich like reading about the poor, the poor about the rich. In Ireland, at any rate, they have liked doing so. Each places its Tír-na-nÓg†, where 'you will get happiness for a penny',[19] its land of unknown adventure, in the kind of life that is just near enough to interest, just far enough to leave the imagination at liberty. Either because he had said all he had to say about the peasantry, or because the cultivated public that read *Fardorougha* and *The Black Prophet*[20] was gone – the best among them in the convict ship, – or because of a growing wish to please the more numerous and less intelligent of the class he had sprung from, or from a combination of all these reasons, Carleton started a series of novels dealing with the life of the gentry. They are almost worthless, except when he touches incidentally on peasant life, as in the jury-room scene in *Willy Reilly*.[21] One or two of them have, for all that, turned out very popular with the Irish uneducated classes. People who love tales of beautiful ladies, supremely brave outlaws, and villains wicked beyond belief, have read fifty editions of *Willy Reilly*. In these novels landlords, agents, and their class are described as falsely as peasants are in the books of Lover and Crocker. In *Valentine M'Clutchy*†, the first novel of his decadence, there is no lack of misdirected power.[22] The land-agent Orangeman, the hypocrite-solicitor, and the old blaspheming landlord who dies in the arms of his drunken mistress, are figures of unforgettable horror. They are the peasant's notion of that splendid laughing world of Lever's. The peasant stands at the roadside, cap in hand, his mouth full of 'your honors' and 'my ladies', his whole voice softened by the courtesy of the powerless, but men like Carleton show the thing that is in his heart. He is not appeased because the foot that passes over him is shod with laughter.

John Banim and his brother Michael, who both have the true peasant accent, are much more unequal writers than Carleton. Unlike him, they covered the peasant life they knew with a melodramatic horde of pirates and wealthy libertines whom they did not know. John Banim, who seems to have invented the manner of *The O'Hara Tales*,[23] lived mostly in London, surrounded by English taste, and had just enough culture to admire and learn and imitate the literary fashion of his age. At times he would write pages, terrible and frank, like all the first half of *The Nowlans*†,[24] and then suddenly seem to remind himself that the public expected certain conventional incidents and sentiments, and what he did his brother Michael copied. Neither had culture enough to tell them to leave the conventionalities alone and follow their own honest natures. For this reason it is mainly the minor characters – personages like the Mayor of Wind-Gap†[25] – that show the Banim genius. They seemed to indulge themselves in these fine creations as though they said, 'The† public will forgive our queer country-bred taste for very truth if we keep it in holes and corners.' Carleton, on the other hand, when he began writing, knew nothing about the public and its tastes. He had little more education than may be picked up at fair greens and chapel greens, and wrote, as a man naturally wants to write, of the things he understood. The Banims' father was a small shopkeeper; Carleton's a peasant, who perforce brought up his son well out of the reach of fashions from over sea. With less education John Banim might have written stories no less complete than those of Carleton, and with more have turned out a great realist – more like those of France and Russia than of England. The first third of *The Nowlans*† is as fine as almost any novel anywhere, and here and there melodrama and realism melt into one and make an artistic unity, like *John Doe*,[26] but much that both he and his brother wrote was of little account.

Neither brother had any trace of Carleton's humor, and John Banim had instead an abiding cold and dry-eyed sadness, produced by ill-health perhaps, wholly different from the tear-dashed melancholy of Carleton's *Black Prophet* – a melancholy as of gray clouds slumbering on the rim of the sea.

In Gerald Griffin,[27] the most finished story-teller among Irish novelists, and later on in Charles Kickham, I think I notice a new accent – not quite clear enough to be wholly distinct; the accent of people who have not the recklessness of the landowning class, nor the violent passions of the peasantry, nor the good frankness of either. The accent of those middle-class people who find Carleton rough and John Banim coarse, who when they write stories cloak all unpleasant matters, and moralize with ease, and have yet a sense of order and comeliness that may some time give Ireland a new literature. Many things are at work to help them: the papers, read by the Irish at home and elsewhere, are in their hands. They are closer to the peasant than to the gentry, for they take all things Irish with conscience, with seriousness. Their main hindrances are a limited and diluted piety, a dread of nature and her abundance, a distrust of unsophisticated life. But for these, Griffin would never have turned aside from his art and left it for the monastery; nor would he have busied himself with any thing so filmy and bloodless as the greater portion of his short stories. As it is, he has written a few perfect tales. The dozen pages or so I have selected seem to me charming, and there are many people who, repelled by the frieze-coated power of Carleton, think his really very fine *Collegians* the best Irish novel.[28] Kickham also, with his idealizing haze, pleases some who do not care for the great Tyrone peasant; not that Kickham was a man naturally given to idealize and cloak the unpleasant, and sophisticate life. His first novel *Sally Cavanagh*†,[29] is direct enough – but having come out of jail, he saw every thing with the rose-spectacles of the returned exile. His great knowledge of Irish life kept him always an historian, though one who cared only to record the tender and humane elements of the life of the common people, and of the small farming and shopkeeping class he came from. When he wrote of the gentry, he fell like Carleton into caricature. The Orangemen, landlords, and agents of *Sally Cavanagh*† and *Knocknagow*†[30] are seldom in any way human, nor are they even artistically true. The loss of accurate copying has always been more destructive to Irish national writers than to the better educated novelists of the gentry. Croker had art enough to give an ideal completeness to his shallowest inventions. Carleton and Banim and Kickham, when once they strayed from the life they had knowledge of, had not art enough to evade the most manifest conventionality and caricature. No modern Irish writer has ever had any thing of the high culture that makes it possible for an author to do as he will with life, to place the head of a beast upon a man, or the head of a man upon a beast, to give to the most grotesque creation the reality of a spiritual existence.

Meanwhile a true literary consciousness – national to the

centre – seems gradually forming out of all this disguising and prettifying, this penumbra of half-culture. We are preparing likely enough for a new Irish literary movement – like that of '48 – that will show itself at the first lull in this storm of politics.[31] Carleton scarcely understood the true tendency of any thing he did. His pages served now one cause, now another, according to some interest or passion of the moment. Things have changed since then. These new folk, limited though they be, are conscious. They have ideas. They understand the purpose of letters in the world. They may yet formulate the Irish culture of the future. To help them, is much obscure feeling for literature diffused throughout the country. The clerks, farmers' sons, and the like, that make up the 'Young Ireland' societies and kindred associations, show an alertness to honor the words 'poet', 'writer', 'orator', not commonly found among their class. Many a poor countryside has its peasant verse-maker. I have seen stories – true histories – by a village shoemaker that only needed a fine convention to take their place in fiction.[32] The school of Davis and Carleton and Ferguson has gone. Most things are changed now – politics are different, life is different. Irish literature is and will be, however, the same in one thing for many a long day – in its nationality, its resolve to celebrate in verse and prose all within the four seest† of Ireland. And why should it do otherwise? A man need not go further than his own hill-side or his own village to find every kind of passion and virtue. As Paracelsus wrote: 'If thou tastest a crust of bread, thou tastest all the stars and all the heavens.'[33]

W. B. Yeats

MARIA EDGEWORTH
1767–1849

Miss Edgeworth was born in the year 1767 at Hare Hatch†,[34] Berkshire. Her father, Richard Lovell Edgeworth, was an Oxford student of a powerful mechanical kind of intelligence. He had come to Oxford from his father's estate in Ireland, his mind choke-full of Rousseau and the French deists,[35] and there fallen in love with a Miss Elers, a lady of German extraction, and married her much against his father's will. He was but twenty years old on the birth of his daughter. When Miss Edgeworth was still a small child her mother died, and her father married again in four months. 'I am not a man of prejudices,' he wrote in later life; 'I have had four wives, the second and third were sisters, and I was in love with the second during the lifetime of the first.'[36] In 1775 she was sent to school at Derby, after a visit to Ireland, in which she had amused herself by cutting out the squares in a checked table-cloth and in trampling through the glass in a number of hot-house frames, delighting in the crash she made. In 1780, she was removed to a fashionable London school. Her holidays were usually spent with Mr Day, the eccentric author of *Sandford and Merton*,[37] whose influence, together with that of her father, started the strange love for the didactic, so harmful to her writings. This unfortunate genius, with her natural talent for the unexpected – witness the hot-house frames, – was ground between these two philosophers, who sought to reduce all things to rule and formula.

At the age of sixteen she returned with her father to Edgeworthstown, the name of the family estate in Longford.[38] The state of the country, its general dilapidation, the character of the people, all greatly moved her and developed the fruitful and sympathetic side of her nature visible later on in *Castle Rackrent*. For some time she acted as her father's agent, who wished to get rid of the middle-man and see things with his own and his daughter's eyes. In this way she learnt to see far down into the causes of Irish discontent. She was all the more at leisure to study the poor people about her, because neither she nor her father sought the company of the drinking and sport-loving squires and squireens[39] of the neighborhood. In 1795 and 1796, amid premonitory muttering of the great rebellion,[40] Miss Edgeworth's first books appeared: a plea for the education of women† and an educational manual called *The Parent's*† *Assistant*, respectively.[41] She began also her *Moral Tales*, not published until 1801. A number of educational books for children came next – *Harry and Lucy, Frank*,† *Rosamond, Early Lessons*,[42] and others, some written by herself, others with help from her father. Fairy tales and all such pleasant impossibilities were to be driven from the nursery and a despotism of the strictly true set up in their place. The nursery, however, has gallantly routed the utilitarian horde. The invasion is as dead as the great outburst of Ninety-eight, amid whose noise it set forth.

After the rebellion Mr Edgeworth entered the Irish Parliament and was among those who voted against the union.[43] In 1800, Miss Edgeworth's imagination burst free from her didacticism and *Castle Rackrent* was written and published. I have spoken of this great novel in the introduction, and need say no more of it here than that its author never perhaps reached again the same tide mark of power and humor. *Belinda* a tale of fashionable life, and the *Essay on Irish Bulls*, followed. The last was the joint work of father and daughter and was planned out as she tells us, 'to show the English public the eloquence and wit and talents of the lower classes of people in Ireland.'[44] In 1802 Mr Edgeworth travelled with his family through France and the Low Countries. His daughter, now a famous writer, saw many foreign celebrities at Paris. Now too, in her thirty-sixth year, she fell in love with a young Swede, a M. Edelcrantz, private secretary to the king.[45] He returned her love, but as neither would leave their own country, they talked to each other of duty, and parted – was she not bound to Edgeworthstown, he to the Swedish court? On returning to Ireland Miss Edgeworth tried hard to forget the Swede in preparing for the press her *Popular Tales*, and in writing *Leonora* a romantic work, intended to please him.[46] Innumerable 'novels with a purpose', archetypes and forerunners of their class, came year after year from her untiring pen. Many were published under the title of *Tales from Fashionable Life*. One of these *The Absentee*,[47] has chapters no less moving than those of *Castle Rackrent*. Macaulay has, indeed, described the scene in which Lord Colambre† discovers himself to his tenantry, as the best thing of its kind since Homer wrote the twenty-second book of the Odyssey.[48]

In 1813 Miss Edgeworth visited London with her father, and was the lion of the season. Byron, who met her at this time, wrote in his journal that she was 'a nice little unassuming "Jeanie Deans" looking body, ... and if not handsome, certainly not ill-looking'.[49] In 1817 Mr Edgeworth died, in his seventy-fourth year. A fortnight before his death he wrote the preface to 'Ormond', one of his daughter's most celebrated stories, and one in which she reached a level never again attained by her.[50] In the succeeding year, with the exception of occasional visits to London and Paris, she continued to live on at Edgeworthstown. In 1820 she completed and published her memoir of her father, a task that had long filled her thoughts. The first volume had been left ready written by Mr Edgeworth himself, the second was her work.[51] *Harry and*† *Lucy*, and *Orlandino*†,[52] and other stories followed at intervals. She was getting old, and her pen worked more slowly. The last years of her life were saddened by the famine. She worked hard at the distribution of relief. The children of Boston subscribed together and sent a hundred and fifty barrels of flour for her poor. This greatly pleased her; she was pleased also because the men who carried the barrels to the shore refused to be paid, and knitted a comforter for each of them.[53]

On May 22, 1849, she fell suddenly ill – pains in the heart being the symptom, – and died after a few hours.

Madame de† Staël said, after reading her *Tales of Fashionable Life*: 'Que Miss Edgeworth etait digne de l'enthousiasme, mais qu'elle s'est perdue dans la triste utilité.'[54] Great genius though she was, she could not persuade herself to trust nature, to set down in tale and novel the emotions and longings and chances that seemed to her pleasant and beautiful. She could not forget the schooling of her father, and of the author of *Sandford and Merton*, and felt bound to see whither every line she wrote tended, to do nothing she could not prove was for the good of man. Here and there, as in *Castle Rackrent*, she has risen above her own intellect, and produced a work of the greatest kind. In the larger number of her writings, one sees how extreme conscientiousness had injured the spontaneity of her nature. She did every thing, no less in life than in novel-writing, with the same elaborate scrupulousness. A relation of mine once got a servant from her.[55] The 'character' filled three sheets of paper. She does the same with the people of her novels. She sends them out into the world with a careful and long-considered judgment attached to each one.

JOHN AND MICHAEL BANIM
MICHAEL, 1796–1874
JOHN, 1798–1842

In the last century there lived in Kilkenny a seller of fishing-tackle and fowling-pieces, named Banim. To him was born in August, 1796, a son, Michael, and in April, 1798, amid the noise of the great rebellion, a second son, John. These two became close friends, and it is in all ways rightful that the same biographical account should serve for both; besides, there is little or no record of Michael except in so far as he comes into the life of his more famous brother.

John Banim got all his schooling in Kilkenny. We first hear of him at a dame's school, kept by a teacher who was 'good-humored, quiet, and fat',[56] unlearned and simple; and next at the English academy of one Charles George Beauchanon, who was learned and far from simple, judging by the account of him under the name of Charles George Buchmahon in *Father Connell*.[57] When ten years old he was moved to a school, famous in its day, taught by a Rev. Mr Magraw, and next to one belonging to a Terence Doyle. But looking back on these times, in later life, it seemed to him that his best education was picked up when reading romances under a hayrick. He busied himself with writing, too, both in prose and in verse. He had turned writer when too small to reach the table comfortably from any chair, and so had been compelled to write on a sheet of paper spread out on the floor. Once every year, a few days before his birthday, it was his custom to solemnly go through the year's† work and condemn it to a birthday burning.

Several of these fires must have flickered up the chimney before he entered, in his thirteenth year, that Kilkenny college described in 'The Fetches'.[58] He there developed a faculty for drawing that decided him to become an artist. Accordingly, when about eighteen, one finds him in Dublin, a student at the art schools at the Royal Dublin Society, and lodging with a certain Oliver Wheeler, who gave him the antitype for the lodging-house keeper in *The Nowlans*†.[59] He was not long in Dublin before the need to turn his art into money drove him down to Kilkenny again and started him as drawing-master.

At one of the schools where he taught was a pretty girl of

seventeen, named Anne D——, the natural daughter of a local squire. She and the young drawing-master fell in love, and thereby began one of the mournfulest love episodes extant. Before long John Banim put on his best clothes and set out to ask her of her father. He found him a violent and bitter old man, who received him with abuse. They parted, quarrelling fiercely; Banim answering in kind the old man's insults. After this Banim found the school doors closed against him. He managed, however, to sit near his sweetheart in chapel, disguised in the hooded cloak of a peasant woman and to thrust into her hands as the people trooped out letters and verses vowing eternal affection. The old squire at last sent a woman, a female relation of the girl, to pretend sympathy and so find out if she still cared for Banim. Quite deceived, she told all, and was at once taken to a place twenty-five miles off, where she would be well out of the way of the young drawing-master and his hooded cloak. The carriage passed by the Banims' shop and John saw it, and running out placed himself before the horses. They were pulled up to prevent his being run over. His eyes met the eyes of Anne D—— for a moment, and then the carriage passed on. He never saw her again. He went in among the fishing-lines and threw himself down in some corner. A messenger came in and laid a package in his hands. It was a miniature of his sweetheart he had painted and given to her. It was returned without any letter or message. Thinking her faithless, he wrote an upbraiding letter. It was the only letter of his she was allowed to see. He wrote many more, and in wholly different mood, but all were intercepted. Months passed; then one day he heard that Anne D—— was dead, and was told that she had fretted herself out of the world. The body lay in a house belonging to her mother's family. He started away riding, but when no more than a mile on his road, dismounted and sent the horse home with a boy he had met with. He could not bear the sitting still on horseback. He walked the rest of the twenty-five miles, but never knew what route he took. It was evening when he went into the farmhouse and stood beside the body. One can imagine the scene: the half-awed whispering of men and women; the young girl there in the midst; the traditional wallflowers about her, and the flickering light of three candles. At first no one noticed the new-comer. At last a half-sister of the dead girl saw him and cried out that he was the murderer of her sister and bid them drive him away. He went out, and going into an outhouse, lay down on a heap of wet straw. He lay there till morning, when the noise of people arriving told him it was time for the funeral. He followed the procession to the graveyard, and when all had gone, lay down upon the grave. He could never remember where he slept that night. Somewhere under the stars, on some ditch side! The next day his brother found him wandering about some ten miles from home, ill and feeble, not having eaten for three days. He led him homeward, neither speaking a word. For a year he merely lived, no more. The night on the wet straw, the fatigue, the despair, the starvation, weakened his constitution permanently, and left there the seeds of the illness that ultimately killed him.

The year 1818 found him somewhat better. He was again able to write and draw, though it was now becoming clear to him that writing, not drawing, was the business of his life. He returned to Dublin and there wrote and published his first book, *The Celt's† Paradise*,[60] a poem on the beautiful old Irish legend of Tír-na-nÓg†, the Gaelic Island of the Blest; a subject that has moved a number of writers, Gaelic and English-speaking, to make their best verses, but wholly unsuitable for Banim's realistic faculty. He next moved over to London and offered a tragedy, he had had for some while on the stocks, to Macready, who accepted it and produced it with great success at Covent Garden Theatre on the 28th of May, 1821.[61] Banim was now twenty-four,[62] and felt he had his foot well fixed on the first rung of the ladder. He returned to Ireland and talked over with Michael a scheme for celebrating the national life in a series of novels that were 'to insinuate through fiction', as Michael has said, 'the causes of Irish discontent, and to insinuate also that if crime were consequent on discontent, it was no great wonder; a conclusion to be arrived at by the reader, not by insisting on it on the part of the author, but by sympathy with the criminals.'[63] Michael had never written any thing but shop accounts, and it was with much difficulty that John persuaded him to contribute to the venture. His persuasions were successful, however. Michael was to become Barnes O'Hara and John, Abel O'Hara, and the series was to be called *The Tales of the O'Hara Family*.

When John returned to London he brought with him a wife aged eighteen. Her father, a Mr Ruth, furnished the least objectionable characteristics of 'Aby Nowlan†' in *The Nowlans†*. For some time London used the pair badly. Mrs Banim fell ill, and what with doctors' bills and the rest, they saw much poverty. 'By the life of Pharaoh, Sir,' John wrote to his brother, 'if I do not ply and tear the brain as wool-combers tear wool, the fire should go out, and the spit cease to turn.'[64] Presently he fell ill himself with a renewal of the wracking pains that followed his visit to the wake and funeral of Anne D——. At last he got somewhat out of his monetary troubles by the publication of some old essays,† *The Revelations of the Dead Alive*, satires on contemporary life by a man who is supposed to have the power of going out of his body in sleep – of projecting his *scin laca, astral body, doppelganger*, or what you will.[65]

Meanwhile, the first volume of O'Hara Tales had been gradually forming itself: John writing steadily at it amid all his troubles; Michael thinking out his contributions while he sold catgut and trout flies, and setting them on paper when the shutters were put up for the night. In 1825 came out in one volume 'Crohoore† of the Billhook†', by Barnes, and 'John Doe', and 'The Fetches', by Abel O'Hara. The book was a great success, and poverty left John's door for a little. In the next four years were published: *The Boyne Water*, an historical romance still much read in Ireland; *The Nowlans†*, the most powerful, and *The Denounced*, the feeblest, of the O'Hara Tales, by John Banim; and *The Croppy*, by Michael.[66] It is not easy, however, to fix where the work of one begins and that of the other ends. It was their custom to write chapters in each other's tales; Michael paying visits to London for the purpose, and John going over to Ireland from time to time, to talk things over with Michael while he was studying the localities of his stories. By the time *The Denounced* was published the health of John Banim was hopelessly wrecked. The feebleness of the book was merely an index of bodily decay. Overwork and constant illness had worn him out. He looked forty, his hair was gray, his face wrinkled, and his step tottering.

He was ordered to France for his health, and while there a play of his, founded on 'The Fetches', was acted in London and condemned by the† *Times* newspaper: 'The perpetuation of such absurd phantasies as fetches and fairies – witches and wizards – is not merely ridiculous, but it is mischievous'; – a remarkable criticism.[67] In 1832 he wrote to his brother: 'My legs are quite gone and I suffer in the extreme, yet I try to work for all that.'[68] He was but thirty-four, and yet it was getting clear enough that his working days were over. The younger Sterling – Carlyle's Sterling – had been a friend of his in London, and now the elder wrote to *The Times* and opened a subscription for him.[69] A public meeting likewise was held in Dublin, at which Sheil spoke and the Lord Mayor presided, and a considerable sum was collected.[70] In 1835 he returned to Kilkenny almost dying, and received an enthusiastic public reception. He lingered on a few years. He made his home in a cottage on Wind-Gap Hill and was called the Mayor of Wind-Gap, after a personage in one of his brother's stories.[71] Too feeble to write, he spent his time gardening. One day he overheard a traveller on the stage coach as it passed by say, 'He will never see the bushes an inch higher,' and heard the driver reply, 'He is booked for the whole journey.' In 1837 he received a small pension from the civil list. In 1842 he died. His brother had started *Father Connell*,[72] and he could not keep his hands off. The work killed him.

Michael Banim survived his brother many years, but wrote nothing of value after his death. He was postmaster of his native town and once mayor. He died in 1874, aged seventy-eight.

John Doe and *The Nowlans*† are, I imagine, the best of John Banim's stories, and *Father Connell* the best of Michael's. Whether it be justifiable to divide the work of one from the work of the other in this way I do not know. They worked constantly, as I have said, upon each other's stories, and were so alike in faculty that it is impossible to fix with confidence the march lands of either. The genius of John Banim was certainly the more vehement and passionate. He had likewise a faculty for verse absent in his brother. His 'Sogarth Aroon' is one of the most beautiful and popular of all Irish poems. The greater number of his verses were, however, of no value.[73]

WILLIAM CARLETON
1798–1869

William Carleton was born on Shrove Tuesday, in the year 1798, when the pike was trying to answer the pitch-cap.[74] He was the youngest of fourteen children. His father, a farmer of the townland† of Prillisk, in the parish of Clogher, County Tyrone, was famous among the neighbors for his great knowledge of all old Gaelic charms, ranns, poems, prophecies, miracle-tales, and tales of ghost and fairy. His mother had the sweetest voice within the range of many baronies. When she sang at a wedding or lifted the keen at a wake, the neighbors would crowd in to hear her, as to some famous *prima donna*. Often, too, when she keened, the other kenners would stand round silent to listen. It was her especial care to know all old Gaelic songs, and many a once noted tune has died with her.

A fit father and mother for a great peasant writer – for one who would be called 'the prose Burns of Ireland'.

As the young Carleton grew up his mind filled itself brimful of his father's stories and his mother's songs. He has recorded how, many times, when his mother sat by her spinning-wheel, singing 'The Trougha', or 'Shule Agra', or some other mournful air, he would go over to her and whisper: 'Mother, don't sing that song; it makes me sorrowful.' Fifty years later he could still hum tunes and sing verses dead on all other lips.

His education, such as it was, was beaten into him by hedge schoolmasters. Like other peasants of his time he learnt to read out of the chap-books – *Freney the Robber, Rogues and Rapparees*; or else, maybe, from the undesirable pages of *Laugh and Be Fat*.[75] He sat under three schoolmasters in succession – Pat Frayne†, called Mat Kavanagh in *Traits and Stories*; O'Beirne of Findramore; and another, whose name Carleton has not recorded, there being naught but evil to say of him. They were a queer race, bred by government in its endeavor to put down Catholic education. The thing being forbidden, the peasantry had sent their children to learn reading, and writing, and a little Latin even, under the 'hips and haws' of the hedges. The sons of ploughmen were hard at work construing Virgil and Horace, so great a joy is there in illegality.

When Carleton was about fourteen he set out as 'a poor

scholar', meaning to travel into Munster in search of more perfect education. 'The poor scholar' was then common enough in Ireland. Many still living remember him and his little bottle of ink. When a boy had shown great attention to his books he would be singled out to be a priest, and a subscription raised to start him on his way to Maynooth. Every peasant's house, as he trudged upon his road, would open its door to him, such honor had learning and piety among the poor. Carleton, however, was plainly intended for nothing of the kind. He did not get farther than Granard, where he dreamed that he was chased by a mad bull, and taking it for an evil omen, went home.

He felt very happy when he came to his own village again, the uncomfortable priestly ambition well done with. He spent his time now in attending all dances, wakes, and weddings, and grew noted as the best dancer and leaper in his district; nor had he many rivals with a spear and shillelah. When he was about nineteen a second pious fit sent him off on a pilgrimage to St Patrick's Purgatory, in Lough Derg. This 'Purgatory', celebrated by Calderón†, is an island where the saint once killed a great serpent, and turned him into stone, and left his rocky semblance visible forever. Upon his return, his opinions, he states, changed considerably, and began slowly drifting into Protestantism.

One day he came to a translation of *Gil Blas*, and was set all agog to see the world and try its chances. Accordingly, he again left his native village, this time not to return. For a while he lingered teaching in Louth, and then starting away again, reached Dublin with the proverbial half-crown in his pocket. After a hard struggle with poverty, in which he turned or tried to turn his hand to many things, he met with Caesar Otway, a well-known anti-papal controversialist, who set him down to write an account of Lough Derg. It was soon written, and published, and well praised. As it now stands, many controversial passages taken out by Carleton's later judgment, it is a tale of the most vivid kind, though its picturesque troops of praying peasants and avowed *votheens*[76] are somewhat injured in simplicity, and also doubtless in truth to nature, by the zeal of the convert.

From this on there is little to record but the publication of his works. The authorities for facts concerning him are few indeed. He married, and eked out his income by teaching his hedge-school Latin. When about thirty he published the *Traits and Stories of the Irish Peasantry*, and become famous in a fashion. Then came *Irish Life and Character*, and *Fardorougha the Miser*, the miser himself being the largest in conception and most finished in execution of all his characters. *The Emigrants of Ahadarra*†, *Valentine M'Clutchy*†, and *The Black Prophet*, with its sombre and passionate dialogue, followed rapidly.[77]

By this time the† 'Young Ireland' movement was in full swing, and 'the National Library', founded by Davis, selling in thousands.[78] Carleton, who had more and more with each succeeding story returned to the beliefs and feelings of his fathers, felt bound to do his part. He wrote a series of short stories in such a style as to be read by the peasantry: 'Paddy Go-Easy'†, a temperance tale, said by Father Mathew to be the best in existence;[79] *Redmond Count O'Hanlon*, the life of a famous outlaw;[80] and *Rody the Rover*, on a favorite theme of his – the secret societies. Rody is an *agent provocateur*, a creature bred in all ages by government in Ireland.[81]

On the death of John Banim, in 1842, an attempt was made to have his pension transferred to Carleton, but some official having discovered that this writer of a temperance tale, read through the whole country like a chap-book, himself drank a deal more than was wholesome, the pension was refused. It might have saved Carleton from years of stumbling decadence brought on by years of hack work. Government has never much minded a drunken magistrate or so, but grows very particular when a man of genius is in question.

Carleton in the latter years of his life wrote little to any good purpose. Poor, feeble stories came from his desk in rapid succession. One or two succeeded, so capricious is public taste; a semi-historical romance of this period being now in its twentieth edition,[82] a success not granted to *Fardorougha* or *The Black Prophet*, both great novels and both out of print. The greater number of the books of his decadence failed, however, and he lived in much poverty almost to his death in 1869. A short time before it he was given the pension refused many years earlier.

SAMUEL LOVER
1797–1868

Samuel Lover was born in Dublin on the 24th of February, 1797. His father was a well-known stock-broker. As young Lover grew up, tales of those innumerable outrages of soldiers and yeomen that had so much to do with bringing on the great rebellion, were dinned into his ears by nurses and servants. Nothing else, perhaps, had so much to do with waking that sympathy with peasant life so visible in his stories. At thirteen he entered his father's office, but spent much of his time, to his father's disgust, in music, painting, verse-writing, and theatricals. At first the angry stock-broker tried obstruction – the paint-box or music-book would get lost mysteriously. Young Lover began more and more to neglect his office-work. When he was eighteen, things came to a climax. He had constructed a marionette show, and his father, unable any longer to bear with such 'frivolities', broke it into pieces with his walking-stick. Its owner, angry in his turn, left the house never to return.

For two years he lived in lodgings, studying art and making his living in some way that has never become known, but live he did, and not without some comfort, finding money enough to buy a guitar and leisure enough to practise it. At the end of the two years he emerged as a rising miniature painter. The Marquis Wellesley, the Duke of Leinster, and Lord Cloncurry sat to him, and Dublin society made him its latest lion. His handsome and mobile face, his numberless stories and good songs, opened all doors. He soon became known to the general public through the song of 'Rory O'More', written at the suggestion of Lady Morgan. Many more followed and repeated its success. Some, such as 'Molly Carew' and 'Widow Macree', are still well known.[83] In 1827 Lover married a Miss Birret, and, in 1834, took advantage of some renewed celebrity gained for him by a miniature of Paganini to move over to London.[84] His two well-known novels, *Rory O'More* and *Handy Andy*, were written and published soon after his arrival.[85] Their immense success induced him henceforth to make literature his main reliance. He wrote a number of dramas now forgotten, an adaptation of *Rory O'More* being the most successful. Indeed,

Rory O'More, as story, song, and stage play, was the triumph of his life.[86] In 1846 he went on a lecturing tour in America, reading selections from his own works. His last picture, *The Kerry Post on Valentine's Day*, was exhibited in Dublin in 1862.[87] He died on July the 6th, 1868.

WILLIAM MAGINN
Born 1794 Died 1842

William Maginn was born in Cork in 1794. He entered Trinity very young, and soon showed signs of the wide learning he was noted for later on. *Blackwood's*† was started in 1817, and Maginn contributed to an early number a translation into Latin of 'Chevy Chase'.[88] For a time he kept a school at Cork, where he came across and befriended Callanan, the first fine translator of old Irish songs, and himself author of some good and well prized verses.[89] In 1832 he married, gave up his school and settled in London, writing for *Blackwood's*† and the then newly started *Standard*, to the success of which he greatly contributed by his political articles. He quarrelled with *Blackwood's*† a little later, and founded in competition *Fraser's Magazine*.[90] In 1838 appeared his *Homeric Ballads*, called by Matthew Arnold 'genuine poems of their sort', but now forgotten.[91] He was all this time constantly in debt through wild living. Dissipation brought him more than once to the debtors' prison, but never did he lose his magnificent serenity. A man who saw him just before his death has thus described him: 'He was quite emaciated and worn away; his hands thin, and very little flesh on his face; his eyes appeared brighter and larger than usual, and his hair wild and disordered. He stretched out his hand and saluted me. He is in ruin, but a glorious ruin nevertheless. . . . He lives a rollicking life, and will write you one of his ablest articles while standing in his shirt or sipping brandy. We talked of Seneca, Homer, Christ, Plato, and Virgil.'[92] He died in 1842, aged forty-eight. He was the origin of Captain Shandon in *Pendennis*.[93] He left behind little beside a great mass of ephemeral articles. 'Father Tom', however, deserves to be long remembered. Its chief personage was a once well-known† Catholic controversialist, Father Tom

Maguire, who shortly before it was written had met in public debate and in the opinion of the multitude routed a Protestant clergyman named Pope.[94]

T. CROFTON CROKER
BORN 1798 DIED 1854

Croker was born in Cork in the year that produced Carleton and John Banim, the year of the great Rebellion. His father was a major in the army, and of course a Protestant. When quite young he was apprenticed to a Cork merchant, but the historian of fairy-land that was to be, stirred already within the mind of the clerk that was, and kept him busy studying local legends and antiquities. In 1818 Major Croker died, and his son started for London to seek his fortune. His namesake, John Wilson Croker, made notorious by Macaulay,[95] a friend but no relation, got him a post in the Admiralty. In 1821 he returned to Ireland, and planned out his first book, *Researches in the South of Ireland*. It was published in 1824. His famous *Fairy Legends* followed in 1825, and was so successful that he wrote immediately a second series.[96] The extract I have taken is from this book, and was considered by his friend and fellow-worker, Keetings, of *The Fairy Mythology*, to be the most valuable, from a folk-lore point of view, of all his writings, as it gives the actual words of a 'fairy man', or village seer.[97]

In 1850 Croker retired from the Admiralty Office on a pension, and lived in London until his death in 1854.

Scott, quoted by Mr Alfred Webb, has described him as 'little as a dwarf, keen-eyed as a hawk, of easy, prepossessing manners, something like Tom Moore'.[98] His work is always humorous and full of 'go', but marred by a constitutional difficulty in believing that any man, unless drunk, could see an apparition, a mode of looking at things more common among educated people in his day than in ours, and at all times destructive to the simplicity and grace of any tale of ghost or goblin that contains it. Nor could he take the peasants themselves quite seriously. The strain to make all things merry and laughable injured his sense of reality. At the same time he had a strong feeling for beauty and romance, and could tell a story better than most men.

GERALD GRIFFIN
Born 1803 – Died 1840

Gerald Griffin was the son of a Limerick brewer. In his seventh year his family moved to Fairylawn, a place on the Shannon, twenty-eight miles from Limerick. Here as time went on he did a deal of shooting and fishing, and acquired that love of legend and historic scenery so visible in his writings. He went to school in the neighborhood, but all that was most vital in his education came probably from his own reading. His favorite author, Virgil, may well have given him that sense of form that marks out his stories from those of other Irish writers. He soon began scribbling tales and poems, and worked on contentedly for some years, encouraged by mother and tutor.

In 1820, the family fortune having gradually dwindled away, his parents were compelled to emigrate to Pennsylvania. They left Gerald, a boy of seventeen, and his two sisters and his younger brother, in charge of their eldest son, a doctor at Adare. Gerald, instead of following his elder brother's example and studying medicine, as he was expected to, began writing for local papers. He now made the acquaintance of John Banim, at that time still obscure like himself.

In 1823, Gerald Griffin composed a tragedy called *Aguire*,[99] and started with it to London, where he remained until 1827, writing plays and stories, and half starving the while. The hard work and poverty of these four years completely wrecked his constitution. Banim, who had also moved over to London, befriended him so far as he would allow him to do so – and that was but little. To write for the stage was his ambition, but that failing he turned his hand to Irish stories, made hopeful by the success of the O'Hara tales, and published *Holland-Tide†*, the volume from which I have taken 'The Knight of the Sheep'.[100] In 1827 he returned home and wrote *Tales of the Munster Festivals*.[101] Next came incomparably his best work, *The Collegians*, the source of Boucicault's *Colleen Bawn*,[102] and the most finished and artistic of all Irish stories. A little later came a historical novel full of research, named *The Wonders*; but the stage remained always his ambition, and, Foster maintains, his true vocation.[103] His now at last rising fame as a novelist brought him little comfort. His novels were constantly perhaps no more than so much wearisome toil to raise the wind. He had always been religious, and amidst his times of toil and care religion grew into a passion. In his later books one feels its presence perpetually, and by no means to the gain of the art. In 1837 he left the world altogether, where clearly he was of most use to his country, and having burnt a number of unpublished works, joined the Christian Brothers,† where he spent his time, according to the custom of the order, in teaching poor children. For three years he 'made his soul' in peace, and then caught fever and died at the North Monastery,† Cork, in 1840, in his thirty-sixth year. A twelvemonth later an early tragedy of his, called *Gisippus*†, was acted with great applause at Covent Garden Theatre, with Macready in the principal part.[104] Miss Mitford has spoken of his life as telling more than all others of 'the broken heart of the man of genius'.[105]

In appearance Gerald Griffin was tall and delicate-looking. It was possible to see in his face the gentle and elegiac temperament that made up, together with a feeble body, a man little capable of shouldering his way.

His novels, though far more polished and complete than those of any other Irishman, are in no way comparable in power and in knowledge of Irish life with those of Carleton and Banim. For all that, their tender sentiment, checkered here and there with feelings of more tragic importance, have won them many friends. He is perhaps, more than all others, the novelist of middle-class Catholic Ireland. In verse, he wrote, beside his tragedies, of which *Gisippus*† alone has been preserved, many popular songs and ballads. They are musical and graceful rather than poetical in any deep sense. His care for finish and completeness, however, might have made him in time a writer of much importance.

CHARLES LEVER
1806–1872

Charles Lever was born on the 31st of August, 1806. His father was a well-known Dublin architect, around whose table were wont to gather many who had been ruined by the union with England and the consequent flight from Dublin of the fashionable and the wealthy. With the exception of stray visits to Galway and Kilkenny – his mother's town, – Lever grew up in this circle, among people whose minds ran ever on the gay and brilliant past, on the period of orators and duellists. At school he does not appear to have been in any way industrious, but busied himself with such matters as organizing his schoolfellows into a regular army, with generals, captains, sergeants, pickets, and the rest, and in helping to lead them to battle against a neighboring school. On one occasion, his side having fired a mine charged with several pounds of gunpowder under the hostile troops, they were all had up before the magistrate and fined. Lever, though little more than entered on his teens, won much honor and glory by addressing the court in favor of his fellows and himself.

He worked hard also at theatricals, being playwright, player, scene-painter, vocalist, and fiddler by turns.

In 1822 he entered Trinity, and, together with his 'chum' Boyle – the original of Webber in *Charles O'Malley*,[106] – lived there through five years of tumultuous high spirits. Like Goldsmith, he wrote street ballads, but, unlike Goldsmith, was not content to creep at night into some by-street to hear them sung,[107] and enjoy in the applause of the crowd a prophecy of fame. Having written some political verses too 'strong' for the trade, Lever went out disguised, together with his friend Boyle, and sang them through the streets. He roused great enthusiasm, and collected no less than thirty-six shillings in halfpence. From this we may judge that the 'strong' verses were against the government.

In 1829 he visited America, and lived for a time among the Canadian Indians. He was formally received into the tribe, and for a little all went well. At last he tired of endless fishing and hunting, and began to long for civilization. He tried, however, to hide his changed feelings, but one day a squaw read his thoughts, and looking fixedly at him, said: 'Your heart, stranger, is not with us now. You wish for your own people, but you will not see them again. Our chief will kill you if you leave us. It is the law of our tribe that none joining us can go away. No, you will never see the pale faces again, nor go back to your own country.'[108] Even if he fled, she told him, and escaped those who would pursue, he could never find the track through the forest. At length Lever grew so ill with longing to get away that the same squaw who had warned him took pity on him. She persuaded an Indian who came every now and then to the camp to barter tobacco and other produce of the settlements, to promise to guide him through the woods for money. By her advice, Lever pretended to be disabled by sickness, and so was left behind among the women when the men went hunting. When all was quiet he and the Indian plunged into the forest. They were pursued, but reached Quebec in safety.

On his return to Europe Lever studied medicine at Gottingen and became Bachelor of Medicine in 1831. Returning to Ireland he commenced practice in the North. In the cholera epidemic of 1832 he won much reputation for skill and devotion. In 1833 the† *Dublin University Magazine*† was started, and Lever was amongst its first contributors. In 1837 *Harry Lorrequer* appeared in its pages, and began his fame as a novelist.[109] From 1837 to 1840 one finds him again out of Ireland, doctoring at Brussels and writing *Charles O'Malley*.[110] Its publication made him at once one of the most important story-tellers of his time. He gave up his practice and returned to Ireland, and was appointed editor of the† *Dublin University Magazine*. About him gathered a circle of writers, some of whom have made their mark in Irish literature. There were among them men like Isaac Butt, the orator and politician; Maxwell and Le Fanu†, the novelists; and Samuel Ferguson, the antiquarian and chief ballad-writer of his day.[111] About him circled these men, the most brilliant of conservative Ireland, in the same period in which the more able spirits of the radical Nationalists drew thought and life from Thomas Davis. Between the two parties – the party of the wits and the party of the thinkers – all that was best in literary Ireland divided itself. Not that the circle who gathered round him had any leader in the sense in which the circle of Davis had. It is the very nature of wit to dissolve all leadership. But Lever was more constantly before the world than any other of his side. Book after book came from his tireless mind. In 1845 he left Ireland, having obtained a diplomatic post at Florence, and spent his remaining years abroad. He died in 1872 at Trieste.

He is the most popular in England of all Irish writers, but has never won a place beside Carleton and Banim, or even Griffin, in the hearts of the Irish people. His books, so full of gayety and animal laughter, are true merely to the life of the party of ascendancy, and to that of their dependants. It will be a long time before the world tires altogether of his gay, witty, reckless personages, though it is gradually learning that they are not typical Irish men and women.

CHARLES KICKHAM
BORN, 1825; DIED, 1882

Charles Kickham, novelist, poet, and Fenian, was the son of a draper in Mullinahonet†, a small town in Tipperary. When Sir Charles Gavan Duffy and Thomas Davis started the *Nation* newspaper, in 1845, he was just twenty – the age when most men begin to form their opinions.[112] The impassioned prose and verse of 'Young Ireland' found him a ready listener, and prepared him to take, together with his kinsman, John O'Mahoney, a prominent part in the attempted insurrection of '48.[113] He was the leading spirit in the Confederate Club at Mullinahonet†, and after the collapse at Ballingarry, a little way from where he lived, he lay in hiding for a time. Soon after, he worked earnestly in the Tenant-Right League, and when that failed gave up all faith in legal agitation, and became one of the leaders of the Fenian movement. John O'Leary, T. C. Luby, and Charles Kickham were the triumvirate appointed to control its action in Ireland.[114] In 1865 he was arrested, and sentenced to fourteen years' penal servitude. He had always had wretched health, and partly on this account was released in four years. He returned to Ireland, and lived there until his death at Blackrock,[115] in 1882.

He was the most lovable of men. Women and children seem especially to have been attached to him. Some one asked him what did he miss most in gaol. 'Children, women, and fires,' he answered.[116] One of the touching things in Kickham's character was an ever-present love for his native town; its mountains and its rivers are often referred to in his writings. A few months before his death, a friend found him gazing intently at the picture of a cow in a Dublin gallery. 'It is so like an old cow at Mullinahone†,' he said.[117] I have seen an unpublished poem of his written in gaol, in which he recalled watching from a bridge at his native place 'the sunset fading' away as though 'quenched by the dew'.[118]

He bore cheerfully from his fourteenth or fifteenth year a burden of partial deafness and blindness, caused by an explosion of a flask of powder. His sentence had to be announced to him through an ear-trumpet, and both deafness and blindness were greatly increased by imprisonment.

Kickham's three novels, *Sally Cavanagh†*, *Knocknagow†*, and *For the Old Land*,[119] are devoted to one subject – a conscientious, laborious study of Irish life and Irish wrongs. *Sally Cavanagh†*, the most impassioned and direct, was written before his imprisonment, the others after. One feels through all he wrote that in him were much humor and character-describing power of wholly Celtic kind, but marred by imperfect training. His books are put together in a hap-hazard kind of way – without beginning, middle, or end. His ballads are much more perfect than his stories. 'Blind Sheehan'† and 'She Dwelt beside the Anner'† will last for many a long day yet.[120]

MISS ROSA MULHOLLAND[121]

Miss Mulholland is the novelist of contemporary Catholic Ireland. She has not the square-built power of our older writers, Banim, Carleton, and their tribe, but has, instead, much fancy and style of a sort commoner in our day than theirs, and a distinction of feeling and thought peculiar to herself.

Introduction ('An Irish Story-teller'), acknowledgement note, 'The Classification of Irish Fairies', and 'Authorities on Irish Folklore' (1891), in *Irish Fairy Tales*, ed. W. B. Yeats (1892)

AN IRISH STORY-TELLER

I am often doubted when I say that the Irish peasantry still believe in fairies. People think I am merely trying to bring back a little of the old dead beautiful world of romance into this century of great engines and spinning-jennies†. Surely the hum of wheels and clatter of printing presses, to let alone the lecturers with their black coats and tumblers of water, have driven away the goblin kingdom and made silent the feet of the little dancers.

Old Biddy Hart at any rate does not think so. Our bran-new opinions have never been heard of under her brown-thatched roof tufted with yellow stonecrop. It is not so long since I sat by the turf fire eating her griddle cake in her cottage on the slope of Benbulben[1] and asking after her friends, the fairies, who inhabit the green thorn-covered hill up there behind her house. How firmly she believed in them! how greatly she feared offending them! For a long time she would give me no answer but 'I always mind my own affairs and they always mind theirs'. A little talk about my great-grandfather who lived all his life in the valley below, and a few words to remind her how I myself was often under her roof when but seven or eight years old loosened her tongue, however.[2] It would be less dangerous at any rate to talk to me of the fairies than it would be to tell some 'Towrow' of them, as she contemptuously called English tourists, for I had lived under the shadow of their own hillsides. She did not forget, however, to remind me to say after we had finished, 'God bless them, Thursday'[3] (that being the day), and so ward off their displeasure, in case they were angry at our notice, for they love to live and dance unknown of men.

Once started, she talked on freely enough, her face glowing in the firelight as she bent over the griddle or stirred the turf, and told how such a one was stolen away from near Coloney village[4] and made to live seven years among 'the gentry', as she calls the fairies for politeness' sake, and how when she came home she had no toes, for she had danced them off; and how such another was taken from the neighbouring village of Grange[5] and compelled to nurse the child of the queen of the fairies a few months before I came. Her news about the creatures is always quite matter-of-fact and detailed, just as if she dealt with any common occurrence: the late fair, or the dance at Rosses[6] last year, when a bottle of whisky was given to the best man, and a cake tied up in ribbons to the best woman dancer. They are, to her, people not so different from herself, only grander and finer in every way. They have the most beautiful parlours and drawing-rooms, she would tell you, as an old man told me once. She has endowed them with all she knows of splendour, although that is not such a great deal, for her imagination is easily pleased. What does not seem to us so very wonderful is wonderful to her, there, where all is so homely under her wood rafters and her thatched ceiling covered with whitewashed canvas. We have pictures and books to help us imagine a splendid fairy world of gold and silver, of crowns and marvellous draperies; but she has only that little picture of St Patrick over the fireplace, the bright-coloured crockery on the dresser, and the sheet of ballads stuffed by her young daughter behind the stone dog on the mantelpiece. Is it strange, then, if her fairies have not the fantastic glories of the fairies you and I are wont to see in picture-books and read of in stories? She will tell you of peasants who met the fairy cavalcade and thought it but a troop of peasants like themselves until it vanished into shadow and night, and of great fairy palaces that were mistaken, until they melted away, for the country seats of rich gentlemen.

Her views of heaven itself have the same homeliness, and she would be quite as naïve about its personages if the chance offered as was the pious Clondalkin laundress who told a friend of mine that she had seen a vision of St Joseph, and that he had 'a lovely shining hat upon him and a shirt-buzzom that was never starched in this world'.[7] She would have mixed some quaint poetry with it, however; for there is a world of difference between Benbulben and Dublinised Clondalkin.

Heaven and Fairyland – to these has Biddy Hart given all she dreams of magnificence, and to them her soul goes out – to the one in love and hope, to the other in love and fear – day after day and season after season; saints and angels, fairies and witches, haunted thorn-trees and holy wells, are to her what books, and plays, and pictures are to you and me. Indeed they are far more; for too many among us grow prosaic and commonplace, but she keeps ever a heart full of music. 'I stand here in the doorway,' she said once to me on a fine day, 'and look at the mountain and think of the goodness of God'; and when she talks of the fairies I have noticed a touch of tenderness in her voice. She loves them because they are always young, always making festival, always far off from the old age that is coming upon her and filling her bones with aches, and because, too, they are so like little children.

Do you think the Irish peasant would be so full of poetry if he had not his fairies? Do you think the peasant girls of Donegal, when they are going to service inland, would kneel down as they do and kiss the sea with their lips if both sea and land were not made lovable to them by beautiful legends and wild sad stories? Do you think the old men would take life so cheerily and mutter their proverb, 'The lake is not burdened by its swan, the steed by its bridle, or a man by the soul that is in him', if the multitude of spirits were not near them?

W. B. Yeats
Clondalkin, July 1891

NOTE

I have to thank Lady Wilde for leave to give 'Seanchan the Bard' from her *Ancient Legends of Ireland* (Ward and Downey),[8] the most poetical and ample collection of Irish folk-lore yet published; Mr Standish O'Grady for leave to give 'The Knighting of Cuchulain'† from that prose epic he has curiously named *History of Ireland, Heroic Period*;[9] Professor Joyce[10] for his 'Fergus O'Mara and the Air Demons'; and Mr Douglas Hyde for his unpublished story, 'The Man who never knew Fear'.

I have included no story that has already appeared in my *Fairy and Folk Tales of the Irish Peasantry* (Camelot Series).[11]

The two volumes make, I believe, a fairly representative collection of Irish folk tales.

CLASSIFICATION OF IRISH FAIRIES

Irish Fairies divide themselves into two great classes: the sociable and the solitary. The first are in the main kindly, and the second full of all uncharitableness.

THE SOCIABLE FAIRIES

These creatures, who go about in troops, and quarrel, and make love, much as men and women do, are divided into land fairies or Sheoques (Ir. *Sidheog*, 'a little fairy'),† and water fairies or Merrows (Ir. *Moruadh*, 'a sea maid'; the masculine is unknown). At the same time I am inclined to think that the term Sheoque may be applied to both upon occasion, for I have heard of a whole village turning out to hear two red-capped water fairies, who were very 'little fairies' indeed, play upon the bagpipes.

1. *The Sheoques.* – The Sheoques proper, however, are the spirits that haunt the sacred thorn bushes and the green raths. All over Ireland are little fields circled by ditches, and supposed to be ancient fortifications and sheepfolds. These are the raths, or forts, or 'royalties', as they are variously called. Here, marrying and giving in marriage, live the land fairies. Many a mortal they are said to have enticed down into their dim world. Many more have listened to their fairy music, till all human cares and joys drifted from their hearts and they became great peasant seers or 'Fairy Doctors', or great peasant musicians or poets like Carolan,[12] who gathered his tunes while sleeping on a fairy rath; or else they died in a year and a day, to live ever after among the fairies. These Sheoques are on the whole good; but

one most malicious habit they have – a habit worthy of a witch. They steal children and leave a withered fairy, a thousand or maybe two thousand years old, instead. Three or four years ago a man wrote to one of the Irish papers, telling of a case in his own village, and how the parish priest made the fairies deliver the stolen child up again. At times full-grown men and women have been taken. Near the village of Coloney, Sligo, I have been told, lives an old woman who was taken in her youth. When she came home at the end of seven years she had no toes, for she had danced them off. Now and then one hears of some real injury being done a person by the land fairies, but then it is nearly always deserved. They are said to have killed two people in the last six months in the County Down district where I am now staying.[13] But then these persons had torn up thorn bushes belonging to the Sheoques.

2. *The Merrows.* – These water fairies are said to be common. I asked a peasant woman once whether the fishermen of her village had ever seen one. 'Indeed, they don't like to see them at all', she answered, 'for they always bring bad weather.' Sometimes the Merrows come out of the sea in the shape of little hornless cows. When in their own shape, they have fishes' tails and wear a red cap called in Irish *cohuleen driuth*.[14] The men among them have, according to Croker, green teeth, green hair, pigs' eyes, and red noses;[15] but their women are beautiful, and sometimes prefer handsome fishermen to their green-haired lovers. Near Bantry, in the last century, lived a woman covered with scales like a fish, who was descended, as the story goes, from such a marriage.[16] I have myself never heard tell of this grotesque appearance of the male Merrows, and think it probably a merely local Munster tradition.

THE SOLITARY FAIRIES

These are nearly all gloomy and terrible in some way. There are, however, some among them who have light hearts and brave attire.

1. *The Lepricaun* (Ir. *Leith bhrogan*, i.e. the one shoe maker[17]). – This creature is seen sitting under a hedge mending a shoe, and one who catches him can make him deliver up his crocks of

gold, for he is a miser of great wealth; but if you take your eyes
off him the creature vanishes like smoke. He is said to be the
child of an evil spirit and a debased fairy, and wears, according
to McAnally, a red coat with seven buttons in each row, and a
cocked-hat,[18] on the point of which he sometimes spins like a
top. In Donegal he goes clad in a great frieze coat.

2. *The Cluricaun* (Ir. *Clobhair-cean* in O'Kearney[19]). – Some
writers consider this to be another name for the Lepricaun,
given him when he has laid aside his shoe-making at night and
goes on the spree. The Cluricauns' occupations are robbing
wine-cellars and riding sheep and shepherds' dogs for a
livelong night, until the morning finds them panting and
mud-covered.

3. *The Gonconer or Ganconagh* (Ir. *Gean-canogh*, i.e. love-talker).
– This is a creature of the Lepricaun type, but, unlike him, is a
great idler. He appears in lonely valleys, always with a pipe in
his mouth, and spends his time in making love to shepherdesses
and milkmaids.

4. *The Far Darrig* (Ir. *Fear Dearg*, i.e. red man). – This is the
practical joker of the other world. The wild Sligo story I give of
'A Fairy Enchantment'[20] was probably his work. Of these
solitary and mainly evil fairies there is no more lubberly wretch
than this same Far Darrig. Like the next phantom, he presides
over evil dreams.

5. *The Pooka* (Ir. *Púca*, a word derived by some from *poc*, a
he-goat). – The Pooka seems of the family of the nightmare. He
has most likely never appeared in human form, the one or two
recorded instances being probably mistakes, he being mixed up
with the Far Darrig. His shape is usually that of a horse, a bull,
a goat, eagle, or ass. His delight is to get a rider, whom he
rushes with through ditches and rivers and over mountains,
and shakes off in the gray of the morning. Especially does he
love to plague a drunkard: a drunkard's sleep is his kingdom.
At times he takes more unexpected forms than those of beast or
bird. The one that haunts the Dun of Coch-na-Phuca in
Kilkenny takes the form of a fleece of wool, and at night rolls out
into the surrounding fields, making a buzzing noise that so
terrifies the cattle that unbroken colts will run to the nearest
man and lay their heads upon his shoulder for protection.

6. *The Dullahan.* – This is a most gruesome thing. He has no

head, or carries it under his arm. Often he is seen driving a black coach called coach-a-bower (Ir. *Coite-bodhar*), drawn by headless horses. It rumbles to your door, and if you open it a basin of blood is thrown in your face. It is an omen of death to the houses where it pauses. Such a coach not very long ago went through Sligo in the gray of the morning, as was told me by a sailor who believed he saw it. In one village I know its rumbling is said to be heard many times in the year.

7. *The Leanhaun Shee* (Ir. *Leanhaun sidhe*, i.e. fairy mistress). – This spirit seeks the love of men. If they refuse, she is their slave; if they consent, they are hers, and can only escape by finding one to take their place. Her lovers waste away, for she lives on their life. Most of the Gaelic poets, down to quite recent times, have had a Leanhaun Shee, for she gives inspiration to her slaves and is indeed the Gaelic muse – this malignant fairy. Her lovers, the Gaelic poets, died young. She grew restless, and carried them away to other worlds, for death does not destroy her power.

8. *The Far Gorta* (man of hunger). – The is an emaciated fairy that goes through the land in famine time, begging and bringing good luck to the giver.

9. *The Banshee* (Ir. *Bean-sidhe*, i.e. fairy woman). – This fairy, like the Far Gorta, differs from the general run of solitary fairies by its generally good disposition. She is perhaps not really one of them at all, but a sociable fairy grown solitary through much sorrow. The name corresponds to the less common Far Shee (Ir. *Fear Sidhe*), a man fairy. She wails, as most people know, over the death of a member of some old Irish family. Sometimes she is an enemy of the house and screams with triumph, but more often a friend. When more than one Banshee comes to cry, the man or woman who is dying must have been very holy or very brave. Occasionally she is most undoubtedly one of the social fairies. Cleena, once an Irish princess and then a Munster goddess, and now a Sheoque, is thus mentioned by the greatest of Irish antiquarians.[21]

O'Donovan, writing in 1849 to a friend, who quotes his words in the *Dublin University Magazine*, says: 'When my grandfather died in Leinster in 1798, Cleena came all the way from Ton Cleena to lament him; but she has not been heard ever since lamenting any of our race, though I believe she still weeps in the mountains of Drumaleague in her own country, where so many of the race of Eoghan More are dying of starvation.'[22] The Banshee on the other hand who cries with triumph is often believed to be no fairy but a ghost of one wronged by an ancestor of the dying. Some say wrongly that she never goes beyond the seas, but dwells always in her own country. Upon the other hand, a distinguished writer on anthropology assures me that he has heard her on 1† December 1867, in Pital, near Libertad, Central America, as he rode through a deep forest. She was dressed in pale yellow, and raised a cry like the cry of a bat. She came to announce the death of his father. This is her cry, written down by him with the help of a Frenchman and a violin.

He saw and heard her again on 5† February 1871, at 16 Devonshire Street, Queen's Square, London. She came this time to announce the death of his eldest child; and in 1884 he again saw and heard her at 28 East Street, Queen's Square, the death of his mother being the cause.[23]

The Banshee is called *badh* or *bowa* in East Munster, and is named *Bachuntha* by Banim in one of his novels.[24]

Other Fairies and Spirits. – Besides the foregoing, we have other solitary fairies, of which too little definite is known to give them each a separate mention. They are the House Spirits, of whom 'Teigue of the Lee' is probably an instance;[25] the Water Sherie, a kind of will-o'-the-wisp; the Sowlth, a formless luminous creature; the Pastha (*Piast-bestia*), the lake dragon, a guardian of hidden treasure; and the Bo men fairies, who live in the marshes of County Down and destroy the unwary. They may be driven away by a blow from a particular kind of sea-weed. I suspect them of being Scotch fairies imported by Scotch settlers. Then there is the great tribe of ghosts called Thivishes in some parts.

These are all the fairies and spirits I have come across in Irish folklore. There are probably many others undiscovered.

W. B. Yeats
Co. Down, June 1891[26]

AUTHORITIES ON IRISH FOLKLORE

Croker's *Legends of the South of Ireland*; Lady Wilde's *Ancient Legends of Ireland*, and *Ancient Charms*; Sir William Wilde's *Irish Popular Superstitions*; McAnally's *Irish Wonders*; *Irish Folkore*, by Lageniensis (Father O'Hanlan); Curtin's† *Myths and Folklore of Ireland*; Douglas Hyde's *Beside the Fire* and his *Leabhar Sgeulaigheachta*; Patrick Kennedy's *Legendary Fictions of the Irish Peasantry*, his *Banks of the Boro*, his *Evenings in† the Duffrey*, and his *Legends of Mount Leinster*; the chap-books, *Royal Fairy Tales*, and *Tales of the Fairies*. There is also much folklore in Carleton's *Traits and Stories*; in Lover's *Legends and Stories of the Irish Peasantry*; in Mr and Mrs S. C. Hall's *Ireland*; in Lady Chatterton's *Rambles in the South of Ireland*; in Gerald Griffin's† *Tales of a Jury Room* in particular, and in his other books in general. It would repay the trouble if some Irish magazine would select from his works the stray legends and scraps of fairy belief. There is much in the *Collegians*. There is also folklore in the chap-book *Hibernian Tales*, and a Banshee story or two will be found in Miss Lefanu's *Memoirs of my Grandmother*, and in Barrington's *Recollections*. There are also stories in Donovan's introduction to the *Four Masters*. The best articles are those in the *Dublin and London Magazine* ('The Fairy Greyhound' is from this collection) for 1827 and 1829, about a dozen in all, and David Fitzgerald's various contributions to the *Revue† Celtique* in our own day, and Miss M'Clintock's articles in the *Dublin University Magazine* for 1878. There are good articles also in the *Dublin University Magazine* for 1839, and much Irish folklore is within the pages of the *Folklore Journal* and the *Folklore Record*, and in the proceedings of the Kilkenny Archaeological Society. The *Penny Journal*, the *Newry Magazine*, *Duffy's Sixpenny Magazine*, and the *Hibernian Magazine*, are also worth a search by any Irish writer on the lookout for subjects for song or ballad. My own articles in the *Scots Observer* and *National Observer* give many gatherings from the little-reaped Connaught fields. I repeat this list of authorities from my *Fairy and Folk Tales of the Irish Peasantry*, – a compilation from some of the sources mentioned, – bringing it down to date and making one or two corrections. The reader who would know Irish tradition should read these books above all others – Lady Wilde's *Ancient Legends*, Douglas Hyde's *Beside the Fire*, and a book not mentioned in the foregoing list, for it deals with the bardic rather than the folk literature, Standish O'Grady's *History of Ireland, Heroic Period* – perhaps the most imaginative book written on any Irish subject in recent decades.[27]

'William Allingham 1824–1889' (1891), in *The Poets and the Poetry of the Century*, ed. Alfred H. Miles (1892)

William Allingham was born in 1824 in Ballyshannon, a little Donegal town, where his ancestors had lived for generations. Here he grew up, filling his mind with all the quaint legends and fancies that linger still in such odd corners of the world, and with that devotion for the place where he was born, felt by few people so intensely as by the Irish. When he was old enough, a small post in the Customs was found for him, and there seemed every likelihood of his spending an obscure life in

> a little town
> Where little folk go up and down.[1]

In his twenty-sixth year his first volume, *Poems*, was issued, and, four years later, in 1854, the first series of those *Day and Night Songs*, which contain so many of his best lyrics. *The Music Master* and a new series of 'Day and Night Songs' followed in 1855.[2] From 1848 it had been his custom to cross over to London every summer. In one of these visits he had met Rossetti, and been introduced by him to Millais and the rest of the pre-Raphaelites. Rossetti and Millais now illustrated *The Music Master* with the fine drawings reprinted in the collected edition of Allingham's works.[3] It was followed by *Laurence Bloomfield* – an agrarian epic – and *Fifty Modern Poems*, containing his last Ballyshannon verses, in 1864 and 1865 respectively.[4] During these years he had also published poems in Ballyshannon itself, by means of broadsheets, which had a wide circulation among the peasantry. The Government considered this local popularity of his verse useful to education, and rewarded him with a pension of £60 a year.

He now left Ballyshannon for London, and either because his

imagination flagged among the London crowds, or because he had said all that was in him to say, or for some other reason not so easy to trace, he ceased to write any poetry as good as the old, and little poetry of any kind. He busied himself with revising, not always happily, his earlier verses, and republishing them from time to time. In 1874 he was appointed editor of *Fraser's*†, and printed in its pages his one prose book, *The Rambles of Patricius Walker*, an account of his journeys through English country places.[5] In the same year he married Miss Helen Paterson, the well-known artist. Among his few poetical ventures in these later years were *Ashby Manor*, a play written in alternate prose and verse, limpid and graceful, but quite lacking in true passion and dramatic energy; and *Evil May Day*, a heavy argumentative experiment in philosophic poetry.[6] He had almost quite lost the light touch and flying fancy of his younger days, and but seldom gave any echo of the old beauty in stray lyric or haphazard snatch of rhyme. The last years of his life were spent mainly at Witley†,[7] where he died in 1889, after a somewhat long illness, brought on by a fall when riding.

To feel the entire fascination of his poetry, it is perhaps necessary to have spent one's childhood, like the present writer, in one of those little seaboard Connaught towns. He has expressed that curious devotion of the people for the earth under their feet, a devotion that is not national, but local, a thing at once more narrow and more idyllic. He sang Ballyshannon and not Ireland. Neither his emotions nor his thoughts took any wide sweep over the world of man and nature. He was the poet of little things and little moments, and of that vague melancholy Lord Palmerston considered peculiar to the peasantry of the wild seaboard where he lived.[8] In one of the rare moments of quaint inspiration that came to him in recent years, he wrote –

> Four ducks on a pond,
> A grass-bank beyond,
> A blue sky of spring,
> White clouds on the wing;
> What a little thing
> To remember for years –
> To remember with tears!

and in the words summed up unconsciously his own poetic personality. The charm of his work is everywhere the charm of stray moments and detached scenes that have moved him; the pilot's daughter in her Sunday frock; the wake with the candles round the corpse, and a cloth under the chin; the ruined Abbey of Asaroe, an old man who was of the blood of those who founded it, watching sadly the crumbling walls; girls sewing and singing under a thorn tree; the hauling in of the salmon nets; the sound of a clarionet through the open and ruddy shutter of a forge, the piano from some larger house, and so on, a rubble of old memories and impressions made beautiful by pensive feeling.[9] Exquisite in short lyrics, this method of his was quite inadequate to keep the interest alive through a long poem. *Laurence Bloomfield*, for all its stray felicities, is dull, and *The Music Master* and 'The Lady of the Sea' are tame and uninventive.[10] He saw neither the great unities of God or of man, of his own spiritual life or of the life of the nation about him, but looked at all through a kaleidoscope full of charming accidents and momentary occurrences. In greater poets everything has relation to the national life or to profound feeling; nothing is an isolated artistic moment; there is a unity everywhere, everything fulfils a purpose that is not its own; the hailstone is a journeyman of God, and the grass blade carries the universe upon its point.[11] But, then, if Allingham had had this greater virtue, he might have lost that which was peculiar to himself, and we might never have had the 'Twilight Voices' or 'Mary Donnelly', or that bitter-sweet exile ballad 'The Winding Banks of Erne'.[12]

W. B. Yeats

'Ellen O'Leary 1831–1889' (1891), in *The Poets and the Poetry of the Century*, ed. Alfred H. Miles (1892)

Miss O'Leary, the Fenian poet, belongs to a type of writers better known in Ireland than in England. Her verses are songs and ballads in the old sense of the word rather than poems and lyrics. Living in a country where the populace are strongly moved by great fundamental passions, she was able to find an audience for her tender and simple rhymes. The streets of her native Tipperary have echoed more than once to some ballad of hers about emigrants and their sorrows, or like theme, sung by the ballad-singers from their little strips of fluttering paper. *The Commercial Journal*, *The Irishman*, and the Fenian organ *The Irish People*,[1] helped also to spread her verse through the country. Her poetry, and the poetry of Casey, and Kickham's *Sally Cavanagh*† and his three or four ballads, made up, indeed, the whole literary product of the Fenian agitation.[2] 'Young Ireland' days had brought their reaction of silence.[3] Simple verse could still, however, find an audience; as it, indeed, always can in Ireland, where the ballad age has not yet gone by. It may be that a troubled history and the smouldering unrest of agitation and conspiracy are good for the making of ballads. If this be so, Miss O'Leary lived amid surroundings of an ideal kind, for all her life she was deep in the councils of Fenianism. Her brother, Mr John O'Leary, is now the most important survivor of the company of men who led the forlorn hope of 1864. O'Leary, Kickham, and Luby formed what was known as the Triumvirate under James Stephens, who bore the singular title of 'Chief Executive'.[4] In 1864 Stephens, O'Leary, Luby, and Kickham were arrested. The escape of Stephens was at once planned, and carried out successfully.[5] Miss O'Leary was the only woman told of the project. From this on she was constantly employed by Stephens carrying messages.

While her brother was awaiting trial, she obeyed without murmur a command that sent her to Paris. Her brother might have been condemned to penal servitude in her absence, but she put her cause before all else. She was back in time, however, to hear the sentence pronounced, and to listen to his characteristic speech: 'I have been found guilty of treason or treason felony. Treason is a foul crime. The poet Dante consigned traitors, I believe, to the ninth circle of hell; but what kind of traitors? Traitors against king, against country, against friends, against benefactors. England is not my country, and I have betrayed no friend, no benefactors. Sidney and Emmet were legal traitors.'[6]

It is impossible to describe Miss O'Leary's life without touching on that of her brother, for he was the most powerful influence she met with. His imprisonment did not, however, abate her political activity. She hid more than one rebel for whom the Government was searching; and when it became necessary to get James Stephens out of the country, raised £200 by a mortgage on some small property she had, to charter a vessel. In 1867, the movement having failed, she went to her native town, and lived there until her brother's return in 1885. He had been five years in prison and fifteen in banishment, but returned still hopeful for Ireland, still waiting the day of deliverance. From 1885 until her death she lived with her brother in Dublin, and their house became a centre of literary endeavour. A little circle of writers who have sought to carry on the ballad literature of Ireland according to the tradition of 1848 drew much of their inspiration from the teaching of Mr O'Leary and his sister,[7] and many of their facts and legends from the books that filled every corner and crevice of Mr O'Leary's rooms. Indeed, no influence in modern Ireland has been more ennobling than that of these two Fenians. Driven by the force of events into hostility to all the dominant parties in Irish politics, they concentrated their influence upon giving to all they met a loftier public spirit and more devoted patriotism. Unionist or Nationalist, Conservative or Liberal, it was nearly all one to them, if they thought you loved Ireland and were ready to seek her prosperity by setting the moral law above all the counsels of expediency. On this last they ever dwelt with most uncompromising insistence.

Miss O'Leary died in 1889, just when she had completed the correction of a collected edition of her poems. It is from this volume, published in 1890 by Sealey, Bryers, and Walker (Lower Abbey Street, Dublin), that the selection has been made.[8]

Poetry such as hers belongs to a primitive country and a young literature. It is exceedingly simple, both in thought and expression. Its very simplicity and sincerity have made it, like much Irish verse, unequal; for when the inspiration fails, the writer has no art to fall back upon. Nor does it know anything of studied adjective and subtle observation. To it the grass is simply green and the sea simply blue; and yet it has, in its degree, the sacred passion of true poetry.

W. B. Yeats

Preface (*c.* 1892) to
The Works of William Blake:
Poetic, Symbolic, and Critical,
ed. Edwin J. Ellis and W. B. Yeats, 3 vols
(1893)

The reader must not expect to find in this account of Blake's myth, or this explanation of his symbolic writings, a substitute for Blake's own works. A paraphrase is given of most of the more difficult poems, but no single thread of interpretation can fully guide the explorer through the intricate paths of a symbolism where most of the figures of speech have a two-fold meaning, and some are employed systematically in a three-fold, or even a four-fold sense. 'Allegory addressed to the intellectual powers while it is altogether hidden from the corporeal understanding is my definition', writes Blake, 'of the most sublime poetry'.[1]

Such allegory fills the 'Prophetic Books',[2] yet it is not so hidden from the corporeal understanding as its author supposed. An explanation, continuous throughout, if not complete for side issues, may be obtained from the enigma itself by the aid of ordinary industry. Such an explanation forms, not perhaps the whole, but certainly the greater part, of the present volumes. Every line, whether written for the 'understanding' or the 'intellect', is based on a line of Blake's own.

Two principal causes have hitherto kept the critics, – among whom must be included Mr Swinburne himself, though he reigns as the one-eyed man of the proverb among the blind, – from attaining a knowledge of what Blake meant.[3]

The first is the solidity of the myth, and its wonderful coherence. The second is the variety of terms in which the sections of it are named.

The foundation of Blake's symbolic system of speech is his conception of the Four-fold in Man, and the covering that concealed this system was a peculiar use of synonyms. The four portions of Humanity are divided under the names of the Four Zoas in the myth,[4] and the reader who does not understand the relation of the Four Zoas to each other, and to each living man, has not made even the first step towards understanding the Symbolic System which is the signature of Blake's genius, and the guarantee of his sanity. Mr Swinburne, Mr Gilchrist, and the brothers, Dante and William Rossetti, deserve well of literature for having brought Blake into the light of day and made his name known throughout the length and breadth of England.[5] But though whatever is accessible to us now was accessible to them when they wrote, including the then unpublished 'Vala', not one chapter, not one clear paragraph about the myth of Four Zoas, is to be found in all that they have published.

With regard to the use of synonyms, which must be understood before the Four Zoas can be traced through their different disguises, the earliest idea of this, as a mere guess, occurred to the editor[6] whose name stands first on the present title-page, in the year 1870. The suggestion arose through a remark in the first edition of Gilchrist's *Life of Blake*, where the poem 'To the Jews', from *Jerusalem*, was printed with a challenge at the beginning, calling on those who could do so, to offer an interpretation.

In the later edition this challenge was withdrawn,[7] probably under the impression that it had not been accepted. The glove, however, had been quietly taken up. 'What if Blake should turn out to use the quarters of London to indicate the points of the compass, as he uses these to group certain qualities of mind associated with certain of the senses and the elements?' This was the idea that presented itself, and eventually led us to shape the master-key that unlocked all the closed doors of the poet's house.

It happened, however, that the idea was fated to be laid aside almost unused for many years. The maker of the lucky guess had only given a week or two of study, and barely succeeded in assuring himself that he was on the right track, when the course of destiny took him to Italy and kept him there, with only brief and busy visits to England and other countries, until a few years ago.[8] In the meantime the other editor had grown up, and become a student of mysticism. He came one day and asked to have Blake explained. Very little could be given him to satisfy so large a demand, but with his eye for symbolic systems, he needed no more to enable him to perceive that here was a myth as well worth study as any that has been offered to the world, since first men learned that myths were briefer and more beautiful than exposition as well as deeper and more companionable. He saw, too, that it was no mere freak of an eccentric mind, but an eddy of that flood-tide of symbolism which attained its tide-mark in the magic of the Middle Ages.

From that moment the collaboration which has produced the present work was begun, and it has gone on, notwithstanding some unforeseen and serious interruptions, for four years. The fellow labourers have not worked hand in hand, but rather have been like sportsmen who pursue the game on different tracks and in the evening divide their spoils. Each has learned in this way that the other was indispensable. The result is not two different views of Blake, so much as one view, reached by two opposite methods of study, worked out in order to satisfy two different forms of mental enjoyment.

Except in connection with the Memoir,[9] very little assistance was to be had from outside. The biographical matter has been added to considerably, the greater part of the space being given to hitherto unpublished facts, while some twenty or thirty pages are condensations of the story as told in the accounts of Blake's life which have already been given to the world. A satisfactory and complete narrative has yet to be written, if all that is now known be set forth at its natural length. But this may well wait. Fresh material comes in from time to time, and now that readers are relieved of their discouraging inability to prove that they are not studying the life or works of a madman, it is probable that much will be done in the near future. A 'Blake Society' would find plenty of occupation. It would probably be able, not only to gather together new facts for the biography, but it might even find some of the lost books by Blake, printed and in manuscript. The Society could also take up the task of interpretation, and work out details, for which space has not been found in this book, large as it is.

Blake's was a complex message – more adapted than any former mystical utterance to a highly complex age. Yet it claims to be but a personal statement of universal truths, 'a system to deliver men from systems'.[10]

The only other European mystics worthy to stand by his side, Swedenborg and Boehme†, were to a large extent sectaries, talking the language of the Churches, and delivering a message intended, before all else, for an age of dogma. They brought the Kingdom of the soul nearer to innumerable men; but now their work is nearly done, and they must soon be put away, reverently, and become, as Blake says, 'the linen clothes folded up'.[11] As the language of spiritual utterance ceases to be theological and becomes literary and poetical, the great truths have to be spoken afresh; and Blake came into the world to speak them, and to announce the new epoch in which poets and poetic thinkers should be once more, as they were in the days of the Hebrew Prophets, the Spiritual leaders of the race. Such leadership was to be of a kind entirely distinct from the 'temporal power' claimed to this day elsewhere. The false idea that a talent or even a genius for verse tends to give a man a right to make laws for the social conduct of other men is nowhere supported in Blake's works. The world in which he would have the poet, *acting as a poet*, seek leadership is the poetic world. That of ordinary conduct should be put on a lower level. It belongs to Time, not to Eternity. It is only so far as conduct affects imagination that it has any importance, or, to use Blake's terms, 'existence'.[12]

The whole of Blake's teaching, – and he was a teacher before all things, – may be summed up in a few words.

Nature, he tells (or rather he reminds) us, is merely a name for one form of mental existence. Art is another and a higher form. But that art may rise to its true place, it must be set free from memory that binds it to Nature.

Nature, – or creation, – is a result of the shrinkage of consciousness, – originally clairvoyant, – under the rule of the five senses, and of argument and law. Consciousness is the result of the divided portions of Universal Mind obtaining perception of one another.

The divisions of mind began to produce matter (as one of its divided moods is called), as soon as it produced contraction (Adam), and opacity (Satan), but its fatal tendency to division had further effects. Contraction divided into male and female, – mental and emotional egotism. This was the 'fall'. Perpetual war is the result. Morality wars on Passion, Reason on Hope, Memory on Inspiration, Matter on Love.

In Imagination only we find a Human Faculty that touches nature at one side, and spirit on the other. Imagination may be described as that which is sent bringing spirit to nature, entering into nature, and seemingly losing its spirit, that nature being revealed as symbol may lose the power to delude.

Imagination is thus the philosophic name of the Saviour, whose symbolic name is Christ, just as Nature is the philosophic name of Satan and Adam. In saying that Christ redeems Adam (and Eve) from becoming Satan, we say that Imagination redeems Reason (and Passion) from becoming Delusion, – or Nature.

The prophets and apostles, priests and missionaries,† of this Redemption are, – or should be, – artists and poets. Art and poetry, by constantly using symbolism, continually remind us that nature itself is a symbol. To remember this, is to be redeemed from nature's death and destruction.

This is Blake's message. He uttered it with the zeal of a man, who saw with spiritual eyes the eternal importance of that which he proclaimed. For this he looked forward to the return of the Golden Age, when 'all that was not inspiration should be cast off from poetry'.[13] Then, wherever† the metaphors and the rhythms of the poet were heard, while the voices of the sects had fallen dumb, should be the new Sinai, from which God should speak in 'Thunder of Thought and flames of fierce desire'.[14]

Edwin J. Ellis
William B. Yeats

Introduction to *Poems of William Blake*, ed. W. B. Yeats (1893, rev. 1905)

Early in the eighteenth century a certain John O'Neil got into debt and difficulties, these latter apparently political to some extent; and escaped both by marrying a woman named Ellen Blake, who kept a shebeen at Rathmines, Dublin, and taking her name. He had a son James, I am told, by a previous wife or mistress, and this son took also the name of Blake, and in due course married, settled in London as a hosier, and became the father of five children, one of whom was the subject of this memoir. John O'Neil had also a son by his wife Ellen; and this son, settling in Malaga, in Spain, entered the wine trade, and became the founder of a family, and from one of this family, Dr Carter Blake, I have the story.[1] James Blake was living over his shop at 28, Broad Street, Golden Square, when, in the year 1757, his son William Blake was born. He had already a son John, the best beloved of father and mother, who grew up to be the black sheep of the family, and he begot afterwards James, who was to pester William with what Tatham calls 'bread and cheese advice',[2] and Robert, whom William came to love like his own soul, and a daughter, of whom we hear little, and among that little not even her name. This family grew up among ideas less conventional than might be looked for in the house of a small shopkeeper. Swedenborgianism was then creeping into England, and the hosier's shop was one of the places where it had found shelter. The prophecies and visions of the new illumination were doubtless a very common subject of talk about the tea-table at night, and must have found ready welcome from William Blake. One prophecy certainly did sink into his mind. Swedenborg had said that the old world ended, and the new began, in the year 1757.[3] From that day forward the old theologies were rolled up like a scroll, and the new Jerusalem came upon the earth. How often this prophecy concerning the year of his birth may have rung in the ears of William Blake we know not; but certainly it could hardly have done other than ring there, when his strange gift began to develop and fill the darkness with shadowy faces and the green meadows with phantom footsteps. He must often have thought that so strange a faculty may well have come not wholly unannounced, that it was the first glimmer of the great new illumination. In later life he called the seeing of visions being in Eden; and in his system Eden came again when the old theology passed away. The profound sanity of his inspiration is proved by his never having, no matter how great the contrast between himself and the blind men and women about him, pronounced himself to be chosen and set apart alone among men. Wiser than Swedenborg, he saw that he had but what all men might have if they would, and that God spoke through him but as He had spoken through the great men of all ages and countries. The first vision we have record of looks strange enough through the clouded glass of Crabb† Robinson's diary. 'God put his forehead to the window'; and Blake, being but four years old, set up a scream.[4] Another authority tells how he strayed later on into the fields at Peckham Rye, and passed a tree full of angels, their bright wings shining among the boughs.[5] There is record, too, of his finding Ezekiel sitting one summer day in the open fields, and of his being beaten by his mother for bringing home so unlikely a story.[6]

His preparation for his great calling went on all the more smoothly in that he was never sent to school. He began early to prove his aphorism, 'The tigers of wrath are wiser than the horses of instruction,'[7] and to govern his life by thought and impulse alone. His father noticing how ill he brooked any kind of authority, and to what great anger he was moved by a blow, resolved to spare him the contest that must needs have arisen between his passionate mood and the narrow pedagogy of the time. He left him to steer his course unaided, and the boy made excellent use of this freedom, reading all that came to hand, poring over Swedenborg, and even, it has been surmised, dipping into profound Boehme, then coming out in translation under the editorship of William Law.[8] Paracelsus, a hero of Blake's later days, has written that 'he who would know the book of Nature must walk with his feet upon its leaves'.[9] Blake began early to fulfil the saying, and to bridge over the gaps in his reading with meditations in the country lanes, and to store his memory with the country sights and sounds that shine and murmur through all his verse. The sulphurous tide of London brick and stone had not then submerged all pleasant walks and kindly solitudes; for a little to the north of Golden Square, and almost abutting upon Oxford Street, were 'the fields of cows by Welling's† Farm';[10] and away westward, at Bayswater, were willow-bordered brooks, where perhaps a stray kingfisher might still be found; and but little to the south, spread far and wide the green lanes and shadowy boscage of Surrey. He had ever close at hand the two things most needed for noble meditation – multitude and solitude.

His father, seeing the imaginative bent of his mind, resolved to make a painter of him; but the boy, hearing how great a premium must be paid for his apprenticeship, said it would be unfair to his brothers and sister, and asked to be set to engraving instead. Accordingly, after three or four years' study at the drawing-school of a certain Parr, whose house stood where now King William Street joins the Strand, we find him working with an engraver called Basire.[11] Basire was an excellent engraver, but belonged to a school then giving way before more graceful if less austere methods. His influence never forsook Blake, who always preserved an enthusiastic remembrance of him and his methods. He was not the master first selected. Blake had been brought to the studio of one Rylands, then at the summit of popularity, but had said, 'Father, I do not like the man's look; he looks as if he would live to be hanged' – a prophecy that was fulfilled twelve years later, when Rylands was hanged for forgery.[12]

Blake worked two years at Basire's house, 31, Great Queen Street (now a carriage-builder's) and just opposite the Freemason's Tavern. Then some trouble arose among the apprentices, and Basire thought best to send him from amongst them. One authority, Malkin, says he did so because Blake 'declined to take part with his master against his fellow-apprentices', and that Basire declared him to be 'too simple and they too cunning';[13] while another authority, Tatham, who probably had his information from Mrs Blake, sets it down to 'matters of intellectual argument' between Blake and his fellows, which sounds likely enough, and rejoices greatly in the change, for, 'had things gone otherwise, he might never have been more than a mere engraver.'[14] Both causes may have weighed with Basire, and certainly it is well for Blake that the change came, though we may doubt if his insurgent will and obstinate heart would ever, despite Tatham, have let him rest content to be a mere inscriber on steel or copper of other men's imaginings, whether 'things had gone otherwise' or no. He was packed off to Westminster Abbey to draw the monuments, pillars, and the like, and was kept there five years. At first he was greatly annoyed by the Westminster students, who had then the right to stray about the Abbey as they would. The man or boy of genius is very generally hated or scorned by the average man or boy until the day come for him to charm them into unwilling homage. Until that day he has often to cry with Blake, 'Why was I not born with a different face?'[15] for his abstracted ways and his strange interests arouse that hatred of the uncommon which lies deep in the common heart. It is said that if you tie a piece of red cloth to a gull's leg its fellow-gulls will peck it to death. Shelley, tormented by the gull-like animosity of his schoolfellows, plunged a pen through the hand of a tormentor. Blake leant out from a scaffolding where he sat at work and flung a Westminster student from a cornice, whither he had climbed the better to tease him. The boy fell heavily upon the stone floor, and Blake went off and laid a formal complaint before the Dean. 'The tigers of wrath' vindicated their wisdom, for the students were ever after shut out of the Abbey. Blake knew well how to temper anger with prudence and make it a harmless and obedient servant. It has been told of him that he once grew angry with a plate he was engraving, and flung it across the room, 'Did you not injure it?' asked some one afterwards. 'I took good care of that', was the reply.[16] Then, too, we have his own aphorism –

> To be in a passion you good may do,
> But no good if a passion is in you.[17]

No matter how enthusiastically he commended enthusiasm, alike of love and of hate, he ever intended the mind to be master over all. He explicitly condemns, likewise, all anger aimed against persons instead of states of mind, though his own practice sometimes but ill conformed to his precept. He, however, held any enthusiastic hatred to be better than the mildness founded upon unbelief and cowardice, for it was his firm conviction that the cold, logical, analytic faculty was the most murderous of all. It was necessary even for the unwise man to grow fierce in the defence of falsehood, 'that enthusiasm and life may not cease'.[18] He is unlikely to have thought out these matters in detail in the early days we write of; but few men have ever mirrored their temperament in their philosophy as clearly as he did, and to his philosophy, accordingly, we must turn again and again.

If Blake learned Nature in his long rambles southward in Surrey, and up northward by Welling's† Farm, he learned to know Art among the tombs and pointed ceilings of the Abbey. Its towers and spire are hieroglyphs for poetic inspiration in more than one of his later drawings. 'Gothic form', he was wont to write, 'is living form';[19] and the shadows of the great Abbey may well have been the shelter that preserved him from the pseudo-classical ideas of his time. In some lines added at a later date to an engraving made now, he compares the great Gothic churches to the tomb of Christ. Christ was his symbolic name for the imagination, and the tomb of Christ could be no other than a shelter, where imagination might sleep in peace until the hour of God should awaken it. What more beautiful shelter could he have found than this ancient Abbey? Outside the 'indefinite' multitude brawled and pushed, and inside the 'definite' forms of art and vision congregated, and were at peace.[20]

One day certain shapes, purporting to be the twelve Apostles, gathered about the altar; and doubtless many another vision appeared likewise, though he probably did not yet begin to think much about their meaning and their message. He was now busy with *Edward III*[21] and other historical fragments, and may have caught something of his historical enthusiasm from the monuments about him. Another inspiration came to him in the works of Chatterton, who, five years his elder, had lately published the poems of 'T. Rowlie'.[22] The 'Bard's Song', at the end of *Edward III* shows the influence of the 'English metamorphosis' very visibly.[23] He must also have read Spenser and the Elizabethan dramatists. This was the only purely literary and purely artistic period of his life; for in a very short time he came to look upon poetry and art as a language for the utterance of conceptions, which, however beautiful, were none the less thought out more for their visionary truth than for their beauty. The change made him a greater poet and a greater artist; for 'He that findeth his life shall lose it, and he that loseth his life for My sake shall find it'.[24]

In his twentieth year his apprenticeship came to an end, and he began engraving and drawing upon his own account. Now,† too, he had the acquaintance of Flaxman and Fuseli,[25] who became his life-long friends, despite one short interruption in the case of the first, brought about by a sudden descent of 'the tigers of wrath'. At this time also he began courting one Polly or Clara Woods, 'a lovely little girl', who took walks with him here and there, and then whistled him down the wind.[26] Many of his descriptions of 'Vala' and other symbolic women, and some few of the illustrations to the 'Prophetic Books', such as the false, smiling face at the bottom of one of the pages of *Vala* (see *WWB* page 5 of the lithographs of *Vala*), and more than one of the lyrics, such as 'Love's Secret', may conceivably owe their inspiration to her.[27] Indubitably a certain type of feminine beauty, at once soft and cruel, emotional and egotistic, filled Blake with a mingled terror and wonder that lasted all his days. And there is no clear evidence of any other woman beside this Clara or Polly Woods and his own good wife, having come at all into his life. The impression made upon him by this girl was quite strong enough to have lasted on; for Tatham has recorded how his love for her made him ill, and how he had to be sent for change of air to the house of the market gardener, Boucher, at Richmond, where he met the girl he was to marry.[28]

The market gardener had a pretty, 'bright-eyed' daughter, named Catherine, who, whenever her mother asked her whom she would marry, was wont to answer, 'I have not yet seen the man.'[29] One night she came into the room where her family were sitting, and saw for the first time a new comer, with young, handsome face and flame-like hair – her own pencil sketch is the authority – and grew upon the moment faint, as the tale has it, from the intuition that she saw her destined husband. She left the room to recover, and upon her return sat down by Blake, and heard from his lips the story of his great love for the false beauty, and of her fickleness and his wretchedness. 'I pity you from my heart,' she cried. 'Do you pity me?' he answered; 'then I love you for that.'[30] Humiliated by his ill-starred love, he was grateful for a little womanly kindness; and from such gratitude, not for the first time upon the earth, sprang a love that lasted until life had passed away. This pretty tale has reflected itself in the great mirror of the 'Prophetic Books'. In them Pity is ever the essential thing in a woman's soul. *The Book of Urizen* describes thus the making of Enitharmon:

> Wonder, awe, fear, astonishment,
> Petrify the eternal myriads
> At the first female form, now separate:
> They called her Pity, and fled.[31]

Enitharmon is 'the vegetable mortal wife of Los; his emanation, yet his wife till the sleep of death is passed'.[32] And the symbolic being Los, though he is Time, and more than one other great abstract thing, is also Blake himself, as may be seen by even a rapid reading of *Milton*.

When Blake had told Catherine Boucher that he loved her, he returned to his work for a year, resolved not to see her until he had put by enough to set up house upon. At the year's end, on August 13th, 1782, they were married, and began housekeeping at 23, Green Street, Leicester Fields, now Leicester Square. Mrs Blake, knowing neither how to read nor write, had to put her mark in the register. In the course of a few years she had profited so well by her husband's teaching that she probably learnt to copy out his manuscripts; for there is little doubt that a certain neat and formal handwriting which crops up here and there is hers, and she certainly helped to colour his illuminated books. She learnt even to see visions, beholding upon one occasion a long procession of English kings and queens pass by with silent tread. She had no children, but repaid her husband for the lack of childish voices by a love that knew no limit and a friendship that knew no flaw. In the day she would often take long walks with him, thirty miles at a stretch being no unusual distance, and having dined at a wayside inn, return under the light of the stars; and often at night, when the presences bade him get up from his bed and write, she would sit beside him, holding his hand.

A year after his marriage his first work, *Poetical† Sketches*, was published at the expense of Flaxman and of some dilettanti friends, who were accustomed to gather at a Rev. Mr Mathew's†, of 28, Rathbone Place.[33] No. 28 is now a chair and umbrella mender's shop, but was then a very fashionable house on the most northernly fringe of London, upon the way to 'the Jew's Harp house and the Green Man†'.[34] The preface tells that the poems were written between the ages of twelve and twenty. He was now twenty-six, and must have been silent for these six years. He was in a period of transition. He had lost interest probably in his purely literary work, and not yet learnt to set his symbolic visions to music. The poems mark an epoch in English literature, for they were the first opening of the long-sealed well of romantic poetry; they, and not the works of Cowper and Thomson† and Chatterton,[35] being the true heralds of our modern poetry of nature and enthusiasm. There is in them no trace of mysticism, but phrases and figures of speech which were soon to pass from the metaphorical to the symbolic stage, and put on mystical significance, are very common. The singer of the 'Mad Song' compares himself to a 'fiend hid in a cloud';[36] and we shall presently hear in definitely mystical poems of 'a child upon a cloud',[37] and of 'My brother John, the evil one, In a black cloud, making his moan';[38] for cloud and vapour became to him a symbol for bodily emotions, and for the body itself. *Edward III* tells of 'golden cities', though as yet the poet knows nothing of the ages of gold, silver, and brass; and tells of the times when the pulse shall begin to beat slow,

> And taste, and touch, and sight, and sound, and smell,
> That sing and dance round Reason's fine-wrought throne,
> Shall flee away, and leave him all forlorn – [39]

though as yet the poet has not learned to count and symbolize these senses, and call them 'the daughters of Albion',[40] and draw them dancing about fallen man among the Druidic monuments of ancient Britain. (See, *Jerusalem*, page 221,[41] and elsewhere.)

A book called by its present owner, Mr Murray, from a phrase in the first paragraph, *An† Island in the Moon*, was written probably soon after the close of the six silent years. It shows in a flickering, feeble way, the dawn of the mystical period. It is a clumsy and slovenly satire upon the dilettanti and triflers who gathered about Mr and Mrs Mathew†, but contains some lyrics not to be found elsewhere, and here reprinted from *The Works of William Blake* (B. Quaritch).[42] The prose, touched now and then with a faint humour, has little but autobiographical interest. Of this there is, however, plenty, for the whole manuscript lightens with a blind fury against the shallow piety and shallow philosophy of his day. The thing should be read once in *The Works*, and then forgotten, for it belongs to the weak side of a strong man, to his petulance, to a certain quarrelsome self-consciousness which took hold upon him at times. There is in it a peculiar and unpleasant poem upon surgery, which was, in all likelihood, his first symbolic verse,[43] and several poems afterwards included in the† *Songs of Innocence*. In 1804 he was to write of being 'again enlightened by the light' which he had 'enjoyed' in his youth, and which had 'for exactly twenty years been closed' from him, 'as by a door and window shutters'.[44] Was this darkening of the spiritual light caused by the awakening of his anger against the men and women of his time? 'The Argument' to *The Marriage of Heaven and Hell*, now soon to be written, tells how 'the just man', the imaginative man that is, walked the vale of mortal life among roses and springs of living water until the 'villain', the unimaginative man, came among the roses and the springs, and then 'the just man' went forth in anger into 'the wilds' among the 'lions' of bitter protest.[45] However this may be, the closing out of the light 'as by a door and window shutters', if Blake's recollection did† not play him false about the twenty years, the writing of *An† Island in† the Moon*, and a quarrel with the Rathbone Place coterie, of which we have some vague record, must have come all very near together.

In 1784, upon the death of his father, William Blake moved into a house next door to the one where he had been born, and which his brother James had now inherited, and started a printseller's shop in partnership with a fellow apprentice, and took his brother Robert for apprentice to engraving. In 1787 Robert fell ill and died, Blake nursing him with such devotion that he is said to have slept for three days when the need for him was over. He had seen his brother's spirit ascending clapping its hands for joy, and might well sleep content.

Soon after the death of Robert, disagreement with his partner brought the print shop to an end, and Blake moved into neighbouring Poland Street, and started what was to prove the great work of his life. One night, a form resembling his brother Robert came to him and taught him how to engrave his poems upon copper, and how to print illustrations and decorative borderings upon the same pages with the poem. In later years he wrote to a friend, 'I know that our deceased friends are more really with us than when they are apparent to our mortal part. Thirteen years ago I lost a brother, and with his spirit I converse daily and hourly in the spirit, and see him in remembrance in the region of my imagination. I hear his advice, and even now write from his dictates. Forgive me for expressing to you my enthusiasm, which I wish all to partake of, since it is to me a source of immortal joy, even in this world. May you continue to be so more and more, and be more and more persuaded, that every mortal loss is an immortal gain. The ruins of time build mansions in eternity.'[46]

He set to work at once to carry out the directions of the spirit. He had now a number of lyrics by him, and began at once printing the† *Songs of Innocence*. He drew the poems upon metal with a varnish chiefly composed of pitch and turpentine. The plate was then placed in a bath of acid, and all the parts not covered by the varnish deeply bitten, until writing and drawing stood up in high relief, ready for ink and roller. He then printed off the sheets in a press for which he paid, Mr Linnell's diary tells us, forty pounds,[47] and afterwards coloured, and in some cases gilded them by hand. All the clean legible text of song and prophecy was written *backward* upon the copper with marvellous accuracy and patience.

In 1789 appeared first the† *Songs of Innocence*, and then *The Book of Thel*, illuminated missals of song in which every page is a window open in Heaven, but open† not as in the days of Noah for the outpouring of the flood 'of time and space', but that we may look into 'the golden age' and 'the imagination that liveth for ever', and talk with those who dwell there by 'Poetry, Painting, and Music, the three powers in man of conversing with Paradise which the flood did not sweep away'.[48] Alas, the poems when printed in plain black and white, wonderful though they be, and full of exultant peace and joyous simplicity, give but a faint shadow of themselves as they are in Blake's own books, where interwoven designs companion them, and gold and yellow tints diffuse themselves over the page like summer clouds. The poems themselves are the morning song of his genius. The thought of the world's sorrow, and that indignation which he has called 'the voice of God',[49] soon began to make hoarse the sweetness, if also to deepen the music of his song. The third book that came from his press, *The Marriage of Heaven and Hell*, dated 1790, has the fierce note which never after wholly died out of his work. It was followed in 1793 by the† *Visions of the Daughters of Albion, America, Europe, Gates of Paradise*, and *The Book of Urizen*; in 1794 by the† *Songs of Experience*; in 1795 by *The Song of Los, Ahania*,[50] and in 1804 by *Jerusalem* and *Milton*. He wrote also a very long poem called *Vala* somewhere between 1797 and 1804 or 1805, but did not publish it, probably because he shrank from the labour and expense. It is the most splendid, as well as the longest, of his mystical works, and was published by Mr E. J. Ellis and myself, for the first time, in *The Works of William Blake*. A conception of its luxuriant beauty can be got from the passages quoted in this volume.[51] There is record too of a 'Bible of Hell', and of this the title-page remains; of an unfinished poem called *The French Revolution*, which was printed in the ordinary way, by a certain Johnston of St Paul's Churchyard; of 'The Gates of Hell, for Children', and of an engraved book called *Outhoun*†.[52] The earlier of the books which have come down to us show the influence of Jacob Boehme and of the kabalistic symbolism, and it is probable that the reading of *The Morning Redness, Mysterium Magnum*, and stray fragments of mediaeval magical philosophy, such as the works of Cornelius Agrippa, then not uncommon in translation, delivered his intellect from the spectral and formal intellect of Swedenborg, and taught him to think about the meaning of his own visions. He may also have met mystics and even students of magic, for there was then an important secret body working in London under three brothers named Falk. The miniature painter Cosway, too, may have come across him, and Cosway kept a house specially for the invocation of spirits.[53] His own illumination probably reached its height between his twentieth and his twenty-seventh year, between the close of his purely literary activity, and the shutting out of the light of the spirit 'as by a door and window shutters'. The six silent years may well have been silent, because the truth was coming upon him, in Boehme's beautiful phrase, 'like a bursting shower'.[54] However this may be, his illumination was before all else a deliverance from Swedenborg. *The Marriage of Heaven and Hell* is certainly a reply to the latter's *Heaven and Hell*, then recently translated, and probably very audible in the talk of his Swedenborgian friend Flaxman, and of his no less Swedenborgian brother James.[55] 'A new heaven is begun,' he writes on one of the first pages, 'and it is now thirty-three years since its advent. The eternal hell revives, and lo, Swedenborg is the angel sitting at the tomb; his writings are the linen clothes folded up.'[56] The creative imagination of William Blake – the Christ in him – had arisen from the tomb in the thirty-third year of his age, the year at which Christ had arisen, and with it had revived hell its activity and heaven its passivity, and the garments of theologic faith which had so long disguised it were thrown away. The fierce invective of a later page about Swedenborg having written no new truth, but all the old falsehoods, combined as it is with a glorification of the older mystics, Boehme and Paracelsus, makes us recognize the wrath of a man against something which had long warped and thwarted him.[57] As years went on he returned again to some extent to the old admiration, though never to the old subjection, until Swedenborg became in *Milton* 'strongest of men', 'Samson shorn by the churches',[58] and in *A† Descriptive Catalogue* a 'visionary' whose 'works' 'are well worth the study of painters and poets', being the 'foundation of grand things'.[59] But it must never be forgotten that whatever Blake borrowed from Swedenborg or Boehme, from mystic or kabalist, he turned to his own purposes, and transferred into a new system, growing like a flower from its own roots, supplementing in many ways, though not controverting in any main matters, the systems of his great predecessors, and that he stands among the mystics of Europe beside Jacob Boehme and the makers of the Kabala, as original as they are and as profound. He is one of those great artificers of God who uttered mysterious truths to a little clan. The others spoke to theologians and magicians, and he speaks to poets and artists. The others drew their symbols from theology and alchemy, and he from the flowers of spring and the leaves of summer; but the message is the same, and the truth uttered is the truth God spake to the red clay at the beginning of the world.

The essentials of the teaching of 'The Prophetic Books' can be best explained by extracts mainly from the 'prose writings', for the language of the books themselves is exceedingly technical. 'God is in the lowest effects as well as in the highest causes,' he wrote on the margin of a copy of Lavater's *Aphorisms*. 'For let it be remembered that creation is God descending according to the weakness of man. Our Lord is the word of God, and everything on earth is the word of God, and in its essence is God.'[60] That portion of creation, however, which we can touch and see with our bodily senses is 'infected' with the power of Satan, one of whose names is 'Opacity';[61] whereas that other portion which we can touch and see with the spiritual senses, and which we call 'imagination', is truly, 'the body of God', and the only reality; but we must struggle to really mount towards that imaginative world, and not allow ourselves to be deceived by 'memory' disguising itself as imagination.[62] We thus mount by poetry, music, and art, which seek for ever 'to cast off all that is not inspiration', and 'the rotten rags of memory', and to become, 'the divine members'.[63] For this reason he says that Christ's apostles were all artists, and that 'Christinity is art', and 'the† whole business of man is the arts', that 'Israel delivered from Egypt is art delivered from nature and imitation';[64] and that we should all engage 'before the world in some mental pursuit'. We must take some portion of the kingdom of darkness, of the void in which we live, and by 'circumcising away the indefinite' with a 'firm and determinate outline', make of that portion a 'tent of God', for we must always remember that God lives alone, 'in minute particulars' in life made beautiful and graceful and vital by imaginative significance, and that all worthy things, all worthy deeds, all worthy thoughts, are works of art or of imagination.[65] In so far as we do such works we drive the mortality, the infection out of the things we touch and see, and make them exist for our spiritual senses – 'the enlarged and numerous senses'; and beholding beauty and truth we see no more 'accident and chance', and the indefinite void 'and a last judgment'† 'passes over us, and the world is consumed', for things are 'burnt up' 'when you cease to behold them'.[66]

'Reason', or argument from the memory and from the sensations of the body, binds us to Satan and opacity, and is the only enemy of God. Sin awakens imagination because it is from emotion, and is therefore dearer to God than reason, which is wholly dead. Sin, however, must be avoided, because we are prisoners, and should keep the rules of our prison house, for 'you cannot have liberty in this world without what you call moral virtue, and you cannot have moral virtue without the subjection of that half of the human race who hate what you call moral virtue'.[67] But let us recognize that these laws are but 'the laws of prudence', and do not let us call them 'the laws of God',[68] for nothing is pleasing to God except the glad invention of beautiful and exalted things. He holds it better indeed for us to break all the commandments than to sink into a dead compliance. Better any form of imaginative evil – any lust or any hate – rather than an unimaginative virtue, for 'the human imagination alone' is 'the divine vision and fruition' 'in which man liveth eternally'. 'It is the human existence itself.'[69] 'I care not whether a man is good or bad,' he makes Los, the 'eternal mind', say in *Jerusalem*,† 'all that I care is whether he is a wise man or a fool. Go, put off holiness and put on intellect.'[70] By intellect he means imagination. He who recognizes imagination for his God need trouble no more about the law, for he will do naught to injure his brother, for we love all which enters truly into our imagination, and by imagination must all life become one, for a man liveth not but in his brother's face and by those 'loves and tears of brothers, sisters, sons, fathers, and friends, which if man ceases to behold he ceases to exist'.[71]

The great contest of imagination with reason is described throughout 'The Prophetic Books' under many symbols, but chiefly under the symbolic conflict of Los, the divine formative principle which comes midway between absolute existence and corporeal life, with Urizen, 'the God of this world'[72] and maker of dead law and blind negation. Blake considered this doctrine to be of the utmost importance, and claimed to have written it under the dictation of spiritual presences. 'I have written this poem from immediate dictation,' he wrote, of *Jerusalem*, 'twelve or sometimes twenty or thirty lines at a time without premeditation, and even against my will. The time it has taken in writing was thus rendered non-existent, and an immense poem exists which seems the labour of a long life, all produced without labour or study.'[73] It is not possible in a short essay like the present to do more than record these things, for to discuss and to consider what these presences were would need many pages. Whatsoever they were, presences or mere imaginings, the words they dictated remain for our wonder and delight. There is not one among these words which is other than significant and precise to the laborious student, and many passages of simple poetry and the marvel of the pictures remain for all who cannot or will not give the needed labour. Merlin's book lies open before us, and if we cannot decipher its mysterious symbols, then we may dream over the melody of evocations that are not for our conjuring, and over the strange colours and woven forms of the spread pages.

In 1793 Blake removed to Hercules Buildings, Lambeth, and besides the illustrating of 'The Prophetic Books' did there much artistic work, notably *Nebuchadnezzar*, a huge water-colour, and *The Lazar House*, and *The Elohim creating Adam*, and a series of designs to Young's *Night Thoughts*†, of which a few were printed with the poem in 1797. The remainder are with Mr Bain, of the Haymarket, who very kindly shows them to Blake's students.[74] The printed designs are, of course, in plain black and white, but the rest are faint luminous sketches in water-colour.†

At Lambeth, too, he saw the one ghost of his life. 'When he was talking on the subject of ghosts,' writes Gilchrist, 'he was wont to say they did not appear much to imaginative men, but only to common minds who did not see the finer spirits. A ghost was a thing seen by the gross bodily eye, a vision by the mental. "Did you ever see a ghost?" asked a friend. "Never but once", was the reply. And it befell thus: Standing one evening at his garden door in Lambeth, and chancing to look up, he saw a horrible grim figure, "scaly-speckled, very awful", stalking downstairs towards him. More frightened than ever before or after, he took to his heels and ran out of the house.'[75]

In 1800 he left London for the first time. Flaxman had introduced him to a certain Hayley, a popular poet of the day, who poured out long streams of verse, always lucid, always rational, always uninspired. He wrote prose too, and was now busy in his turreted country house putting together a life of Cowper. Blake was invited to engrave the illustrations, and to set up house in the neighbourhood.[76] At first all went well. The village of Felpham seemed an entirely beautiful place, beloved of God and of the spirits. Blake met all manner of kings and poets and prophets walking in shadowy multitudes on the edge of the sea, 'majestic shadows, grey but luminous, and superior to the common height of man'.[77] Other and more gentle beings appeared likewise. 'Did you ever see a fairy's funeral?' said Blake to a lady who sat next him at some gathering at Hayley's or elsewhere. 'Never, sir', was the answer. 'I have,' he replied; 'but not before last night. I was writing alone in my garden; there was a great stillness among the branches and flowers, and more than common sweetness in the air; I heard a low and pleasant sound, and I knew not whence it came. At last I saw the broad leaf of a flower move, and underneath I saw a procession of creatures of the size and colour of green and grey grasshoppers, bearing a body laid out on a rose leaf, which they buried with songs and disappeared.'[78] He has elsewhere described the fairies as 'the rulers of the vegetable world',[79] and 'vegetable' was with him a technical term meaning 'bodily' and sensuous. Jacob Boehme is also said to have had a vision of the fairies.[80]

After a while patronage became more than he could bear, and kind worldly Hayley a burden more insistent and persistent than the grasshopper of old.[81] Not only did Hayley himself give the prophet, who was his guest, little but mechanical work, but he sought out excellent ladies, kindly and worldly like himself, who wanted miniatures and painted fire-screens. Before long Blake began to hurl at his head petulant epigrams†, though there were times now and afterwards when the worldliness disappeared, and the kindliness remained alone visible to him, and then he would say that Hayley had kept him safe by his good will through spiritual terror and contests 'not known to men on earth', but which had else made the three years he spent at Felpham 'the darkest years that ever mortal suffered'.[82] Towards the last an event occurred which awoke all his slumbering gratitude. One evening he found a soldier in his garden, and not knowing that he had been put there to dig by his own gardener, asked him with all politeness to be gone. The man refused with threats, and Blake, getting angry, caught him by the elbows, and, despite his endeavour to spar, forced him away down the road to the village tavern where he was quartered. The soldier avenged himself by swearing that Blake had cursed the King, and vowed help to Bonaparte should he come over. Blake was arrested. Hayley came forward and bailed him out, and though suffering from a fall from his horse at the time, gave at the trial evidence as to character. The case was tried at the Chichester Quarter Sessions on the 11th of June, 1804, the verdict of 'not guilty' awakening tumultuous applause in court. One old man remembered long afterwards Blake's flashing eyes. The soldier, whose name was Scofield, appears in *Jerusalem* as a symbol for Adam, presumably because 'honest indignation', which is 'the voice of God', turned him from the garden.[83] Blake held all 'natural events' to be but symbolic messages from the unknown powers. The people of Felpham remember Hayley to this day, and tradition has wrapped him about with a kind of mythological wonder, having a suggestiveness which looks like a survival from some wild tavern talk of Blake's. He had two wives, they say, and kept one in a wood with her leg chained to a tree-trunk. Blake would have made this mean the captivity of half his imagination in 'the vegetable world', which is Satan's kingdom, and all nothing. The popular voice has in very truth done for Hayley what Blake himself did for Scofield. It has given him a place in mythology.

In 1804 he returned to London and took a house in South Molton Street,[84] and there engraved *Jerusalem* and *Milton*. These, with the exception of *The Ghost of Abel*, a dramatic fragment written very early, but not appearing until 1822, were the last poems published by him. He continued until the end of his life to find occasional purchasers for these and other 'Prophetic Books', but never any to read and understand. He did not, however, cease to write. 'I have written more than Voltaire or Rousseau,' he said, in one of the last years of his life; 'six or seven epic poems as long as Homer, and twenty tragedies as long as *Macbeth*. . . . I write when commanded by the spirits, and the moment I have written, I see the words fly about the room in all directions. It is then published, and the spirits can read.'[85]

Henceforth his published works were to be wholly pictorial. He was now conscious that the 'light' so long hid from him 'as by a door and window shutters' was come again, and foresaw a great period of artistic creation; for had he not conquered 'the spectrous fiend' which had marred his power and obscured his inspiration?[86] The first works of this new and better period were done for a certain Cromeck, a publisher, who set him to illustrate Blair's *Grave*.[87] These illustrations must always remain among his greatest. They are much less illustrations of Blair than expressions of his own moods and visions. We see the body and soul rushing into each other's arms at the last day, the soul hovering over the body and exploring the recesses of the grave, and the good and bad appearing before the judgment seat of God, not as these things appeared to the orthodox eyes of Blair, but as they appeared to the mystical eyes of William Blake.[88] The body and soul are in one aspect corporeal energy and spiritual love, and in another reason and passion, and their union is not that bodily arising from the dead, dreamed of by the orthodox, but that final peace of God wherein body and soul cry 'thither' with one voice. The grave was in his eyes the sleep of reason, and the last judgment no high session of a personal law-giver, but the 'casting out' of 'nature' and 'corporeal understanding'.[89]

Cromeck gave these designs into the hands of Schiavonetti, an excellent engraver, but a follower of the fashionable school of 'blots and blurs', of soft shadows and broken lights, and not of the unfashionable school of 'firm and determinate outline' to which Blake belonged.[90] Blake likewise had been promised the engraving, and the choice of another was a serious money loss to him. The result was a quarrel, which grew to the utmost vehemence when Cromeck added the further wrong of setting Stothard to paint for engraving a picture of *The Canterbury Pilgrims*, having taken the idea from seeing Blake at work on the same subject with like intentions. Blake tried to vindicate himself by an exhibition of his paintings, *The Canterbury Pilgrims* among them. The exhibition was held at his brother James', in Golden Square, in 1809, and proved an utter failure.[91] I give many extracts from the printed catalogue and from an address to the public, which never got beyond the MS. stage. Both catalogue and address are full of magnificent and subtle irony and of violent and petulant anger. He would not moderate his passion, for he was ever combative against a time which loved moderation, compromise, and measured phrase, because it was a time of 'unbelief and fear' and of imaginative dearth. Had he not said, 'Bring† out number, weight, and measure in a time of dearth'? and with him there was no dearth; and also that 'the road of excess leads to the palace of wisdom'?[92] His fault was not that he did not moderate his passion, but that he did not feel the error he so often warns himself against, of being angry with individuals instead of 'states' of mind. The evil he denounced was really evil, but the men he denounced did not really personify that evil.[93] The turbulent heart of the mystic could not but feel wrath against a time that knew not him or his. No wonder that he should fall, from sheer despair of making any man understand his subtle philosophy of life, into many an unsubtle unphilosophical rhapsody of hate when too angry even to hide himself in storm clouds of paradox. He had probably never seen any good painting of the Florentine and Flemish schools, but holding them to be the source of the art of his day, denounced them with violence. Had they not sacrificed the intellectual outline to indefinite lights and shadows, and renounced imaginative things for what seemed to him unimaginative copying of corporeal life and lifeless matter? Were they not his enemies in all things, and the enemies of Raphael and Angelo and Dürer†?[94] He made, in a blind hopeless way, something of the same protest made afterwards by the pre-Raphaelites with more success.[95] They saw nothing but an artistic issue, and were at peace; whereas he saw in every issue the whole contest of light and darkness, and found no peace. To him the universe seemed filled with an intense excitement at once infinitesimal and infinite, for in every grass blade, in every atom of dust,[96] Los, the 'eternal mind',[97] warred upon dragon Urizen, 'the God of this world'. The 'dots and lozenges',[98] and the 'indefinite' shadows of engraver or painter, took upon them portentous meanings to his visionary eyes. 'I know that the great majority of Englishmen are fond of the indefinite,' he writes to a correspondent, 'which they measure by Newton's doctrine of the fluxions of an atom, a thing which does not exist' (that is to say, belongs to reason, not to imagination; to nature, not to mind). 'These are politicians, and think that Republican art' (a system of thought or art which gives every one of the parts separate individuality and separate rights as in a Republic) 'is inimical to their atom, for a line or lineament is not formed by chance. A line is a line in its minutest subdivisions, straight or crooked. It is itself, not intermeasurable by anything else. . . . But since the French Revolution Englishmen are all intermeasurable by one another, certainly a happy state of agreement in which I for one do not agree.'[99] 'The dots or lozenges', 'the blots and blurs', have no individuality when taken apart, and what is true of them is true also of the men for whom 'the blots and blurs' are made; for are not all things symbolic, and is not art the greatest of symbols? In his philosophy, as expounded in 'The Prophetic Books', he had a place for everything, even for 'nature' and the corporeal hindrance, but he left a place for the highest only in his interpretation of the philosophy, and forgot that we must never be partisans, not even partisans of the spirit.

For a time now his purse was very empty, he and his wife, if Cromeck is to be believed, which he probably is not, living for a time on 10s. a week,[100] and it might, perhaps, have kept empty to the end had not he met in 1818 John Linnell, the landscape painter, and found in him the most generous patron of his life. Now, too, he made the acquaintance of another good friend, John Varley, 'the father of modern water-colour',[101] and did for him a series of drawings of his spiritual visitants: *The Ghost of a Flea* (a symbol of the rapacious man), *The Man who built the Pyramids* (a symbol probably of the man of worldly power, for Egypt is nature or the world, and the pyramids a glory of Egypt), and many others. In 1821 he moved from Poland Street to Fountain Court, and made for Mr Linnell the famous series of designs, to Job, which is perhaps his masterpiece.[102] Their austere majesty, too well known to need any description here, contrasts with the fanciful prettiness and delicate grace of his early work. Life had touched his imagination with melancholy. He received £100 for the plates, and was to get another £100 out of the profits of publication. He got £50 of this second £100 before his death, the slow sale not making a bigger sum possible. In 1822 he painted a very fine series of water-colours illustrating *Paradise Lost* for Mr Linnell,[103] filling them with the peculiarities of his own illumination as usual, and in 1825 began an immense series of designs to Dante† for the same friend, sketching them in water-colour and engraving seven. Of those he engraved, *Francesco and Paola* is the most perfect and the most moving, and must always haunt the memory with a beauty at once tender and august.[104] Had he lived to finish the whole series, or even the hundred and odd drawings he began, it had surely been the veritable crown of his labours as an artist; but he was to pass the gate he had called 'of pearl and gold', and to stand where Dante stood by Beatrice, and to enter the great white Rose before his hands had half transcribed the story of that other mystic traveller.[105] In 1827 he fell ill of a strange complaint, a shivering and sinking, which told him he had not long to live. He wrote to a friend, 'I have been very near the gates of death, and have returned very weak, and an old man, feeble and tottering, but not in spirit and life, not in the real man, the imagination which liveth for ever. In that I grow stronger and stronger as this foolish body decays'; and then passed on to discuss matters of business, and matters of engraving and politics, but soon burst out again. 'Flaxman is gone, and we must soon follow every one to his own eternal house, leaving the delusions of Goddess Nature and her laws to get into freedom from all the laws of the numbers – into the mind in which every one is king and priest in his own house. God grant it on earth as it is in heaven.'[106]

'On the day of his death,' writes a friend who had his account from Mrs Blake, 'he composed songs to his Maker, so sweetly to the ear of his Catherine, that, when she stood to hear him, he, looking upon her most affectionately, said, "My beloved! they are *not mine. No!* They are *not* mine."† He told her they would not be parted; he should always be about her to take care of her.'[107] Another account says, 'He† said he was going to that country he had all his life wished to see, and expressed himself happy, hoping for salvation through Jesus Christ. Just before he died his countenance became fair, his eyes brightened and he burst out into singing of the things he saw in heaven.'[108] 'He made the rafters ring,' said Tatham.[109] 'The death of a saint,' said a poor woman who had come in to help Mrs Blake.[110]

The wife continued to believe him always with her in the spirit, even calling out to him at times as if he were but a few yards away; but, none the less, fretted herself into the grave, surviving him only two years.[111] No spiritual companionship could make up for the lack of daily communion in the common things of life, for are we not one half 'phantoms of the earth and water'?[112] She left his designs and unpublished manuscripts, of which there were, according to Allan Cunningham, a hundred volumes ready for the press, to Tatham, who had shown her no little friendliness. Tatham was an 'angel' in the Irvingite Church,[113] and coming to hold that the designs and poems alike were inspired by the devil, pronounced sentence upon them, and gave up two days to their burning. 'I have', wrote Blake, 'always found that angels have the vanity to speak of themselves as the only wise; this they do with a confident insolence sprouting from systematic reasoning.'[114] Though Tatham, bound in by systematic theology, did him well nigh the greatest wrong one man can do another, none the less is Tatham's MS. life of Blake a long cry of admiration. He speaks of 'his noble and elastic mind', of his profound and beautiful talk, and of his varied knowledge. Yet, alas, could he only have convinced himself that it was not for him to judge whether, when Blake wrote of vision 'a bad cause' – to use his own phrase – 'made a bad book',†[115] we might still have that account of Genesis, 'as understood by a Christian visionary', of which a passage, when read out, seemed 'striking', even to conventional Crabb† Robinson, and perhaps 'The Book of Moonlight', a work upon art, though for this I do not greatly long, and the *Outhoun*†, and many lyrics and designs, whereof the very names are dead.[116] Blake himself would have felt little anger, for he had thought of burning his MSS† himself, holding, perhaps as Boehme held, and Swedenborg also, that there were many great things best unuttered within earshot of the world. Boehme held himself permitted to speak of much only among his 'schoolfellows'; and Blake held there were listeners in other worlds than this. He knew, despite the neglect and scorn of his time, that fame even upon the earth would be granted him, and that his work was done, for the Eternal Powers do not labour in vain.

> Re-engraved time after time,
> Ever in their youthful prime;
> My designs unchanged remain,
> Time may rage but rage in vain.
> For above Time's troubled fountains,
> On the great Atlantic mountains,
> In my golden house on high,
> There they shine eternally.[117]

W. B. Yeats

'Modern Irish Poetry'
(1894; rev. 1899, *c.* 1903, 1908), repr. from
A Book of Irish Verse Selected from Modern Writers,
ed. W. B. Yeats (1895, rev. 1900)

The Irish Celt is sociable, as may be known from his proverb, 'It is better to be quarreling than to be lonely,'[1] and the Irish poets of the nineteenth century have made songs abundantly when friends and rebels have been at hand to applaud. The Irish poets of the eighteenth century found both at a Limerick hostelry, above whose door was written a rhyming welcome in Gaelic to all passing poets, whether their pockets were full or empty. Its owner, himself a famous poet, entertained his fellows as long as his money lasted, and then took to minding the hens and chickens of an old peasant woman for a living, and ended his days in rags, but not, one imagines, without content. Among his friends and guests had been Red O'Sullivan, Gaelic O'Sullivan, blind O'Heffernan, and many another, and their songs had made the people, crushed by the disasters of the Boyne and Aughrim,[2] remember their ancient greatness.

The bardic order, with its perfect artifice and imperfect art, had gone down in the wars of the seventeenth century, and poetry had found shelter amid the turf smoke of the cabins. The powers that history commemorates are but the coarse effects of influences delicate and vague as the beginning of twilight, and these influences were to be woven like a web about the hearts of men by farm-labourers, pedlars, potato-diggers, hedge-schoolmasters, and grinders at the quern, poor wastrels who put the troubles of their native land, or their own happy or unhappy loves, into songs of an extreme beauty. But in the midst of this beauty was a flitting incoherence, a fitful dying out of the sense, as though the passion had become too great for words, as must needs be when life is the master and not the slave of the singer.

English-speaking Ireland had meanwhile no poetic voice, for Goldsmith had chosen to celebrate English scenery and manners; and Swift was but an Irishman by what Mr Balfour has called the visitation of God, and much against his will; and Congreve by education and early association; while Parnell, Denham, and Roscommon were poets but to their own time.[3] Nor did the coming with the new century of the fame of Moore set the balance even, for his Irish melodies are too often artificial and mechanical in their style when separated from the music that gave them wings. Whatever he had of high poetry is in 'The Light of other Days', and in 'At the Mid Hour of Night', which express what Matthew Arnold has taught us to call 'the Celtic melancholy', with so much of delicate beauty in the meaning and in the wavering or steady rhythm that one knows not where to find their like in literature.[4] His more artificial and mechanical verse, because of the ancient music that makes it seem natural and vivid, and because it has remembered so many beloved names and events and places, has had the influence which might have belonged to these exquisite verses had he written none but these.

An honest style did not come into English-speaking Ireland until Callanan wrote three or four naive translations from the Gaelic. 'Shule Aroon' and 'Kathleen O'More'[5] had indeed been written for a good while, but had no more influence than Moore's best verses. Now, however, the lead of Callanan was followed by a number of translators, and they in turn by the poets of Young Ireland, who mingled a little learned from the Gaelic ballad-writers with a great deal learned from Scott, Macaulay, and Campbell, and turned poetry once again into a principal means for spreading ideas of nationality and patriotism.[6] They were full of earnestness, but never understood that, though a poet may govern his life by his enthusiasms, he must, when he sits down at his desk, but use them as the potter the clay. Their thoughts were a little insincere, because they lived in the half-illusions of their admirable ideals; and their rhythms not seldom mechanical, because their purpose was served when they had satisfied the dull ears of the common man. They had no time to listen to the voice of the insatiable artist, who stands erect, or lies asleep waiting until a breath arouses him, in the heart of every

craftsman. Life was their master, as it had been the master of
the poets who gathered in the Limerick hostelry, though it
conquered them not by unreasoned love for a woman, or for
native land, but by reasoned enthusiasm, and practical energy.
No man was more sincere, no man had a less mechanical mind
than Thomas Davis, and yet he is often a little insincere and
mechanical in his verse. When he sat down to write he had so
great a desire to make the peasantry courageous and powerful
that he half believed them already 'the finest peasantry upon
the earth',[7] and wrote not a few such verses as –

> Lead him to fight for native land,
>   His is no courage cold and wary;
> The toops live not that could withstand
>   The headlong charge of Tipperary – [8]

and to-day we are paying the reckoning with much bombast.
His little book has many things of this kind, and yet we honour
it for its public spirit, and recognize its powerful influence with
gratitude. He was in the main an orator influencing men's acts,
and not a poet shaping their emotions, and the bulk of his
influence has been good. He was, indeed, a poet of much
tenderness in the simple love-songs 'The Marriage', 'A Plea for
Love', and 'Mary Bhan Astór', and, but for his ideal of a
fisherman defying a foreign soldiery, would have been as good
in 'The Boatman of Kinsale'; and once or twice when he
touched upon some historic sorrow he forgot his hopes for the
future and his lessons for the present, and made moving verse.[9]

His contemporary, Clarence Mangan, kept out of public life
and its half-illusions by a passion for books, and for drink and
opium, made an imaginative and powerful style. He translated
from the German, and imitated Oriental poetry, but little that
he did on any but Irish subjects has a lasting interest. He is
usually classed with the Young Ireland poets, because he
contributed to their periodicals and shared their political
views; but his style was formed before their movement began,
and he found it the more easy for this reason, perhaps, to give
sincere expression to the mood which he had chosen, the only
sincerity literature knows of; and with happiness and
cultivation might have displaced Moore. But as it was,

whenever he had no fine ancient song to inspire him, he fell into rhetoric which was only lifted out of commonplace by an arid intensity. In his 'Irish National Hymn', 'Soul and Country',[10] and the like, we look into a mind full of parched sands where the sweet dews have never fallen. A miserable man may think well and express himself with great vehemence, but he cannot make beautiful things, for Aphrodite never rises from any but a tide of joy. Mangan knew nothing of the happiness of the outer man, and it was only when prolonging the tragic exultation of some dead bard that he knew the unearthly happiness which clouds the outer man with sorrow, and is the fountain of impassioned art. Like those who had gone before him, he was the slave of life, for he had nothing of the self-knowledge, the power of selection, the harmony of mind, which enables the poet to be its master, and to mould the world to a trumpet for his lips. But O'Hussey's Ode over his outcast chief must live for generations because of the passion that moves through its powerful images and its mournful, wayward, and fierce rhythms.

> Though he were even a wolf ranging the round green
>   woods,
> Though he were even a pleasant salmon in the
>   unchainable sea,
> Though he were a wild mountain eagle, he could scarce
>   bear, he,
>   This sharp, sore sleet, these howling floods.[11]

Edward Walsh, a village schoolmaster, who hovered, like Mangan, on the edge of the Young Ireland movement, did many beautiful translations from the Gaelic; and Michael Doheny, while out 'on his keeping' in the mountains after the collapse at Ballingarry, made one of the most moving of ballads;[12] but in the main the poets who gathered about Thomas Davis, and whose work has come down to us in *The Spirit of the Nation*, were of practical and political, not of literary, importance.

Meanwhile Samuel Ferguson, William Allingham, and Aubrey de Vere[13] were working apart from politics; Ferguson selecting his subjects from the traditions of the bardic age, and Allingham from those of his native Ballyshannon, and Aubrey de Vere wavering between English, Irish, and Catholic tradition. They were wiser than Young Ireland in the choice of their models, for, while drawing not less from purely Irish sources, they turned to the great poets of the world, Aubrey de Vere owing something of his gravity to Wordsworth, Ferguson much of his simplicity to Homer, while Allingham had trained an ear, too delicate to catch the tune of but a single master, upon the lyric poetry of many lands. Allingham was the best artist, but Ferguson had the more ample imagination, the more epic aim. He had not the subtlety of feeling, the variety of cadence of a great lyric poet, but he has touched, here and there, an epic vastness and *naïveté*, as in the description in *Congal* of the mire-stiffened mantle of the giant spectre Mananan mac Lir striking against his calves with as loud a noise as the mainsail of a ship 'when with the coil of all its ropes it beats the sounding mast'.[14] He is frequently dull, for he often lacked the 'minutely appropriate words'[15] necessary to embody those fine changes of feeling which enthral the attention; but his sense of weight and size, of action and tumult, has set him apart and solitary, an epic figure in a lyric age.

Allingham, whose pleasant destiny has made him the poet of his native town, and put 'The Winding Banks of Erne' into the mouths of the ballad-singers of Ballyshannon,[16] is, on the other hand, a master of 'minutely appropriate words', and can wring from the luxurious sadness of the lover, from the austere sadness of old age, the last golden drop of beauty; but amid action and tumult he can but fold his hands. He is the poet of the melancholy peasantry of the West, and, as years go on, and voluminous histories and copious romances drop under the horizon, will take his place among those minor immortals who have put their souls into little songs to humble the proud.

The poetry of Aubrey de Vere has less architecture than the poetry of Ferguson and Allingham, and more meditation. Indeed, his few but ever memorable successes are enchanted islands in gray seas of stately impersonal reverie and description, which drift by and leave no definite recollection. One needs, perhaps, to perfectly enjoy him, a Dominican habit, a cloister, and a breviary.

These three poets published much of their best work before and during the Fenian movement, which, like Young Ireland, had its poets, though but a small number. Charles Kickham, one of the 'triumvirate' that controlled it in Ireland; John Casey, a clerk in a flour-mill; and Ellen O'Leary, the sister of Mr John O'Leary, were at times very excellent.[17] Their verse lacks, curiously enough, the oratorical vehemence of Young Ireland, and is plaintive and idyllic. The agrarian movement that followed produced but little poetry, and of that little all is forgotten but a vehement poem by Fanny Parnell and a couple of songs by T. D. Sullivan, who is a good song-writer, though not, as the writer has read on an election placard, 'one of the greatest poets who ever moved the heart of man.'[18] But while Nationalist verse has ceased to be a portion of the propaganda of a party, it has been written, and is being written, under the influence of the Nationalist newspapers and of Young Ireland societies and the like. With an exacting conscience, and better models than Thomas Moore and the Young Irelanders, such beautiful enthusiasm could not fail to make some beautiful verses. But, as things are, the rhythms are mechanical, and the metaphors conventional; and inspiration is too often worshipped as a Familiar who labours while you sleep, or forget, or do many worthy things which are not spiritual things.

For the most part, the Irishman of our times loves so deeply those arts which build up a gallant personality, rapid writing, ready talking, effective speaking to crowds,[19] that he has no thought for the arts which consume the personality in solitude. He loves the mortal arts which have given him a lure to take the hearts of men, and shrinks from the immortal, which could but divide him from his fellows. And in this century, he who does not strive to be a perfect craftsman achieves nothing. The poor peasant of the eighteenth century could make fine ballads by abandoning himself to the joy or sorrow of the moment, as the reeds abandon themselves to the wind which sighs through them, because he had about him a world where all was old enough to be steeped in emotion. But we cannot take to ourselves, by merely thrusting out our hands, all we need of pomp and symbol, and if we have not the desire of artistic perfection for an ark, the deluge[20] of incoherence, vulgarity, and triviality will pass over our heads. If we had no other symbols but the tumult of the sea, the rusted gold of the thatch, the redness of the quicken-berry, and had never known the rhetoric of the platform and of the newspaper, we could do without laborious selection and rejection; but, even then, though we might do much that would be delightful, that would inspire coming times, it would not have the manner of the greatest poetry.

Here[21] and there, the Nationalist newspapers and the Young Ireland societies have trained a writer who, though busy with the old models, has some imaginative energy; while the more literary writers, the successors of Allingham and Ferguson and De Vere, are generally more anxious to influence and understand Irish thought than any of their predecessors who did not take the substance of their poetry from politics. They are distinguished too by their deliberate art, and by their preoccupation with spiritual passions and memories.

The poetry of Lionel Johnson and Mrs Hinkson is Catholic and devout, but Lionel Johnson's is lofty and austere,[22] and like De Vere's never long forgets the greatness of his Church and the interior life whose expression it is, while Mrs Hinkson is happiest when she puts emotions, that have the innocence of childhood, into symbols and metaphors from the green world about her. She has no reverie nor speculation, but a devout tenderness like that of St Francis for weak instinctive things, old gardeners, old fishermen, birds among the leaves, birds tossed upon the waters. Miss Hopper belongs to that school of writers which embodies passions, that are not the less spiritual because no Church has put them into prayers, in stories and symbols from old Celtic poetry and mythology. The poetry of AE†, at its best, finds its symbols and its stories in the soul itself, and has a more disembodied ecstasy than any poetry of our time.[23] He is the chief poet of the school of Irish mystics, in which there are many poets besides many who have heard the words, 'If ye know these things, happy are ye if ye do them,'[24] and thought the labours that bring the mystic vision more important than the labours of any craft.

Mr Herbert Trench and Mrs Shorter and 'Moira O'Neill'[25] are more interested in the picturesqueness of the world than in religion. Mr Trench and Mrs Shorter have put old Irish stories into vigorous modern rhyme, and have written, the one in her 'Ceann Dubh Deelish' and the other in 'Come, let us make Love deathless', lyrics that should become a lasting part of

Irish lyric poetry. 'Moira O'Neill' has written pretty lyrics of Antrim life;[26] but one discovers that Mrs Hinkson or Miss Hopper, although their work is probably less popular, comes nearer to the peasant passion, when one compares their work and hers with that Gaelic song translated so beautifully by Dr Sigerson, where a ragged man of the roads, having lost all else, is yet thankful for 'the great love gift of sorrow', or with many songs translated by Dr Hyde in his *Love Songs of Connacht*, or by Lady Gregory in her *Poets and Dreamers*.[27]

Except some few Catholic and mystical poets and Professor Dowden[28] in one or two poems, no Irishman living in Ireland has sung excellently of any but a theme from Irish experience, Irish history, or Irish tradition. Trinity College, which desires to be English, has been the mother of many verse writers and of few poets; and this can only be because she has set herself against the national genius, and taught her children to imitate alien styles and choose out alien themes, for it is not possible to believe that the educated Irishman alone is prosaic and uninventive. Her few poets have been awakened by the influence of the farm-labourers, potato-diggers, pedlars, and hedge-schoolmasters of the eighteenth century, and their imitators in this, and not by a scholastic life, which, for reasons easy for all to understand and for many to forgive, has refused the ideals of Ireland, while those of England are but far-off murmurs. An enemy to all enthusiasms, because all enthusiasms seemed her enemies, she has taught her children to look neither to the world about them, nor into their own souls, where some dangerous fire might slumber.

To remember that in Ireland the professional and landed classes have been through the mould of Trinity College or of English universities, and are ignorant of the very names of the best Irish writers, is to know how strong a wind blows from the ancient legends of Ireland, how vigorous an impulse to create is in her heart to-day. Deserted by the classes from among whom has come the bulk of the world's intellect, she struggles on, gradually ridding herself of incoherence and triviality, and slowly building up a literature in English, which, whether important or unimportant, grows always more unlike others; nor does it seem as if she would long lack a living literature in Gaelic, for the movement for the preservation of Gaelic, which has been so much more successful than anybody foresaw, has already its poets. Dr Hyde has written Gaelic poems which pass from mouth to mouth in the west of Ireland. The country people have themselves fitted them to ancient airs, and many that can neither read nor write sing them in Donegal and Connemara and Galway. I have, indeed, but little doubt that Ireland, communing with herself in Gaelic more and more, but speaking to foreign countries in English, will lead many that are sick with theories and with trivial emotion to some sweet well-waters of primeval poetry.

P.S. – This essay, written in 1895, though revised from time to time, sounds strangely to my ears to-day.[29] I still admire much that I then admired, but if I rewrote it now I should take more pleasure in the temper of our writers and deal more sternly with their achievement. The magnanimous integrity of their politics, and their own gallant impetuous minds, needed no commendation among the young Irishmen for whom I wrote, and a very little dispraise of their verses seemed an attack upon the nation itself. Taylor, the orator, a man of genius and of great learning, never forgave me what I have said of Davis here and elsewhere,[30] and it is easier for me to understand his anger in this year than thirteen years ago when the lofty thought of men like Taylor and O'Leary was the strength of Irish nationality. A new tradition is being built up on Gaelic poetry and romance and on the writings of the school I belong to, but the very strength of the new foundations, their lack of obvious generalization, their instinctive nature, the impossibility of ill-educated minds shaping the finer material, has for the moment marred the moral temper among those who are young enough to feel the change.

April, 1908

'Lionel Johnson'
(1898; rev. 1900, 1908), repr. from
A Treasury of Irish Poetry in the English Tongue,
ed. Stopford A. Brooke and T. W. Rolleston
(1900)

Contemporary Irish poets believe in a spiritual life, invisible and troubling, and express this belief in their poetry. Contemporary English poets are interested in the glory of the world, like Mr Rudyard Kipling; or in the order of the world, like Mr William Watson; or in the passion of the world, like Mr John Davidson; or in the pleasure of the world, like Mr Arthur Symons.[1] Mr Francis Thompson, who has fallen under the shadow of Mr Coventry Patmore, the poet of an older time and in protest against that time, is alone preoccupied with a spiritual life;[2] and even he, except at rare moments, has less living fervour of belief than pleasure in the gleaming and scented and coloured symbols that are the footsteps where the belief of others has trodden. Ireland, upon the other hand, is creating in English a poetry as full of spiritual ardour as the poetry that praised in Gaelic *The Country of the Two Mists*, and *The Country of the Young*, and *The Country of the Living Heart*.[3]

'AE'†[4] has written an ecstatic pantheistic poetry which reveals in all things a kind of scented flame consuming them from within. Miss Hopper, an unequal writer, whose best verses are delicate and distinguished, has no clear vision of spiritual things, but makes material things as frail and fragile as if they were but smouldering leaves, that we stirred in some mid-world of dreams, as 'the gossips' in her poem 'stir their lives' red ashes'.[5] Mrs Hinkson, uninteresting at her worst, as only uncritical and unspeculative writers are uninteresting, has sometimes expressed an impassioned and instinctive Catholicism in poems that are, as I believe, as perfect as they

111

are beautiful,[6] while Mr Lionel Johnson has in his poetry completed the trinity of the spiritual virtues by adding Stoicism to Ecstasy and Asceticism.[7] He has renounced the world and built up a twilight world instead, where all the colours are like the colours in the rainbow that is cast by the moon, and all the people as far from modern tumults as the people upon fading and dropping tapestries. He has so little interest in our pains and pleasures, and is so wrapped up in his own world, that one comes from his books wearied and exalted, as though one had posed for some noble action in a strange *tableau vivant* that cast its painful stillness upon the mind instead of the body. He might have cried with Axel, 'As for living, our servants will do that for us.'[8] As Axel chose to die, he has chosen to live among his books and between two memories – the religious tradition of the Church of Rome and the political tradition of Ireland.[9] From these he gazes upon the future, and whether he write of Sertorius or of Lucretius, or of Parnell or of 'Ireland's dead', or of '98, or of St Columba or of Leo XIII†,[10] it is always with the same cold or scornful ecstasy. He has made a world full of altar lights and golden vestures, and murmured Latin and incense clouds, and autumn winds and dead leaves, where one wanders remembering martyrdoms and courtesies that the world has forgotten.

His ecstasy is the ecstasy of combat, not of submission to the Divine will; and even when he remembers that 'the old Saints prevail', he sees the 'one ancient Priest'[11] who alone offers the Sacrifice, and remembers the loneliness of the Saints. Had he not this ecstasy of combat, he would be the poet of those peaceful and unhappy souls, who, in the symbolism of a living Irish visionary,[12] are compelled to inhabit when they die a shadowy island Paradise in the West, where the moon always shines, and a mist is always on the face of the moon, and a music of many sighs is always in the air, because they renounced the joy of the world without accepting the joy of God.

1898†

'AE'†
(1898; rev. 1900), in
A Treasury of Irish Poetry in the English Tongue,
ed. Stopford A. Brooke and T. W. Rolleston
(1900)

Some dozen years ago a little body of young men hired a room
in Dublin, and began to read papers to one another on the
Vedas and the Upanishads and the Neo-Platonists, and on
modern mystics and spiritualists. They had no scholarship,
and they spoke and wrote badly, but they discussed great
problems ardently and simply and unconventionally, as men
perhaps discussed great problems in the mediaeval
Universities. When they were scattered by their different trades
and professions, others took up the discussions where they
dropped them, moving the meetings, for the most part, from
back street to back street; and now two writers of genius – 'AE'†
and 'John Eglinton' – seem to have found among them, without
perhaps agreeing with them in everything, that simplicity of
mind and that belief in high things, less common in Dublin
than elsewhere in Ireland, for whose lack imagination
perishes.[1] 'John Eglinton' in *Two Essays on the Remnant* and in
the essays he has published in the little monthly magazine they
print and bind themselves, analyses the spiritual elements that
are transforming and dissolving the modern world; while
'AE'†, in *Homeward: Songs by the Way* and in *The Earth Breath*,[2]
repeats over again the revelation of a spiritual world that has
been the revelation of mystics in all ages, but with a richness of
colour and a subtlety of rhythm that are of our age. Plotinus
wrote: 'In the particular acts of human life it is not the interior
soul and the true man, but the exterior shadow of the man
alone, which laments and weeps, performing his part on the
earth, as in a more ample and extended scene, in which many

113

shadows of souls and phantom forms appear;'[3] and so these
poems cry out that 'for every deep filled with stars' there 'are
stars and deeps within',[4] and that 'our thought' is but 'the echo
of a deeper being', and that 'we kiss because God once for
beauty sought amid a world of dreams',[5] and that we rise by
'the symbol charioted' 'through loved things' to 'love's own
ways'.[6] They are full of the sadness that has fallen upon all
mystics, when they have first come to understand that there is
an invisible beauty from which they are divided by visible
things. How can one be interested in the rising and in the
setting of the sun, and in the work men do under the sun, when
the mistress that one loves is hidden behind the gates of death,
and it may be behind a thousand gates beside – gate beyond
gate?

> What of all the will to do?
>   It has vanished long ago,
> For a dream-shaft pierced it through
>   From the Unknown Archer's bow.
>
> What of all the soul to think?
>   Some one offered it a cup
> Filled with a diviner drink;
>   And the flame has burned it up.
>
> What of all the hope to climb?
>   Only in the self we grope
> To the misty end of time:
>   Truth has put an end to hope.[7]

It is this invisible beauty that makes the planets 'break in
woods and flowers and steams' and 'shake' the winds from
them 'as the leaves from off the rose', and that 'kindles' all
souls and lures them 'through the gates of birth and death', and
in whose heart we will all rest when 'the shepherd of the ages
draws his misty hordes away through the glimmering deeps to
silence' and to 'the awful fold'.[8] But this invisible beauty
kindles evil as well as good, for its shadow is 'the fount of
shadowy beauty' that pours out those things 'the heart', the
merely mortal part of us, 'would be', and 'chases' them in

'endless flight'. All emotions are double, for either we choose 'the shadowy beauty', and our soul weeps, or the invisible beauty that is 'our high ancestral self', and the body weeps.[9]

These poems, the most delicate and subtle that any Irishman of our time has written, seem to me all the more interesting because their writer has not come from any of our seats of literature and scholarship, but from among sectaries and visionaries whose ardour of belief and simplicity of mind have been his encouragement and his inspiration.

W. B. Yeats

'Nora Hopper' (1898; rev. 1900), in
A Treasury of Irish Poetry in the English Tongue, ed. Stopford A. Brooke and T. W. Rolleston (1900)

Modern poetry grows weary of using over and over again the personages and stories and metaphors that have come to us through Greece and Rome, or from Wales and Brittany through the Middle Ages, and has found new life in the Norse and German legends. The Irish legends, in popular tradition and in old Gaelic literature, are more numerous and as beautiful, and alone among great European legends have the beauty and wonder of altogether new things. May one not say, then, without saying anything improbable, that they will have a predominant influence in the coming century, and that their influence will pass through many countries?

The latest of a little group of contemporary writers, who have begun to found their work upon them, as the Trouvères†[1] founded theirs upon the legends of Arthur and his knights, is Miss Nora Hopper, whose two books,[2] though they have many of the faults of youth, have at their best an extraordinary delicacy and charm. I got *Ballads in Prose* when it came out, two or three years ago, and it haunted me as few new books have ever haunted me, for it spoke in strange wayward stories and birdlike little verses of things and of persons I remembered or had dreamed of; it did not speak with the too emphatic manner that sometimes mars the more powerful stories Miss Fiona Macleod[3] has told of like things and persons, but softly – more murmuring than speaking. Even now, when the first enchantment is gone and I see faults I was blind to, I cannot go by certain brown bogs covered with white tufts of bog-cotton – places where the world seems to become faint and fragile – without remembering the verses her Daluan – a kind of Irish

116

Pan – sings among the bogs; and when once I remember them, they run in my head for hours –

All the way to Tir na n'Og are many roads that run,
But the darkest road is trodden by the King of Ireland's son.
The world wears on to sundown, and love is lost and won,
But he recks not of loss or gain, the King of Ireland's son.
He follows on for ever, when all your chase is done,
He follows after shadows – the King of Ireland's son.[4]

One does not know why he sings it, or why he dies on November Eve, or why the men cry over him 'Daluan is dead – dead! Daluan is dead!' and the women, 'Da Mort is king,' for 'Duluan' is but Monday and 'Da Mort' is but Tuesday;[5] nor does one well know why any of her best stories, 'Boholaun† and I', 'The Gifts of Aodh and Una', 'The Four Kings', or 'Aonan-na-Righ',†[6] shaped itself into the strange, drifting, dreamy thing it is, and one is content not to know. They delight us by their mystery, as ornament full of lines, too deeply interwoven to weary us with a discoverable secret, delights us with its mystery; and as ornament is full of strange beasts and trees and flowers, that were once the symbols of great religions, and are now mixing one with another, and changing into new shapes, this book is full of old beliefs and stories, mixing and changing in an enchanted dream. Their very mystery, that has left them so little to please the mortal passionate part of us, which delights in the broad noon-light men need if they would merely act and live, has given them that melancholy which is almost wisdom.

A great part of *Quicken Boughs* was probably written before *Ballads in Prose*; for, though it is all verse, it has few verses of the same precise and delicate music as those scattered among the stories in the earlier book. But 'Phyllis and Damon' is perfect in its kind, while 'The Dark Man'[7] gives beautiful words to that desire of spiritual beauty and happiness which runs through so much modern true poetry. It is founded upon the belief, common in Ireland, that certain persons are, as it is called, 'away' or more with the fairies than with us, and that 'dark' or blind people can see what we cannot.

W. B. Yeats

'Althea Gyles',
in *A Treasury of Irish Poetry in the English Tongue*,
ed. Stopford A. Brooke and T. W. Rolleston
(1900)

Miss Althea Gyles may come to be one of the most important of
the little group of Irish poets who seek to express indirectly
through myths and symbols, or directly in little lyrics full of
prayers and lamentations, the desire of the soul for spiritual
beauty and happiness. She has done, besides the lyric I quote,
which is charming in form and substance, a small number of
poems full of original symbolism and spiritual ardour, though
as yet lacking in rhythmical subtlety.[1] Her drawings and
book-covers, in which precise symbolism never interferes with
beauty of design, are as yet her most satisfactory expression of
herself.[2]

    W. B. Yeats

'Thoughts on Lady Gregory's Translations': Prefaces (1902, 1903; rev. 1905, 1908, 1912), repr. from Lady Gregory, *Cuchulain of Muirthemne* (1902) and *Gods and Fighting Men* (1904)

I
CUCHULAIN AND HIS CYCLE

The Church when it was most powerful taught learned and unlearned to climb, as it were, to the great moral realities through hierarchies of Cherubim and Seraphim, through clouds of Saints and Angels who had all their precise duties and privileges. The story-tellers of Ireland, perhaps of every primitive country, imagined as fine a fellowship, only it was to the aesthetic realities they would have had us climb. They created for learned and unlearned alike, a communion of heroes, a cloud of stalwart witnesses; but because they were as much excited as a monk over his prayers, they did not think sufficiently about the shape of the poem and the story. We have to get a little weary or a little distrustful of our subject, perhaps, before we can lie awake thinking how to make the most of it. They were more anxious to describe energetic characters, and to invent beautiful stories, than to express themselves with perfect dramatic logic or in perfectly-ordered words. They shared their characters and their stories, their very images, with one another, and handed them down from generation to generation; for nobody, even when he had added some new trait, or some new incident, thought of claiming for himself what so obviously lived its own merry or mournful life. The maker of images or worker in mosaic who first put Christ upon a cross would have as soon claimed as his own a thought which was perhaps put into his mind by Christ himself. The Irish poets had also, it may be, what seemed a supernatural sanction, for a chief poet had to understand not only innumerable kinds

of poetry, but how to keep himself for nine days in a trance.[1]
Surely they believed or half believed in the historical reality of
even their wildest imaginations. And so soon as Christianity
made their hearers desire a chronology that would run side by
side with that of the Bible, they delighted in arranging their
Kings and Queens, the shadows of forgotten mythologies, in
long lines that ascended to Adam and his Garden. Those who
listened to them must have felt as if the living were like rabbits
digging their burrows under walls that had been built by Gods
and Giants, or like swallows building their nests in the stone
mouths of immense images, carved by nobody knows who. It is
no wonder that one sometimes hears about men who saw in a
vision ivy-leaves that were greater than shields, and blackbirds
whose thighs were like the thighs of oxen.[2] The fruit of all those
stories, unless indeed the finest activities of the mind are but a
pastime, is the quick intelligence, the abundant imagination,
the courtly manners of the Irish country-people.

†

William Morris came to Dublin when I was a boy, and I had
some talk with him about these old stories. He had intended to
lecture upon them, but 'the ladies and gentlemen' – he put a
communistic fervour of hatred into the phrase – knew nothing
about them. He spoke of the Irish account of the battle of
Clontarf and of the Norse account, and said, that one saw the
Norse and Irish tempers in the two accounts.[3] The Norseman
was interested in the way things are done, but the Irishman
turned aside, evidently well pleased to be out of so dull a
business, to describe beautiful supernatural events. He was
thinking, I suppose, of the young man who came from Aoibhill
of the Grey Rock, giving up immortal love and youth, that he
might fight and die by Murrough's side.[4] He said that the
Norseman had the dramatic temper, and the Irishman had the
lyrical. I think I should have said with Professor Ker, epical
and romantic[5] rather than dramatic and lyrical, but his words,
which have so great an authority, mark the distinction very
well, and not only between Irish and Norse, but between Irish
and other un-Celtic literatures. The Irish story-teller could not
interest himself with an unbroken interest in the way men like
himself burned a house, or won wives no more wonderful than

themselves. His mind constantly escaped out of daily circumstance, as a bough that has been held down by a weak hand suddenly straightens itself out. His imagination was always running to Tír-na-nÓg†, to the Land of Promise,[6] which is as near to the country-people of to-day as it was to Cuchulain[7] and his companions. His belief in its nearness† cherished in its turn the lyrical temper, which is always athirst for an emotion, a beauty which cannot be found in its perfection upon earth, or only for a moment. His imagination, which had not been able to believe in Cuchulain's greatness, until it had brought the Great Queen, the red-eyebrowed goddess,[8] to woo him upon the battlefield, could not be satisfied with a friendship less romantic and lyrical than that of Cuchulain and Ferdiad,[9] who kissed one another after the day's fighting, or with a love less romantic and lyrical than that of Baile and Aillinn, who died at the report of one another's deaths, and married in Tír-na-nÓg.†[10] His art, too, is often at its greatest when it is most extravagant, for he only feels himself among solid things, among things with fixed laws and satisfying purposes, when he has reshaped the world according to his heart's desire. He understands as well as Blake that the ruins of time build mansions in eternity,[11] and he never allows anything† that we can see and handle† to remain long unchanged. The characters must remain the same, but the strength of Fergus may change so greatly, that he, who a moment before was merely a strong man among many, becomes the master of Three Blows that would destroy an army, did they not cut off the heads of three little hills instead, and his sword, which a fool had been able to steal out of its sheath, has of a sudden the likeness of a rainbow.[12] A wandering lyric moon must knead and kindle perpetually that moving world of cloaks made out of the fleeces of Manannan†;[13] of armed men who change themselves into sea-birds;[14] of goddesses who become crows;[15] of trees that bear fruit and flower at the same time.[16] The great emotions of love, terror,† and friendship must alone remain untroubled by the moon in that world which is still the world of the Irish country-people, who do not open their eyes very wide at the most miraculous change, at the most sudden enchantment. Its events, and things, and people are wild, and are like unbroken horses, that are so much more beautiful than horses that have learned to run between shafts. One thinks of actual life, when one reads those Norse stories, which had shadows of their decadence, so necessary were the proportions of actual life to their efforts, when a dying man remembered his heroism enough to look down at his wound and say, 'Those broad spears are coming into fashion';[17] but the Irish stories make us understand why some Greek writer called myths the activities of the daemons.[18] The great virtues, the great joys, the great privations, come in the myths, and, as it were, take mankind between their naked arms, and without putting off their divinity. Poets have chosen their themes more often from stories that are all, or half, mythological, than from history or stories that give one the sensation of history, understanding, as I think, that the imagination which remembers the proportions of life is but a long wooing, and that it has to forget them before it becomes the torch and the marriage-bed.

†

One finds, as one expects, in the work of men who were not troubled about any probabilities or necessities but those of emotion itself, an immense variety of incident and character and of ways of expressing emotion. Cuchulain fights man after man during the quest of the Brown Bull,[19] and not one of those fights is like another, and not one is lacking in emotion or strangeness; and when one thinks imagination can do no more, the story of the Two Bulls,[20] emblematic of all contests, suddenly lifts romance into prophecy. The characters too have a distinctness we do not find among the people of the *Mabinogion*, perhaps not even among the people of the *Morte D'Arthur*.[21] We know we shall be long forgetting Cuchulain, whose life is vehement and full of pleasure, as though he always remembered that it was to be soon over; or the dreamy Fergus who betrays the sons of Usnach for a feast, without ceasing to be noble; or Conall† who is fierce and friendly and trustworthy,[22] but has not the sap of divinity that makes Cuchulain mysterious to men, and beloved of women. Women indeed, with their lamentations for lovers and husbands and sons, and for fallen rooftrees and lost wealth, give the stories their most beautiful sentences; and, after Cuchulain, one thinks

most of certain great queens – of angry, amorous Maeve, with
her long, pale face; of Findabair, her daughter, who dies of
shame and of pity;[23] of Deirdre, who might be some mild
modern housewife but for her prophetic wisdom. If one does
not set Deirdre's lamentations[24] among the greatest lyric
poems of the world, I think one may be certain that the
wine-press of the poets has been trodden for one in vain; and yet
I think it may be proud Emer, Cuchulain's fitting wife, who will
linger longest in the memory. What a pure flame burns in her
always, whether she is the newly-married wife fighting for
precedence, fierce as some beautiful bird;† or the confident
housewife, who would awaken her husband from his magic
sleep with mocking words; or the great queen who would get
him out of the tightening net of his doom, by sending him into
the Valley of the Deaf, with Niamh, his mistress, because he
will be more obedient to her;[25] or the woman whom sorrow has
set with Helen and Iseult and Brunnhilda, and Deirdre, to
share their immortality in the rosary of the poets.[26]

'"And oh! my love!" she said, "we were often in one
another's company, and it was happy for us; for if the world had
been searched from the rising of the sun to sunset, the like
would never have been found in one place, of the Black
Sainglain and the Grey of Macha, and Laeg the chariot-driver,
and myself and Cuchulain."

'And after that Emer bade Conall† to make a wide, very deep
grave for Cuchulain; and she laid herself down beside her
gentle comrade, and she put her mouth to his mouth, and she
said: "Love of my life, my friend, my sweetheart, my one choice
of the men of the earth, many is the woman, wed or unwed,
envied me until to-day; and now I will not stay living after
you."'[27]

†

To us Irish, these personages should be very moving, very
important, for they lived in the places where we ride and go
marketing, and sometimes they have met one another on the
hills that cast their shadows upon our doors at evening. If we
will but tell these stories to our children the Land will begin
again to be a Holy Land, as it was before men gave their hearts
to Greece and Rome and Judea. When I was a child I had only

to climb the hill behind the house to see long, blue, ragged hills flowing along the southern horizon. What beauty was lost to me, what depth of emotion is still perhaps lacking in me, because nobody told me, not even the merchant captains who knew everything, that Cruachan of the Enchantments lay behind those long, blue, ragged hills![28]

March 1902[†]

II
FION AND HIS CYCLE

A few months ago I was on the bare Hill of Allen, 'wide Almhuin of Leinster', where Finn and the Fianna are said to have had their house,[29] although there are no earthen mounds there like those that mark the sites of old houses on so many hills. A hot sun beat down upon flowering gorse and flowerless heather; and on every side except the east, where there were green trees and distant hills, one saw a level horizon and brown boglands with a few green places and here and there the glitter of water. One could imagine that had it been twilight and not early afternoon, and had there been vapours drifting and frothing where there were now but shadows of clouds, it would have set stirring in one, as few places even in Ireland can, a thought that is peculiar to Celtic romance, as I think, a thought of a mystery coming not as with Gothic nations out of the pressure of darkness, but out of great spaces and windy light. The hill of Teamhair, or Tara,[30] as it is now called, with its green mounds and its partly-wooded sides, and its more gradual slope set among fat grazing lands, with great trees in the hedgerows, had brought before one imaginations, not of heroes who were in their youth for hundreds of years, or of women who came to them in the likeness of hunted fawns,[31] but of kings that lived brief and politic lives, and of the five white roads that carried their armies to the lesser kingdoms of Ireland, or brought to the great fair that had given Teamhair its sovereignty all that sought justice or pleasure or had goods to barter.

†

It is certain that we must not confuse these kings, as did the medieval chroniclers, with those half-divine kings of Almhuin. The chroniclers, perhaps because they loved tradition too well to cast out utterly much that they dreaded as Christians, and perhaps because popular imagination had begun the mixture, have mixed one with another ingeniously, making Finn the head of a kind of Militia under Cormac MacArt, who is supposed to have reigned at Teamhair in the second century, and making Grania, who travels to enchanted houses under the cloak of Aengus, god of Love, and keeps her troubling beauty longer than did Helen hers, Cormac's daughter, and giving the stories of the Fianna, although the impossible has thrust its proud finger into them all, a curious air of precise history.[32] It is only when we separate the stories from that medieval pedantry, that we recognise one of the oldest worlds that man has imagined, an older world certainly than we find in the stories of Cuchulain, who lived, according to the chroniclers, about the time of the birth of Christ.[33] They are far better known, and we may be certain of the antiquity of incidents that are known in one form or another to every Gaelic-speaking countryman in Ireland or in the Highlands of Scotland. Sometimes a labourer digging near to a cromlech, or Bed of Diarmuid and Grania as it is called,[34] will tell you a tradition that seems older and more barbaric than any description of their adventures or of themselves in written text or in story that has taken form in the mouths of professed story-tellers. Finn and the Fianna found welcome among the court poets later than did Cuchulain; and one finds memories of Danish invasions and standing armies mixed with the imaginations of hunters and solitary fighters among great woods. We never hear of Cuchulain delighting in the hunt or in woodland things; and one imagines that the story-teller would have thought it unworthy in so great a man, who lived a well-ordered, elaborate life, and could delight in his chariot and his chariot-driver and his barley-fed horses. If he is in the woods before dawn we are not told that he cannot know the leaves of the hazel from the leaves of the oak; and when Emer laments him no wild creature comes into her thoughts but the cuckoo that cries over cultivated fields. His story must have come out of a time when the wild wood was giving way to pasture and tillage, and men had no longer a reason to consider every cry of the birds or change of the night. Finn, who was always in the woods, whose battles were but hours amid years of hunting, delighted in the 'cackling of ducks from the Lake of the Three Narrows; the scolding talk of the blackbird of Doire an Cairn; the bellowing of the ox from the Valley of the Berries; the whistle of the eagle from the Valley of Victories or from the rough branches of the Ridge of the Stream; the grouse of the heather of Cruachan; the call of the otter of Druim re Coir'.[35] When sorrow comes upon the queens of the stories, they have sympathy for the wild birds and beasts that are like themselves: 'Credhe wife of Cael came with the others and went looking through the bodies for her comely comrade, and crying as she went. And as she was searching she saw a crane of the meadows and her two nestlings, and the cunning beast the fox watching the nestlings; and when the crane covered one of the birds to save it, he would make a rush at the other bird, the way she had to stretch herself out over the birds; and she would sooner have got her own death by the fox than the nestlings to be killed by him. And Credhe was looking at that, and she said: "It is no wonder I to have such love for my comely sweetheart, and the bird in that distress about her nestlings."'[36]

†

One often hears of a horse that shivers with terror, or of a dog that howls at something a man's eyes cannot see, and men who live primitive lives where instinct does the work of reason are fully conscious of many things that we cannot perceive at all. As life becomes more orderly, more deliberate, the supernatural world sinks farther away. Although the gods come to Cuchulain, and although he is the son of one of the greatest of them, their country and his are far apart, and they come to him as god to mortal; but Finn is their equal. He is continually in their houses; he meets with Bodb Dearg, and Aengus, and Manannan†, now as friend with friend, now as with an enemy he overcomes in battle; and when he has need of their help his messenger can say: 'There is not a king's son or a prince, or a leader of the Fianna of Ireland, without having a wife or a mother or a foster-mother or a sweetheart of the Tuatha de

Danaan.'[37] When the Fianna are broken up at last, after hundreds of years of hunting, it is doubtful that he dies at all, and certain that he comes again in some other shape, and Oisin, his son, is made king over a divine country. The birds and beasts that cross his path in the woods have been fighting-men or great enchanters or fair women, and in a moment can take some beautiful or terrible shape. We think of him and of his people as great-bodied men with large movements, that seem, as it were, flowing out of some deep below the shallow stream of personal impulse, men that have broad brows and quiet eyes full of confidence in a good luck that proves every day afresh that they are a portion of the strength of things. They are hardly so much individual men as portions of universal nature, like the clouds that shape themselves and reshape themselves momentarily, or like a bird between two boughs, or like the gods that have given the apples and the nuts; and yet this but brings them the nearer to us, for we can remake them in our image when we will, and the woods are the more beautiful for the thought. Do we not always fancy hunters to be something like this, and is not that why we think them poetical when we meet them of a sudden, as in these lines in *Pauline*?

> An old hunter
> Talking with gods; or a high-crested chief
> Sailing with troops of friends to Tenedos?[38]

†

One must not expect in these stories the epic lineaments, the many incidents woven into one great event of, let us say, the story of the War for the Brown Bull of Cuailgne, or that of the last gathering at Muirthemne.[39] Even *Diarmuid and Grania*, which is a long story, has nothing of the clear outlines of *Deirdre*, and is indeed but a succession of detached episodes.[40] The men who imagined the Fianna had the imagination of children, and as soon as they had invented one wonder, heaped another on top of it. Children – or, at any rate, it is so I remember my own childhood – do not understand large design, and they delight in little shut-in places where they can play at houses more than in great expanses where a country-side takes, as it were, the impression of a thought. The wild creatures and the green

things are more to them than to us, for they creep towards our
light by little holes and crevices. When they imagine a country
for themselves it is always a country where you can wander
without aim, and where you can never know from one place
what another will be like, or know from the one day's adventure
what may meet you with to-morrow's sun.

†

Children play at being great and wonderful people, at the
ambitions they will put away for one reason or another before
they grow into ordinary men and women. Mankind as a whole
had a like dream once; everybody and nobody built up the
dream bit by bit, and the ancient story-tellers are there to make
us remember what mankind would have been like, had not fear
and the failing will and the laws of nature tripped up its heels.
The Fianna and their like are themselves so full of power, and
they are set in a world so fluctuating and dream-like, that
nothing can hold them from being all that the heart desires.

I have read in a fabulous book that Adam had but to imagine
a bird and it was born into life, and that he created all things out
of himself by nothing more important than an unflagging
fancy;[41] and heroes who can make a ship out of a shaving have
but little less of the divine prerogatives.[42] They have no
speculative thoughts to wander through eternity and waste
heroic blood; but how could that be otherwise? for it is at all
times the proud angels who sit thinking upon the hill-side and
not the people of Eden. One morning we meet them hunting a
stag that is 'as joyful as the leaves of a tree in summer-time';[43]
and whatever they do, whether they listen to the harp or follow
an enchanter over-sea, they do for the sake of joy, their joy in
one another, or their joy in pride and movement; and even their
battles are fought more because of their delight in a good fighter
than because of any gain that is in victory. They live always as if
they were playing a game; and so far as they have any
deliberate purpose at all, it is that they may become great
gentlemen and be worthy of the songs of the poets. It has been
said, and I think the Japanese were the first to say it, that the
four essential virtues are to be generous among the weak, and
truthful among one's friends, and brave among one's enemies,
and courteous at all times; and if we understand by courtesy not

merely the gentleness the story-tellers have celebrated, but a delight in courtly things, in beautiful clothing and in beautiful verse, one understands that it was no formal succession of trials that bound the Fianna to one another. Only the Table Round, that is indeed, as it seems, a rivulet from the same well-head, is bound in a like fellowship, and there the four heroic virtues are troubled by the abstract virtues of the cloister. Every now and then some noble knight builds a cell upon the hill-side, or leaves kind women and joyful knights to seek the vision of the Grail in lonely adventures. But when Oisin or some kingly forerunner – Bran, son of Febal,[44] or the like – rides or sails in an enchanted ship to some divine country, he but looks for a more delighted companionship, or to be in love with faces that will never fade. No thought of any life greater than that of love, and the companionship of those that have drawn their swords upon the darkness of the world, ever troubles their delight in one another as it troubles Iseult amid her love, or Arthur amid his battles. It is an ailment of our speculation that thought, when it is not the planning of something, or the doing of something, or some memory of a plain circumstance, separates us from one another because it makes us always more unlike, and because no thought passes through another's ear unchanged. Companionship can only be perfect when it is founded on things, for things are always the same under the hand, and at last one comes to hear with envy the voices of boys lighting a lantern to ensnare moths, or of the maids chattering in the kitchen about the fox that carried off a turkey before breakfast. Lady Gregory's book of tales is full of fellowship untroubled like theirs, and made noble by a courtesy that has gone perhaps out of the world. I do not know in literature better friends and lovers. When one of the Fianna finds Osgar dying the proud death of a young man, and asks is it well with him, he is answered, 'I am as you would have me be.'[45] The very heroism of the Fianna is indeed but their pride and joy in one another, their good fellowship. Goll, old and savage, and letting himself die of hunger in a cave because he is angry and sorry, can speak lovely words to the wife whose help he refuses. ' "† It it best as it is," he said, "and I never took the advice of a woman east or west, and I never will take it. And oh, sweet-voiced queen," he said, "what ails you to be fretting after me? And remember now your silver and your gold, and your silks . . . and do not be crying tears after me, queen with the white hands," he said, "but remember your constant lover Aodh, son of the best woman of the world, that came from Spain asking for you, and that I fought on Corcar-an-Dearg; and go to him now," he said, "for it is bad when a woman is without a good man." [46]

†

They have no asceticism, but they are more visionary than any ascetic, and their invisible life is but the life about them made more perfect and more lasting, and the invisible people are their own images in the water. Their gods may have been much besides this, for we know them from fragments of mythology picked out with trouble from a fantastic history running backward to Adam and Eve, and many things that may have seemed wicked to the monks who imagined that history, may have been altered or left out; but this they must have been essentially, for the old stories are confirmed by apparitions among the country-people to-day. The Men of Dea fought against the mis-shapen Fomor, as Finn fights against the Cat-Heads and the Dog-Heads; [47] and when they are overcome at last by men, they make themselves houses in the hearts of hills that are like the houses of men. When they call men to their houses and to their Country-Under-Wave† they promise them all that they have upon earth, only in greater abundance. The god Midhir sings to Queen Etain in one of the most beautiful of the stories: 'The young never grow old; the fields and the flowers are as pleasant to be looking at as the blackbird's eggs; warm streams of mead and wine flow through that country; there is no care or no sorrow on any person; we see others, but we ourselves are not seen.' [48] These gods are indeed more wise and beautiful than men; but men, when they are great men, are stronger than they are, for men are, as it were, the foaming tide-line of their sea. One remembers the Druid who answered, when someone asked him who made the world, 'The Druids made it.' [49] All was indeed but one life flowing everywhere, and taking one quality here, another there. It sometimes seems as if there is a kind of day and night of religion, and that a period when the influences are those that shape the world is followed by a period when the greater power is in influences that would lure the soul out of the world, out of the body. When Oisin is speaking with St Patrick of the friends and the life he has outlived, he can but cry out constantly against a religion that has no meaning for him. He laments, and the country-people have remembered his words for centuries: 'I will cry my fill, but not for God, but because Finn and the Fianna are not living.'[50]

†

Old writers had an admirable symbolism that attributed certain energies to the influence of the sun, and certain others to the lunar influence. To lunar influence belong all thoughts and emotions that were created by the community, by the common people, by nobody knows who, and to the sun all that came from the high disciplined or individual kingly mind. I myself imagine a marriage of the sun and moon in the arts I take most pleasure in; and now bride and bridegroom but exchange, as it were, full cups of gold and silver, and now they are one in a mystical embrace. From the moon come the folk-songs imagined by reapers and spinners out of the common impulse of their labour, and made not by putting words together, but by mixing verses and phrases, and the folk-tales made by the capricious mixing of incidents known to everybody in new ways as one deals out cards, never getting the same hand twice over. When one hears some fine story, one never knows whether it has not been hazard that put the last touch of adventure. Such poetry, as it seems to me, desires an infinity of wonder or emotion, for where there is no individual mind there is no measurer-out, no marker-in of limits. The poor fisher has no possession of the world and no responsibility for it; and if he dreams of a love-gift better than the brown shawl that seems too common for poetry, why should he not dream of a glove made from the skin of a bird, or shoes made from the skin of a herring, or a coat made from the glittering garment of the salmon?[51] Was it not Aeschylus who said he but served up fragments from the banquet of Homer?[52] – but Homer himself found the great banquet on† an earthen floor and under a broken roof. We do not know who at the foundation of the world made the banquet for the first time, or who put the pack of cards into rough hands; but we do know that, unless those that have made many inventions are about to change the nature of poetry, we may have to go where Homer went if we are to sing a new song. Is it because all that is under the moon thirsts to escape out of bounds, to lose itself in some unbounded tidal stream, that the songs of the folk are mournful, and that the story of the Fianna, whenever the queens lament for their lovers, reminds us of songs that are still sung in country-places? Their grief, even when it is to be brief like Grania's, goes up into the waste places of the sky. But in supreme art, or in supreme life there is the influence of the sun too, and the sun brings with it, as old writers tell us, not merely discipline but joy; for its discipline is not of the kind the multitudes impose upon us by their weight and pressure, but the expression of the individual soul, turning itself into a pure fire and imposing its own pattern, its own music, upon the heaviness and the dumbness that is in others and in itself. When we have drunk the cold cup of the moon's intoxication, we thirst for something beyond ourselves, and the mind flows outward to a natural immensity; but if we have drunk from the hot cup of the sun, our own fulness awakens, we desire little, for wherever one goes one's heart goes too; and if any ask what music is the sweetest, we can but answer, as Finn answered, 'What happens.'[53] And yet the songs and stories that have come from either influence are a part, neither less than the other, of the pleasure that is the bride-bed of poetry.

†

Gaelic-speaking Ireland, because its art has been made, not by the artist choosing his material from wherever he has a mind to, but by adding a little to something which it has taken generations to invent, has always had a popular literature. We cannot say how much that literature has done for the vigour of the race, for who can count the hands its praise of kings and high-hearted queens made hot upon the sword-hilt, or the amorous eyes it made lustful for strength and beauty? We remember indeed that when the farming people and the labourers of the towns made their last attempt to cast out England by force of arms they named themselves after the companions of Finn.[54] Even when Gaelic has gone and the poetry with it, something of the habit of mind remains in ways of speech and thought and 'come-all-ye's'[55] and poetical sayings; nor is it only among the poor that the old thought has been for strength or weakness. Surely these old stories, whether of Finn or Cuchulain, helped to sing the old Irish and the old Norman-Irish aristocracy to their end. They heard their hereditary poets and story-tellers, and they took to horse and died fighting against Elizabeth or against Cromwell; and when an English-speaking aristocracy had their place, it listened to no poetry indeed, but it felt about it in the popular mind an exacting and ancient tribunal, and began a play that had for spectators men and women that loved the high wasteful virtues. I do not think that their own mixed blood or the habit of their time need take all, or nearly all, credit or discredit for the impulse that made those gentlemen of the eighteenth century fight duels over pocket-handkerchiefs, and set out to play ball against the gates of Jerusalem for a wager, and scatter money before the public eye;[56] and at last, after an epoch of such eloquence the world has hardly seen its like, lose their public spirit and their high heart, and grow querulous and selfish, as men do who have played life out not heartily but with noise and tumult. Had they known the people and the game a little better, they might have created an aristocracy in an age that has lost the understanding of the word. When one reads of the Fianna, or of Cuchulain, or of any of their like, one remembers that the fine life is always a part played finely before fine spectators. There also one notices the hot cup and the cold cup of intoxication; and when the fine spectators have ended, surely the fine players grow weary, and aristocratic life is ended. When O'Connell covered with a dark glove the hand that had killed a man in the duelling-field, he played his part;[57] and when Alexander stayed his army marching to the conquest of the world that he might contemplate the beauty of a plane-tree, he played his part.[58] When Osgar complained,† as he lay dying,† of the keening of the women and the old fighting-men, he too played his part: ' "No man ever knew any heart in me," he said, "but a heart of twisted horn, and it covered with iron; but the howling of the dogs beside me," he said, "and the keening of the old fighting-men and the crying of the women one after another, those are the things that are vexing me." '†[59] If we would create a great community – and what other game is worth the labour? – we must recreate the old foundations of life, not as they existed in that splendid misunderstanding of the eighteenth century, but as they must always exist when the finest minds and Ned the beggar and Seaghan the fool[60] think about the same thing, although they may not think the same thought about it.

†

When I asked the little boy who had shown me the pathway up the Hill of Allen if he knew stories of Finn and Oisin, he said he did not, but that he had often heard his grandfather telling them to his mother in Irish. He did not know Irish, but he was learning it at school, and all the little boys he knew were learning it. In a little while he will know enough stories of Finn and Oisin to tell them to his children some day. It is the owners of the land whose children might never have known what would give them so much happiness. But now they can read Lady Gregory's book to their children, and it will make Slieve-na-Mon†, Allen, and Benbulben,[61] the great mountain that showed itself before me every day through all my childhood and was yet unpeopled, and half the country-sides of south and west, as populous with memories as her *Cuchulain of Muirthemne*† will have made Dundealgan and Emain Macha and Muirthemne;[62] and after a while somebody may even take them to some famous place and say, 'This land where your fathers lived proudly and finely should be dear and dear and again dear'; and perhaps when many names have grown musical to their ears, a more imaginative love will have taught them a better service.

III

I praise but in brief words the noble writing of these books, for words that praise a book, wherein something is done supremely well, remain, to sound in the ears of a later generation, like the foolish sound of church bells from the tower of a church when every pew is full.

1903

Preface to
The Love Songs of Connacht: Being the Fourth Chapter of the Songs of Connacht,
collected and tr. Douglas Hyde (1904)

This little book, the fourth chapter of the still unfinished Songs of Connacht, was the first book that made known to readers that had no Irish, the poetry of the Irish country people.[1] There had been other translators, but they had a formal eighteenth century style, that took what Dr Hyde would call the 'sap and pleasure'[2] out of simple thought and emotion. Their horses were always steeds and their cows kine, and their rhythms had the formal monotony or the oratorical energy of that middle class literature that comes more out of will and reason than out of imagination and sympathy. Dr Hyde's prose translations, printed at the end of this book, are I think even better than his verse ones; for even he cannot always escape from the influence of his predecessors when he rhymes in English. His imagination is indeed at its best only when he writes in Irish or in that beautiful English of the country people who remember too much Irish to talk like a newspaper, and I commend his prose comments on the poems to all who can delight in fine prose. He wrote them in Irish first, and they are printed in Irish with the Irish text of the poems in the ordinary editions of his book.

W. B. Yeats

Preface to Lionel Johnson,
'Poetry and Patriotism', in *Poetry and Ireland: Essays by W. B. Yeats and Lionel Johnson* (1908)

The following essay was delivered as a lecture,[1] and I have left out those unimportant opening words, which a lecturer finds necessary, that his audience may grow used to his voice and his appearance.

Lionel Johnson was small but delicately made, and with great dignity of manner, and he spoke with so much music that what had been in another monotony, became nobility of style. His reading or speaking of poetry befitted his own particularly, that had from scholarship and from the loneliness and gravity of his mind an air of high lineage, but even poor verses were beautiful upon his lips. I think no man ever saw him angry or petulant, or till his infirmity had grown on him,[2] shaken from his self possession, and it often seemed as if he played at life, as if it were an elaborate ritual that would soon be over. I am certain he had prevision of his end, and that he was himself that mystic and cavalier who sang:

> Go from me: I am one of those, who fall.
> What! hath no cold wind swept your heart at all,
> In my sad company? before the end,
> Go from me, dear my friend!

> Yours are the victories of light: your feet
> Rest from good toil, where rest is brave and sweet.
> But after warfare in a mourning gloom,
> I rest in clouds of doom.

> Have you not read so, looking in these eyes,
> Is it the common light of the pure skies,
> Lights up their shadowy depths? the end is set:
> Though the end be not yet.[3]

Preface to John M. Synge,
Deirdre of the Sorrows: A Play (1910)

It was Synge's practice to write many complete versions of a play, distinguishing them with letters, and running half through the alphabet before he finished.[1] He read me a version of this play the year before his death, and would have made several more,† always altering and enriching.[2] He felt that the story, as he had told it, required a grotesque element mixed into its lyrical melancholy to give contrast and create an impression of solidity, and had begun this mixing with the character of Owen, who would have had some part in the first act also, where he was to have entered Lavarcham's cottage with Conchubor.[3] Conchubor would have taken a knife from his belt to cut himself free from threads of silk that caught in brooch or pin as he leant over Deirdre's embroidery frame, and forgotten this knife behind him. Owen was to have found it and stolen it. Synge asked that either I or Lady Gregory should write some few words to make this possible, but after writing in a passage we were little satisfied and thought it better to have the play performed, as it is printed here, with no word of ours. When Owen killed himself in the second act, he was to have done it with Conchubor's knife.[4] He did not speak to me of any other alteration, but it is probable that he would have altered till the structure had become as strong and varied as in his other plays; and had he lived to do that, *Deirdre of the Sorrows* would have been his master-work, so much beauty is there in its course, and such wild nobleness in its end, and so poignant is an emotion and wisdom that were his own preparation for death.

W. B. Yeats
April, 1910

Introduction to
Selections from the Writings of Lord Dunsany (1912)

I

Lady Wilde once told me that when she was a young girl she was stopped in some Dublin street by a great crowd and turned into a shop to escape from it. She stayed there some time and the crowd still passed. She asked the shopman what it was, and he said, 'the funeral of Thomas Davis, a poet.'[1] She had never heard of Davis; but because she thought a country that so honoured a poet must be worth something, she became interested in Ireland and was soon a famous patriotic poet herself, being, as she once said to me half in mockery, an eagle in her youth. That age will be an age of romance for a hundred years to come. Its poetry slid into men's ears so smoothly that a man still living, though a very old man now, heard men singing at the railway stations he passed upon a journey into the country the verses he had published but that morning in a Dublin newspaper; and yet we should not regret too often that it has vanished, and left us poets even more unpopular than are our kind elsewhere in Europe; for now that we are unpopular we escape from crowds, from noises in the street, from voices that sing out of tune, from bad paper made one knows not from what refuse, from evil-smelling gum, from covers of emerald green, from that ideal of reliable, invariable men and women, which would forbid saint and connoisseur who always, the one in his simple, the other in his elaborate way, do what is unaccountable, and forbid life itself which, being, as the definition says, the only thing that moves itself, is always without precedent. When our age too has passed, when its moments also, that are so common and many, seem scarce and precious, students will perhaps open these books, printed by village girls at Dundrum, as curiously as at twenty years I opened the books of history and ballad verse of the old 'Library of Ireland'.[2] They will notice that this new 'Library', where I have gathered so much that seems to me representative or beautiful, unlike the old, is intended for few people, and written by men and women with that ideal condemned by 'Mary of the Nation', who wished, as she said, to make no elaborate beauty and to write nothing but what a peasant could understand.[3] If they are philosophic or phantastic, it may even amuse them to find some analogy of the old with O'Connell's hearty eloquence, his winged dart shot always into the midst of the people, his mood of comedy; and of the new, with that lonely and haughty person below whose tragic shadow we of modern Ireland began to write.[4]

II

The melancholy, the philosophic irony, the elaborate music of a play by John Synge, the simplicity, the sense of splendour of living in Lady Gregory's lamentation of Emer, Mr James Stephens when he makes the sea waves 'Tramp with banners on the shore' are as much typical of our thoughts and day, as was 'She dwelt beside the Anner with mild eyes like the dawn', or any stanza of 'The† Pretty Girl of Loch Dan', or any novel of Charles Lever's of a time that sought to bring Irish men and women into one nation by means of simple patriotism and a genial taste for oratory and anecdotes.[5] A like change passed over Ferrara's brick and stone when its great Duke, where there had been but narrow medieval streets, made many palaces and threw out one straight and wide street, as Carducci said, to meet the Muses.[6] Doubtless the men of 'Perdóndaris that famous city'[7] have such antiquity of manners and of culture that it is of small moment should they please themselves with some tavern humour; but we must needs cling to 'our foolish Irish pride'[8] and form an etiquette, if we would not have our people crunch their chicken bones with too convenient teeth, and make our intellect architectural that we may not see them turn domestic and effusive nor nag at one another in narrow streets.

III

Some of the writers of our school have intended, so far as any creative art can have deliberate intention, to make this change, a change having more meaning and implications than a few sentences can define. When I was first moved by Lord Dunsany's work I thought that he would more help this change if he could bring his imagination into the old Irish legendary world instead of those magic lands of his with their vague Eastern air;[9] but even as I urged him I knew that he could not, without losing his rich beauty of careless suggestion, and the persons and images that for ancestry have all those romantic ideas that are somewhere in the background of all our minds. He could not have made Slieve-na-Mon[10] nor Slieve Fua incredible and phantastic enough, because that prolonged study of a past age, necessary before he could separate them from modern association, would have changed the spontaneity of his mood to something learned, premeditated, and scientific.

When we approach subtle elaborate emotions we can but give our minds up to play or become as superstitious as an old woman, for we cannot hope to understand. It is one of my superstitions that we became entangled in a dream some twenty years ago; but I do not know whether this dream was born in Ireland from the beliefs of the country men and women, or whether we but gave ourselves up to a foreign habit as our spirited Georgian fathers did to gambling, sometimes lying, as their history has it, on the roadside naked, but for the heap of straw they had pulled over them, till they could wager a lock of hair or the paring of a nail against what might set them up in clothes again.[11] Whether it came from Slieve-na-Mon or Mount Abora, AE† found it with his gods and I in my *Land of Heart's Desire*, which no longer pleases me much.[12] And then it seemed far enough till Mr Edward Martyn discovered his ragged Peg Inerney,[13] who for all that was a queen in faery; but soon John Synge was to see all the world as a withered and witless place in comparison with the dazzle of that dream; and now Lord Dunsany has seen it once more and as simply as if he were a child imagining adventures for the knights and ladies that rode out over the drawbridges in the piece of old tapestry in its mother's room. But to persuade others that it is all but one dream, or to persuade them that Lord Dunsany has his part in that change I have described I have but my superstition and this series of little books where I have set his tender, pathetic, haughty fancies among books by Lady Gregory, by AE†, by Dr Douglas Hyde, by John Synge, and by myself.[14] His work which seems today so much on the outside, as it were, of life and daily interest, may yet seem to those students I have imagined rooted in both. Did not the Maeterlinck of *Pelleas and Melisande* seem to be outside life? and now he has so influenced other writers, he has been so much written about, he has been associated with so much celebrated music, he has been talked about by so many charming ladies, that he is less a vapour than that Dumas *fils* who wrote of such a living Paris.[15] And has not Edgar Allan† Poe, having entered the imagination of Baudelaire, touched that of Europe?[16] for there are seeds still carried upon a tree, and seeds so light they drift upon the wind and yet can prove that they, give them but time, carry a big tree. Had I read 'The Fall of Babbulkund' or 'Idle Days on the Yann'[17] when a boy I had perhaps been changed for better or worse, and looked to that first reading as the creation of my world; for when we are young the less circumstantial, the further from common life a book is, the more does it touch our hearts and make us dream. We are idle, unhappy and exorbitant, and like the young Blake admit no city beautiful that is not paved with gold and silver.[18]

IV

These plays and stories have for their continual theme the passing away of gods and men and cities before the mysterious power which is sometimes called by some great god's name but more often 'Time'. His travellers, who travel by so many rivers and deserts and listen to sounding names none heard before, come back with no tale that does not tell of vague rebellion against that power, and all the beautiful things they have seen get something of their charm from the pathos of fragility. This poet who has imagined colours, ceremonies and incredible processions that never passed before the eyes of Edgar Allan† Poe or of De Quincey, and remembered as much fabulous beauty as Sir John Mandeville,[19] has yet never wearied of the most universal of emotions and the one most constantly associated with the sense of beauty; and when we come to examine those astonishments that seemed so alien we find that he has but transfigured with beauty the common sights of the world. He describes the dance in the air of large butterflies as we have seen it in the sun-steeped air of noon. 'And they danced but danced idly, on the wings of the air, as some haughty queen of distant conquered lands might in her poverty and exile dance in some encampment of the gipsies for the mere bread to live by, but beyond this would never abate her pride to dance for one fragment more.'[20] He can show us the movement of sand, as we have seen it where the sea shore meets the grass, but so changed that it becomes the deserts of the world: 'and all that night the desert said many things softly and in a whisper but I knew not what he said. Only the sand knew and arose and was troubled and lay down again and the wind knew. Then, as the hours of the night went by, these two discovered the foot-tracks wherewith we had disturbed the holy desert and they troubled over them and covered them up; and then the wind lay down and the sand rested.'[21] Or he will invent some incredible sound that will yet call before us the strange sounds of the night, as when he says, 'sometimes some monster of the river coughed'.[22] And how he can play upon our fears with that great gate of his carved from a single ivory tusk dropped by some terrible beast;[23] or with his tribe of wanderers that pass about the city telling one another tales that we know to be terrible from the blanched faces of the listeners though they tell them in an unknown tongue;[24] or with his stone gods of the mountain, for 'when we see rock walking it is terrible' 'rock should not walk in the evening'.[25]

Yet say what I will, so strange is the pleasure that they give, so hard to analyse and describe, I do not know why these stories and plays delight me. Now they set me thinking of some old Irish jewel work, now of a sword covered with Indian Arabesques that hangs in a friend's hall, now of St Mark's at Venice, now of cloud palaces at the sundown; but more often still of a strange country or state of the soul that once for a few weeks I entered in deep sleep and after lost and have ever mourned and desired.

v

Not all Lord Dunsany's moods delight me, for he writes out of a careless abundance; and from the moment I first read him I have wished to have between two covers something of all the moods that do. I believe that I have it in this book, which I have just been reading aloud to an imaginative young girl more French than English, whose understanding, that of a child and of a woman, and expressed not in words but in her face, has doubled my own.[26] Some of my selections, those that I have called 'A Miracle' and 'The Castle of Time' are passages from stories of some length, and I give but the first act of *Argimēnēs*, a play in the repertory of the Abbey Theatre, but each selection can be read I think with no thoughts but of itself. If 'Idle Days on the Yann' is a fragment it was left so by its author, and if I am moved to complain I shall remember that perhaps not even his imagination could have found adventures worthy of a traveller who had passed 'memorable, holy Golnuz, and heard the pilgrims praying,' and smelt burned poppies in Mandaroon.[27]

W. B. Yeats
Normandy 1912

Preface to
Rabindranath Tagore, *The Post Office*,
tr. Devabrata Mukerjea (1914)

When this little play was performed in London a year ago by
the Irish players,[1] some friends of mine discovered much
detailed allegory, the Headman being one principle of social
life, the Curdseller or the Gaffer another; but the meaning is
less intellectual, more emotional and simple.[2] The deliverance
sought and won by the dying child is the same deliverance
which rose before his imagination, Mr Tagore has said, when
once in the early dawn he heard, amid the noise of a crowd
returning from some festival, this line out of an old village song,
'Ferryman, take me to the other shore of the river.' It may come
at any moment of life, though the child discovers it in death, for
it always comes at the moment when the 'I', seeking no longer
for gains that cannot be 'assimilated with its spirit', is able to
say, 'All my work is thine'.[3] On the stage the little play shows
that it is very perfectly constructed, and conveys to the right
audience an emotion of gentleness and peace.

W. B. Yeats

Preface (1921) to
John M. Synge,
Shingu Gikyoku Zenshu
('Collected Plays of Synge'),
tr. Mineko Matsumura (1923)

So I am to write 'a few words of preface' to introduce the plays of John Synge,[1] who had in his mind so much of all that is most ancient in my country, to your countrymen, whose ancient poetry has come to mean so much to me† now that Mr Waley† and others have published their translations.[2] When I read the plays and essays of John Synge I go back at moments to our Middle Ages† and even further back, but as I go back, though I find much beauty at the journey's end, I am all the time among poor unlucky people, who live in thatched cottages among stony fields by the side of a bleak ocean, or on the slopes of bare wind-swept† mountains. In your Noh plays† or in that diary of one of your court ladies† of the eleventh century that I was reading yesterday,[3] I find beliefs and attitudes† of mind not very different but I find them among happy cultivated people. Once or twice when I have read some Japanese poem or play I have wished that Synge were living. How like it is,† in its story† or emotional quality, to something he has recorded in his book on the Aran Islands† or in his *Well of the Saints* or in his *Riders to the Sea*,†[4] or that Lady Gregory or I have found in Galway or in Sligo. The story of your Nishikigi for instance exists among us but as a mere anecdote,† which no poet has changed into great poetry.[5] Shortly before his last illness Synge told me that he meant to write no more peasant plays† and his last play, his unfinished *Deirdre of the Sorrows* is about old Irish kings and queens though written in the peasant dialect; and had he lived I think he would have been helped by your literature as I have been helped by it.[6] He told me once that he got no pleasure from the success of his plays in England, and I think the one or two continental productions of his *Playboy* that took place just before his death meant little to him,[7] but I am certain that the translation† of his plays into Japanese would have given him very great pleasure.

W. B. Yeats
December 1921

Introduction to
Oscar Wilde, *The Happy Prince and Other Fairy Tales* (1923)

When I was lecturing in Boston a little before the War an Arab refugee told me that Oscar Wilde's works had been translated into Arabian and that his *Happy Prince and Other Tales* had been the most popular: 'They are our own literature,' he said. I had already heard that 'The Soul of Man under Socialism' was much read in the Young China party;[1] and for long after I found myself meditating upon the strange destiny of certain books. My mind went back to the late eighties when I was but just arrived in London with the manuscript of my first book of poems,[2] and when nothing of Wilde's had been published except his poems and 'The Happy Prince'. I remember the reviews were generally very hostile to his work, for Wilde's aesthetic movement was a recent event and London journalists were still in a rage with his knee breeches, his pose – and it may be with his bitter speeches about themselves; while men of letters saw nothing in his prose but imitations of Walter Pater or in his verse but imitations of Swinburne and Rossetti.[3] Never did any man seem to write more deliberately for the smallest possible audience or in a style more artificial, and that audience contained nobody it seemed but a few women of fashion who invited guests to listen to his conversation and two or three young painters who continued the tradition of Rossetti. And then in the midst of my meditation it was as though I heard him saying with that slow precise, rhythmical elocution of his, 'I have a vast public in Samarkand.'[4] Perhaps they do not speak Arabian in Samarkand, but whatever name he had chosen he would have chosen it for its sound and for its suggestion of romance. His vogue in China would have touched him even more nearly, and I can almost hear his voice speaking of jade and powdered lacquer. Indeed, when I remember him with

147

pleasure it it always the talker I remember, either as I have heard him at W. E. Henley's or in his own house or in some passage in a play, where there is some stroke of wit which had first come to him in conversation or might so have come.[5] He was certainly the greatest talker of his time. 'We Irish', he had said to me, 'are too poetical to be poets, we are a nation of brilliant failures, but we are the greatest talkers since the Greeks.' He talked as good Irish talkers always do – though with a manner and music that he had learnt from Pater or Flaubert[6] – and as no good English talker has ever talked. He had no practical interest, no cause to defend, no information to give, nor was he the gay jester whose very practical purpose is our pleasure. Behind his words was the whole power of his intellect, but that intellect had given itself to pure contemplation. I know two or three such men in Ireland to-day, and one of them is an unknown man who lurched into my carriage in a Wicklow train two or three years ago: 'First class carriage, third class ticket, do it on principle,' he began, and then, speaking of a friend of his killed in the war, burst out with, 'Why are so many dead that should be alive and so many alive that should be dead?' For twenty minutes of drunken speech he talked as Shakespeare's people talked, never turning away for a moment from the fundamental and insoluble; and he told me one story that Wilde would have told with delight. Then too I think of a doctor and of a priest with whom I have talked in many places, but especially on a remote Connemara sea coast where, day after day, their minds, more learned in all the poetry of the world than mine, and vehement with phantasy, played with the fundamental and the insoluble.[7]

The further Wilde goes in his writings from the method of speech, from improvisation, from sympathy with some especial audience the less original he is, the less accomplished. I think 'The Soul of Man under Socialism' is sometimes profound because there are so many quotations in it from his conversation; and that *The Happy Prince and Other Tales* is charming and amusing because he told its stories, (his children were still young at that time) and that *A House of Pomegranates*[8] is over-decorated and seldom amusing because he wrote its stories; and because when he wrote, except when he wrote for actors, he no longer thought of a special audience. In

'The Happy Prince' or 'The Selfish Giant' or 'The Remarkable Rocket' there is nothing that does not help the story, nothing indeed that is not story; but in 'The Birthday of the Infanta' there is hardly any story worth the telling. 'The Fisherman and his Soul', from the same book, has indeed so good a story that I am certain that he told it many times; and, that I may enjoy it, I try to imagine it as it must have been when he spoke it, half consciously watching that he might not bore by a repeated effect or an unnecessary description, some child or some little company of young painters or writers. Only when I so imagine it do I discover that the incident of the young fisherman's dissatisfaction with his mermaid mistress, upon hearing a description of a girl dancing with bare feet was witty, charming and characteristic. The young fisherman had resisted many great temptations, but never before had he seen so plainly that she had no feet. In the written story that incident is so lost in decorations that we let it pass unnoticed at a first reading, yet it is the crisis of the tale. To enjoy it I must hear his voice once more, and listen once more to that incomparable talker.

I arrived in London after a long visit to Ireland a few months before his great disaster[9] and said to some friend of his, 'What is Wilde doing?' 'Oh,' said his friend, 'he is very melancholy, he gets up about two in the afternoon, for he tries to sleep away as much of life as possible, and he has made up a story which he calls the best story in the world and says that he repeats it to himself after every meal and upon going to bed at night.' He then told me the story and I believe I can trust my memory to recall his very words: 'Christ came over a white plain to a purple city, and, as He went through a street, He heard voices above His head. He looked up and saw a young man lying drunk upon a window-sill. Christ said, "Why do you waste your soul in drunkenness?" and the young man answered, "Lord, I was a leper and you healed me. What else can I do?" A little further on He saw a young man following a harlot with glittering eyes, and said,† "Why do you dissolve your soul in debauchery?" and the young man answered, "Lord, I was blind and you healed me. What else can I do?" In the middle of the city He found an old man crouched upon the ground weeping and said, "Why do you weep?" and the old man answered, "Lord, I was dead and you raised me into life – what else can I do but weep?"' I, too, think that is one of the best stories in the world, though I do not like, and did not like when I first heard it, 'white plain',† 'purple city', 'glittering eyes'. It has definiteness, the simplicity of great sculpture, it adds something new to the imagination of the world, it suddenly confronts the mind – as does all great art – with the fundamental and the insoluble. It puts into almost as few as possible words a melancholy that comes upon a man at the moment of triumph, the only moment when a man without dreading some secret bias, envy, disappointment, jealousy, can ask himself what is the value of life. Wilde, when I knew him first, was almost a poor man. 'People think I am successful,' he said, or some such words, 'but at this moment I do not know how to earn even a few shillings.' And now he had three plays running at once,[10] had earned it was said ten thousand pounds in a year: 'Lord, I was dead and you raised me into life, what else can I do but weep?'

The other day I found at the end of one of his volumes, in a section called 'Poems in Prose', that very story expanded to fifty or sixty lines, and by such description as 'Fair pillars of marble', 'the loud noise of many lutes', 'the hall of chalcedony and the hall of jasper', 'torches of cedar', 'One whose face and raiment were painted and whose feet were shod with pearls.'[11] The influence of painting upon English literature which began with the poetry of Keats had now reached its climax, because all educated England was overshadowed by Whistler, by Burne-Jones, by Rossetti; and Wilde – a provincial like myself – found in that influence something of the mystery, something of the excitement, of a religious cult and of a cult that promised an impossible distinction.[12] It was precisely because he was not of it by birth and by early association that he caught up phrases and adjectives for their own sake, and not because they were a natural part of his design, and spoke them to others as though it were his duty to pass on some password, sign or countersign. When his downfall came he had discovered his natural style in *The Importance of Being Earnest*, constrained to that discovery by the rigorous† technique of the stage, and was about to give to the English theatre comedies which would have been to our own age what the comedies of Goldsmith and of Sheridan were to theirs. He had already but one rival – Mr Bernard Shaw –

whose provincialism led him not to Walter Pater but to Karl Marx, and who, for all his longer life and his greater imaginative energy, has never cast off completely the accidental and the soluble.[13]

Preface to
John Butler Yeats, *Early Memories:*
Some Chapters of Autobiography (1923)

My father died in New York on February 2nd, 1922, at the end
of his eighty-second† year. He died after a few hours'† illness
brought on, as it seemed, by a long walk in the cold of a New
York winter. He awoke in the middle of the night to find his
friends Mrs Foster and Mr John Quinn sitting beside his bed
and after a few words of pleasure at the sight said to Mrs
Foster,† 'Remember you have promised me a sitting in the
morning.' These were his last words for he dropped off to sleep
and died in his sleep.[1] He had gone to America some ten or
twelve years before to be near my eldest sister who had an
exhibition of embroidery there, and though she left after a few
months he stayed on.[2] 'At last,' he said,† 'I have found a place
where people do not eat too much at dinner to talk afterwards.'
As he grew infirm his family and his friends constantly begged
him to return, but, though he promised as constantly and
would even fix the day of sailing, he would always ask for a few
weeks more. He lived in a little French hotel in 29th Street
where there is a café and night after night sat there, sketch book
in hand, surrounded by his friends, painters and writers for the
most part, who came to hear his conversation.[3] He seemed to
work as hard as in his early days, and drew with pen or pencil
innumerable portraits with vigour, and subtlety. He painted a
certain number in oils, and worked for several years at a large
portrait of himself, commissioned by Mr John Quinn. I have
not seen this portrait, but expect to find that he had worked too
long upon it and, as often happened in his middle life when, in a
vacillation† prolonged through many months it may be, he
would scrape out every morning what he had painted the day
before, that the form is blurred, the composition confused, and
the colour muddy.[4] Yet in his letters he constantly spoke of this

picture as his masterpiece, insisted again and again, as I had heard him insist when I was a boy, that he had found what he had been seeking all his life. This growing skill had been his chief argument against return to Ireland, for the portrait that displayed it must not be endangered by a change of light. The most natural among the fine minds that I have known,† he had been preoccupied all his life with the immediate present and what he thought his growing skill, but began towards its end, as I suppose we all do, to compare the present to the remote past. When I noticed how often his letters referred to long dead relations and friends, 'those lost people' as he called them in one letter, I persuaded him to begin his autobiography.[5] He wrote, though with difficulty and a little against the grain, the biographical fragment in this book. When his account of friends and relations had come to an end the difficulty increased, and finding it more amusing to put the present into letters, or conversation, he put off the next chapter from day to day. Everything that happened, the death or marriage of an acquaintance, the discovery of a new friend, stirred his imagination; and his letters, now that his conversation can be heard no more, are indeed the fullest expression of a wisdom where there is always beauty. Yet this biographical fragment has its measure of wisdom and beauty, and I am pleased to think that when my son has reached his eighteenth birthday he will be able to say,† 'Though my grandfather was born a hundred years ago, and I have never seen his face, I know him from his book and think of him with affection.'[6]

W. B. Yeats
June, 1923

Preface (1923) to
Oliver St John Gogarty,
An Offering of Swans and Other Poems (1924)

Oliver Gogarty telephoned to me at the Savile Club a few months ago to know where he could buy two swans. Up to his neck in its ice-cold water he had promised two swans to the Liffey if permitted to land in safety.[1] I made inquiries, and was able to report in a couple of days that there were certainly swans for sale at a well-known English country house, and probably at the Zoological Gardens. He had been kidnapped by armed men from his house in Dublin between seven and eight in the evening, hurried into a motor, and driven to a deserted house on the banks of the Liffey near Chapelizod. As he was not blindfolded it seemed unlikely that he would return. 'Death by shooting is a very good death,' said one of the armed men. 'Isn't it a fine thing to die to a flash,' said another armed man. 'Have we any chance of a Republic, Senator?' said a third. They sent a man to report on their success†, and while waiting his return Oliver Gogarty played bodily feebleness that they might relax their care, and the restless movements of terror that they, alarmed lest his clatter reached the road, might bid him take off his boots. He saw his moment, plunged into the river and escaped in the darkness, not hearing in the roar of flooded water the shots fired at random. Forced for his safety to leave Ireland for a time, he practised his profession in London, and I wonder if it was the excitement of escape, or the new surroundings, his occasional visits to old English country houses, that brought a new sense of English lyric tradition and changed a wit into a poet. The witty sayings that we all repeated, the Rabelaisian verse that we all copied rose out of so great a confused exuberance that I, at any rate, might have foreseen the miracle. Yet no, for a miracle is self-begotten and, though afterwards we may offer swans to Helicon,[2] by its very nature something we cannot foresee or premeditate. Its only rule is that it follows, more often than otherwise, the discovery of a region or a rhythm where a man may escape out of himself. Oliver Gogarty has discovered the rhythm of Herrick and of Fletcher, something different from himself and yet akin to himself; and I have been murmuring his 'Non Dolet', his 'Begone, Sweet Ghost', and his 'Good Luck'.[3] Here are but a few pages, that a few months have made, and there are careless lines now and again, traces of the old confused exuberance. He never stops long at his best, but how beautiful that best is, how noble, how joyous!

W. B. Yeats
August 30th, 1923†

Preface (1924) to
Jean Marie Matthias Philippe
Auguste Count de Villiers de l'Isle-Adam,
Axel, tr. H. P. R. Finberg (1925)

Before I went to Paris in 1894 I had read with great difficulty, for I had little French – almost as learned men read newly-discovered Babylonian cylinders – the *Axel* of Villiers de l'Isle-Adam.[1] That play seemed all the more profound, all the more beautiful, because I was never quite certain that I had read a page correctly. I was quite certain, however, that it was about those things that most occupied my thought and the thought of my friends, for we were perpetually thinking and talking about the value of life, and sometimes one or other of us – Lionel Johnson perhaps – would say, like Axel, that it had no value.[2] It did not move me because I thought it a great masterpiece, but because it seemed part of a religious rite, the ceremony perhaps of some secret Order wherein my generation had been initiated. Even those strange sentences so much in the manner of my time – 'as to living, our servants will do that for us'; 'O to veil you with my hair where you will breathe the spirit of dead roses' – did not seem so important as the symbols: the forest castle, the treasure, the lamp that had burned before Solomon.[3] Now that I have read it all again in Mr Finberg's translation and recalled that first impression, I can see how those symbols became a part of me, and for years to come dominated my imagination, and when I point out this fault or that – the monotonous piling-up of pictures in the last scene, the too abundant debates with the Commander or with Janus – I but discover there is no escape, that I am still dominated. Is it only because I opened the book for the first time when I had the vivid senses of youth that I must see that tower room always, and hear always that thunder?

Axel or its theme filled the minds of my Paris friends; my host

Macgregor Mathers, magician and mystic, talked of the Rosy Cross, and condemned the Sar Péladan for founding a Rosicrucian Order of his own, and bringing its roses to Notre Dame to be blessed.[4] The Latin Quarter had become virtuous, and notorious young women talked of their virginity. 'Villiers de l'Isle-Adam', Rémy de Gourmont wrote, 'has opened the doors of the unknown with a crash, and a generation has gone through them to the Infinite.'[5] But when I met Verlaine he insisted, having evidently forgotten all about it, that Villiers meant that nothing mattered but love, and added, 'He was flighty, but what French he wrote!'[6] I met frequently at a friend's house the wealthy Russian woman who had arranged for the play's performance, and I remember her vehemence, her vitality, as she paced to and fro kicking the floor-rugs from her way, and denouncing Ibsen for his lack of morals;[7] and that a young sculptor, who had tried to represent in stone forms like those painted by Gustave Moreau, sat at a little table in the corner modelling a bust of the actor who was to take the principal part.[8] The Sar Péladan had commended portraits that were 'to the spiritual glory of the sitter'.[9] The Russian had in her box upon the night of the performance her three divorced husbands, with whom she remained on the most excellent terms.[10] I was in the midst of one of those artistic movements that have the intensity of religious revivals in Wales and are such a temptation to the artist in his solitude. I have in front of me an article which I wrote at the time, and I find sentence after sentence of revivalist thoughts that leave me a little ashamed.[11] I wrote that we had grown tired 'of the photographing of life' and 'returned to symbolism', that these realists must be compelled to follow science into the obscurity of the schools, that 'the puppet plays of M. Maeterlinck have been followed by a still more remarkable portent.[12] Thirty thousand francs and enthusiastic actors have been found to produce the *Axel* of his master, Villiers de l'Isle-Adam. On February 26th a crowded audience of artists and men of letters listened, and on the whole with enthusiasm, from two o'clock until ten minutes to seven to this drama, which is written in prose as elevated as poetry, and in which all the characters are symbols, and all the events allegories. It is nothing to the point that the general public have since shown that they will have none of *Axel*, and that the critics have denounced it . . . and called the young generation both morbid and gloomy. One fat old critic,[13] when the Magician of the Rosy Cross began to denounce the life of pleasure and to utter the ancient doctrine of the spirit, turned round with his back to the stage and looked at the pretty girls through his opera-glass. Have we not proved, he doubtless thought, that nothing is fit for the stage except the opinions that everybody believes, the feelings that everybody shares, the wit which everybody understands? – and yet they have brought Dr Ibsen and the intellect on to the boards, and now here comes Villiers de l'Isle-Adam and that still more unwholesome thing the soul.'

I then go on to suggest with a prudence that surprises me that, should the play be brought to England, the second and third acts should be 'enormously reduced in length. The second act especially dragged greatly. The situation is exceedingly dramatic, and with much of the dialogue left out would be very powerful. The third act, though very interesting to anyone familiar with the problems and philosophy it deals with, must inevitably as it stands bore and bewilder the natural man with no sufficient counterbalancing advantage. There was no question of the dramatic power of the other acts; even the hostile critics have admitted this.' And then I wind up by commending the players and producers because they have not forgotten that an actor can be at times 'a reverent reciter of majestic words'.

On my return to London I tried to arrange a performance there, and Miss Florence Farr, who was producing *Arms and the Man* and my *Land of Heart's Desire*, offered her theatre for nothing, but the London public was thought unprepared, being in its first enthusiasm for Jones and Pinero.[14]

W. B. Yeats
September 20th, 1924

Introduction to *The Midnight Court*†, from Brian Merriman and Donagh Rua Macnamara, *The Midnight Court and The Adventures of a Luckless Fellow*, tr. Percy Arland Ussher (1926)

Months ago Mr Ussher asked me to introduce his translation of 'The Midnight Court'. I had seen a few pages in an Irish magazine; praised its vitality; my words had been repeated; and because I could discover no reason for refusal that did not make me a little ashamed, I consented. Yet I could wish that a Gaelic scholar had been found, or failing that some man of known sobriety of manner and of mind – Professor Trench of Trinity College let us say – to introduce to the Irish reading public this vital, extravagant, immoral, preposterous poem.[1]

Brian Mac Giolla Meidhre – or to put it in English, Brian Merriman – wrote in Gaelic, one final and three internal rhymes in every line, pouring all his mediaeval abundance into that narrow neck. He was born early in the eighteenth century, somewhere in Clare, even now the most turbulent of counties, and the countrymen of Clare and of many parts of Munster have repeated his poem† down to our own day. Yet this poem which is so characteristically Gaelic and mediaeval is founded upon 'Cadenus and Vanessa',[2] read perhaps in some country gentleman's library. The shepherds and nymphs of Jonathan Swift plead by counsel before Venus:

> Accusing the false creature man.
> The brief with weighty crimes was charged
> On which the pleader much enlarged,
> That Cupid now has lost his art,
> Or blunt the point of every dart.

Men have made marriage mercenary and love an intrigue; but the shepherds' counsel answers that the fault lies with women who have changed love for 'gross desire' and care but for 'fops and fools and rakes'.[3] Venus finds the matter so weighty that she calls the Muses and the Graces to her assistance and consults her books of law – Ovid, Virgil, Tibullus, Cowley, Waller[4] – continuously adjourns the court for sixteen years, and then after the failure of an experiment gives the case in favour of the women. The experiment is the creation of Vanessa, who instead of becoming all men's idol and reformer, all women's example, repels both by her learning and falls in love with her tutor Swift.

The Gaelic poet changed a dead to a living mythology, and called men and women to plead before Eevell of Craglee, the chief of Munster spirits†, and gave her court reality by seeing it as a vision upon a mid-summer day under a Munster tree. No countryman of that time doubted, nor in all probability did the poet doubt, the existence of Eevell, a famous figure to every story-teller.[5] The mediaeval convention of a dream or vision has served the turn of innumerable licentious rhymers in Gaelic and other languages, of Irish Jacobites who have substituted some personification of Ireland, some Dark Rosaleen, for a mortal mistress, of learned poets who call before our eyes an elaborate allegory of courtly love. I think of Chaucer's 'Romaunt of the Rose', his 'Book of the Duchess', and of two later poems that used to be called his, 'Chaucer's Dream' and 'The Complaint of the Black Knight'.[6] But in all these the vision comes in May.

> That it was May, me thoughte tho,
> It is fyve yere or more ago;
> That it was May, thus dreamed me
> In tyme of love and jolitie
> That all things ginneth waxen gay.[7]

One wonders if there is some Gaelic precedent for changing the spring festival for that of summer, the May-day singing of the birds to the silence of summer fields. Had Mac Giolla Meidhre before his mind the fires of St John's Night, for all through Munster men and women leaped the fires that they might be fruitful, and after scattered the ashes that the fields might be fruitful also.[8] Certainly it is not possible to read his verses without being shocked and horrified as city onlookers were perhaps shocked and horrified at the free speech and buffoonery of some traditional country festival.

He wrote at a moment of national discouragement, the penal laws were still in force through weakening, the old order was a vivid memory but with the failure of the last Jacobite rising hope of its return had vanished, and no new political dream had come.[9] The state of Ireland is described: 'Her land purloined, her law decayed ... pastures with weeds o'ergrown, her ground untilled ... hirelings holding the upper hand', and worst of all – and this the fairy court has been summoned to investigate – 'the lads and lasses have left off breeding.' Are the men or the women to blame? A woman speaks first, and it is Swift's argument but uttered with voluble country extravagance, and as she speaks one calls up a Munster hearth, farmers sitting round at the day's end, some old farmer famous through all the countryside for this long recitation, speaking or singing with dramatic gesture. If a man marries, the girl declares, he does not choose a young girl but some rich scold 'with a hairless crown and a snotty nose'. Then she describes her own beauty and asks if she is not more fit for marriage? She has gone everywhere 'bedizened from top to toe', but because she lacks money nobody will look at her and she is single still –†

> After all I have spent upon readers of palms
> And tellers of tea-leaves and sellers of charms.[10]

Then an old man replies, and heaps upon her and upon her poverty-stricken father and family all manner of abuse: he is the champion of the men, and he will show where the blame lies. He tells of his own marriage. He was a man of substance but has been ruined by his wife who gave herself up to every sort of dissipation – Swift's argument again. A child was born, but when he asked to see the child the women tried to cover it up, and when he did see it, it was too fine, too handsome and vigorous to be a child of his. And now Swift is forgotten and

dramatic propriety, the poet speaks through the old man's
mouth and asks Eevell of Craglee to abolish marriage that such
children may be born in plenty.

> For why call a Priest in to bind and to bless
> Since Mary the Mother of God did conceive
> Without calling the Clergy or begging their leave,
> The love-gotten children are famed as the flower
> Of man's procreation and nature's power,
> For love is a lustier sire than law,
> And has made them sound without fault or flaw
> And better and braver in heart and head
> Than the puny breed of the marriage bed.[11]

The bastard's speech in *Lear* is floating through his mind
mixed up doubtless with old stories of Diarmuid's and
Cuchulain's† loves, and old dialogues where Oisin railed at
Patrick; but there is something more, an air of personal
conviction that is of his age, something that makes his words –
spoken to that audience – more than the last song of Irish
paganism.[12] One remembers that Burns is about to write his
beautiful defiant 'Welcome to his love-begotten Daughter†' and
that Blake who is defiant in thought alone meditates perhaps
his *Marriage of Heaven and Hell*.[13] The girl replies to the old man
that if he were not so old and crazed she would break his bones,
and that if his wife is unfaithful what better could he expect
seeing that she was starved into marrying him. However, she
has her own solution. Let all the handsome young priests be
compelled to marry. Then Eevell† of Craglee gives her
judgment†, the Priests are left to the Pope who will order them
into marriage one of these days, but let all other young men
marry or be stripped and beaten by her spirits, and let all old
bachelors be tortured by the spinsters. The poem ends by the
girl falling upon the poet and beating him because he is
unmarried. He is ugly and humped, she says, but might look as
well as another in the dark.

Standish Hayes O'Grady has described 'The† Midnight†
Court' as the best poem written in Gaelic,[14] and as I
read Mr Ussher's translation I have felt, without sharing what
seems to me an extravagant opinion, that Mac† Giolla

Meidhre, had political circumstances been different, might have founded a modern Gaelic literature. Mac Conmara†, or Macnamara, though his poem is of historical importance, does not interest me so much.[15] He knew Irish and Latin only, knew nothing of his own age, saw vividly but could not reflect upon what he saw, and so remained an amusing provincial figure.

1926

Prefatory letter to the Medici Society, in William Blake, *Songs of Innocence*, illus. Jacynth Parsons (1927)

To
The Medici Society.

Dear Sirs,

A Dublin maker of beautiful stained glass brought to my house last night a sixteen-year-old English girl with a face of still intensity, her black plaited hair falling between her shoulders.[1] He laid a large portfolio on a table in the middle of the room, but as I had already refused to write that preface for her drawings I carried the portfolio to a table in a distant corner. Those present were a Free State officer, a distinguished dramatist, a country gentleman with imperfect sight who has the history of modern Italy read to him for five hours a day because he thinks it is like that of modern Ireland.[2] We arranged our talk unconsciously that it might contain incidents to amuse a young girl fresh from Grimm's goblins and *Treasure Island*.[3] Somebody told stories of our civil war, I pointed to the bullet hole in the study door and hinted at all the Free State officer could tell if he were not silent and gloomy. Presently he said Republicans were bound to win the general election in September, and do all kinds of horrible things, and in a minute we had exchanged civil war for politics. But I am old and impatient and have listened to one theme or the other most Monday evenings these five years.[4] So I brought the portfolio back into the middle of the room and for the rest of the evening we talked of nothing but these pictures which reveal a most accomplished artist and a dreaming child. It is natural that she should picture pretty children playing among the squirrels, but not that she should draw hands and feet like that; make hair coil in those great heavy folds where there is so much nature and so much pattern; discover the poignant emotion of those two figures half lost in the dark wood; or the strange austere beauty of that dark Indian woman sitting under her tree of life, a dark child upon her knees, suggesting so much mysterious intellect.[5] William Blake† would not have grudged her his *Songs of Innocence*, nor thought that having his magnificent ornament they needed no other. He would have understood that she had read until certain of his songs – 'The Little Boy Found', 'Another's Sorrow',[6] most of all perhaps – became her own songs and needed her own ornament.

I had to explain to those about the table that only a task continued from day to day had momentum enough to overcome my indolence, that I intended to write nothing but philosophy for a year, that being no art critic I had not knowledge enough to judge this painting with the precision that gives judgment authority, that I hated writing prefaces and wrote one[7] a couple of years ago so badly that I have had spasms of remorse ever since. No, you must forgive me and not fancy that I lack astonished admiration because I refuse to write one single word.

W. B. Yeats

Introduction to *The Coinage of Saorstát Éireann*† (1928)

As the most famous and beautiful coins are the coins of the Greek Colonies, especially of those in Sicily, we decided to send photographs of some of these, and one coin of Carthage, to our selected artists, and to ask them, as far as possible, to take them as a model.[1] But the Greek coins had two advantages that ours could not have, one side need not balance the other, and either could be stamped in high relief, whereas ours must pitch and spin to please the gambler, and pack into rolls to please the banker.

We asked advice as to symbols, and were recommended by the public: round towers, wolf-hounds, shamrocks, single or in wreaths, and the Treaty Stone of Limerick; and advised by the Society of Antiquaries to avoid patriotic emblems altogether, for even the shamrock emblem was not a hundred years old.[2] We would have avoided them in any case, for we had to choose such forms as permit an artist to display all his capacity for design and expression, and as Ireland is the first modern State to design an entire coinage, not one coin now and another years later, as old wears out or the public changes its taste, it seemed best to give the coins some relation to one another. The most beautiful Greek coins are those that represent some god or goddess, as a boy or girl, or those that represent animals or some simple object like a wheat-ear. Those beautiful forms, when they are re-named Hibernia or Liberty, would grow empty and academic, and the wheat-ear had been adopted by several modern nations. If we decided upon birds and beasts, the artist, the experience of centuries has shown, might achieve a masterpiece, and might, or so it seemed to us, please those that would look longer at each coin than anybody else, artists and children. Besides, what better symbols could we find for this horse-riding, salmon-fishing, cattle-raising country?

III

We might have chosen figures from the history of Ireland, saints or national leaders, but a decision of the Executive Council excluded modern men, and no portraits have come down to us of St Brigid or King Brian.[3] The artist, to escape academical convention, would have invented a characteristic but unrecognisable head. I have before me a Swedish silver coin and a Swedish bronze medal, both masterly, that display the head of their mediaeval King, Gustavus Vasa. But those marked features were as familiar to the people as the incidents of his life, the theme of two famous plays.[4] But even had we such a figure a modern artist might prefer not to suggest some existing knowledge, but to create new beauty by an arrangement of lines.

IV

But how should the Government choose its artists? What advice should we give? It should reject a competition open to everybody. No good artist would spend day after day designing, and perhaps get nothing by it. There should be but a few competitors, and whether a man's work were chosen or not he should be paid something, and he should know, that he might have some guarantee of our intelligence, against whom he competed. We thought seven would be enough, and that of these three should be Irish. We had hoped to persuade Charles Shannon, a master of design, whose impressive caps and robes the Benchers of the King's Inn† had rejected in favour of wig and gown, to make one of these, but he refused, and that left us two Dublin sculptors of repute, Albert Power and Oliver Sheppard, and Jerome Connor arrived lately from New York.[5] Before choosing the other four we collected examples of modern coinage with the help of various Embassies or of our friends. When we found anything to admire – the Italian coin with the wheat-ear or that with the Fascist emblem; the silver Swedish coin with the head of Gustavus Vasa; the American bison coin[6] – we found out the artist's name and asked for other specimens of his work, if we did not know it already. We also examined the work of various medallists, and, much as we admired the silver Gustavus Vasa, we preferred a bronze Gustavus Vasa by the great Swedish sculptor† Carl Milles. Carl Milles and Ivan Meštrović†, sculptor† and medallist, have expressed in their work a violent rhythmical† energy unknown to past ages, and seem to many the foremost sculptors of our day.[7] We wrote to both these and to James E. Fraser, designer† of the bison and of some beautiful architectural sculpture,[8] and to Publio Morbiducci, designer of the coin with the Fascist emblem,[9] but Fraser refused, and Meštrović† did not reply until it was too late.[10] We substituted for Fraser the American sculptor† Manship, the creator of a Diana and her dogs, stylised and noble.[11] But as yet we had no Englishman, and could think of no one among the well-known names that we admired both as sculptor† and medallist. After some hesitation, for Charles Ricketts had recommended S. W. Carline, designer of a powerful Zeebrugge medal, and of a charming medal struck to the honour of Flinders Petrie, we selected, on the recommendation of the Secretary of the British School at Rome, Percy Metcalfe, a young sculptor as yet but little known.[12]

V

Because when an artist takes up a task for the first time he must sometimes experiment before he has mastered the new technique, we advised that the artist himself should make every alteration necessary, and that, if he had to go to London or elsewhere for the purpose, his expenses should be paid. An Irish artist had made an excellent design for the seal of the Dublin National Gallery, and that design, founded upon the seal of an Irish abbey, had been altered by the Mint, round academic contours substituted for the planes and straight lines of a mediaeval design.[13] One remembers the rage of Blake when his designs came smooth and lifeless from the hands of an engraver whose work had been substituted for his.[14] The Deputy Master of the Mint has commended and recommended to other nations a precaution which protects the artist, set to a new task and not as yet a craftsman, from the craftsman who can never be an artist.

VI

We refused to see the designs until we saw them all together. The name of each artist, if the model had been signed, was covered with stamp paper. The models were laid upon tables, with the exception of one set, fastened to a board, which stood upright on the mantelpiece. We had expected to recognise the work of the different artists by its† style, but we recognised only the powerful handling of Milles on the board over the mantelpiece. One set of designs seemed far to exceed the others as decorations filling each its circular space, and this set, the work of Percy Metcalfe, had so marked a style, and was so excellent throughout, that it seemed undesirable to mix its designs with those of any other artist.[15] Though we voted coin by coin, I think we were all convinced of this. I was distressed by my conviction. I had been certain that we could mix the work of three or four different artists, and that this would make our coinage more interesting, and had written to Milles, or to some friend of his, that it was unthinkable that we should not take at least one coin from so great an artist. Nobody could lay aside without a pang so much fine work, and our Government, had it invited designs, without competition, from either Morbiducci or Manship, would have been lucky to get such work as theirs. Manship's Ram and Morbiducci's Bull are magnificent;[16] Manship's an entirely new creation, Morbiducci's a re-creation of the Bull in the Greek coin we had sent him as an example. That I may understand the energy and imagination of the designs of Milles[17] I tell myself that they have been dug out of Sicilian earth, that they passed to and fro in the Mediterranean traffic two thousand years and more ago, and thereupon I discover that his strange bull, his two horses, that angry woodcock, have a supernatural energy. But all are cut in high relief, all suggest more primitive dies than we use today, and turned into coins would neither pitch nor pack.

What can I say of the Irish artists who had all done well in some department of their craft – Sheppard's *O'Leary* at the Municipal Gallery, and Power's *Kettle* at the Dublin National Gallery, are known, and Connor's *Emmet* may become known[18] – except that had some powerful master of design been brought to Dublin years ago, and set to teach there, Dublin would have made a better show? Sir William Orpen affected Dublin painting, not merely because he gave it technical knowledge, but because he brought into a Dublin Art School the contagion of his vigour.[19] The work of Metcalfe, Milles, Morbiducci, Manship, displays the vigour of their minds, and the forms of their designs symbolise that vigour, and our own is renewed at the spectacle.

VII

As certain of the beasts represent our most important industry, they were submitted to the Minister for Agriculture and his experts, and we awaited the results with alarm. I have not been to Chartres Cathedral for years, but remember somewhere outside the great doors figures of angels or saints, whose spiritual dignity and architectural effect depend upon bodies much longer in proportion to the length of their heads than a man's body ever was.[20] The artist who must fill a given space and suggest some spiritual quality or rhythmical movement finds it necessary to suppress or exaggerate. Art, as some French critic has said, is appropriate exaggeration.[21] The expert on horse-flesh or bull-flesh, or swine-flesh, on the other hand, is bound to see his subject inanimate and isolated. The coins have suffered less than we feared. The horse, as first drawn, was more alive than the later version, for when the hind legs were brought more under the body and the head lowered, in obedience to technical opinion, it lost muscular tension; we passed from the open country to the show-ground.[22] But, on the

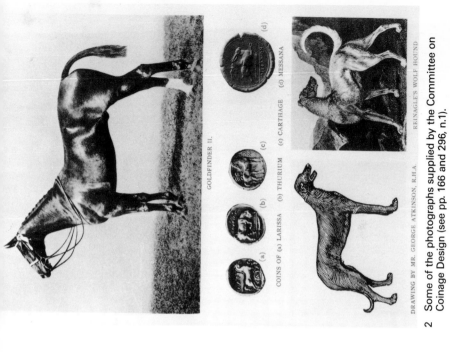

GOLDFINDER II.

COINS OF (a) LARISSA   (b) THURIUM   (c) CARTHAGE   (d) MESSANA

DRAWING BY MR. GEORGE ATKINSON, R.H.A.   REINAGLE'S WOLF HOUND

2 Some of the photographs supplied by the Committee on Coinage Design (see pp. 166 and 296, n.1).

1 Jacynth Parsons, 'The Little Black Boy', water-colour illustration (1926) to William Blake's poem (see pp. 165 and 295, n.5).

3   Coin designs by Carl Milles (see pp. 168–70; 297, n.7; 298, n.17).

4   Coin design by Ivan Meštrović (see pp. 168 and 297, nn.7 and 10).

5 Coin designs by Percy Metcalfe, as submitted (see pp. 169–70 and 298, nn. 15 and 22).

6 Coin designs by Percy Metcalfe, revised, as minted (see pp. 170 and 298, n. 22).

other hand, it is something to know that we have upon our half-crown a representation of an Irish hunter, perfect in all its points, and can add the horseman's pleasure to that of the children and the artists. The first bull had to go, though one of the finest of all the designs, because it might have upset, considered as an ideal, the eugenics of the farmyard, but the new bull is as fine, in a different way. I sigh, however, over the pig, though I admit that the state of the market for pig's cheeks† made the old design impossible. A design is like a musical composition, alter some detail and all has to be altered. With the round cheek of the pig went the lifted head, the look of insolence and of wisdom, and the comfortable round bodies of the little pigs. We have instead querulous and harassed animals, better merchandise but less living.[23]

Preface (1929) to
Oliver St John Gogarty, *Wild Apples* (1930)

I

Some years ago I made a selection from Oliver Gogarty's poetry for the Cuala Press; and now I make another from what he has published between that and now.[1] Oliver Gogarty is a careless writer, often writing first drafts of poems rather than poems but often with animation and beauty. He is much like that in his conversation; except that his conversation is wittier and profounder when public events excite him, whereas public events – some incursion of Augustus John, perhaps, benumb his poetry.[2]

Why am I content to search through so many careless verses for what is excellent? I do not think that it is merely because they are excellent, I think I am not so disinterested; but because he gives me something that I need and at this moment of time. The other day I was reading Lawrence's description in his *Revolt of the Desert* of his bodyguard of young Arabs: 'men proud of themselves, and without families . . . dressed like a bed of tulips'; and because brought up in that soft twilight – 'magic casements'; 'syren there' – come down from the great Liberal Romantics, I recognised my opposite, and was startled and excited.[3] The great Romantics had a sense of duty and could hymn duty upon occasion, but little sense of a hardship borne and chosen out of pride and joy.[4] Some Elizabethans had that indeed, though Chapman alone constantly, and after that nobody – until Landor;[5] and after that nobody except when some great Romantic forgot, perhaps under the influence of the Classics, his self-forgetting emotion, and wrote out of character. But certainly nobody craved for it as we do, who sometimes feel as if no other theme touched us. I find it in every poem of Oliver Gogarty that delights me, in the whole poem, or in some astringent adjective. It is in his description of his own

172

verses when he compares them to apples and calls them 'a tart crop',[6] often in his praise of women:

> She does not know her hair
> Is golden with an hint
> Of Trojan ashes in't.[7]

and almost too deliberately there when he longs to have brought for some lovely daughter of Dervorgilla's† sake:

> Knights of the air and the submarine men cruising
>   Trained through a lifetime.
>
> Brought the implacable hand with law-breakers,
> Drilled the Too-many and broken their effrontery†,
> Broken the dream of the men of a few acres
>   Ruling a country;
>
> Brought the long day with its leisure and its duty,
> Built once again the limestone lordly houses:
> Founded on steel is the edifice of Beauty,
>   Steel it arouses.[8]

II

The other day I was asked why a certain man did not live at Boar's Hill, that pleasant neighbourhood where so many writers live,[9] and replied,† 'We Anglo-Irish hate to surrender the solitude we have inherited', and then began to wonder what I meant. I ran over the lives of my friends, of Swift and Berkeley, and saw that all, as befits scattered men in an ignorant country, were solitaries. Even Shaw, who has toiled at public meetings and committee meetings that he might grow into an effective superficial man of the streets, has made the wastrels of *Heartbreak House* cry when they hear the whirr of a Zeppelin overhead,† 'Turn on all the lights.'[10] Unlike those Fabian friends of his he desires and doubtless dreads inexplicable useless adventure. And Synge sang of himself as 'Almost forgetting human words',[11] and it was his solitude that

got him into trouble; and heaven knows into what foul weather
Oliver Gogarty's Anglo-Irish muse has launched the gayest of
its butterflies. Yet I recommend Irish Anthologists to select
'Aphorism' which being clear and inexplicable, will be most
misjudged. I would be certain of its immortality had it a more
learned rhythm and, as it is I have not been able to forget these
two years, that Ringsend whore's drunken complaint, that little
red lamp before some holy picture, that music at the end:†

> And up the back-garden
> The sound comes to me
> Of the lapsing, unsoilable
> Whispering sea.[12]

III

Oliver Gogarty may console himself for he keeps good
company. An Arab king sent a man to Lawrence, saying that as
he had just given him a hundred lashes for excess of
individuality – he had killed an enemy in court under the eye of
the judge – he was exactly the man Lawrence wanted for his
bodyguard.[13] Yes, we shall be forgiven our butterflies.

W. B. Yeats

'Anglo-Irish Ballads',
by F. R. Higgins[1] and W. B. Yeats,
in *Broadsides: A Collection of Old and New Songs*
(1935)

I

The earliest Anglo-Irish ballads we know anything about were made at the beginning of the eighteenth century. Gaelic civilisation had been defeated at the Boyne.[2] Increasing numbers began to speak English words that found no reverberation in their minds; those minds had no sounding-box left, they were all strings. Many of these Irish ballads, translations or original poems, were the work of hedge schoolmasters, packed with Latin mythology and long words derived from the Latin, but all were sung to Gaelic music, all showed the influence of Gaelic pronunciation and metre – 'e' in Gaelic must always sound like 'a':

> O, were I Hector that noble victor who died a victim to
> Grecian skill;
> O, were I Paris whose deeds are various an arbitrator on
> Ida's hill;
> I'd range through Asia, likewise Arabia, Pennsylvania
> seeking for you
> The burning regions like sage Orpheus to see your face, my
> sweet Colleen Rue.[3]

Their speech, apart from its pedantry, is like that of the Europeanised Indians, the speech of men who have perhaps fluent English yet understand nothing of the words but their dictionary meaning. Then come original ballads, some purged, some unpurged of pedantry:

175

I'll sell my rock, I'll sell my reel,
When flax is spun I'll sell my wheel,
To buy my love a sword of steel.
Gotheen mavourneen slaun.[4]

But the pedantry has never died; the 'Boys of Mullabaun'
might have been written at any time during the last two
hundred years:

To end my lamentations I am in consternation;
No one can roam for recreation until the day do dawn;
Without a hesitation we're charged with combination
And sent for transportation with the Boys of Mullabaun.[5]

From the great houses or through wandering labourers
came Scotch and English ballads. Goldsmith heard 'Barbara
Allen' sung in the Midlands,[6] one of the present writers heard it
sung by a girl out of a Dublin slum; it had come down, one knows
not how long, from mother to daughter:[7] but these ballads,
generally in the towns, always in the country cottages, are sung
to Irish music, their rhythm modified, sometimes enriched, by
the new notes. In town and country alike, as in the old English
carols, every song is a narrative. So and so is telling the story of
his life, so and so did this or that. Perhaps popular Gaelic
literature had always been narrative. The song that expresses
emotion only, the pure lyric, the song of love or grief, had
reached Ireland after the twelfth century as it had all Europe,
from the South of France, but in Ireland it remained in
noblemen's houses, or among the pupils in the Monasteries.
Among the cottages the twelfth century lingered and still
lingers. The street songs were more dramatic in their narrative,
the singer had to shout, clatter-bones in hand, to draw the
attention of the passer-by.[8] One thinks of 'Johnny I hardly
Knew Ye', magnificent in gaiety and horror, of the
'Kilmainham Minut', of 'The Night Before Larry Was
Stretched'; nor were the song-makers always of the people.[9]
Goldsmith while still at College wrote ballads for five shillings
a-piece,[10] Swift's political lampoons were still sung in the
Coombe when Sir Walter Scott visited Ireland,[11] and one of the
present writers remembers a libel action about a song some

Dublin shop-keeper wrote upon an enemy and committed to the street singers.[12]

At the close of the eighteenth century Dublin street singers had some wealth and much influence; a political ballad had more effect than a speech. Lever, while a college student, disguised himself, turned street singer, and returned at evening with thirty shillings.[13] One attributes to this period 'The Croppy Boy', 'The Shan Van Vocht', perhaps 'The Wearing of the Green'.[14]

The political ballads have never ceased to be written and sung, the Boer war created many, recent events not so many, but it is to Cardinal MacHale, 'the Lion of the West', the Land League, the Phoenix Park Murders, Parnell, that the popular mind goes back:

> The American Eagle
> It burst asunder
> When it saw the Blackbird of Avondale.[15]

Some of the ballads may have been danced, for one of the present writers saw at Rosses Point, County Sligo, a man dance a ballad called 'The Rocky Road to Dublin', but if so the Gaelic dance, no expression, no movement above the waist, the Gaelic dance as we know it, was not the only dance.

> But he dances there
> As if his kin were dead,
> Clay in his thoughts,
> And lightning in his tread.[16]

The dancer at Rosses Point used his whole body; he went by steamer, swayed his body as the steamer tossed on the waves, came at last to the rocky road, wherever that is, moved his feet as if climbing over great rocks.

II

Both town and country ballads get their characteristics from the music. Because that music permits, like much Asiatic music, quarter-tones, the stress will sometimes lack sharpness, certainty. In 'The Groves of Blarney' the third line

> Being banks of posies that spontaneous grow there[17]

halts because the stress falling upon 'spontaneous' carries too many syllables. Sung to Irish music all runs smoothly; the stress, though falling mainly upon the second syllable, enriches the whole word. A singer cannot indeed sing it adequately if he does not like words for their own sake however little he understands them. If he sang to a musician trained in modern music he would be condemned for the imperfection of his ear, yet no rich-sounding two or three syllabled word can be spoken or sung without quarter-tones. When Florence Farr spoke or sang to her psaltery her mastery of the subtle rhythm of words made her out of tune to ears responsive alone to the modern rhythm of notes.[18] On the other hand, a reader who knows nothing of Irish music finds that line in 'The Groves of Blarney' unmetrical; a pæon or foot of four syllables, is not permissible in English ballad metre. Sometimes a poet accustomed, like Tom Moore, to Irish music, can, while avoiding unmetrical effects, give a line lingering, wavering poignancy. Consider:

> In the mid hour of night when the stars are weeping I fly
> To the lone vale we loved, when life shone warm in thine
>   eye.[19]

The† stress falling on 'mid', or 'weep', on 'lone', on 'warm', syllables not sufficiently isolated to sustain it, compels us to speak 'mid hour' 'are weeping' 'lone vale' 'shone warm' slowly, prolonging the syllables; it is as though the stress suffused itself like a drop of dye. This poem, and perhaps one other, are the only poems of Moore that have the poet's rhythm; his musician Stephenson[20] made Irish tunes conform to modern notation, and Moore, a man without background, tradition, felt himself free to invent or copy mechanical, facile rhythm –

> The young May moon is shining bright.†[21]

'Moore'†, William Morris said once†, 'is a great song writer.

He is not a poet, he has not the poet's rhythm.'[22] The present writers add that he was half way to the music hall, to the rhymed burlesque, to the Gilbert and Sullivan opera, to the hurdy-gurdy rhyme of the mechanised town, equivalent of Mutt and Jeff and the comic figures upon the posters.[23] Neither his songs nor those of 'Young Ireland', nor any songs set by professional musicians, have become folk-lore as have the songs of such recent poets as Graves, Fahy, Campbell and Colum;[24] he is confined to the schoolroom, the concert platform; ears trained by country singers reject him.

The quarter-tones in Japanese music permit speech to rise imperceptibly into song, and because Irish songs close on three beats on a single note the singer will sometimes speak the last three words – an effect imitated on the Abbey stage when the last words of a song by Zozimus were spoken, then caught up and shouted by the stage crowd.[25]

A study of our music might unite music and speech once more. Modern verse copies daily speech, rejects no word because it is prosaic, modern, abstract, so long as it is in general use. One of the present writers had to change the word 'politic' in a song because it was 'unsingable',[26] but a country singer would not have found it 'unsingable', might indeed have taken a particular pleasure in it. No word effective in speech should perhaps be unsingable. To the country singer the words are more important than the music; he will sing different poems to the same tune, should they run to some tune he has forgotten he is told to 'word it out', or speak the poem. All Gaelic poems, or all but a few modern exceptions, were written to some tune, whatever tune came to mind perhaps; the words themselves had sufficient novelty.[27]

If what is called the gapped scale, if the wide space left unmeasured by the mathematical ear where the voice can rise wavering, quivering, through its quarter-tones,[28] is necessary if we are to preserve in song the natural rhythm of words, one understands why the Greeks murdered the man who added a fourth string to the lyre.[29]

III

Frederic† Myers suggested once that a poet may hear musical notes, not through the ear, but through the nerves of the tongue.[30] One of the writers of this essay is accustomed to write his poetry, when it has a marked stanzaic movement, to Irish tunes; he is a musician and knows what he is doing. The other cannot recognise a tune when he hears it, yet wrote in early life poems to simple tunes, sometimes of his own composition; the 'Song of the Old Mother' to a tune in the gapped scale. Mr Arnold Dolmetsch took them down, and others from Mr Laurence Binyon incapable also of recognising a tune when he hears it. The reciter of a poem, not less than its creator, will sometimes speak it to a tune. Mr Dolmetsch took down the notes of a recitation by Mr A. H. Bullen the Elizabethan scholar, also incapable of recognising a tune when he heard it. Some of these tunes can be found at the end of 'Speaking to the Psaltery' in *Essays* by W. B. Yeats.[31]

There is a possibility that the simple metres based on lines of three and four accents, eight or six syllables, all that constitute what Mr G. M. Young calls the fundamental 'sing-song of the language',[32] come to the poet's tongue with their appropriate tunes; that when a poet has not grown up in a country civilisation hearing these tunes sung by servants and nurses, his musical sense is changed. Mr Young has suggested that such a change is taking place in England and America where civilisation grows more and more a town civilisation. It seems possible, though he does not say so, that the tongue may lose that part of its function which is related to sound, not merely its sensitiveness to tune but its subconscious memory of a music that flourished when the Greeks murdered their man. A distinguished poet, who has written admirably upon other occasions writes:

> Our half-thought thoughts divide in sifted wisps
> Against the basic facts repatterned without pause,
> I can no more gather my mind up in my fist. . . .[33]

He may interest the mind, he is describing a journey by rail with some accuracy, but he does not give pleasure to the tongue.

What change of language did to the hedge schoolmasters†, town civilisation does to us all in some measure, imposing upon popular arts a mechanical pattern of sound and shape, upon the arts of the intellectual classes a stark individuality, a bundle of dry sticks. Mr Young suggests that poetry is seeking a relation with instrumental music; he points out that certain American writers, anxious to create a popular poetry, write their poems to jazz tunes.[34] Some recent philosophical poems by their richness of suggestion, by their strange emotion, make the present writers fancy a relation, not yet fully conscious, with great instrumental music:

> Beneath a thundery glaze
> The raindrops fall.
>
> What is this new oppression of my heart?
>
> Have I not looked upon this scene before!
> These leafy dromedaries
> Dark green,
> Painted upon that wall
> Of livid sky
> Where vacancy's bright silent spiders crawl!
>
> The hills' pure outlined contours on that light
> Empty my soul.
> I watch those spidery lines
> Bright violet.
>
> And there's a poisonous cloud as dark as jet
> Pouring from heaven.[35]

F. R. Higgins
W. B. Yeats

Introduction (1935) to
Selections from the Poems of Dorothy Wellesley†
(1936)

Some months ago, when recovering in bed from a long illness, I read many anthologies, skipping every name known to me, discovering poetry written since I read everybody, being young. It was perhaps my illness that made me hard to please, for almost all seemed clay-cold, clay-heavy; I thought at my worst moments, 'I have read too much abstract philosophy; I can no longer understand the poetry of other men.' Then, in an anthology edited by Sir John Squire, I found poems signed Dorothy Wellesley.[1] Though she is well known among the younger poets and critics, I had never heard of her. My eyes filled with tears. I read in excitement that was the more delightful because it showed I had not lost my understanding of poetry. I had opened the book in the middle of a poem called 'Walled Garden':

> Blue lilies, sprung† between three oceans, said:
> 'Grinding, and half atilt
> The light-swung boulders rock upon the veldt:
> We bloom† by lions dead
> Of old age in the wild.'†[2]

Three laboured lines, two Elizabethan in their frenzied grandeur, their rich simplicity of rhythm. Then came 'Horses', well known I think†, certainly well known among my Dublin friends, though I had never heard of it. I found in passage after passage a like grandeur, a powerful, onrushing, masculine rhythm; no accident this time but a work of accomplished skill:

> Who, in the garden-pony carrying skeps
> Of grass or fallen leaves, his knees gone slack,
> Round belly, hollow back,
> Sees the Mongolian Tarpan of the Steppes?

Or, in the Shire with plaits and feathered feet,
The war-horse† like the wind the Tartar knew?
Or, in the Suffolk Punch, spells out anew
The wild grey asses fleet
With stripe from head to tail, and moderate ears?[3]

No poet of my generation would have written 'moderate' exactly there; a long period closes, the ear, expecting some poetic word, is checked, delighted to be so checked, by the precision of good prose. Elsewhere in the author's work I discover that precision. Face to face with the problem that has perplexed us all, she can unite a modern subject and vocabulary with traditional richness.

We do not think only of the noises in the streets, of the smoke of the black country, of the contents of museums, of the misery of the unemployed; Homer and Shakespeare were not more in our fathers' minds than they are in ours. An old diplomatist took me fishing for white trout – alas, I caught nothing – said between casts, 'Odysseus is always with me.'[4] We must remain natural, writing of those things that belong to our civilisation, that are always with us, yet give point and accent from our own research. I was delighted to find a writer who explored the picturesque among flowers, fishes, shells, serpents, trees, horses, or for its sake returned to the imaginations of her childhood. The crooked mirror of Edith Sitwell's intensity transforms like imaginations into a scene for the Russian ballet or, in her more grotesque moods, for Aubrey Beardsley's later satiric art;[5] but Dorothy Wellesley presents the actual child, not merely in such amusing snatches as 'Great-grandmama', 'Sheep', 'England',[6] but in descriptions like that in 'The Lost Forest', where the green light of the leaves is sea-water flowing among the trunks, while congers nose the daffodils, a flight of fishes perch upon a cherry bough.[7]

I sent somebody to Bumpus's[8] for *Poems of Ten Years*, found that this selection of picturesque detail, this going back, was not a mere literary device, but a love that seemed a part of character for undisturbed Nature, a hatred for the abstract, the mechanical, the invented. This love, this hatred, gave its own intensity to poems often beautiful, often obscure, sometimes ill-constructed, but seemed without purpose or philosophy.

Then I came upon 'Matrix', a long meditation, perhaps the most moving philosophic poem of our time – (Herbert Read's 'Mutations of the Phoenix' is too obscure, Turner's *Seven Days of the Sun*,† a collection of fragments, some of the exquisite beauty) – and discovered that it was moving precisely because its wisdom, like that of the sphinx, was animal below the waist.[9] In its vivid, powerful, abrupt lines, passion burst into thought without renouncing its uterine darkness. I had a moment's jealousy; I had thought of expending my last years on philosophic verse, but knew now that I was too old. Only those in vigorous life can have such hatred of the trivial light. Here was something new or very old, the philosophy of the Vedanta or of Plotinus[10] with a terror not of their time before human destiny; yet its author had never read Plotinus or the Indian thinkers. I was certain of that because of omissions, of an emphasis impossible had she some logical system in mind – knew that terror itself had made poem and philosophy. If man ever had knowledge or wisdom it was in the dark of the womb, sang the lines, or before he was conceived; in the hush of night are we not conscious of the unconceived? There must be an escape; death is no escape because the dead cannot forget that they have lived, and must dread, through bread and food, to enter into the body once more, finding there 'the† reiteration of birth'.[11] The Greek solution is touched upon lightly as though it passed through the mind for a moment, then all is passion once again:

> Earth, back to the earth.
>
> Out of her beauty at birth,
> Out of her I came
> To lose all that I knew:
> Though somehow at birth I died,
> One night she will teach me anew:
> Peace? The same
> As a woman's†, a mother's
> Breast undenied, to console
> The small bones built in the womb,
> The womb that loathed the bones,
> And cast out the soul.[12]

I asked a visitor to find out who was called, or called herself 'Dorothy Wellesley'; was it name or pseudonym? – I learnt to my surprise that she was neither harassed journalist nor teacher. Flaubert talked of writing a story called 'La Spirale'†[13] about a man who dreamed more and more magnificently as his daily circumstance reached abject poverty, celebrated asleep his marriage to a princess. Balzac thought we writers are at our best when confined during formative years to what the eighteenth century called the garrets and cellars.[14]

It seems fitting, that thought in mind, to close this essay murmuring, with better reason than Coleridge knew, 'Where learnt you that heroic measure?'[15]

1935

Introduction (1936) to
Margot Ruddock, *The Lemon Tree* (1937)

[I]

I was in Majorca, breakfasting in bed at 7.30 when my wife announced that Margot Collis had arrived[1] – a† woman in whom I had some two years before divined a frustrated tragic genius. She had asked my help to found a poets' theatre.[2] Of distinguished beauty of face and limb, a successful provincial actress, managing her own company, she had come to London hoping to get work on the London stage.[3] Her father's name was Ruddock, and she wishes, when we speak of her as a poet, to be called Margot Ruddock. I brought her to Dulac the painter, and Ashton the creator and producer of ballets,[4] subtle technical minds with an instinctive knowledge of the next step in whatever art they discussed. I asked her to recite some poems. She had all the tricks of the professional elocutionist, but rehearsed by Ashton and Dulac substituted a musical clarity pleasant to a poet's ear. In a few days she had lost it and returned unconsciously to the tricks, but what can be done once can be done again.[5] I had never seen her act, but after thirty years' experience I know from the mind of man and woman what they can do† upon the stage when they have found their legs, judging that mind perhaps from the way they sink into a chair or lift a cup. There was something hard, tight, screwed-up, in her, but were that dissolved by success she might be a great actress, for she possessed a quality rare upon the stage or, if found there, left unemployed – intellectual passion. She had set her heart upon my *Player Queen* where the principal character might give the opportunity she had lacked, seemed indeed in some senses of the word herself.

I gave Margot Ruddock permission to arrange for a performance of The† *Player Queen* wherever she could, said all I

186

cared about was that she should play the principal part, and returned to Ireland. Such a performance was arranged for, but for some reason I have never fathomed, Margot Ruddock, or, to use her stage name, Margot Collis, had but a minor part which she played with beauty and distinction.[6]

Meanwhile I had discovered her poetry. She sent me passionate, incoherent improvisations, power struggling with that ignorance of books and of arts which has made the modern theatre what it is. I criticized her with some vehemence and the improvisations became coherent poems. I selected 'The Child Compassion', 'Autumn', which have something of Emily Brontë's† intensity, and some others for an anthology I have compiled for the Oxford University Press.[7] She wrote from time to time, most letters contained a poem or poems, but these poems seemed to have lost form; had she fallen back as after the Ashton and Dulac rehearsal? It was not now a falling back into convention but an obsession by her own essential quality; passion followed passion with such rapidity that she had no time for deliberate choice; she seemed indifferent to scansion, even to syntax. I got angry and told her to stop writing.[8] After that almost every day brought some big packet of verse; I was busy with Shree Purohit Swami, we were translating the Upanishads†; I left the packets unopened, or thrust the contents into some drawer unread. And now she had come to defy me and to cover my table with her thoughts. I sat down with boredom but was soon amazed at my own blindness and laziness. Here in broken sentences, in ejaculations, in fragments of all kinds was a power of expression of spiritual suffering unique in her generation.[9] 'O Song, song harshened, I have leashed you to harshness.' . . . 'I will shut out all but myself and grind, grind myself down to the bone.' . . . 'Follow, follow lest that which you love vanishes, Let it go, let it go.'† . . . 'Shape me to Eternal Damnation to rid me of the phlegm that spits itself from unbearable cold.' . . . 'Bleed on, bleed on, soul, because I shall not cease to knife you until you are white and dry.' . . . 'Almost I tasted ecstasy and then came the Blare, and drowned perfection in perfection.' . . . 'I cannot endure it when I see you asleep, having carefully tucked your teddy bear beside you. I cannot endure it. Even if you would have been born anyhow. Even if you did choose me. Even if it was because I

cannot endure it you chose me!' . . .† 'Good nature, sweet
nature and you'll have to be crushed. You shall not be; by God
you shall not be. Whatever you do I will see that you are not
crushed. I will not stand that you be crushed.' 'Feed the cat!
feed the cat, you can't starve people though they can starve you.
Might as well eat as I feed the cat; now the cat wants my food.'
'Consider and consider and always come back to what you said
in a flash and to what you knew when you saw it.' 'Give me
power to choose to keep wisdom.' 'I will scald myself to cool.'

'O sky harshen, O wind blow cold,
O crags of stony thought be steep
That mind may ache and bleed,
That mind be scattered to the wind.'

'All is true of all
For all that is is true;
But Truth is not;
To become Truth
Is not to be.'

'Grief is not in Truth
But Truth in grief must live grief
Yet know no grief;
For Truth is proof against all but itself.'

'When all thought is gathered into the heart
And set out to ripen like good fruit;
And that which might have been eaten withered,
And that which were better withered eaten;
I sit and sit
And marvel at the itch of it.'

'I have counted all that may happen
And it will not happen,
I have said all that shall be
And it will not be.'

'O song, no tears but thine
Be sung, no thought

That is not secret
Shut out all others
For all earth must lie
But thou, and I.'

June 1936

II

Margot Ruddock left for Barcelona and a few days later the British Consul there wired that she had fallen out of a window and broken her knee-cap.[10] My wife and I went to Barcelona and found her in the Clinica Evangelica where she had been brought the night before. She was sitting up in bed writing an account of her experiences. She has added since, mainly at my suggestion, four or five explanatory sentences, and crossed out a word here and there.[11] Her dominant thought, during those wanderings from house to house, street to street, had been, she said a few weeks ago, that God died and suffered in everything that we ate and in everything that we did. She was undergoing an experience perhaps well known once in Europe and in Asia, though in† every individual it must take a different form. Some old Indian writer has said, 'The Yogi must often seem mad, must often be mad.'[12] But she was sane when I saw her in Barcelona; her main thought the trouble she was causing, or had caused, and she has remained sane.

I publish on my own responsibility what she then wrote; the first pride of authorship passed she would have preferred to hide it or destroy it. Some of her friends and mine think that its publication may injure her, but I am not of that opinion. The story that appeared in the Press, her supposed attempt at suicide,[13] will soon be forgotten, is already forgotten perhaps, but all her life some like story would have followed her; far better that the true story should be known seeing that it lacks neither nobility nor strangeness. Though her poems, their descriptions of what old poets have called the 'razor's edge',[14] despite their occasional technical imperfection, have in a still greater measure that nobility and strangeness, they gain, like many lyrical poems when their origin is known, a second beauty, passing as it were out of literature into life.

There are only twenty little poems in this book, all written with great difficulty over a considerable space of time, and if she writes more it will be perhaps upon some different theme. The mystic who has found or approached ecstasy, whether in the midst of order or disorder, must return into the life of the world to test or employ knowingly or unknowingly his new knowledge. Margot Ruddock may become Margot Collis again, and forget amid the excitement of the Boards that more perilous excitement.

W. B. Yeats
December 1936

'Music and Poetry', by W. B. Yeats and Dorothy Wellesley,[1] in *Broadsides: A Collection of New Irish and English Songs* (1937)

We fix a quarrel upon the concert platform. We must win if poetry is to get back its public.

Poetry, apart from some topical accident, has never had many readers; but all through the East to-day, and all through Europe yesterday, it has and has had many hearers. Music that wants of us nothing but images that suggest sound, cannot be our music; and bad poetry, as Mozart pointed out does that as well as, or better than good;[2] such music can but dislocate, wherever there is syntax and elaborate rhythm. The poet, his ear attentive to his own art, hears with derision most settings of his work, or, if the work be not his own but some famous masterpiece, with blind rage. And yet there are old songs that melt him into tears.

Somebody has said that the poet who writes for a composer should 'eschew all attempts to write poetry';[3] yet did not Sappho and Pindar attempt it, and even a folk song begins somewhere?[4] It seems that seventeenth century makers of madrigals started the trouble with musical constructions out of all relation to poetic rhythm and sense. Then Glück tried to summon music back to both by a revival of Greek tragedy. Then Purcell in certain operas; Dryden's *King Arthur* was written for such treatment; left the poetical rhythm and sense to the actors, pushing on his musical constructions here and there like the gilded chariots and chairs in some stage scene invented by Inigo Jones. But the balance was not found. The art of Wagner, claimed once for the final art, suggests to the eyes and ears of a poet almost admirable plots, situations full of musical suggestion; but not less clearly to his mind an impression of wet sound and words dead and dry as a besom.[5] W. J. Turner has suggested that Mozart is comparatively unpopular in Italy, because where his language is known he cannot lift his dead and dry words.[6]

Yet there must be some right balance between sound and word. One of the two poets who sign these words heard lately and with great excitement some popular Czecho-Slovakian music, drums and big wind; an heroic dance or a march. Every now and then some sentence was spoken half a dozen times. He did not know the language, but through his imagination passed a line from a German War poem: 'The trooper lies under his horse.'[7] The sentence was spoken vehemently and naturally; was not always the same, but was always repeated, or so it seemed, the same number of times. Then during the Mass the word 'Amen' is taken up and played with like a ball;[8] and it has been suggested that the secret Jewish name of God was a way of carolling the four vowels that constitute the word Jehovah when written in Hebrew.[9] The same poet has based a dramatic form upon the Noh drama of Japan;[10] contemplative emotion left to singers who can satisfy the poet's ear, exposition of plot to actors, climax of the whole to dancers; in one play at the beginning and end a scenic dance. Tradition has shown that music and the dance, unlike music and the words, can elaborate themselves, dance into its utmost, music into all but its utmost subtlety, and yet keep their union. He does not say that he has succeeded, but that his experiment should be repeated.

Even the most modern musician must recognise that there is an ancient art of song, no more superseded than the art of Giotto;[11] that in this ancient art the words first catch the attention, stand as it were in the foreground; whereas in his own art, conceived in the seventeenth century and not yet fully born, music must first catch the attention, stand as it were in the foreground, and that it cannot be fully born until he, no corpse carrier, can make word and sound altogether alive.

The art of the concert platform is a parvenu, it is upon trial, it should be convicted, and the majority of men are upon our side. There is an old poet in Malabar whose most famous poem laments his deafness; he sings, as we understand singing, to a whole people.[12] Tagore sings to men he 'keeps near him for the purpose';[13] then come the minstrels, and then to these other minstrels. The broadcasts sent out from Delhi, in the vernacular tongues of India, are almost altogether sung or spoken poetry; and everywhere throughout the East, competent authority assures us, the harlots sing as we would have them sing.

The concert platform has wronged the poets by masticating their well-made words and turning them into spittle; wronged and insulted, by example and the arrogant criticism it encourages, all that still consider song a natural expression of life, singing because in love, or miserable, or happy, or because their heads are empty. Aristotle bids us think like wise men but express ourselves like the common people,[14] but what if genius and a great vested interest thrive upon the degradation of the mother tongue?

We can do little, but we can sing, or persuade our friends to sing, traditional songs, or songs by new poets set in the traditional way. There should be no accompaniment,[15] because where words are the object an accompaniment can but distract attention, and because the musician who claims to translate the emotion of the poet into another vehicle is a liar. Sustaining notes there have been and may be again; a pause, dramatic or between verses, may admit flute or string, clapping hands, cracking fingers or whistling mouth. We reject all professional singers because no mouth trained to the modern scale can articulate poetry. We must be content with butchers and bakers and those few persons who sing from delight in words.[16]

W. B. Yeats
Dorothy Wellesley

APPENDIXES

Appendix 1 Notes by Yeats (and/or Douglas Hyde) to items other than Yeats's introduction and headnotes, *Fairy and Folk Tales of the Irish Peasantry*, ed. W. B. Yeats (1888) pp. 38, 131n, 150, 150n, 160n, 161n, 168n, 207n, 213n, 220–2nn, 295n, 299 (probably written by Douglas Hyde), 309n (revised by Yeats), 320–1, 323–6. See the textual introduction, pp. 318–19 below, for a list of exclusions.

Sir Samuel Ferguson [note (p. 320) to 'The Fairy Well of Lagnanay' (pp. 13–16) and 'The Fairy Thorn' (pp. 38–40)].

Many in Ireland consider Sir Samuel Ferguson their greatest poet. The English reader will most likely never have heard his name, for Anglo-Irish critics, who have found English audience, being more Anglo than Irish, have been content to follow English opinion instead of leading it, in all matters concerning Ireland.

[Endnote (p. 38) to Samuel Lover, 'The White Trout; A Legend of Cong' (pp. 35–7).]

[†These trout stories are common all over Ireland. Many holy wells are haunted by such blessed trout. There is a trout in a well on the border of Lough Gill, Sligo, that some paganish person put once on the gridiron. It carries the marks to this day. Long ago, the saint who sanctified the well put that trout there. Nowadays it is only visible to the pious, who have done due penance.]

Legend of Knockgrafton [note (pp. 320–1) to Thomas Crofton Croker, 'The Legend of Knockgrafton' (pp. 40–5)].

Moat does not mean a place with water, but a tumulus or barrow. The words *La Luan Da Mort agus Da Dardeen* are Gaelic for 'Monday, Tuesday, and Wednesday too.' Da Hena is Thursday. Story-tellers, in telling this tale, says Croker, sing these words to the following music – according to Croker, music of a very ancient kind[1]:

Lu - an, da Mort, au-gus da Dar-dine. Da Lu - an, da Mort, da

Lu - an, da Mort, da Lu - an, da Mort, au-gus da Dar - dine.

Mr Douglas Hyde has heard the story in Connaught, with the song of the fairy given as 'Peean Peean daw feean, Peean go leh agus leffin' (*pighin, pighin, dà phighin, pighin go ieith agus leith phighin*)†, which in English means, 'a penny, a penny, twopence, a penny and a half, and a halfpenny.'

Cusheen Loo [supplement (p. 320) to a headnote (p. 33) to 'Cusheen Loo', tr. from the Irish by J. J. Callanan].

Forts, otherwise raths or royalties, are circular ditches enclosing a little field, where, in most cases, if you dig down you come to stone chambers, their bee-hive roofs and walls made of unmortared stone. In these little fields the ancient Celts fortified themselves and their cattle, in winter retreating into the stone chambers, where also they were buried. The people call them Dane's forts, from a misunderstanding of the word *Danān* (*Tuath-de-Danān*)†. The fairies have taken up their abode therein, guarding them from all disturbance. Whoever roots them up soon finds his cattle falling sick, or his family or himself. Near the raths are sometimes found flint arrow-heads; these are called 'fairy darts', and are supposed to have been flung by the fairies, when angry, at men or cattle.

Stolen Child [note (p. 321) to W. B. Yeats, 'The Stolen Child' (pp. 59–60)].

The places mentioned are round about Sligo. Further Rosses is a very noted fairy locality. There is here a little point of rocks where, if anyone falls asleep, there is danger of their waking silly, the fairies having carried off their souls.

[Footnote (p. 131) to the word 'farrel' in Letitia Maclintock, 'Grace Connor' (pp. 130–2).]

When a large, round, flat griddle cake is divided into triangular cuts, each of these cuts is called a farrel, farli, or parli.

[Endnote (p. 150) to Letitia Maclintock, 'Bewitched Butter (Donegal)' (pp. 149–50).]

[†There is hardly a village in Ireland where the milk is not thus believed to have been stolen times upon times. There are many counter-charms. Sometimes the coulter of a plough will be heated red-hot, and the witch will rush in, crying out that she is burning. A new horse-shoe or donkey-shoe, heated and put under the churn, with three straws, if possible, stolen at midnight from over the witches' door, is quite infallible. – Ed.]

[Footnote (p. 150) to the word 'Moiley's' in Letitia Maclintock, 'Bewitched Butter (Donegal)' (pp. 149–50).]
    In Connaught called a 'mweeal' cow – i.e., a cow without horns. Irish *maol*, literally, blunt. When the new hammerless breech-loaders came into use two or three years ago, Mr Douglas Hyde heard a Connaught gentleman speak of them as the 'mweeal' guns, because they had no cocks.

[Footnote (p. 160) to the phrase 'a piece of horse-shoe nailed on the threshold' in 'Bewitched Butter (Queen's County)' (pp. 155–65), from *Dublin University Magazine*, 1839.]
    It was once a common practice in Ireland to nail a piece of horse-shoe on the threshold of the door, as a preservative against the influence of the fairies, who, it is thought, dare not enter any house thus guarded. This custom, however, is much on the wane, but still it is prevalent in some of the more uncivilised districts of the country.

[Footnote (p. 161) to the phrase 'an aged red-haired woman' in 'Bewitched Butter (Queen's County)' (pp. 155–65), from *Dublin University Magazine*, 1839.]
    Red-haired people are thought to possess magic power.

[Footnote (p. 168) to the name 'Shemus Rua (Red James)' in Patrick Kennedy, 'The Witches' Excursion' (pp. 168–70).]
    Irish, *Séumus Ruadh*. The Celtic vocal organs are unable to pronounce the letter j, hence they make Shon or Shawn of John, or Shamus of James, etc.

[Footnote (p. 207) to the word 'ganconers' in 'Loughleagh (Lake of Healing)' (pp. 206–11), from *Dublin and London Magazine*, 1825.]
    Ir. *gean-canach* – i.e., love-talker, a kind of fairy appearing in lonesome valleys, a dudeen (tobacco-pipe) in his mouth, making love to milk-maids, etc.

The Gonconer or Gancanagh [Gean-canach]†. [Note (pp. 323–4) by Douglas Hyde to the word 'ganconers' (p. 207) in 'Loughleagh (Lake of Healing)', repr. from *Dublin and London Magazine*, 1825. This note, although not by Yeats, is included because in 1891 Yeats used 'Ganconagh' as a pseudonym in the publication of his novel and short story, *John Sherman and Dhoya* (1891); for Yeats's definition of the word, see p. 63 above.]

O'Kearney, a Louthman, deeply versed in Irish lore, writes of the *gean-cānach* (love-talker) that he is 'another diminutive being of the same tribe as the Lepracaun, but, unlike him, he personated love and idleness, and always appeared with a dudeen in his jaw in lonesome valleys, and it was his custom to make love to shepherdesses and milkmaids. It was considered very unlucky to meet him, and whoever was known to have ruined his fortune by devotion to the fair sex was said to have met a *gean-cānach*. The dudeen, or ancient Irish tobacco pipe, found in our raths, etc., is still popularly called a *gean-cānach*'s† pipe.'

The word is not to be found in dictionaries, nor does this spirit appear to be well known, if known at all, in Connacht. The word is pronounced *gánconâgh*.

In the MS. marked R. I. A. 23/E.13 in the Roy' Ir. Ac., there is a long poem describing such a fairy hurling-match as the one in the story, only the fairies described as the *shiagh*, or host, wore plaids and bonnets, like Highlanders. After the hurling the fairies have a hunt, in which the poet takes part, and they swept with great rapidity through half Ireland. The poem ends with the line –

'S gur shiubhail me na cûig cúig cûige's gan fúm acht buachallân buidhe;

'and I had travelled the five provinces with nothing under me but a yellow bohalawn (rag-weed)'. [*Note by Mr Douglas Hyde*.]

[Footnote (p. 213) to the author in Giraldus Cambrensis, 'The Phantom Isle' (p. 213).]

'Giraldus Cambrensis' was born in 1146, and wrote a celebrated account of Ireland.

[Glossary footnotes (p. 220) to the words *shoneen* (l. 3) and *Sleiveens* (l. 6) in W. B. Yeats, 'The Priest of Coloony' (pp. 220–1).]

Shoneen – i.e., upstart.
Sleiveen – i.e., mean fellow.

[Footnote (p. 221) to W. B. Yeats, 'The Priest of Coloony' (pp. 220–1).]

[†Coloony is a few miles south of the town of Sligo. Father O'Hart lived there in the last century, and was greatly beloved. These lines accurately record the tradition. No one who has held the stolen land has prospered. It has changed owners many times.]

Father John O'Hart [note (p. 324) to W. B. Yeats, 'The Priest of Coloony' (pp. 220–1)].

Father O'Rorke is the priest of the parishes of Ballysadare and Kilvarnet, and it is from his learnedly and faithfully and sympathetically written history of these parishes that I have taken the story of Father John, who had been priest of these parishes, dying in the year 1739. Coloony is a village in Kilvarnet.

Some sayings of Father John's have come down. Once when he was sorrowing greatly for the death of his brother, the people said to him, 'Why do you sorrow so for your brother when you forbid us to keen?' 'Nature', he answered, 'forces me, but ye force nature'. His memory and influence survives, in the fact that to the present day there has been no keening in Coloony.

He was a friend of the celebrated poet and musician, Carolan.

Shoneen and Sleiveen [note (p. 324) to W. B. Yeats, 'The Priest of Coloony' (pp. 220–1)].

Shoneen is the diminutive of *shone* (Ir. *Seón*)†. There are two Irish names for John – one is *Shone*, the other is *Shawn* (Ir. *Seághan*)†. Shone is the 'grandest' of the two, and is applied to the gentry. Hence *Shoneen* means 'a little gentry John', and is applied to upstarts and 'big' farmers, who ape the rank of gentleman.

Sleiveen, not to be found in the dictionaries, is a comical Irish word (at least in Connaught) for a rogue. It probably comes from *sliabh*, a mountain, meaning primarily a mountaineer, and in a secondary sense, on the principle that mountaineers are worse than anybody else, a rogue. I am indebted to Mr Douglas Hyde for these details, as for many others.

[Footnote (p. 222) to Thomas Crofton Croker, 'The Story of the Little Bird' (pp. 222–3).]

Amulet, 1827. T. C. Croker wrote this, he says, word for word as he heard it from an old woman at a holy well.[2]

Demon Cat [note (p. 325) to Lady Wilde, 'The Demon Cat' (pp. 229–30)].

In Ireland one hears much of Demon Cats. The father of one of the present editors of the *Fortnightly* had such a cat, say county Dublin peasantry. One day the priest dined with him, and objecting to see a cat fed before Christians, said something over it that made it go up the chimney in a flame of fire. 'I will have the law on you for doing such a thing to my cat,' said the father of the editor. 'Would you like to see your cat?' said the priest. 'I would', said he, and the priest brought it up, covered with chains, through the hearth-rug, straight out of hell. The Irish devil does not object to these undignified shapes. The Irish devil is not a dignified person. He has no whiff of sulphureous majesty about him. A centaur of the ragamuffin, jeering and shaking his tatters, at once the butt and terror of the saints!

A Legend of Knockmany [note (p. 325) to William Carleton, 'A Legend of
Knockmany' (pp. 266–79)].

Carleton says – 'Of the grey stone mentioned in this legend, there is a very
striking and melancholy anecdote to be told. Some twelve or thirteen years
ago, a gentleman in the vicinity of the site of it was building a house, and, in
defiance of the legend and curse connected with it, he resolved to break it up
and use it. It was with some difficulty, however, that he could succeed in
getting his labourers to have anything to do with its mutilation. Two men,
however, undertook to blast it, but, somehow, the process of ignition being
mismanaged, it exploded prematurely, and one of them was killed. This
coincidence was held as a fulfilment of the curse mentioned in the legend. I
have heard that it remains in that mutilated state to the present day, no other
person being found who had the hardihood to touch it. This stone, before it
was disfigured, exactly resembled that which the country people term a
miscaun of butter, which is precisely the shape of a complete prism, a
circumstance, no doubt, which, in the fertile imagination of the old Senachies,
gave rise to the superstition annexed to it.'

[Footnote (p. 295) to Patrick Kennedy, 'The Enchantment of Gearoidh
Iarla' (pp. 294–6).]

The last time *Gearoidh Iarla* appeared the horse-shoes were as thin as
a sixpence.

[Endnote (p. 299), probably by Douglas Hyde, to 'Munachar and
Manachar', tr. Douglas Hyde (pp. 296–9).]

There is some tale like this in almost every language. It resembles that
given in that splendid work of industry and patriotism, Campbell's *Tales of the
West Highlands* under the name of *Moonachug and Meenachug*. 'The English
House that Jack built', says Campbell, 'has eleven steps, the Scotch Old
Woman with the Silver Penny has twelve, the Novsk Cock and Hen A-nutting
has twelve, ten of which are double. The German story in Grimm has five or
six, all single ideas.' This, however, is longer than any of them. It sometimes
varies a little in the telling, and the actors' names are sometimes *Suracha* and
Muracha, and the crow is sometimes a gull, who, instead of *daub! daub!* says *cuir
cré rua lesh!*

[Footnote (p. 309) to 'The Story of Conn-eda; or, The Golden Apples of
Lough Erne', tr. Nicholas O'Kearney (pp. 306–18).]

The Firbolgs believed their elysium to be under water. The peasantry still
believe many lakes to be peopled. – See section on *T'yeer na n-Oge*.

Some Authorities on Irish Folk-Lore[3] [pp. 325–6].

Croker's *Legends of the South of Ireland*. Lady Wilde's *Ancient Legends of Ireland*.
Sir William Wilde's *Irish Popular Superstitions*. McAnally's *Irish Wonders. Irish*

Folk-Lore, by Lageniensis. Lover's *Legends and Stories of the Irish Peasantry*. Patrick Kennedy's *Legendary Fictions of the Irish Celts, Banks of the Boro, Legends of Mount Leinster*, and *Banks of the Duffrey*; Carleton's† *Traits and Stories of the Irish Peasantry*; and the chap-books, *Royal Fairy Tales, Hibernian Tales*, and *Tales of the Fairies*. Besides these there are many books on general subjects, containing stray folk-lore, such as Mr and Mrs S. C. Hall's *Ireland*; Lady Chatterton's *Rambles in the South of Ireland*; Gerald Griffin's *Tales of a Jury-room*; and the *Leadbeater Papers*. For banshee stories see Barrington's *Recollections* and Miss Lefanu's *Memoirs of my Grandmother*. In O'Donovan's introduction to the *Four Masters* are several tales. The principal magazine articles are in the *Dublin and London Magazine* for 1825–1828 (Sir William Wilde calls this the best collection of Irish folk-lore in existence); and in the *Dublin University Magazine* for 1839 and 1878, those in '78 being by Miss Maclintock. The *Folk-Lore Journal* and the *Folk-Lore Record* contain much Irish folk-lore, as also do the *Ossianic Society*'s publications and the proceedings of the *Kilkenny Archaeological Society*. Old Irish magazines, such as the *Penny Journal, Newry Magazine*, and *Duffy's Sixpenny Magazine* and *Hibernian Magazine*, have much scattered through them. Among the peasantry are immense quantities of ungathered legends and beliefs.

Appendix 2 Notes by Yeats to items other than his introduction and headnotes, *Representative Irish Tales*, ed. W. B. Yeats (1891) I, 178, 190; II, 157–9, 331. See the textual introduction, p. 320 below, for a list of exclusions.

[Footnote (I, 178) to an excerpt from Michael Banim, *The Mayor of Wind-gap*.]
In Kilkenny, Banim means. To this day the custom is universal in the west of Ireland. – Ed.

[Endnote (I, 190) to an excerpt from Michael Banim, *The Mayor of Wind-gap*, chs 2 and 5.]
Throughout the novel the 'sthrange man' and the Mayor of Wind-gap are confronted as the good and evil powers of the tale. In the first we have Banim at his most melodramatic; in the second, keeping close to life, and describing a personage who had really lived at Wind-gap a little before his day, he has given us one of the most beautiful characters in fiction.

[Endnote (II, 157–9) to Thomas Crofton Croker, 'The Confessions of Tom Bourke'.]
Note: Croker has, perhaps, slandered our 'fairy doctors'. It was the custom of his day to take nothing 'supernatural' seriously. He could not drive out of his head the notion that every man who saw a spirit was commonly drunk as a piper. Things have changed since then. I quote the following from Lady Wilde's *Ancient Legends*,[1] as it describes a 'fairy doctor' of wholly other type.

'He never touched beer, spirits, or meat, in all his life, but has lived entirely on bread, fruit, and vegetables. A man who knew him thus describes him: "Winter and summer his dress is the same, merely a flannel shirt and coat. He will pay his share at a feast, but neither eats nor drinks of the food and drink set before him. He speaks no English, and never could be made to learn the English tongue, though he says it might be used with great effect to curse one's enemy. He holds a burial-ground sacred, and would not carry away so much as a leaf of ivy from a grave. And he maintains that the people are right to keep to their ancient usages, such as never to dig a grave on a Monday; and to carry the coffin three times round the grave, following the course of the sun, for then the dead rest in peace. Like the people, also, he holds suicides as accursed; for they believe that all its dead turn over on their faces if a suicide is laid amongst them.

'"Though well off, he never, even in his youth, thought of taking a wife; nor was he ever known to love a woman. He stands quite apart from life, and by this means holds his power over the mysteries. No money will tempt him to impart his knowledge to another, for if he did he would be struck dead – so he believes. He would not touch a hazel stick, but carries an ash wand, which he holds in his hand when he prays, laid across his knees; and the whole of his life is devoted to works of grace and charity, and though now an old man, he has never had a day's sickness. No one has ever seen him in a rage, nor heard an angry word from his lips but once, and then being under great irritation, he recited the Lord's Prayer backwards as an imprecation on his enemy. Before his death he will reveal the mystery of his power, but not till the hand of death is on him for certain." When he does reveal it, we may be sure it will be to one person only – his successor.'

[Headnote (II, 331) to the anonymous 'The Jackdaw'.]

The following is from an old chapbook called *The Hibernian Tales*. I quote it not so much for its own sake, though it is not altogether unamusing, as for its value as a representative of the chapbook literature, once the main reading of the people.

Appendix 3   Notes by Yeats (or of untraced origin) to items other than his introduction, *Irish Fairy Tales*, ed. W. B. Yeats (1892) pp. 70, 115, 153, 190.

[Footnote (p. 70) to the word 'Rath' in 'The Fairy Greyhound' (pp. 69–76).]

Raths are little fields enclosed by circular ditches. They are thought to be the sheepfolds and dwellings of an ancient people.

[Footnote (p. 115) to the phrase 'not a chapel, but a lonely old fort' in Patrick Weston Joyce, 'Fergus O'Mara and the Air-Demons' (pp. 112–22).]

A fort is the same as a rath (see p. 70); a few are fenced in with unmortared stone walls instead of clay ditches.

[Footnote (p. 153) to the phrase 'white-headed boy' in Gerald Griffin†, 'Owney and Owney-na-peak' (pp. 151–81).]
White-haired boy, a curious Irish phrase for the favourite child.

[Footnote (p. 190) to the word 'gaesa' in Standish James O'Grady, 'The Knighting of Cuculain'.]
Curious vows taken by the ancient warriors. Hardly anything definite is known of them. – Ed.

Appendix 4   Acknowledgements, *Poems of William Blake*, ed. W. B. Yeats, 2nd edn (1905) p. 1.

I have to thank Mr E. J. Ellis for lending me his copy of 'the MS. book',[1] and for kindly reading the proofs of my introduction;† Mr Fairfax Murray for leave to reprint three lyrics from *An Island in† the Moon*; and Dr Carter Blake for information about Blake's ancestry.[2]

Appendix 5   *Poems of William Blake*, ed. W. B. Yeats, 2nd edn (1905) notes on pp. 261–77.

The *Poetical Sketches*. Page 1. – The original edition has the following preface:

Advertisement

'The following Sketches were the production of untutored youth, commenced in his twelfth, and occasionally resumed by the author till his twentieth year; since which time, his talents having been wholly directed to the attainment of excellence in his profession, he has been deprived of the leisure requisite to such a revisal of these sheets as might have rendered them less unfit to meet the public eye.

'Conscious of the irregularities and defects found on almost every page, his friends have still believed that they possessed a poetical originality which merited some respite from oblivion. These opinions remain, however, to be now re-proved or confirmed by a less partial public.'

Mr Dante Rossetti endeavoured to make some, at any rate, of the corrections which Blake could not – or, one is inclined to suspect, would not –

make, and made a number of metrical emendations in the selection of the *Sketches* given in Gilchrist's *Life and Works of William Blake*. He made these with admirable judgment, but when they were made, the poems, taken as a whole, were well nigh as irregular as at the outset.

There seems no logical position between leaving the poems as they are, with all their slips of rhythm, and making alterations of a very sweeping nature, which would be out of place in a working text like the present. The present editor has accordingly simply reprinted Blake's own text, not even retaining the very small number of emendations made by Mr W. M. Rossetti. He has, however, to economize space, left out several poems altogether, holding them mere boyish experiments, with here and there some line or passage of beauty. The poems left out are: 'Fair Elenor', 'Gwin, King of Norway', 'Prologue to Edward the Fourth', and four prose poems called 'Prologue to King John', 'The Couch of Death', 'Contemplation', and 'Samson', respectively. 'A War Song', though scare worthy of a place in the body of the book, is interesting enough for quotation here.

A War Song: To Englishmen.

Prepare, prepare the iron helm of war,
Bring forth the lots, cast in the spacious orb;
The Angel of Fate turns them with mighty hands,
And casts them out upon the darkened earth!
    Prepare, prepare!

Prepare your hearts for Death's cold hand! prepare
Your souls for flight, your bodies for the earth!
Prepare your arms for glorious victory!
Prepare your eyes to meet a holy God!
    Prepare, prepare!

Whose fatal scroll is that? Methinks 'tis mine!
Why sinks my heart, why faltereth my tongue?
Had I three lives, I'd die in such a cause,
And rise, with ghosts, over the well-fought field.
    Prepare, prepare!

The arrows of Almighty God are drawn!
Angels of Death stand in the low'ring heavens!
Thousands of souls must seek the realms of light,
And walk together on the clouds of heaven!
    Prepare, prepare!

Soldiers, prepare! Our cause is Heaven's cause;
Soldiers, prepare! Be worthy of our cause:
Prepare to meet our fathers in the sky:
Prepare, O troops that are to fall to-day!
    Prepare, prepare!

Alfred shall smile, and make his heart rejoice;
The Norman William and the learned Clerk,
And Lion-Heart, and black-browed Edward with
His loyal queen, shall rise, and welcome us!
                    Prepare, prepare!

'Samson' is seen at its best in this direction to Delilah: 'Go on, fair traitress; do thy guileful work; ere once again the changing moon her circuit hath performed, thou shalt overcome and conquer him by force unconquerable, and wrest his secret from him. Call thine alluring arts and honest-seeming brow, the holy kiss of love and the transparent tear; put on fair linen that with the lily vies, purple and silver; neglect thy hair, to seem more lovely in thy loose attire; put on thy country's pride deceit; and eyes of love decked in mild sorrow; and sell thy lord for gold.'

Songs† of Innocence and Experience. Pages 47 to 85. – Messrs Dante and William Rossetti, in the second volume of Gilchrist's *Life of Blake*, and in the Aldine edition of the poems[1] respectively, have made several grammatical and metrical emendations. The original text is here restored. 'The Nurse's Song' and 'The Little Boy Lost' are to be found imbedded in that curious prose narrative, *An Island in† the Moon*, in slightly different form from that in the† *Songs of Innocence*; and 'The Clod† and the Pebble', 'The Garden of Love', 'A† Poison Tree', 'Infant Sorrow', 'Earth's Answer', 'London', 'The Lily', 'Nurse's Song', 'The Tiger', 'The Human Image', 'The Sick Rose', 'The Little Vagabond', 'Holy Thursday', 'The Angel', 'The Fly', and a part of 'The Chimney-Sweeper', from the *Songs of Experience*, are to be found in a more or less different shape in a note-book usually spoken of by Blake's biographers and editors as 'the MS. book'.

Songs of Innocence and *Songs† of Experience* were latterly bound together by Blake under the title of the† *Songs of Innocence and of Experience, Shewing† the Two Contrary States of the Human Soul*. 'The MS. book' gives the following verses with the note that they are a 'Motto† for the Songs of Innocence and of† Experience'.

The Good are attracted by men's perceptions,
    And think not for themselves,
Till Experience teaches them to catch
    And to cage the Fairies and Elves.

And then the Knave begins to snarl,
    And the Hypocrite to howl;
And all his good friends show their private end,
    And the Eagle is known from the Owl.

Strange lines that are clear enough to the student of Blake's philosophy; but at most a perspicuous gloom to the rest of mankind. The excision of 'his' from the last line but one would make them a little more intelligible. The third and fourth lines should be compared with 'Opportunity', page 120.

'The Tiger'. Page 74. – The MS. book contains the following first draft for 'The Tiger'. The editor has restored, where necessary for the sense, occasional words which were crossed out by Blake. The poem will be found exactly as it is in the MS. book with the crossed out words in italics, and several alternative readings, at page 92, vol. iii., of *The Works of William Blake*. He is at present merely anxious to give it in the form pleasantest for the eye and the memory without the interruption of italics and alternative readings.

The Tiger.

Tiger, Tiger, burning bright
In the forests of the night,
What immortal hand or eye
Dare frame thy fearful symmetry?

In what distant deeps or skies
Burned the fire within thine eyes?
On what wings dared he aspire?
What the hand dared seize the fire?

And what shoulder and what art
Could twist the sinews of thy heart?
And when thy heart began to beat,
What dread hand and what dread feet

Could filch it from the furnace deep,
And in thy hornèd ribs dare steep
In the well of sanguine woe
*　　*　　*　　*　　*　　*　　*

In what clay and in what mould
Were thine eyes of fury rolled
*　　*　　*　　*　　*　　*　　*

Where the hammer, where the chain,
In what furnace was thy brain?
What the anvil? what dread grasp
Dared thy deadly terrors clasp?

Tiger, Tiger, burning bright
In the forests of the night,
What immortal hand or eye
Dare frame thy fearful symmetry?

There is also an interesting variant upon this couplet –

Did He smile His work to see,
Did He who made the lamb make thee?

in which 'laugh' is substituted for 'smile'.

Mr Gilchrist and Mr Rossetti give a version slightly different from the one found by Mr Ellis and the present editor in the MS. book, and claim for it also MS. authority.

When Blake altered and copied out the poem for engraving he altogether omitted the unfinished fourth verse, and forgot to make the last line of the third a complete sentence. Mr D. G. Rossetti did this for him by substituting 'formed' for 'and'; but Malkin, who probably had Blake's authority, prints 'forged'.

'The Garden of Love'. Page 76. – Mr Rossetti inserts at the beginning of this poem two verses, which are here printed in the† 'Ideas of Good and Evil', as a separate poem called 'Thistles and Thorns'. He found them in the MS. book, and forgot to notice the long line which Blake had drawn to divide them from 'The Garden of Love' which followed.

'The Little Vagabond'. Page 76. – The MS. book gives instead of line 9 'Such usage in heaven never do well', 'The poor parsons with wind like a blown bladder swell'.

'London'. Page 77. – Compare with the 'blackening church'†, and 'marriage hearse', in this poem, the use of the same terms in the following detached quatrain from the MS. book. It is called there 'An Ancient Proverb'.

> Remove away that blackening church,
> Remove away that marriage-hearse,
> Remove away that man of blood,
> You'll quite remove that ancient curse.

'Infant Sorrow'. Page 79. – The MS. book continues this poem as follows:

> When I saw that rage was vain,
> And to sulk would nothing gain;
> Turning many a trick and wile,
> I began to soothe† and smile.
>
> And I soothed day after day,
> Till upon the ground I lay;
> And I smiled night after night,
> Seeking only for delight.
>
> And I saw before me shine
> Clusters of the wandering vine;
> And many a lovely flower and tree
> Stretched their blossoms out to me.

My father, then, with holy book, (? look)[2]
In his hands a holy book,
Pronouncèd curses on my head,
And bound me in a myrtle shade.

So I smote him – and his gore
Stained the roots my myrtle bore;
But the time of youth is fled,
And grey hairs are on my head.

'Cradle† Song'. Page 82. – This was never included by Blake in any engraved edition of the† *Songs of Experience*, but it is an obvious pendant to 'Cradle† Song' in the† *Songs of Innocence*. The editor accordingly follows Mr Rossetti and Mr Gilchrist in printing here from the MS. book.

'To Tirzah'†. Page 84. – In engraved *Songs* the words 'to be raised a spiritual body' are written at the end of the poem.

'The Voice of the Ancient Bard'. Page 85. – This poem has hitherto been printed at the end of the† *Songs of Innocence*. The editor, however, follows a copy of the† *Songs* sold by Mrs Blake after Blake's death to a Mr Edwards, which was probably the last engraved, in placing it at the end of the† *Songs of Experience*, where it forms a natural pendant to 'The voice of the bard, who present, past, and future sees', at the beginning.

'Ideas of Good and Evil'. Page 89. – The MS. Book has upon its title-page[3] the above inscription, which was possibly a first and rejected attempt towards a title for the poems afterwards called the† *Songs of Innocence and of*† *Experience*, but probably a first thought for a title of the† *Songs of Experience* alone, 'experience' and eating the fruit of the Tree of Knowledge of Good and Evil being one and the same in Blake's philosophy. The first possibility is made unlikely by the fact that the MS. book contains none of the† *Songs of Innocence*, which therefore probably preceded it. If this be so, it must† have been begun between 1789 and 1794. He kept it by him well-nigh all his life, and jotted down in it a record of all manner of wayward moods and fancies. The title 'Ideas of Good and Evil' was probably soon forgotten, but, having at any rate his partial sanction, may well serve us better than such unmeaning and uncomely titles as 'Later Poems' or 'Miscellaneous† Poems'. The editor follows the example of Gilchrist's book in including under the title poems from other sources than the MS. book. The sources are letters, the engraved copy of *The Gates of Paradise*, the newly discovered *An Island in*† *the Moon*, and what the author of the note on page 85 of Gilchrist's second volume has called 'another small autograph collection of different matter somewhat more fairly copied' than the MS. book. This 'autograph collection' has vanished for the present, having defied all the efforts of Mr Ellis and the present writer to discover it. It is to be hoped that it has not vanished for good and all, for the editor of the poems in Gilchrist and the editor of the Aldine edition have with a timidity which was perhaps natural in introducing for the first time an eccentric author whom the bulk of readers held to be mad, and whose meaning they themselves but partially understood, permitted themselves far too numerous transpositions, alterations, and omissions in printing from still accessible sources. The editor of the Gilchrist text, in the case of this now inaccessible 'autograph collection' also, admits to having found it 'necessary' to 'omit, transpose, or combine', that he might 'lessen obscurity', but claims to have done so far less than in printing from the MS. book, and his principles were certainly adopted in the main by Mr W. M. Rossetti in the Aldine edition. A comparison of the text given here of poems like 'The Grey Monk', and poems like that which the present writer has called 'Spectre and Emanation', with the text given in either Mr Gilchrist's or Mr Rossetti's book, will show how much has been sacrificed in the battle with 'obscurity'. The student of Blake's philosophy knows well that what seems most obscure is usually most characteristic, and grudges any clearness gained at the expense of his author's meaning. He finds it even harder to forgive those cases where Mr Rossetti did not confine himself to the right he claimed to 'omit, transpose, or combine',† but substituted, in the name of lucidity, words of his own for Blake's carefully selected words. These substitutions are, however, few, and probably arose from bewilderment over the strangeness of the terms, combined with the difficulty of reading the well-nigh illegible MS. Mr Rossetti may well have refused to believe his eyes when he came, in 'The Everlasting Gospel', for instance, to 'anti-Christ, creeping Jesus', and have convinced himself that Blake meant to write 'anti-Christ, aping Jesus'. His sin was not so much editorial, for almost any ordinary editor would have made a mistake as human, but that sin, which he shares with a large portion of the human race, of having no feeling for mystical terms. Whatever he may have done ill in these matters is more than balanced by the great service he has done Blake in other ways. In the following selection, a few lyrics given in the Aldine or in Mr Shepherd's edition[4] are excluded and others included which have not appeared in either of these books. The added lyrics are, 'The Pilgrim', 'A Song of Sorrow', and 'Old English Hospitality', from *An Island in*† *the Moon*. The excluded poems are 'La Fayette',[5] 'To Mrs Butts', 'Seed Sowing', 'Idolatry', 'Long John Brown and Little Mary Bell', 'Song by an Old Shepherd', and 'Song by a Shepherd', and well nigh all 'the epigrams and satirical pieces on art and artists'. None of these poems, howsoever curious and biographically interesting they be, have poetical value anything like equal to the selections from 'The Prophetic Books', made possible by leaving them out. In many cases Blake gave no title to his poems, and the editor has ventured more than once to differ from the titles chosen by Mr W. M. Rossetti and to substitute titles of his own. He has never, however, done this except when the old title seemed obviously misleading, uncharacteristic, or ungainly.

Blake's own text of the† 'Ideas of Good and Evil' has been restored in the present volume in every case where the original MS. is still accessible. The restorations are not always to the advantage of the poem, though in some cases they certainly are; and it is possible that the editors of the future may prefer to make a few of those corrections which Blake would doubtless have made had he re-copied for the press his rough first drafts, and to keep a mid-track between the much modified version of Messrs Dante and William Rossetti and the present literal text.

'Auguries of Innocence'. Page 90. – See note to 'Proverbs'.

'To Mr Butts'.[6] Page 92. – From a letter to Mr Butts from Felpham.

'To Mrs Flaxman'.[7] Page 95. – From a letter to Flaxman from Felpham.

'Proverbs'.[8] Page 96. – This is one of the poems taken from that other 'small autograph collection' mentioned in Gilchrist. Mr Herne Shepherd gives in *Blake's Poems and Songs of Innocence* (Pickering and Chatto) a version different in the order of the verses, and in having several grammatical and one or two obvious metrical slips, not present in the version given by Mr Dante Rossetti in Gilchrist's book. Even if Mr Shepherd gave the text with accuracy, it is impossible to say in the absence of the manuscript how far he read Blake's *intentions* correctly. The poem is a series of magnificent proverbs and epigrams, rather than a poem with middle, beginning, and end, and Blake in all likelihood set these proverbs and epigrams down in order of composition, and not in order of thought and subject. The manuscript was never corrected for the press, and may have been little more than a series of notes to help his own memory. Mr D. G. Rossetti may therefore, in putting the lines in order of thought and subject, have gone really nearer to Blake's own intention than Mr Herne Shepherd in printing them in the order of the manuscript. One is the more ready to believe this, because the poem as arranged by Mr Rossetti was incomparably finer than Mr Shepherd's version. The writer has, therefore, adopted Mr Rossetti's version. Mr Rossetti has also left out several couplets given by Shepherd. The writer at first thought of restoring these, but on second thought prints them here, as they would assuredly mar with their clumsy rhythm and loose structure the magnificent sweetness and power of one of the greatest of all Blake's poems.

The couplet –

> Every tear in every eye
> Becomes a babe in eternity –

was continued as follows –

This is caught by females aright,
And return'd to its own delight.

a little further down came the lines –

The babe that weeps the rod beneath,
Writes revenge in realms of death;

and towards the end of the poem –

To be in a passion you good may do,
But no good if a passion is in you.

In one matter, however, the editor has differed both from the version of Mr Herne Shepherd and Mr Gilchrist. He is entirely convinced that the title 'Auguries of Innocence', refers only to the first four lines of this version. Blake was most exact in the use of terms, and would never have called either 'The harlot's cry from the street', or 'The whore and gambler by the state licensed', or 'The questioner who sits so sly', or 'The wanton boy who kills the fly', or well nigh any of the things mentioned in this poem, 'Auguries of Innocence'.

He did, upon the other hand, hold that 'Innocence' or the state of youthful poetic imagination was none other than to 'see a world in a grain of sand' and 'a heaven in a wild flower'. Neither Mr Rossetti nor Mr Shepherd believed Blake to use words with philosophical precision, but held him a vague dreamer carried away by his imagination, and may well have never given two thoughts to anything except the imaginative charm of the title. We have already seen how Mr W. M. Rossetti tacked on to 'The Garden of Love' two verses which Blake had clearly marked off as a separate poem. In this case, too, there was probably a line drawn between the first quatrain and the rest of the poem, and even if there were not, the internal evidence is itself conclusive. The editor has, therefore, printed the 'Auguries of Innocence' as a poem by itself, and called the lines thus separated from them 'Proverbs', as that is a title used by Blake in *The Marriage of Heaven and Hell* for short gnomic sayings of the kind.

'In a Myrtle Shade'. Page 103. – The poem printed is the final version chosen by Blake, but the MS. book contains two other versions which are not uninteresting. The first should be compared with the poem quoted in the notes to 'Infant Sorrow'. It is as follows:

To a lovely myrtle bound,
Blossoms showering all around

O how weak and weary I
Underneath my myrtle lie,
Like to dung upon the ground,
Underneath my myrtle bound.

Why should I be bound to thee,
O my lovely myrtle tree?
Love, free love, cannot be bound
To any tree that grows on ground.

Oft my myrtle sighed in vain,
To behold my heavy chain;
Oft my father saw us sigh,
And laughed at our simplicity.

So I smote him, and his gore
Stained the roots my myrtle bore;
But the time of youth is fled,
And grey hairs are on my head.

The second version is:

To my Myrtle.

Why should I be bound to thee,
O my lovely myrtle tree?
Love, free love, cannot be bound
To any tree that grows on ground.
To a lovely myrtle bound,
Blossom showering all around,
Underneath my myrtle bound,
O how weak and weary I
Underneath my myrtle lie.

There is written beside these versions in pencil a stanza, now almost illegible, of which the following words can be made out:

Deceit to seeming   *   *   *
*   *   *   *   refined
To everything but interest blind,
And   *   *   *   fetters every mind,
And forges fetters of the mind.

We give this fragment because it was the origin of a stanza interpolated in Gilchrist's book in the middle of the poem I call 'Freedom and Captivity'. It was no doubt more legible than at present when Mr D. G. Rossetti copied it out, and the word that looks more like 'seeming' may perhaps be really 'secrecy'. His reading, too, of the lines, which are now quite illegible, is probably to be trusted. His version is as follows:

Deceit to secrecy inclined
Moves, lawful, courteous and refined,
To everything but interest blind,
And forges fetters for the mind.

'The Two Thrones'.[9] Page 104. – This poem, which is given no title by Blake, is called 'Mammon', and is much edited in Mr W. M. Rossetti's edition. It is here given exactly as in the MS. book.

'The Two Kinds of Riches'.[10] Page 105. – The MS. book gives no title.

'The Grey Monk'. Page 109. – This poem was originally intended, as the MS. book shows, to have been the latter half of a poem of fourteen stanzas, which began with the line, 'I saw a monk of Constantine.' Blake changed this first line into 'I saw a monk of Charlemagne', made a few other alterations here and there, and divided the poem into two parts. To the first half of four stanzas he added three stanzas, and printed it in the preface to chap. iii. of *Jerusalem* (see page 201). The second half he left without change or addition. The arrangement of the verses in the Aldine edition is quite arbitrary. Mr Rossetti has made the second stanza in Blake's MS. the third in his version, and the third the fourth, and the fourth the fifth, and the fifth the seventh, and the seventh the ninth, and left out Blake's own ninth stanza altogether. He has also imported a stanza from 'The Monk of Charlemagne', and made it the second stanza. Mr Rossetti made no secret of his transposition and suppression, so that no great blame attaches to him in this matter. He had to introduce Blake to an unwilling generation, and thought it best to lop off many an obtrusive knot and branch.

'The Everlasting Gospel'. Page 110. – Mr Rossetti has by a slip of the pen claimed to give this poem 'in full' (see Aldine edition, page 144), and has not only not done so, but has given passages out of the order intended by Blake, and printed words here and there which are not in Blake at all. The poem is not given in full in the present book; for it is not possible to do so without many repetitions, for Blake never made a final text. The MS. book contains three different versions of a large portion of the poem, and it is not possible to keep wholly to any one of these without sacrificing many fine passages. Blake left, however, pretty clear directions for a great part of the text-making, and these directions were ignored by Mr Rossetti. The short fragment which begins the poem both in the present and in the Aldine text was probably intended to be a private dedication apparently to Stothard, and not a part of the poem at all. The present editor follows Mr Rossetti in leaving out two ungainly lines about the length of Stothard's nose and the shortness of Blake's (see *Works of William Blake*, vol. ii, page 44). Had Blake ever printed the dedication he also would doubtless have suppressed these lines. The poem was intended by him to begin with the lines which open 'Was Jesus humble, or did He give any proofs of humility?' for he has written the title above them. Mr Rossetti puts these lines almost at the very end. There are two other versions of the first part of the poem, and passages are here added from one of these versions. There still remain two fragments, the one is marked by Blake as containing '94 lines', though later additions slightly increased its length, and the other contains 48 lines, and is printed on a slip of paper at the end of the book. There is a mark at the foot of the '94 line' fragment signifying that it is to follow the lines over which Blake had written the title. It begins, 'Was Jesus chaste', and ends, 'For dust and clay is the serpent's meat, That never was meant for man to eat.' The 48 line fragment begins, 'Was Jesus born of a virgin pure', and ends, 'God's righteous law that lost its prey'. There still remains a couplet, 'I am sure this Jesus will not do Either for Christian or for Jew.' Blake marks it to follow the '94 lines', but this mark may have been made before the writing of the lines beginning 'Was Jesus born of a virgin pure', for certainly its place is at the end of all. There are also a few fragmentary lines here and there of whose place no indication is given. All the fragments are given separately in *The Works of William Blake*.

'To Nobodaddy'†. Page 120. – Printed by Mr Rossetti without Blake's quaint title. In a later version Blake changed the last line to 'Gains females' loud applause'.

'Cupid'.[11] Page 122. – The MS. book gives the following fifth stanza:

> 'Twas the Greeks' love of war
> Turned Cupid into a boy,
> And woman into a statue of stone:
> Away flew every joy.

'Spectre and Emanation'.[12] Page 129. – Mr Dante Rossetti read this as primarily a love poem, and was led by this mistake into calling it 'Broken Love'. Blake gives no title, but 'Spectre and Emanation' is his technical expression for reason and emotion, active and passive, masculine and feminine, past and future, body and soul, and all the other duads of his complex system. Both Mr Dante Gabriel Rossetti in Gilchrist's *Life of Blake*, and Mr W. M. Rossetti in the Aldine, adopt an arrangement of the verses not to be found in the MS. book.

The verses in the text are those numbered by Blake as part of the poem. There are, however, certain other verses which were apparently rejected by him. They are as follows:

> O'er my sins thou dost sit and moan,
> Hast thou no sins of thine own?
> O'er my sins thou dost sit and weep,
> And lull thy own sins fast asleep.

> What transgressions I commit
> Are for thy transgression fit:
> They thy harlots, thou their slave;
> And thy bed becomes their grave.

Poor, pale, pitiable form
That I follow in a storm!
Iron tears and groans of lead
Bind around my aching head.

'Los the Terrible'.[13] Page 136. – This extract from a letter to Mr Butts, dated
November, 1802, and described as having been 'composed above a twelve
month ago, while walking from Felpham to Levant, to meet my sister', has no
title in the original. 'Los the Terrible' describes the subject of the poem, which
is Los in his malevolent rather than in his more usual benevolent aspect.

Tiriel. Page 147. – The style of the poem, which resembles rather that of 'The
Mental Traveller' than the more vehement and broken style of the later
prophetic poems, makes it clear that *Tiriel* belongs to an earlier period than
any other of the prophetic books. It was probably followed by *The Ghost of
Abel*! Mr Rossetti says: 'The† handwriting appears to me to belong to no late
period of his life. This character of handwriting prevails up to near the close of
the poem. With the words (in section 8), "I am Tiriel, King of the West"†, a
new and less precise kind of handwriting begins; clearly indicating, I think,
that Blake, after an interval of some years, took up the poem and finished it,
perhaps in much more summary fashion than he at first intended.' The style of
the later lines seems to the present writer to be much later than the style of the
rest of the poem. It is more directly mystical, more of a direct appeal from the
soul of Blake to the soul of the reader, and much more wholly dependent upon
mystical knowledge for its interest. The rest of the poem has a certain interest
and meaning as a story, but this latter page is as purely mystical as *Europe*, or
America, or *Jerusalem*. It is symbolical rather than allegorical.

Thel. Page 169. – This poem was engraved in 1789. The engraved copy begins
'The daughters of Mne Seraphim', Blake having apparently thought of
writing 'The daughters of Mnetha', Mnetha being the name given in his
system to the Mother of All. The letters 'Mne' are scratched out in the
Bodleian copy, and it it possible that Blake got into the habit of reading 'Mne'
as 'the', and of so giving the rhythm the syllable it requires.

The Marriage of Heaven and Hell. Page 176. – This poem was engraved in 1790,
and is a reply to the then recently translated *Heaven and Hell* of Swedenborg.†

Visions of the Daughters of Albion. Page 194. – This poem was engraved in 1793,
and is not only one of the most beautiful but one of the most subtle and
difficult of 'the prophetic books'.

[*The Book of*] *Ahania*. Page 207. – This poem was engraved in 1795.† There is a
copy, the only one extant, of Blake's edition, in the library of Lord Houghton.

Vala. Page 218. – This poem was never engraved by Blake.† It was probably written during the last three or four years of the century. The manuscript was given by Blake to his friend Linnell, the landscape painter, but at what date is not now known. The extracts given are from the second and eighth books respectively.

Jerusalem. Page 221. – It is dated 1804, but Blake was probably at work upon it both before and after that date.

Milton. Page 233. – Also dated 1804, but like *Jerusalem*, probably not finished until a later date. It was originally intended to run to twelve books, but Blake finished it in two.

On his Picture of the Canterbury Pilgrims. Page 239. – From the *Descriptive Catalogue* which was published in 1809.

Identity. Page 250. – From a number of disordered notes in the MS. book which seem to have been intended as an introduction to his description of his picture of *The Last Judgment*.

Minute Knowledge. Page 251. – From Blake's sequel to his description of the picture of *The Last Judgment*.

The Nature of a Last Judgment. Page 251. – From the same source with the last.

Why Men enter Heaven. Page 252. – From the same source with the last.

Learning without Imagination. Page 253. – From the description, in the *Descriptive Catalogue*, of the picture of *A Spirit vaulting from a Cloud*.

Form and Substance are One. Page 253 – From the scraps of a 'Public Address' which are scattered about the MS. book, and which were printed by Gilchrist in a somewhat arbitrary order.

Good and Evil. Page 253. – From the sequel to his description of the picture of *The Last Judgment*.

The Clearness of Vision. Page 254. – From the description in the *Descriptive Catalogue*, of his picture *The Bard from Gray*.

Outline in Art and Life. Page 254. – From the description, in the *Descriptive Catalogue*, of *Ruth – a Drawing*.

The Tree of Good and Evil. Page 255. – From the sequel to his description of the picture of *The Last Judgment*. It is omitted in Gilchrist perhaps because Blake himself drew a line through it. It was probably objected to by Blake simply because it added to the obscurity, without greatly helping the argument, of his 'sequel', and not because he disapproved of it in itself, for it states more shortly and explicitly than elsewhere a fundamental conception of his.

There is no Natural Religion, I, II. Pages 255, 256. – From the engraved, but undated, and illustrated tractates.

Appendix 6 Passage on contemporary Irish poets, in Introduction (dated 5 Aug 1894), *A Book of Irish Verse Selected from Modern Writers*, ed. W. B. Yeats, 1st edn (1895) pp. xxiii–xxiv. The passage was heavily revised for the 2nd edn (1900).

Here and there, however, the Societies have trained up a young writer, who, though busy with the old models, has, like 'Iris Olkyn',[1] imaginative energy; and many have come to them from without, and brought with them deliberate craftsmanship. There is, indeed, more of unity in Irish literary life to-day than when Ferguson, Allingham, and Mr Aubrey de Vere were doing their best work. They had not much in common with the Ireland of their day, while their successors, Dr Hyde, Mr Lionel Johnson, Mr Rolleston, and Mrs Hinkson are trying to understand and influence Irish opinion. Dr Hyde is, before all else, a translator and scholar; Mr Rolleston has written but little verse;[2] and it is too soon to measure the height and depth of Mr Johnson's impassioned eloquence; but Mrs Hinkson has published four books of poems, two being very admirable. One remembers her piteous and poignant 'Children of Lir', her quaint and humorous 'Iona',[3] and places her with Allingham and De Vere. She has no revery, no speculation, but a Franciscan tenderness for weak instinctive things, – old gardeners, old fishermen, birds in the leaves, birds tossed upon the waters.

A little mystical movement – the only heretical movement, if we can call a mixed horde of Christians and pagans heretics – which disordered Ireland has found time to create – has lately begun to make poets, and of these the most interesting are Mr Charles Weekes, who recently published, but immediately withdrew, a curious and subtle book;[4] and 'AE'†, an exquisite though still imperfect craftsman, who has put a distinctive mood of the little group into haunting stanzas –

> What of all the will to do?
>   It vanished long ago,
> For a dream-shaft pierced it through
>   From the Unknown Archer's bow.
>
> What of all the soul to think?
>   Some one offered it a cup
> Filled with a diviner drink,
>   And the flame has burned it up.
>
> What of all the hope to climb?
>   Only in the self we grope
> To the misty end of time:
>   Truth has put an end to hope.[5]

Except these mystics and Prof. Dowden at an odd moment, no Irishman. . . .

Appendix 7 *A Book of Irish Verse Selected from Modern Writers,* ed. W. B. Yeats, 1st edn (1895) notes on pp. 250–7.

Page xxi, lines 21 to 25. [For the text of this note and annotation to it, see p. 272, note 19 below.]

Page 1 [Oliver Goldsmith', 'Old Age' from the 'Deserted Village']. 'The deserted village' is Lissoy, near Ballymahon, and Sir Walter Scott tells of a hawthorn there which has been cut up into toothpicks by Goldsmith enthusiasts; but the feeling and atmosphere of the poem are unmistakably English.

Page 8 [Richard Allen Milliken, 'The Groves of Blarney']. Some verses in 'The Epicurean' were put into French by Théophile Gautier for the French translation, and back again into English by Mr Robert Bridges. If any Irish reader who thinks Moore a great poet, will compare his verses with the results of this double distillation, and notice the gradual disappearance of their vague rhythms and loose phrases, he will be the less angry with the introduction to this book. Moore wrote as follows –

You, who would try
    Yon terrible track,
To live or to die,
    But ne'er to turn back.

You, who aspire
    To be purified there,
By the terror of fire,
    Of water, and air, –

If danger, and pain,
    And death you despise,
On – for again
    Into light you shall rise:

Rise into light
    With the secret divine,
Now shrouded from sight
    By a veil of the shrine.

These lines are certainly less amazing than the scrannel piping of his usual
anapaests; but few will hold them to be 'of their own arduous fullness
reverent'! Théophile Gautier sets them to his instrument in this fashion,

Vous qui voulez courir
La terrible carrière,
Il faut vivre ou mourir,
San regard en arrière:

Vous qui voulez tenter
L'onde, l'air, et la flamme,
Terreurs à surmonter
Pour épurer votre âme,

Si, méprisant la mort,
Votre foi reste entière,
En avant! – le coeur fort
Reverra la lumière.

Et lira sur l'autel
Le mot du grand mystère,
Qu'au profane mortel
Dérobe un voile austère.

Then comes Mr Robert Bridges, and lifts them into the rapture and precision
of poetry –

O youth whose hope is high,
Who dost to truth aspire,
Whether thou live or die,
O look not back nor tire.

Thou that are bold to fly
Through tempest, flood, and fire,
Nor doest not shrink to try
Thy heart in torments dire:

If thou canst Death defy,
If thy faith is entire,
Press onward, for thine eye
Shall see thy heart's desire.

Beauty and love are nigh,
And with their deathless quire –
Soon shall thine eager cry
Be numbered and expire.

Page 27 [James Clarence Mangan, 'Dark Rosaleen' (from the Irish)]. 'Dark Rosaleen' is one of the old names of Ireland. Mangan's translation is very free; as a rule when he tried to translate literally, as in 'The Munster Bards', all glimmer of inspiration left him.

Page 32, line 20 [Mangan, 'Lament for the Princes of Tyrone and Tyrconnell' (from the Irish): 'The Mount whereon the martyr-saint/Was crucified']. 'This passage is not exactly a blunder, though at first it may seem one: the poet supposes the grave itself transferred to Ireland, and he naturally includes in the transference the whole of the immediate locality about the grave' (Mangan note).

Page 47, line 6 [Mangan, 'Prince Alfrid's Itinerary through Ireland' (from the Irish): 'And in every one of the five (provinces of Ireland) I found']. The two Meaths once formed a distinct province.[1]

Page 55, line 7 [Mangan, 'The Nameless One': 'That there was once one whose blood ran lightning']. This poem is an account of Mangan's own life, and is, I think, redeemed out of rhetoric by its intensity. The following poem, 'Siberia', describes, perhaps, his own life under a symbol.

Page 59 [Gerald Griffin, 'Hy-Brasail']. Hy Brasail, or Teer-Nan-Oge, is the island of the blessed, the paradise of ancient Ireland. It is still thought to be seen from time to time glimmering far off.

Page 61 [Edward Walsh, 'Mo Craoibhin Cno' (from the Irish)]. *Mo Craoibhin Cno* means my cluster of nuts, and is pronounced *Mo Chreevin Knō*.

Page 64 [*sic*, 63] [Walsh, 'Maigréad Ni Chealleadh']. Mr O'Keefe has sent the writer a Gaelic version of this poem, possibly by Walsh himself. A correspondent of his got it from an old peasant who had not a word of English. A well-known Gaelic scholar pronounces it a translation, and not the original of the present poem. *Mairgréad ni Chealleadh* is pronounced *Mairgréd nei Kealley*. The *Ceanabhan*, pronounced *Kanovan*, is the bog cotton, and the *Monadan* is a plant with a red berry found on marshy mountains.

Page 69 [Michael Doheny, 'A cuisle geal mo chroidhe']. *A cuisle geal mo chroidhe*, pronounced *A cushla gal mo chre*, means 'bright pulse of my heart'.

Page 74 [Ferguson, 'The Welshmen of Tirawley']. Sir Samuel Ferguson introduces the poem as follows: Several Welsh families, associates in the

Several Welsh families, associates in the invasion of Strongbow, settled in the West of Ireland. Of these, the principal, whose names have been preserved by the Irish antiquarians, were the Walshes, Joyces, Heils (*a quibus* MacHale), Lawlesses, Tolmyns, Lynotts, and Barretts, which last drew their pedigree from Walynes, son of Guyndally, the *Ard Maor*, or High Steward of the Lordship of Camelot, and had their chief seats in the territory of the two Bacs, in the barony of Tirawley, and county of Mayo. *Clochan-na-n'all*, i.e. 'The Blind Men's Stepping-stones', are still pointed out on the Duvowen river, about four miles north of Crossmolina, in the townland of Garranard; and *Tubber-na-Scorney*, or 'Scrags Well', in the opposite townland of Carns, in the same barony. For a curious *terrier* or applotment[2] of the Mac William's revenue, as acquired under the circumstances stated in the legend preserved by Mac Firbis, see Dr O'Donovan's highly-learned and interesting 'Genealogies, &c. of Hy. Fiachrach', in the publications of the *Irish Archaeological Society* – a great monument of antiquarian and topographical erudition.[3]

Page 90, line 6 [Ferguson, 'The Welshmen of Tirawley': 'That the sons of William Conquer']. 'William Conquer' was William Fitzadelm De Burgh, the Conqueror of Connaught.

Page 91, line 4 [Ferguson, 'Aideen's Grave']. Sir Samuel Ferguson introduces the poem as follows:

Aideen, daughter of Angus of Ben-Edar (now the Hill of Howth), died of grief for the loss of her husband, Oscar, son of Ossian, who was slain at the battle of Gavra (*Gowra*, near Tara in Meath), A.D. 284. Oscar was entombed in the rath or earthen fortress that occupied part of the field of battle, the rest of the slain being cast in a pit outside. Aideen is said to have been buried on Howth, near the mansion of her father, and poetical tradition represents the Fenian heroes as present at her obsequies. The Cromlech in Howth Park has been supposed to be her sepulchre. It stands under the summits from which the poet Atharne is said to have launched his invectives against the people of Leinster, until, by the blighting effect of his satires, they were compelled to make him atonement for the death of his son.

Page 99 [Ferguson, 'Deirdre's Lament for the Sons of Usnach' (from the Irish)]. 'There was then no man in the host of Ulster that could be found who would put the sons of Usnach to death, so loved were they of the people and nobles. But in the house of Conor was one called Mainé Rough Hand, son of the king of Lochlen, and Naesi had slain his father and two brothers, and he undertook to be their executioner†. So the sons of Usnach were then slain, and the men of Ulster, when they beheld their death, sent forth their heavy shouts of sorrow and lamentation. Then Deirdre fell down beside their bodies wailing and weeping, and she tore her hair and garments and bestowed kisses on their lifeless lips and bitterly bemoaned them. And a grave was opened for them, and Deirdre, standing by it, with her hair dishevelled and shedding tears abundantly, chanted their funeral song.' (*Hibernian Nights' Entertainments*†.)

Page 102 [Ferguson, 'The Fair Hills of Ireland' (from the Irish)]. *Uileacan Dubh O'*, pronounced *Uileacaun Doov O*, is a phrase of lamentation.

Page 108, line 16 [Ferguson, 'The Fairy Well of Lagnanay': 'I wish I were with Anna Grace!']. 'Anna Grace' is the heroine of another ballad by Ferguson. She also was stolen by the Fairies.

Page 112, line 6 [Ferguson, 'On the Death of Thomas Davis': 'Thomas Davis, is thy toil']. Thomas Davis had an Irish father and a Welsh mother, and Emily Brontë an Irish father and a Cornish mother, and there seems no reason for including the first and excluding the second. I find, perhaps fancifully, an Irish vehemence in 'Remembrance'. Several of the Irish poets have been of mixed Irish-Celtic and British-Celtic blood. William Blake has been recently claimed as of Irish descent, upon the evidence of Dr Carter Blake;[4] and if, in the course of years, that claim becomes generally accepted, he should be included also in Irish anthologies.

Page 119, line 13 [Aubrey de Vere, 'The Little Black Rose shall be red at last']. 'The Little† Black Rose' is but another form of 'Dark Rosaleen', and has a like significance. 'The Silk of the Kine' is also an old name for Ireland.

Page 138 [Thomas Davis, 'Maire Bhan Astór']. *Maire Bhan Astór* is pronounced *Mauria vaun a-stór*, and means 'Fair Mary, my treasure'.

Page 140 [Davis, 'O! the Marriage']. *Mo bhuachaill*, pronounced *mo Vohil*, means 'my boy'.

Page 174 [Thomas D'Arcy McGee, 'The Gogan Saor']. The Goban Saor, the mason Goban, is a familiar personage in Irish folk-lore, and the reputed builder of the round towers.

Pasge 191 [Alfred Perceval Graves, 'Father O'Flynn']. *Slainté*, '[†your] health'.

Page 207 [Katharine Tynan Hinkson, 'The Children of Lir']. 'And their step-mother, being jealous of their father's great love for them, cast upon the king's children, by sorcery, the shape of swans, and bade them go roaming, even till Patrick's mass-bell should sound in Erin; but no farther in time than that did her power extend.' – *The Fate of the Children of Lir*.

Page 222 [Lionel Johnson, 'The Red Wind']. The wind was one of the deities of the Pagan Irish. 'The murmuring of the Red Wind from the East,' says an old poem, 'is heard in its course by the strong as well as the weak; it is the wind that wastes the bottom of the trees, and injurious to man is that red wind.'

Page 226 [Johnson, 'Can Doov Deelish']. *Can Doov Deelish* means 'dear black head'.

Page 231 ['Shule Aroon' (anonymous)]. The chorus is pronounced *Shoo-il, shoo-il, shoo-il, a rooin, Shoo-il go socair, ogus shoo-il go kiune, Shoo-il go den durrus ogus euli liom, Iss go de too, mo vourneen, slaun*, and means –

> Move, move, move, O treasure,
> Move quietly and move gently,
> Move to the door, and fly with me,
> And mayest thou go, my darling, safe!

Page 232 ['The Shan Van Vocht' (anonymous)]. *Shan van vocht,* meaning 'little old woman'†, is a name for Ireland.

Page 235 ['The Wearing of the Green' (anonymous)]. This is not the most ancient form of the ballad, but it is the form into which it was recast by Boucicault, and which has long taken the place of all others.

Page 237, line 2 ['The Rakes of Mallow' (anonymous): 'Breaking windows, damning, sinking']. 'Sinking', violent swearing.

Appendix 8   Preface (1899), *A Book of Irish Verse Selected from Modern Writers,* ed. W. B. Yeats, 2nd edn (1900) pp. xiii–xv.

I have not found it possible to revise this book as completely as I should have wished. I have corrected a bad mistake of a copyist,[1] and added a few pages of new verses towards the end, and softened some phrases in the introduction which seemed a little petulant in form, and written in a few more to describe writers who have appeared during the last four years, and that is about all. I compiled it towards the end of a long indignant argument, carried on in the committee rooms of our literary societies, and in certain newspapers between a few writers of our new movement, who judged Irish literature by literary standards, and a number of people, a few of whom were writers, who judged it by its patriotism and by its political effect; and I hope my opinions may have value as part of an argument which may awaken again. The Young Ireland writers wrote to give the peasantry a literature in English in place of the literature they were losing with Gaelic, and these methods, which have shaped the literary thought of Ireland to our time, could not be the same as the methods of a movement which, so far as it is more than an instinctive expression of certain moods of the soul, endeavours to create a reading class among the more leisured classes, which will preoccupy itself with Ireland and the needs of Ireland. The peasants in eastern counties have their Young Ireland poetry, which is always good teaching and sometimes good poetry, and the peasants of the western counties have beautiful poems and stories in Gaelic, while our more leisured classes read little about any country, and nothing about Ireland. We cannot move these classes from an apathy, come from their separation from the land they live in, by writing about politics or about Gaelic, but we may move them by becoming men of letters and expressing primary emotions and truths in ways appropriate to this country. One carries on the traditions of Thomas Davis, towards whom our eyes must always turn, not less than the traditions of good literature, which are the morality of the man of letters, when one is content, like AE,† with fewer readers that one may follow a more hidden beauty; or when one endeavours, as I have endeavoured in this book, to separate what has literary value from what has only a patriotic and political value, no matter how sacred it has become to us.

The reader who would begin a serious study of modern Irish literature shoud do so with Mr Stopford Brooke's and Mr Rolleston's exhaustive anthology.

W. B. Y.
August 15, 1899

Appendix 9   Excerpt from acknowledgements, *A Book of Irish Verse Selected from Modern Writers*, ed. W. B. Yeats, 2nd edn (1900) p. [xxxii].

Two writers are excluded whom he would gladly have included – Casey, because the copyright holders have refused permission, and Mr George Armstrong, because his 'Songs of Wicklow', when interesting, are too long for this book.[1]

Appendix 10   Sections I and II of 'Lady Gregory's *Cuchulain of Muirthemne*', *Discoveries. Edmund Spenser. Poetry and Tradition; and Other Essays*, vol. VIII of *The Collected Works in Verse and Prose of William Butler Yeats* (1908) pp. 133–6.

I

I think this book is the best that has come out of Ireland in my time. Perhaps I should say that it is the best book that has ever come out of Ireland; for the stories which it tells are a chief part of Ireland's gift to the imagination of the world – and it tells them perfectly for the first time. Translators from the Irish have hitherto retold one story or the other from some one version, and not often with any fine understanding of English, of those changes of rhythm, for instance, that are changes of the sense. They have translated the best and fullest manuscripts they knew, as accurately as they could, and that is all we have the right to expect from the first translators of a difficult and old literature. But few of the stories really begin to exist as great works of imagination until somebody has taken the best bits out of many manuscripts. Sometimes, as in Lady Gregory's version of *Deirdre*, a dozen manuscripts have to give their best before the beads are ready for the necklace. It has been as necessary also to leave out as to add, for generations of copyists, who had often but little sympathy with the stories they copied, have mixed versions together in a clumsy fashion, often repeating one incident several times, and every century has ornamented what was once a simple story with its own often extravagant ornament. One does not perhaps exaggerate when one says that no story has come down to us in the form it had when the story-teller told it in the winter evenings. Lady Gregory has done her work of compression and selection at once so firmly and so reverently that I cannot believe that anybody, except now and then for a scientific purpose, will need another text than this, or than the version[1] of it the Gaelic League has begun to publish in Modern Irish. When she has added her translations from other cycles, she will have given Ireland its *Mabinogion*, its *Morte D'Arthur*, its *Nibelungenlied*.[2] She has already put a great mass of stories, in which the ancient heart of Ireland still lives, into a shape at once harmonious and characteristic; and without writing more than a very few sentences of her own to link together incidents or thoughts taken from different manuscripts, without adding more indeed than the story-teller must often have added to amend the hesitation of a moment. Perhaps more than all she had discovered a fitting dialect to tell them in. Some years ago I wrote some stories of mediaeval Irish life,[3] and as I wrote I was sometimes made wretched by the thought that I knew of no kind of English that befitted them as the language of Morris's prose stories – that lovely crooked language – befitted his journeys to woods and wells beyond the world.[4] I knew of no language to write about Ireland in but our too smooth, too straight, too logical modern English; but now Lady Gregory has discovered a speech as beautiful as that of Morris, and a living speech into the bargain. As she lived among her people she grew to love the beautiful speech of those who think in Irish, and to understand that it is as true a dialect of English as the dialect that Burns wrote in.[5] It is some hundreds of years old, and age gives a language authority. One finds in it the vocabulary of the translators of the Bible, joined to an idiom which makes it tender, compassionate, and complaisant, like the Irish language itself. It is certainly well suited to clothe a literature which never ceased to be folk-lore even when it was recited in the Courts of Kings.

II

Lady Gregory could with less trouble have made a book that would have better pleased the hasty reader. She could have plucked away details, smoothed out characteristics till she had left nothing but the bare stories; but a book of that kind would never have called up the past, or stirred the imagination of a painter or a poet, and would be as little thought of in a few years as if it had been a popular novel.

The abundance of what may seem at first irrelevant invention in a story like the death of Conaire,[6] is essential if we are to recall a time when people were in love with a story, and gave themselves up to imagination as if to a lover. One may think there are too many lyrical outbursts, or too many enigmatical symbols here and there in some other story, but delight will always overtake one in the end. One comes to accept without reserve an art that is half epical, half lyrical, like that of the historical parts of the Bible, the art of a time when perhaps men passed more readily than they do now from one mood to another, and found it harder than we do to keep to the mood in which one tots up figures or banters a friend.

Appendix 11   Endnote, titled 'Note by W. B. Yeats on the Conversation of Cuchulain and Emer (Page 23)',[1] to p. 23 ('The Courting of Emer: Cuchulain's Riddles'), Lady Gregory, *Cuchulain of Muirthemne: The Story of the Men of the Red Branch of Ulster* (1902) pp. 351–3.

This conversation, so full of strange mythological information, is an example of the poet speech of ancient Ireland. One comes upon this speech here and there in other stories and poems. One finds it in the poem attributed to Ailbhe, daughter of Cormac Mac Art, and quoted by O'Curry in 'MS. Materials', of which one verse is an allusion to a story given in Lady Gregory's book:

> The apple tree of high Aillinn,
> The yew of Baile of little land,
> Though they are put into lays,
> Rough people do not understand them.[2]

One finds it too in the poems which Brian, Son of Tuireann, chanted when he did not wish to be wholly understood. 'That is a good poem, but I do not understand a word of its meaning,' said the kings before whom he chanted;[3] but his obscurity was more in a roundabout way of speaking than in mythological allusions. There is a description of a banquet, quoted by Professor Kuno Meyer, where hens' eggs are spoken of as 'gravel of Glenn Ai', and leek, as 'a tear of a fair woman', and some eatable seaweed, dulse, perhaps, as a 'net of the plains of Rein' – that is to say, of the sea – and so on. He quotes also a poem that calls the sallow 'the strength of bees', and the hawthorn 'the barking of hounds', and the gooseberry bush 'the sweetest of trees', and the yew, 'the oldest of trees'.[4]

This poet speech somewhat resembles the Icelandic court poetry, as it is called, which certainly required alike for the writing and understanding of it a great traditional culture. Its descriptions of shields and tapestry, and its praises of Kings, that were first written, it seems, about the tenth century, depended for their effects on just this heaping up of mythological allusions, and the 'Eddas' were written to be a granary for the makers of such poems.[5] But by the fourteenth and fifteenth centuries they have come to be as irritating to the new Christian poets and writers who stood outside their tradition, as are the more esoteric kinds of modern verse to unlettered readers. They were called 'obscure', and 'speaking in riddles', and the like.

It has sometimes been thought that the Irish poet speech was indeed but a copy of this court poetry, but Professor York Powell contradicts this, and thinks it is not unlikely that the Irish poems influenced the Icelandic, and made them more mythological and obscure.[6]

I am not scholar enough to judge the Scandinavian verse, but the Irish poet speech seems to me at worst an over-abundance of the esoterism which is an essential element in all admirable literature, and I think it a folly to make light of it, as a recent writer has done.[7] Even now, verse no less full of symbol and myth seems to me as legitimate as, let us say, a religious picture full of symbolic detail, or the symbolic ornament of a Cathedral.

Nash's –

> Brightness falls from the air,
> Queens have died young and fair,
> Dust hath closed Helen's eye –[8]

must seem as empty as a Scald's song,[9] or the talk of Cuchulain and Emer, to one who has never heard of Helen, or even to one who did not fall in love with her when he was a young man. And if we were not accustomed to be stirred by Greek myth, even without remembering it very fully, 'Berenice's ever burning hair'[10] would not stir the blood, and especially if it were put into some foreign tongue, losing those resounding 'b's' on the way.

The mythological events Cuchulain speaks of give mystery to the scenery of the tales, and when they are connected with the battle of Magh Tuireadh, the most tremendous of mythological battles,[11] or anything else we know much about, they are full of poetic meaning or historical interest. The hills that had the shape of a sow's back at the coming of the Children of Miled, remind one of Borlase's conviction that the pig was the symbol of the mythological ancestry of the Firbolg, which the Children of Miled were to bring into subjection, and of his suggestion that the magical pigs that Maeve numbered were some Firbolg tribe that Maeve put down in war.[12] And everywhere that esoteric speech brings the odour of the wild woods into our nostrils.

The earlier we get, the more copious does this traditional and symbolical element in literature become. Till Greece and Rome created a new culture, a sense of the importance of man, all that we understand by humanism, nobody wrote history, nobody described anything as we understand description. One called up the image of a thing by comparing it with something else, and partly because one was less interested in man, who did not seem to be important, than in divine revelations, in changes among the heavens and the gods, which can hardly be expressed at all, and only by myth, by symbol, by enigma. One was always losing oneself in the unknown, and rushing to the limits of the world. Imagination was all in all. Is not poetry, when all is said, but a little of this habit of mind caught as in the beryl stone of a Wizard?[13]

Appendix 12   Section VIII of 'What We Did or Tried to Do' (1928), in *Coinage of Saorstát Éireann 1928* [Jan 1929?] pp. 6–7.

I have given here my own opinions and impressions, and I have no doubt my Committee differs from some, but I know no other way of writing. We had all our points of view, though I can only remember one decision that was not unanimous. A member had to be out-voted because he wanted to substitute a harrier for a wolf-hound on the ground that on the only occasion known to him when hare and wolf-hound met the wolf-hound ran away. I am sorry that our meetings have come to an end, for we learned to like each other well.

What remains to be said is said in the name of the whole Committee. Our work could not have been done so quickly nor so well had not the Department of Finance chosen Mr MacCauley† for our Secretary. Courteous, able and patient he has a sense of order that fills me with wonder.

W. B. Yeats

Appendix 13 Introduction (prefatory paragraph), *Selections from the Poems of Dorothy Wellesley* (1936) p. vii.

In this little book Lady Gerald Wellesley has, at my persuasion, collected from her *Poems of Ten Years* and from unpublished work, such poems as best represent her talent, altering, condensing, omitting much, not less rich in poetical experience. At my suggestion she has put first her latest poem, which seems as profound in thought as it is swift in movement.[1]

Appendix 14 Anonymous headnote to the untitled introduction, Dorothy Wellesley, *The Poets and Other Poems* (1943) p. 3.

The following introduction by W. B. Yeats was written for a selection he had made from a volume called *Poems of Ten Years*. This choice of his was published under the title of *Selections from the Poems of Dorothy Wellesley: with an Introduction by W. B. Yeats and a Portrait by Sir William Rothenstein*. Unfortunately most of the edition was destroyed by fire during the great London air raids. In the circumstances it may be of interest to reprint this here, as an instance of his own taste in styles and subjects, and also of the generosity of a great Poet towards the work of one of whom he then knew nothing beyond her poems.

Appendix 15 Letter from Yeats to In-sŏb Jung [Zŏng],[1] 8 Sept 1936, published as front matter to *An Anthology of Modern Poems in Korea: (100 Poets and 100 Poems)*, ed. and tr. In[-]sob Zŏng (1948) p. 3.

I thank you very much for showing me your volume of translations from modern Korean poets. I do not think you should have any difficulty in finding a publisher. I notice a delightful little poem of your own about a girl, a comb and a ring.[2]

NOTES

FAIRY AND FOLK TALES

1. Richard Corbett (1582–1635), 'A proper new Ballad, entituled The Faeryes Farewell; or, God-a-Mercy Will', ll. 21–4 and 34–5, *The Poems of Richard Corbet, Late Bishop of Oxford and Norwich*, 4th edn, ed. Octavius Gilchrist (London: Longman, Hurst, Rees and Orme, 1807) pp. 214–15: '. . . Or Ciss . . . merrily merrily went theyre tabor, / And nimbly went theyre toes. . . . Theyre songs were Ave Maryes.' J. A. W. Bennett and H. R. Trevor-Roper (eds), *The Poems of Richard Corbett* (Oxford: Clarendon Press, 1955), date this poem *c.* 1620 (p. 128).
2. Rosses Point, Co. Sligo, five miles north-west of Sligo.
3. William Hazlitt's *The Spirit of the Age; or, Contemporary Portraits* (1825), a collection of essays on writers of the day, gave wide currency to the phrase 'the spirit of the age'. In 1844 Richard Henry Horne prepared *A New Spirit of the Age* (London: Smith, Elder). The phrase often was set in quotation marks, as for example in a review by James Smetham in 1869, quoted in Alexander Gilchrist, *Life of William Blake with Selections from his Poems and Other Writings*, 2nd edn, 2 vols (London: Macmillan, 1880) II, 321.
4. Giraldus Cambrensis (Giraldus de Barri, 1146?–1220?), *The Topography of Ireland* (1187), tr. Thomas Forester, in *The Historical Works of Giraldus Cambrensis*, ed. Thomas Wright (London: Bohn, 1863) ch. xix ('How the Irish are very ignorant of the rudiments of the faith'), pp. 134–5, *et passim*.
5. Innistor (Tor Inis, Tower Island): Tory Island, off the north-west coast of Co. Donegal; see Eugene O'Curry, *On the Manners and Customs of the Ancient Irish: A Series of Lectures*, ed. W. K. Sullivan (London: Williams and Norgate, 1873) II, 186.
6. Cromlech: ancient Irish stone tomb formed of one great flat stone lying on the tops of several large standing stones; a dolmen.
    Pillar-stone: variously used by the ancient Irish to mark graves and boundaries.
7. Holy-eve night: Samhain Eve or All Hallows Night or Halloween (31 October).
8. Alexander Rose, 'Parish of Dungiven [Co. Londonderry]', in *A Statistical Account, or Parochial Survey of Ireland, Drawn up from Communications of the Clergy*, comp. William Shaw Mason (1774–1853) (Dublin: Cumming and Neray Mahon, 1814) I, 318 ('Seanachies'), 317–18 ('Ossian's Poems'):

The poems attributed to Ossian, and other bardic remains, are still repeated here by the old Seanachies, (as they are called) with visible exultation. . . . A curious evidence of the accuracy of tradition, in preserving these remains, may be noticed: two of the poems transcribed [from these seanachies at Dungiven], namely Deirdri (the Darthula of Macpherson) and Tailc, had been already published, from southern manuscripts, in a volume entitled – Transactions of the Gaelic Society: this book, which was accidentally in the writer's possession, afforded an opportunity of comparing the poems taken from *viva voce* recitation, with the printed copy; and strange as it may seem, they were found to agree together word for word, with the exception, however, of a few lines in Deirdri, and four entire stanzas in Tailc, which the written record had evidently lost, and tradition preserved. . . .

The Gaelic Society reference is to Theophilus O'Flanagan, 'Deirdri, or, The Lamentable Fate of the Sons of Usnach, An Dramatic Irish Tale, One of the Three Tragic Stories of Erin; Literally Translated into English, from an Original Gaelic Manuscript, with Notes and Observations: To which is Annexed, the Old Historic Account of the Facts on which the Story is Founded', *Transactions of the Gaelic Society of Dublin*, I (1808) 1–179. Yeats's reference to the Royal Dublin Society is a mistake, presumably for the British Museum (BL, Egerton 1782). In 1899 Douglas Hyde explained that the older of the two versions that O'Flanagan had published in 1808 'agrees closely with that contained in "Egerton 1782" of the British Museum, but neither of the manuscripts which he used is now known to exist' ('Déirdre', *Zeitschrift für celtische Philologie*, 2 [1899] 138).

9. Castlehacket, Co. Galway, is four miles west of Tuam. Yeats further explained, in a note to the 'Kidnappers' section in the second edition of *The Celtic Twilight* (London: Bullen, 1902), that the Hackets 'were descended from a man and a spirit' and 'were notable for beauty' (p. 124; *Myth* 74).

10. Henry R. Montgomery (ed.), *Specimens of the Early Native Poetry of Ireland, in English Metrical Translations* (Dublin: McGlashan, 1846), attributed 'the celebrated song of "Eileen a Roon"' to Carol O'Daly, brother of the famed religious bard Donogha Mór O'Daly (d. 1244 in Boyle, Co. Roscommon). Montgomery's account continues: 'Like many other of our ancient songs, it has been plagiarised in Scotland, under the title of "Robin Adair"' (p. 99). The specific John O'Daly to whom Yeats here refers is untraced; Lissadell, Co. Sligo, had been the home of Murray O'Daly, a thirteenth-century poet, mentioned in William G. Wood-Martin, *History of Sligo, County and Town, from the Earliest Ages to the Close of the Reign of Queen Elizabeth* (Dublin: Hodges, Figgis, 1882) I, 181–2.

Edward Bunting published the old Irish air '*Eibhlin a Ruin*' ('Ellen a Roone') in *The Ancient Music of Ireland* (Dublin: Hodges and Smith, 1840) pp. 94–5 (no. 123), noting that the air was anonymous and that Gerald O'Daly, an Irish harpist, probably only adapted Irish words to it. The tune 'Eileen Aroon' was popularised in Scotland by the blind Irish harpist Dennis A. Hempson (1695–1807), born in Co. Londonderry. The title 'Robin Adair' came from an Irish parody in 1734, and the modern words of 'Robin Adair' were written by Caroline Keppel, *c.* 1750. In the nineteenth century, the Irish poet Thomas Moore (1779–1852) set the lyric 'Erin, the Tear and the Smile' to the 'Eileen Aroon' air, and Gerald Griffin (1803–40), Irish novelist and poet, wrote a lyric titled 'Eileen Aroon', collected in *Irish Minstrelsy: Being a Selection of Irish Songs, Lyrics, and Ballads,* ed. H. Halliday Sparling (London: Scott, 1888) pp. 341–3.

11. George Frederick Handel (Georg Friedrich Händel, 1685–1759) lived in Dublin from November 1741 to August 1742. Handel's praise of 'Eileen Aroon' is mentioned in Montgomery, *Specimens of the Early Native Poetry of Ireland,* p. 99: 'Handel and [Francesco] Geminiani [(1674?–1762?)], the great composers, united in eulogy of it. The former is stated to have declared that he would be rather the author of that simple air than of the most elaborate composition he had ever published.'

12. [Yeats's note:] He lived some time in Dublin, and heard it then.

13. O'Donoghue of Ross, an ancient chieftain, traditionally reappears at early dawn on May Day at Lough Leane (the Lake of Killarney), Co. Kerry. See Thomas Crofton Croker, 'The Legend of O'Donoghue', in *Fairy Legends and Traditions of the South of Ireland* [1st ser.] (London: Murray, 1825) pp. 353–9.

14. Paddy Flynn (described in 'A Teller of Tales' in *The Celtic Twilight*), of Ballisodare, Co. Sligo, four miles south of Sligo. Drumahair (Dromahair), Co. Leitrim, is two miles south of Lough Gill and one mile from the border of Co. Sligo. Drumcliff, Co. Sligo, is four miles north of Sligo.

15. Paddy Flynn was Yeats's source for this anecdote of St Columba (or Columcille, 521–97), Irish abbot and missionary, and his mother, Ethne, daughter of Mac-naue; it is not recorded in the standard *Life of Columba* by St Adamnan (625?–704). See Yeats's remark in a letter to Father Matthew Russell, 5 July [1888]: 'I looked up the Columbkille prophesies but did not find the picturesque one I heard down in the country' (*CL1* 80). See also 'Teller of Tales', in *The Celtic Twilight* (*Myth* 5), and note 14 above.

16. See the 'Banshee' section of this introduction, p. 16 above.

17. Thomas à Kempis (Thomas Hamerken, 1380–1471) is the reputed author of *The Imitation of Christ*; the reference is presumably to book I, chap. xx ('Of the Love of Solitude and Silence'), but is not a specific quotation.

18. For Thomas Crofton Croker and Samuel Lover, see pp. 51–2 and 49–50 above.

19. For the Young Ireland writers and the rising in July 1848, see pp. 56 above and 240, note 21 and 249, note 113 below. The Great Famine, caused by potato blight, lasted from 1845 to 1848.

20. The 'Ghosts' section of *FFT* includes 'The Fate of Frank M'Kenna' (pp. 139–45) by William Carleton (1794–1869).

21. For Patrick Kennedy (1801–73), see p. 253, note 27 below. Lady Jane Francesca Elgee Wilde (1824–96), *Ancient Legends, Mystic Charms and Superstitions of Ireland*, 2 vols (London: Ward and Downey, 1887–8).

22. For Letitia Maclintock and for *Leabhar Sgeuluigheachta* (1889), by Douglas Hyde (1860,1949), see note 32 and 253–4, note 27 below.

23. Edward Walsh (1805–50) and Jeremiah (or James) Callanan (1795–1829) translated Irish folk materials.

24. Sassanach (Sassenach): Gaelic name for Saxon (or English).

25. For *The Royal Fairy Tales*, *The [Royal] Hibernian Tales* and *The Tales of the Fairies*, see p. 253, note 27 below.

26. [Yeats's note:] *Phaedrus*. Jowett's translation. (Clarendon Press.)

27. Boreas, the North Wind, carried off Orithyia, the daughter of Erechtheus, legendary King of Athens.

28. Artemis, the Greek goddess, is often portrayed as a virgin huntress; her companion Pharmacia is known only from this legend. Areopagus is a hill to the west of the Acropolis in Athens.

29. A saying of the oracle of Apollo at Delphi.

30. Typho (Typhon): a hundred-headed monster.

31. *Phaedrus*, III.229–30, in *The Dialogues of Plato*, tr. Benjamin Jowett (1817–93) (Oxford: Clarendon Press, 1871) I, 563–4: '. . . Ilissus. . . . believe that the . . . quarter of a mile . . . temple of Agra, and . . . of altar. . . . I don't recollect; but I wish that you would tell me whether you . . . tale. Socrates. The wise are doubtful, and if, like them, I also doubted, there would be nothing very strange in that. I. . . . locality, as according . . . story she. . . . these explanations are . . . to give them. . . . and impossible monstrosities and marvels of nature. And . . . them all to. . . . says; and I should be absurd indeed, if while I am still in ignorance of myself I were to . . . business. And therefore I. . . . I indeed a . . . of a gentler . . . Nature. . . .'

32. Patrick Kennedy, 'The Kildare Pooka', 'The Witches' Excursion', 'The Long Spoon', 'The Enchantment of Gearoiddh Iarla', in *Legendary Fictions of the Irish Celts* (London: Macmillan, 1866); 'The Twelve Wild Geese', 'The Lazy Beauty and Her Aunts' and 'The Haughty Princess', in *The Fireside Stories of Ireland* (Dublin: M'Glashan and Gill, and Patrick Kennedy, 1870).

The five items by Letitia Maclintock (also spelled 'M'Clintock' and 'McClintock', b. 1835) are 'A Donegal Fairy', 'Jamie Freel and the Young Lady: A Donegal Tale', 'Far Darrig in Donegal', 'Grace Connor', and 'Bewitched Butter (Donegal)'; they are from her 'Folk-lore of the County Donegal', *Dublin University Magazine*, 88 (Nov 1876) 607–14 (anonymous), and 89 (Feb 1877) 241–9. Lady Wilde, ['The Black Lamb'] (in 'The Dance of the Dead'), 'The Horned Women', 'The Priest's Soul' and 'The Demon Cat', in *Ancient Legends* (1887–8). William Allingham, 'The Fairies', 'The Lepracaun, or, Fairy Shoemaker' and 'A Dream', in *Irish Songs and Poems* (London: Reeves and Turner, 1887). Samuel Ferguson, 'The Fairy Well', *Blackwood's Edinburgh Magazine*, 33 (Apr 1833) 667, and 'The Fairy Thorn', in *Lays of the Western Gael, and other Poems* (Dublin: Sealey, Bryers and Walker, 1888). W. B. Yeats,

'The Stolen Child', and Ellen O'Leary, 'A Legend of Tyrone', in *Poems and Ballads of Young Ireland: 1888* (Dublin: Gill, 1888).

33. Tírechán, 'Life of Saint Patrick' (7th c.), in *The Patrician Texts in the Book of Armagh*, ed. and tr. Ludwig Bieler (Dublin: Institute for Advanced Studies, 1979) pp. 142–3 (B.26.3): 'deorum terrenorum'. Yeats's immediate source probably was Sir William Robert Wilde, *Irish Popular Superstitions* (Dublin: McGlashan, 1852) p. 125.

34. Untraced; for a generally similar statement see Kennedy, *The Fireside Stories of Ireland*, p. 131.

35. [Yeats's note:] Occultists, from Paracelsus to Eliphas† Levi, divide the nature spirits into gnomes, sylphs, salamanders, undines; or earth, air, fire, and water spirits. Their emperors, according to Eliphas†, are named Cob, Paralda, Djin, Hicks respectively.[35a] The gnomes are covetous, and of the melancholic temperament. Their usual height is but two spans, though they can elongate themselves into giants. The sylphs are capricious, and of the bilious temperament. They are in size and strength much greater than men, as becomes the people of the winds. The salamanders are wrathful, and in temperament sanguine. In appearance they are long, lean, and dry. The undines are soft, cold, fickle, and phlegmatic. In appearance they are like man. The salamanders and sylphs have no fixed dwellings.

It has been held by many that somewhere out of the void there is a perpetual dribble of souls; that these souls pass through many shapes before they incarnate as men – hence the nature spirits. They are invisible – except at rare moments and times; they inhabit the interior elements, while we live upon the outer and the gross. Some float perpetually through space, and the motion of the planets drives them hither and thither in currents. Hence some Rosicrucians have thought astrology may foretell many things; for a tide of them flowing around the earth arouses there, emotions and changes, according to its nature.

Besides those of human appearance are many animal and bird-like shapes. It has been noticed that from these latter entirely come the familiars seen by Indian braves when they go fasting in the forest, seeking the instruction of the spirits. Though all at times are friendly to men – to some men – 'They have', says Paracelsus, 'an aversion to self-conceited and opinionated persons, such as dogmatists, scientists, drunkards, and gluttons, and against vulgar and quarrelsome people of all kinds; but they love natural men, who are simple-minded and childlike, innocent and sincere, and the less there is of vanity and hypocrisy in a man, the easier will it be to approach them; but otherwise they are as shy as wild animals.'[35b]

35a. Éliphas Lévi (Alphonse Louis Constant, 1810–75), *Dogme et rituel de l'haute magie* (1856), tr. Arthur E. Waite, in *The Mysteries of Magic: a Digest of the writings of Éliphas Lévi with Biographical and Critical Essay* (1st edn 1886), 2nd edn (London: Paul, Trench, Trübner, 1897), pp. 173, 178: 'Gob' (*vice* 'Cob') and 'Nicksa' (*vice* 'Hicks').

35b. Philippus Aureolus Paracelsus (Theophrastus Bombastus von Hohenheim, 1493?–1541), Swiss alchemist and physician, gave these descriptions of the elemental spirits in his *A Book on Nymphs, Sylphs, Pygmies and Salamanders and on the Other Spirits* (posthumously publ. 1566), Tractus II, 'About their Abode', quoted in Franz Hartmann, *The Life of Philippus Theophrastus, Bombast of Hohenheim, Known by the Name of Paracelsus and the Substance of his Teachings concerning Cosmology, Anthropology, Pneumatology, Magic and Sorcery, Medicine, Alchemy and Astrology, Philosophy and Theosophy* (London: Redway, 1887), pp. 99–101 (citing *Philosophia Occulta*). The quoted passage (pp. 100–1) reads: '. . . The Elementals have an aversion against self-conceited . . . child-like . . . is vanity . . . be for him to. . . .'

36. For 'pooka', see pp. 15–16 below; for 'fetch', see p. 17 above and p. 245, note 67 below.

37. The anonymous Irish air 'The Pretty Girl Milking the Cow' is printed in Edward Bunting, *A General Collection of the Ancient Music of Ireland* (London: Clementi, 1809) I, 59, and, as 'Pretty Girl milking the Cows', in John O'Daly, *The Poets and Poetry of Munster: A Selection of Irish Songs by the Poets of the Last Century*, tr. James Clarence Mangan (Dublin: O'Daly, 1849), p. 82. For 'The Pretty Girl Milking the Cow' as a fairy tune and the fairy music of Torlough O'Carolan (1670–1753), a Gaelic musician and poet, see Lady Wilde, *Ancient Legends*, I, 273–4 ('The Fairy Rath') and 253 ('The Sidhe Race').

38. See pp. 94 and 266, note 78 below.

39. Lady Wilde, *Ancient Legends*, I, 73 ('The Trial by Fire'): '. . . Saints, . . .'

40. Giraldus Cambrensis, *Topography of Ireland* (see note 4 above), p. 74 (ch. xii): '. . . phantom; insomuch that. . . .'

41. Lady Wilde, *Ancient Legends*, I, 11 (Intro.) and I, 68–70 ('The Fairy Race'), says every seven years rather than every year.

42. See Kennedy, *Legendary Fictions*, pp. 121–2. Bantry, Co. Cork, is at the head of Bantry Bay.

43. [Yeats's note:] The trooping fairies wear green jackets, the solitary ones red. On the red jacket of the Lepracaun, according to McAnally, are seven rows of buttons – seven buttons in each row. On the western coast, he says, the red jacket is covered by a frieze one, and in Ulster the creature wears a cocked hat, and when he is up to anything unusually mischievous, leaps on to a wall and spins, balancing himself on the point of the hat with his heels in the air. McAnally tells how once a peasant saw a battle between the green jacket fairies and the red. When the green jackets began to win, so delighted was he to see the green above the red, he gave a great shout. In a moment all vanished and he was flung into the ditch.[43a]

43a. David Rice McAnally, Jr (1810–95), *Irish Wonders: The Ghosts, Giants, Pookas, Demons, Leprechawns, Banshees, Fairies, Witches, Widows, Old Maids, and Other Marvels of the Emerald Isle: Popular Tales as Told by the People* (London: Ward, Lock, 1888), pp. 142, 140, 141.

44. Nicholas O'Kearney, Introduction (1855) to *Feis Tighe Chonain Chinn-Shleibhe; or, The Festivities at the House of Conan of Ceann-Sleibhe, in the County of Clare*, Transactions of the Ossianic Society, 2 (1854) (publ. Dublin: O'Daly, for the Ossianic Society, 1855) 17.

45. Croker, *Fairy Legends* (1825) p. 214 (endnote to 'The Little Shoe'); Croker places it in Kilkenny, not Tipperary.
46. O'Kearney, *Festivities*, p. 19: 'Clobhar-ceann'.
47. Thomas Crofton Croker, *Fairy Legends and Traditions of the South of Ireland*, 2nd ser., 2 vols in 1 (London: Murray, 1828) ı, 109 (endnote to 'Hanlon's Mill' [1827]).
48. Untraced; the index of *The Times* (London) for 1807 does not mention such an incident.
49. [Two notes by Yeats:]

Banshee's Cry.
Mr and Mrs S. C. Hall give the following notation of the cry:[49a]

Omens.
   We have other omens beside the Banshee and the Dullahan and the Coach-a-Bower. I know one family where death is announced by the cracking of a whip. Some families are attended by phantoms of ravens or other birds. When McManus, of '48 celebrity, was sitting by his dying brother, a bird of vulture-like appearance came through the window and lighted on the breast of the dying man. The two watched in terror, not daring to drive it off. It crouched there, bright-eyed, till the soul left the body. It was considered a most evil omen. Lefanu worked this into a tale.[49b] I have good authority for tracing its origin to McManus and his brother.

49a. Samuel Carter Hall and Anna Maria Fielding Hall, *Ireland: Its Scenery, Character, &c.* (1st edn 1841–3), new edn (London: Virtue, 1860) ııı, 106.
49b. Terence Bellew MacManus (1823–60), Young Irelander and Fenian, joined William Smith O'Brien in the unsuccessful Young Ireland rising at Ballingarry, Co. Tipperary, in July 1848.
      The Irish novelist Joseph Sheridan LeFanu (1814–73) used an owl in a similar scene in his story 'The Watcher', in *Ghost Stories and Tales of Mystery* (Dublin: McGlashan, 1851), pp. 54–9; slightly revised as 'The Familiar', in *In a Glass Darkly* (London: Bentley, 1872) ı, 193–202.
50. Lady Wilde, *Ancient Legends*, ı, 225 ('The Dead'): 'In the Islands. . . . they also forbid crying for the dead until three hours have passed by, lest the wail of the mourners should waken the dogs who are waiting to devour the souls of men before they can reach the throne of God.' Lady Wilde also mentioned this in her introduction (ı, 15–16).
51. Lady Wilde, *Ancient Legends*, ı, 222 ('The Dead').

52. Joseph Ferguson, 'Parish of Ballymoyer [Co. Armagh]', in *A Statistical Account of Ireland*, comp. William Shaw Mason (Dublin: Cumming, 1816) II, 83: 'A girl chasing a butterfly was chid by her companions, saying, "that may be the soul of your grandfather." Upon enquiry it was found, that a butterfly hovering near a corpse, was regarded as a sign of its everlasting happiness.'

53. [Yeats's note:] The last trial for witchcraft in Ireland – there were never very many – is thus given in MacSkimin's *History of Carrickfergus*: '"†1711, March 31st, Janet Mean, of Braid-island; Janet Latimer, Irish-quarter, Carrickfergus; Janet Millar, Scotch-quarter, Carrickfergus; Margaret Mitchel, Kilroot; Catharine M'Calmond, Janet Liston, *alias* Seller, Elizabeth Seller, and Janet Carson, the four last from Island Magee, were tried here, in the County of Antrim Court, for witchcraft."

'Their alleged crime was tormenting a young woman, called Mary Dunbar, about eighteen years of age, at the house of James Hattridge, Island Magee, and at other places to which she was removed. The circumstances sworn on the trial were as follows:

'"The afflicted person being, in the month of February, 1711, in the house of James Hattridge, Island Magee (which had been for some time believed to be haunted by evil spirits), found an apron on the parlour floor, that had been missing some time, tied with *five strange knots*, which she loosened.

'"On the following day she was suddenly seized with a violent pain in her thigh, and afterwards fell into fits and ravings; and, on recovering, said she was tormented by several women, whose dress and personal appearance she minutely described. Shortly after, she was again seized with the like fits, and on recovering she accused five other women of tormenting her, describing them also. The accused persons being brought from different parts of the country, she appeared to suffer extreme fear and additional torture as they approached the house.

'"It was also deposed that strange noises, as of whistling, scratching, etc., were heard in the house, and that a sulphureous smell was observed in the rooms; that stones, turf, and the like were thrown about the house, and the coverlets, etc., frequently taken off the beds and made up in the shape of a corpse; and that a bolster once walked out of a room into the kitchen with a night-gown about it! It likewise appeared in evidence that in some of her fits three strong men were scarcely able to hold her in the bed; that at times she vomited feathers, cotton yarn, pins, and buttons; and that on one occasion she slid off the bed and was laid on the floor, as if supported and drawn by an invincible power. The afflicted person was unable to give any evidence on the trial, being during that time dumb, but had no violent fit during its continuance."

'In defence of the accused, it appeared that they were mostly sober, industrious people, who attended public worship, could repeat the Lord's Prayer, and had been known to pray both in public and private; and that some of them had lately received communion.

'Judge Upton charged the jury, and observed on the regular

attendance of accused at public worship; remarking that he thought it improbable that real witches could so far retain the form of religion as to frequent the religious worship of God, both publicly and privately, which had been proved in favour of the accused. He concluded by giving his opinion "that the jury could not bring them in guilty upon the sole testimony of the afflicted person's visionary images". He was followed by Judge Macarthy, who differed from him in opinion, "and thought the jury might, from the evidence, bring them in guilty", which they accordingly did.

'This trial lasted from six o'clock in the morning till two in the afternoon; and the prisoners were sentenced to be imprisoned twelve months, and to stand four times in the pillory of Carrickfergus.

'Tradition says that the people were much exasperated against these unfortunate persons, who were severely pelted in the pillory with boiled cabbage stalks and the like, by which one of them had an eye beaten out.'[53a]

53a. Samuel M'Skimin (1774–1843), *The History and Antiquities of the County of the Town of Carrickfergus, from the Earliest Records to the Present Time* (1st edn privately printed 1811), 2nd edn (Belfast: Smyth, 1823), pp. 72–3, 74–5: '. . . alias. . . . on their trial . . . apron in the. . . . with the like &c. frequently . . . night gown. . . . an invisible power. . . .'
'. . . received the communion. . . . observed the . . . of the accused on public. . . . boiled eggs, cabbage. . . .' In addition to those changes, Yeats altered the punctuation in twenty-nine instances and the capitalisation of two words. M'Skimin does not identify his source, except to say he is quoting 'from a rare manuscript' (p. 74 n. 1).

54. Lady Wilde, *Ancient Legends*, I, 191–2 ('An Irish Adept of the Islands'): '. . . meat, in. . . . same, merely. . . . Monday; and. . . . dead who have been recently buried turn. . . . off he . . . wife, nor. . . . impart this knowledge. . . . knees, and . . . charity." [paragraph division] Though . . . man he. . . . once; and . . . backwards, as. . . .' Innis Sark (Inishark) is off the coast of Connemara, Co. Galway.

55. Giraldus Cambrensis, *Topography of Ireland*, pp. 79–84 (ch. xix).

56. Kennedy, *Legendary Fictions*, p. 114.

57. [Yeats's note:] '*Tir-na-n-óg*', Mr Douglas Hyde writes, ' "The Country of the Young", is the place where the Irish peasant will tell you *geabhaedh tu an sonas aer pighin*, "you will get happiness for a penny", so cheap and common it will be. It is sometimes, but not often, called *Tir-na-hóige*,† the "Land of Youth". Crofton Croker writes it, *Thierna-na-noge*,[57a] which is an unfortunate mistake of his, *Thierna* meaning a lord, not a country. This unlucky blunder is, like many others of the same sort where Irish words are concerned, in danger of becoming stereotyped, as the name of Iona has been, from mere clerical carelessness.'

57a. Croker, *Fairy Legends* (1825), pp. 321 (section title: 'Thierna na Oge'), 337 (endnote to 'The Legend of Lough Gur').

58. This ancedote from the brief travels in Ireland, 15 May – 17 July 1644, of François le Gouz de la Boullaye (1610?–1669?) is reported in his *The Tour of the French Traveller M. de la Boullaye le Gouz in Ireland, A.D. 1644*, ed. and

tr. Thomas Crofton Croker (London: Boone, 1837) p. 4, which is an excerpt from *Les Voyages et observations du sieur de la Boullaye le Gouz* (Paris, 1653).

59. Aldfrid (Aldfrith, Ealhfrith), King of Northumbria (reigned 685–704), was educated in Ireland, where he was known as Flann Fionn. These are the first and third quatrains of his poem known as 'Prince Aldfrid's Itinerary through Ireland', which he wrote in Irish, using Irish metre. The translation is that of James Clarence Mangan in *Specimens of the Early Native Poetry of Ireland* (see n. 10 above), ed. Montgomery, pp. 61–2: '. . . Inisfail . . . clerics. . . . wheat and . . . feast and. . . .'

60. Giraldus Cambrensis, *Topography of Ireland*, p. 146 (ch. xxxii): 'Our nation may seem barbarous, uncivilized, and cruel, they have always shewn great honour and reverence to their ecclesiastics, and never on any occasion raised their hands against God's saints. But there is now come into a land a people who know how to make martyrs [perhaps an allusion to Thomas à Becket (1118?–70)], and have frequently done it. Henceforth Ireland will have its martyrs, as well as other countries.'

WILLIAM CARLETON

1. Prillisk is just outside the town of Clogher, twenty-four miles south of Omagh, Co. Tyrone.
2. Rann: (Irish) quatrain, verse, or stanza.
3. William Carleton, Introduction to *Traits and Stories of the Irish Peasantry*, new edn (Dublin: Curry, 1843) I, x: '. . . sing it for you; but . . . wife: *the Irish melts into the tune, but the English doesn't.*'

   For the air and for the words, in Irish and English, of the opening verse of 'Bean an Fhir Ruadh' ('The Red-haired Man's Wife'), see John O'Daly, *The Poets and Poetry of Munster: A Selection of Irish Songs by the Poets of the Last Century*, tr. James Clarence Mangan (Dublin: O'Daly, 1849) pp. 166–7. Carleton used the title for a novel, *The Red-Haired Man's Wife*, which he wrote in 1867 and which was published posthumously in 1870 in the *Carlow College Magazine*, with replacements for the portions of the manuscript that had been destroyed in a fire.

4. Carleton was born in 1794, not 1798, on 4 March, according to his tombstone, or 'on Shrove Tuesday, the 20th of February', according to his autobiography in *The Life of William Carleton: Being his Autobiography and Letters; and an Account of his Life and Writings, from the Point at which the Autobiography Breaks Off*, ed. David J. O'Donoghue (London: Downey, 1896) I, 2. A birth date of 1798 was given in *Chambers's Cyclopaedia of English Literature*, ed. Robert Chambers, 4th edn, rev. Robert Carruthers (London and Edinburgh: Chambers, 1892) II, 315 and in the earlier editions.

   For the pitch-cap, an instrument of torture used against Irish rebels in the Rising of 1798, see William E. H. Lecky, *A History of Ireland in the Eighteenth Century* (London: Longmans, Green, 1892) IV, 272: 'Some soldiers of the North Cork Militia are said to have invented the pitched cap of linen or thick brown paper, which was fastened with burning pitch to the victim's head and could not be torn off without tearing the hair or lacerating the skin.'

5. 'Shuile Agra' was published by the Cuala Press in *A Broadside*, 7, no. 5 (Oct 1914) [1]. For 'Trougha' see a note by David J. O'Donoghue to the *Life of William Carleton*, 1, 9n: ' "The Green Woods of Truagh" is the name this air is known by.' Edward Bunting published an air 'The Green Woods of Truigha' in *A General Collection of the Ancient Music of Ireland* (London: Clementi, 1809) 1, 42. Carleton's ballad 'Sir Turlough, or the Church-yard Bride', which is based on a local legend from the barony of Truagh, Co. Monaghan, has the refrain 'By the bonnie green woods of Killeevy'; it was published in the *Dublin Literary Gazette* and collected in *The Ballad Poetry of Ireland*, ed. Charles Gavan Duffy (Dublin: Duffy, 1845) pp. 54–6. The quotations are from Carleton, Introduction to *Traits and Stories* (1843) 1, x, xi: '. . . singing the *Trougha*, or *Shuil agra*, or . . . that song; it makes. . . .'

6. Carleton remarked in his introduction to *Traits and Stories* (1843): 'At this day I am in possession of Irish airs, which none of our best antiquaries in Irish music have ever heard, except through me, and of which neither they nor I myself know the names' (1, xi).

7. Andrew Magrath, the *Mangaire Súgach* ('Jolly Pedlar') (fl. late 18th c.), wrote a popular song to the air of 'Craoibín Aoibhinn Áluinn Óg' ('Fair Excellent Young Maid') in which the opening stanza says that he was invited to Cnoc Firinn in Co. Limerick by Donn, 'chief of the Munster Fairies' (O'Daly, *The Poets and Poetry of Munster*, pp. 20–1).

8. (As Mat Kavanagh) in 'The Hedge School, and the Abduction of Mat Kavanagh' and (as Pat Frayne) in 'Ned M'Keown', *Traits and Stories of the Irish Peasantry* (1830); (as Pat Frayne) in 'Master and Scholar: Being the Wonderful History of "Sam" and Pat Frayne; or, A Thirst after Knowledge', *Illustrated London Magazine*, 2 (1854) 198–206. Charles McGoldrick was model for the schoolmaster in 'The Poor Scholar', *Traits and Stories of the Irish Peasantry*, 2nd ser. (1833).

9. Granard, Co. Longford, twelve miles north-west of Longford, is about fifty miles from Clogher.

10. Carleton, Introduction to *Traits and Stories of the Irish Peasantry*, new edn (Dublin: Curry, 1843) 1, xiv: 'Oh, why . . . go? maybe . . . again!'

11. Lough Derg, Co. Donegal; see p. 240, note 17 below.

12. *The Adventures of Gil Blas of Santillane* (1715–35), a picaresque novel by Alain René Le Sage.

13. Ten miles south-west of Dundalk, Co. Louth.

14. The farmer was Pierce Murphy; the Lynch family was burned in Wildgoose Lodge, four miles from Carrickmacross, Co. Monaghan; the ringleader, Paddy Devaun (Patrick 'Devann' in Carleton's story 'Wildgoose Lodge' and endnote), was executed at the village of Correagh, Co. Louth. The quotations are from Carleton's autobiography in *Life of William Carleton* (1, 135: 'God be merciful to the soul of my poor marthyr') and his endnote to 'Wildgoose Lodge', in *Traits and Stories* (1844) 11, 336: 'Poor Paddy!' Yeats included 'Wildgoose Lodge' in *Stories from Carleton*, pp. 183–99, and in *Representative Irish Tales* (1891) 1, 197–232.

The Ribbon Societies, which began in 1826, were local agrarian secret societies that used intimidation and violence to protect tenant-farmers from exploitation by landowners and to protest the payment of tithes.

15. Caesar Otway (1779?–1842), Protestant minister, travel writer, and editor of the *Christian Examiner*, the *Dublin Penny Journal* and the *Dublin University Magazine*. William (and later John) Rigby were gun-makers in Suffolk Street, Dublin.

16. *The Purgatory of Saint Patrick* (*El Purgatorio de San Patricio*), a verse drama by the Spanish dramatist and poet Pedro Calderón de la Barca (1600–81). An English translation by Denis Florence was published in 1853.

17. 'A Pilgrimage to Patrick's Purgatory', *Christian Examiner and Church of Ireland Magazine*, 6 (1828) 268–86, 343–62; repr. as 'Lough Dearg Pilgrim' in *Father Butler: The Lough Dearg Pilgrim, being Sketches of Irish Manners* (Dublin: Curry, 1829) pp. 201–302. For Otway and the revisions see Barbara Hayley, *Carleton's Traits and Stories and the 19th Century Anglo-Irish Tradition* (Gerrards Cross, Bucks: Smythe, 1983) pp. 334ff.

18. *Traits and Stories* (1830 and 1833).

19. *Fardorougha the Miser; or, The Convicts of Lisnamona* (Dublin: Curry, 1839); published in serial form 1837–8 in the *Dublin University Magazine*.

20. *Valentine M'Clutchy, the Irish Agent; or, Chronicles of the Castle Cumber Property* (Dublin: Duffy, 1845).

21. Thomas Osborne Davis (1814–45), Irish poet and journalist, was a leader of the Young Ireland movement, which fostered political and cultural Irish nationalism through a successful weekly newspaper, *The Nation*, which Davis helped found, and the inexpensive books in the Duffy's Library of Ireland series; see p. 246, note 78 below. James Hardiman's *Irish Minstrelsy; or, Bardic Remains of Ireland*, 2 vols (London: Robins, 1831), which included English translations, was one of the important early collection of Irish poems and songs; see, for example, Samuel Ferguson (1810–86), Irish poet and antiquarian, 'Appendix to Articles on Hardiman's Minstrelsy', *Dublin University Magazine*, 4 (Nov 1834) 530–42.

22. *Art Maguire: or, The Broke Pledge: A Narrative* (Dublin: Duffy, 1845) (based on an earlier short story, 'The Broken Oath', published 1828 in the *Christian Examiner*); *Para Sastha; or, The History of Paddy Go-Easy and his Wife Nancy*, Duffy's Library of Ireland, no. 6 (Dublin: Duffy, 1845); *Rody the Rover; or, The Ribbonman*, Duffy's Library of Ireland, no. 5 (Dublin: Duffy, 1845).

23. The Irish novelist John Banim died in 1842; see pp. 41–5 above for Yeats's biographical sketch of him, in *Representative Irish Tales* (1891). 'Tubber Derg, or the Red Well', *Traits and Stories* (1833) (expanded version of 'The Landlord and Tenant, an Authentic Story', published April 1831 in the *National Magazine*); 'The Dream of a Broken Heart', [*Dublin*] *University Review and Quarterly Magazine*, 1 (1833) 341–62.

24. Charles J. Kickham, *For the Old Land: A Tale of Twenty Years Ago* (Dublin: Gill, 1886), chs viii (excerpt)–xi; rev. edn (Dublin: Gill, 1904) pp. 66–90. Yeats chose that scene as the single piece by Kickham in *Representative Irish Tales* (1891).

25. *The Black Prophet: A Tale of the Irish Famine* (Dublin: Duffy; Belfast: Simms and M'Intyre, 1847); published in serial form 1846 in the *Dublin University Magazine*.

REPRESENTATIVE IRISH TALES

1. Thomas Crofton Croker (1798–1854), Samuel Lover (1797–1868), Charles James Lever (1806–72), William Carleton (1794–1869), Charles J. Kickham (1828–82), John Banim (1798–1842) and Michael Banim (1796–1874).
2. A Hell Fire Club was founded in 1735 in Dublin by Richard Parsons, Earl of Rosse. Yeats knew the following account by John Edward Walsh in *Sketches of Ireland Sixty Years Ago* (Dublin: McGlashan, 1847) pp. 11–12:

    Among the gentry of the period was a class called 'Bucks,' whose whole enjoyment, and the business of whose life seemed to consist in eccentricity and violence. Some of the Bucks associated together under the name of the 'Hell-fire Club;' and among other infernal proceedings, it is reported that they set fire to the apartment in which they met, and endured the flames with incredible obstinacy, till they were forced out of the house; in derision, as they asserted, of the threatened torments of a future state. On other occasions, in mockery of religion, they administered to one another the sacred rites of the church in a manner too indecent for description.

3. Samuel Lover, 'Barny O'Reirdon, the Navigator', *Legends and Stories of Ireland*, 2nd ser. (London: Baldwin and Cradock, 1834); Yeats included this story in *Representative Irish Tales*.
4. Samuel Lover's novel *Handy Andy: A Tale of Irish Life* (London: Lover, 1842).
5. Yeats included Lover's poem 'The "Whistlin' Thief"' in *BIV*.
6. Sidhe: fairies.
7. Croker, 'The Priest's Supper' and 'Daniel O'Rourke', in *Fairy Legends and Traditions of the South of Ireland* [1st ser.] (London: Murray, 1825) pp. 37–46, 277–94. For 'gods of the earth', see pp. 10 and 233, note 33 above.
8. Croker, 'The Confessions of Tom Bourke', in *Fairy Legends* (1825) pp. 105–36. Yeats also included this story in *FFT* (1888).
9. Dullahans: headless coachmen: Thivishes: ghosts. Sowlths: formless, luminous spirits. Bowas: banshees. Water Sheries: will-o'-the-wisp spirits. See pp. 63–5 above.
10. [Samuel Ferguson], 'Father Tom and the Pope: or, A Night at the Vatican', *Blackwood's Magazine*, 43 (May 1838) 614–17. This story was sometimes attributed, as by Yeats here, to William Maginn (1794–1842) or to John Fisher Murray (1811–65). Father Matthew Russell mentioned Yeats's misattribution in a review in the *Irish Monthly*, 9 (July 1891) 379

(*CL1* 187 n. 4); Yeats subsequently attributed it to Ferguson (Yeats to the Editor of the Dublin *Daily Express*, 27 Feb 1895, *CL1* 441–2; see also 'Irish National Literature, IV: A List of the Best Irish Books', *UP1*, 386). For Father Tom Maguire, see p. 247, note 94 below.

11. William Carleton, *Traits and Stories of the Irish Peasantry* (1830 and 1833).

12. Maria Edgeworth, *Castle Rackrent* (London: Johnson, 1800).

13. Maria Edgeworth, *The Absentee*, in *Tales of Fashionable Life*, vols. V and VI (London: Johnson, 1812). See also note 47 below.

14. See p. 240, note 15 above.

15. Rath: prehistoric hill fort. For an expanded definition, see p. 61 above.

16. William Carleton, 'The Poor Scholar', 'Tubber Derg, or the Red Well' (1831), and 'Wildgoose Lodge' (1830), in *Traits and Stories*, 2nd ser. (1833).

17. Samuel Ferguson (1810–86), Irish poet and antiquarian. For Thomas Osborne Davis see p. 240, note 21 above.

18. *Fardorougha the Miser; or The Convicts of Lisnamona* (Dublin: Curry, 1839).

19. See Yeats's note on Tír-na-nÓg, the Irish folk paradise, the Country of the Young, in *FFT*, p. 237, note 57 above, where he acknowledges this quotation from Douglas Hyde.

20. *The Black Prophet: A Tale of the Irish Famine* (Dublin: Duffy; Belfast: Simms and M'Intyre, 1847); published in serial form 1846 in the *Dublin University Magazine*.

21. *Willy Reilly and His Dear Colleen Bawn: A Tale Founded upon Fact* (London: Hope, 1855).

22. *Valentine M'Clutchy, the Irish Agent; or, Chronicles of the Castle Cumber Property* (Dublin: Duffy, 1845).

23. *Tales by the O'Hara Family* was the series title for many of the works of John and Michael Banim.

24. *Tales by the O'Hara Family: The Nowlans, and Peter of the Castle*, 2nd ser. (London: Colburn, 1826).

25. A character in *The Mayor of Wind-Gap, and Canvassing* (London: Saunders and Otley, 1835); see p. 45 above and p. 246, note 71 below.

26. In *Tales, by the O'Hara Family* [1st ser.] (London: Simpkin and Marshall, 1825).

27. Gerald Griffin (1803–40).

28. *The Collegians; or, The Colleen Bawn: A Tale of Garryowen* (London: Saunders and Otley, 1829); Yeats chose an excerpt from ch. 16 for *Representative Irish Tales*.

29. Charles Kickham, *Sally Cavanagh; or, The Untenanted Graves: A Tale of Tipperary* (Dublin: Kelly, 1869).

30. *Knocknagow; or, The Homes of Tipperary* (Dublin, 1873).

31. For the Young Ireland movement of 1842–8, see p. 240, note 21 above and p. 271, note 6 below.

32. Pat Gogarty (*c.* 1849–91), of Whitehall, between Greenhills and Clondalkin, Co. Dublin, five miles south-west of Dublin; see Yeats's letters to Katharine Tynan, 14 Mar [1888], and to John O'Leary [8 Aug 1889] (*CL1* 54, 180).

33. The sixteenth-century alchemist and physician Paracelsus often

emphasized the connection of macrocosm and microcosm. The quotation is untraced; Yeats later used it in a letter to the editor of *United Ireland*, 14 May 1892 (*UP1* 224, *CL1* 299), as a motto on the title-page of *The Countess Kathleen and Various Legends and Lyrics* (London: Unwin; Boston: Roberts, 1892) (Wade, nos 6, 7; see Yeats to T. Fisher Unwin, [?]28 Apr [1892], *CL1* 293–4), and as an epigraph to *Poems* (London: Unwin, 1895) p. iv (verso of title-page; Wade, no. 15) and *Poems* (London: Unwin, 1899) p. vi (verso of title-page; Wade, no. 17).

34. Her parents lived in Hare Hatch, a hamlet near Maidenhead; she was born at her grandfather's house in Black Bourton, sixteen miles west of Oxford. The copy-text reads: 'Hare Hack'.

35. Prominent French deists included Voltaire (1694–1778); for a time, Denis Diderot (1713–84); and, to some extent, Jean Jacques Rousseau (1712–78).

36. Untraced. He made several similar statements in his memoirs, written 1808–10, published as the first volume of *Memoirs of Richard Lovell Edgeworth, Esq. Begun by Himself and Concluded by his Daughter, Maria Edgeworth* (London: Hunter, 1820).

37. Thomas Day's *History of Sandford and Merton* (3 vols, 1783–9), a novel for young readers, reflects his admiration for Rousseau's naturalism. Day was a close friend of Richard Lovell Edgeworth.

38. Maria Edgeworth was fifteen years old in 1782 when her family went to Edgeworthstown (or Mostrim), Co. Longford, eight miles east of Longford.

39. Squireens: (Irish slang) petty squires. See the amusing definition in John Edward Walsh, *Sketches of Ireland Sixty Years Ago* (see p. 241, note 2 above) p. 34: '. . . A class of men abounding in Ireland, called "squireens." They were the younger sons or connexions of respectable families, having little or no patrimony of their own, but who scorned to *demean* themselves by any *useful* or profitable pursuit.'

40. The Irish Rising of 1798.

41. Her first published work, *Letters for Literary Ladies, and An Essay on the Noble Science of Self-Justification* (London: Johnson, 1795), advocated advanced learning for women. Her second published work was a collection of stories, *The Parent's Assistant; or, Stories for Children* (London: Johnson, 1796).

42. *Moral Tales for Young People* (London: Johnson, 1801); *Harry and Lucy: Parts I and II of Early Lessons, Rosamond: Parts III–V of Early Lessons*, and *Frank: Parts VI–IX of Early Lessons* (London: Johnson, 1801).

43. The Act of Union (1800) dissolved the Irish Parliament.

44. *Belinda* (London: Johnson, 1801). *Essay on Irish Bulls* (London: Johnson, 1802) reports and explains Irish comic verbal blunders or 'bulls'. The quotation is from *Memoirs of Richard Lovell Edgeworth, Esq.*, II, 336: '. . . to shew the . . . eloquence, wit, and. . . .'

45. Abraham Niclas Clewberg Edelcrantz (1756–1821), administrator of royal theatres for King Gustav III of Sweden. Chevalier Edelcrantz met Maria Edgeworth while he was travelling through Europe to examine new inventions that might be used in Sweden.

46. *Popular Tales* (London: Johnson, 1805); *Leonora* (London: Johnson, 1806).
47. *Tales of Fashionable Life*, 6 vols (London: Johnson, 1809–12), I: *Ennui* (1809), II: *Almeria, Madame de Fleury. The Dun* (1809), III: *Manoeuvring* (1809), IV: *Vivian* (1812), V: *Emile de Coulanges. The Absentee* (1812), VI: *The Absentee* [concluded] (1812).
48. Thomas Babington Macaulay (1800–59); see George Otto Trevelyan, *The Life and Letters of Lord Macaulay* (London: Longmans, Green, 1876) II, 234: 'Macaulay on one occasion pronounces that the scene in the Absentee, where Lord Colambre discovers himself to his tenantry and to their oppressor, is the best thing of the sort since the opening of the Twenty-second book of the Odyssey', where Odysseus reveals himself to the suitors.
49. Byron met her at the London home of Sir Humphry Davy on 17 May 1813; Jeanie Deans is the pure-hearted and somewhat plain-featured young heroine in Sir Walter Scott's *The Heart of Midlothian* (1818). The quotation is from Byron's journal, 19 Jan 1821: *Byron's Letters and Journals*, ed. Leslie A. Marchand (Cambridge, Mass.: Harvard University Press, 1978) VIII, 30 ('. . . "Jeanie Deans"-looking bodie," as we Scotch say – and, if. . . .').
50. Richard Lovell Edgeworth's note to the reader is dated 31 May 1817, in Maria Edgeworth, *Harrington: A Tale; and Ormond: A Tale* (London: Johnson, 1817) I, i–iv.
51. *Memoirs of Richard Lovell Edgeworth, Esq.* (see note 36 above).
52. *Harry and Lucy Concluded: The Last Part of Early Lessons* (London: Hunter, 1825); *Orlandino* (Edinburgh: Chambers, 1848).
53. The Great Famine of 1845 to 1848. Yeats here followed the account in the Maria Edgeworth entry of the *Dictionary of National Biography*: 'Some of her admirers in Boston sent a hundred and fifty barrels of flour addressed to "Miss Edgeworth for her poor." The porters who carried it ashore refused to be paid, and she sent to each of them a woollen comforter knitted by herself' (VI, 382). For a more accurate version see Augustus J. C. Hare (ed.), *The Life and Letters of Maria Edgeworth* (London: Arnold, 1894) II, 328: 'The children of Boston . . . raised a subscription for her, and sent a hundred and fifty pounds of flour and rice. They were simply inscribed – "To Miss Edgeworth, for her poor." Nothing, in her long life, ever pleased or gratified her more.' See also Hare's note to the entry for 22 March 1847: 'The Irish porters who carried the seed corn sent from Philadelphia to the shore for embarkation refused to be paid.'
54. 'That Miss Edgeworth was worthy of enthusiasm, but she got lost in dreary usefulness.' This remark by the French writer Mme Anne Louise Germaine de Staël (1766–1817) was reported by Étienne Dumont (1759–1829), French utilitarian, penologist and man of letters, in a letter to Maria Edgeworth, 1 Nov 1813, quoted in Grace A. L. Oliver, *A Study of Maria Edgeworth*, 3rd edn (Boston: Williams, 1882) p. 352: '. . . était. . . .' See also Marilyn Butler, *Maria Edgeworth: A Literary Biography* (Oxford: Clarendon Press, 1972) p. 223. For *Tales of Fashionable Life* see note 47 above.
55. Untraced.

56. Untraced.
57. *Father Connell* (London: Newby and Boone, 1842).
58. Earlier students of Kilkenny College included Jonathan Swift (1667–1745), William Congreve (1670–1729), George Farquhar (1678–1707) and George Berkeley (1685–1753); the school is described in 'The Fetches', in *Tales, by the O'Hara Family*, [1st ser.], 3 vols (London: Simpkin and Marshall, 1825) II, 135–43.
59. *The Nowlans* (London: Colburn, 1826).
60. *The Celt's Paradise* (poem) (London: Warren, 1821).
61. *Damon and Pythias*, a tragedy in five acts, performed with William Charles Macready (1793–1873) as Damon and Charles Kemble (1775–1854) as Pythias. Banim's script was revised by Richard Lalor Sheil (1791–1851), Irish dramatist and Roman Catholic politician. According to a review in *The Times*, 29 May 1821 (p. 3), 'the tragedy was received throughout with very great applause'. It was acted seven times and was published (London: Warren, 1821). John Genest described it as 'indifferent' in *Some Account of the English Stage from the Restoration in 1660 to 1830* (Bath: Carrington, 1832) IX, 111.
62. In fact he was twenty-three years old.
63. Untraced.
64. 22 Dec 1822, quoted in Patrick Joseph Murray, *The Life of John Banim, the Irish Novelist* (New York: Sadlier, 1869) p. 127: '. . . sir, if . . . and tease the brain, as wool-combers tease wool . . . spit could not turn.'
65. *The Revelations of the Dead Alive* (London: Simpkin and Marshall, 1824). 'Scin Laeca' is an 'outer casing, or emanation, or larva' that a person 'can (involuntarily in most cases) project' – Patrick Kennedy, *Legendary Fictions of the Irish Celts* (London: Macmillan, 1866) p. 188.
66. *Tales, by the O'Hara Family* (1825); the introductory letter (II, 111–34) to 'The Fetches' is signed 'Abel O'Hara'. *The Boyne Water: A Tale* (London: Simpkin and Marshall, 1826). *The Denounced; or, The Last Baron of Crana* (London: Colburn and Bentley, 1830). *The Croppy: A Tale of 1798* (London: Colburn, 1828).
67. Banim, in the story 'The Fetches', defined the term: 'In Ireland, a Fetch is the supernatural facsimile of some individual, which comes to insure to its original, a happy longevity, or immediate dissolution: if seen in the morning the one event is predicted; if, in the evening, the other' – *Tales, by the O'Hara Family* (1825) II, 128.

    The play was *The Death Fetch; or, the Student of Gottingen*, performed at the English Opera House, London, 25 July – 5 Aug 1826. *The Times*, 26 July 1826, described it as 'a new operatic romance . . . by Mr. Benham [*sic*]' (p. 2, col. e). The comment about fairies is in that same review and is accurately quoted in Murray, *Life of John Banim*, p. 231: '. . . perpetuation of the idea of such absurd. . . .'

68. 20 Jan 1832, quoted in Murray, *Life of John Banim*, p. 232: '. . . gone, and . . . suffer agony in. . . .'
69. John Sterling (1806–44), of whom Thomas Carlyle wrote a biography, *The Life of John Sterling* (1851, 1852); his father, Edward Sterling (1773–1847), was an editorial writer (famed as 'the Thunderer') for *The*

Times and was Irish. A subscription for Banim was proposed in an unsigned article, 'Mr. Banim', in *The Times*, 14 Jan 1833 (p. 3, col. e). Banim's letter of thanks, dated 20 Jan 1833, was published in *The Times*, 24 Jan 1833 (p. 5, col. b).

70. Lord Mayor Archer presided at the Banim subscription meeting in Dublin, 31 Jan 1833. For Richard Lalor Sheil, who gave the opening speech, see note 61 above.

71. The title character of Michael Banim's *The Mayor of Wind-Gap* (1835) is the old man Maurteen Maher; see Michael Banim, Introduction to *The Mayor of Wind-Gap and Canvassing*, new edn (Dublin: Duffy, 1865) p. iii.

72. *Father Connell* (London: Newby and Boone, 1842).

73. 'Soggarth Aroon' ('Priest Dear') is the only poem by John Banim that Yeats included either in his article 'Popular Ballad Poetry of Ireland' (1887–8, publ. 1889; *UP1* 159–61) or in *BIV*.

74. Because this biographical sketch of Carleton is a direct condensation of Yeats's earlier introduction to *Stories from Carleton* (1889), I have annotated here only the few items that are additions to the earlier introduction, pp. 23–8 above.

75. *The Life and Adventures of J[ames] Freney . . . with an Account of Several Other Noted Highway Men* (Dublin: Warren, n.d.). *Irish Rogues and Rapparees* is mentioned, together with a chap-book on Freney, in a list of reading books used in the hedge schools, by Hely Dutton, *Statistical Survey of the Country of Clare with Observations on the Means of Improvement* (Dublin: Dublin Society, 1808) p. 236; it is also mentioned by Patrick Kennedy in *The Fireside Stories of Ireland* (Dublin: M'Glashan and Gill, and Patrick Kennedy, 1870) p. 167, note to p. 98. *Laugh and Be Fat . . . Being the Best Collection of Funny Jokes, and Humorous Tales*, 10th edn (Dublin, 1783).

76. Votheen (voteen): religious devotee, usually applied only to foolish or hypocritical devotees.

77. *The Emigrants of Ahadarra: A Tale of Irish Life* (Belfast: Simms and M'Intyre, 1848). For *Valentine M'Clutchy* and *The Black Prophet*, see notes 20 and 25 above.

78. Thomas Osborne Davis (see p. 240, note 21 above) is sometimes credited with founding the 'Library of Ireland' series of shilling volumes on Irish topics; in fact the series was founded by Charles Gavan Duffy (1816–1903), an Irish publisher, journalist, politician and poet, in 1845. See Charles Gavan Duffy, *Young Ireland: A Fragment of Irish History: 1840–1845* (1880; repr. Dublin: Gill, 1884), pp. 241n and 287.

79. *Parra Sastha; or, The History of Paddy Go-Easy*, Duffy's Library of Ireland, no. 6 (Dublin: Duffy, 1845). The Rev. Theobald Mathew (1790–1856) was a prominent Irish temperance leader.

80. *Redmond, Count O'Hanlon, the Irish Rapparee: An Historical Tale* (Dublin: Duffy, 1862). Redmond O'Hanlon (d. 1681) led a band of outlaws in Counties Tyrone and Armagh after he was dispossessed of his property under the Cromwellian settlement. The French called him Count O'Hanlon.

81. *Rody the Rover; or, The Ribbonman*, Duffy's Library of Ireland, no. 5 (Dublin: Duffy, 1845); for the Ribbon Societies, see pp. 239–40, note 14 above.

82. *Willy Reilly and His Dear Coleen Bawn;* see note 21 above.

83. 'Rory O'More; or, Good Omens', 'Molly Carew', and 'Widow Machree', *The Poetical Works of Samuel Lover* (New York: Sadlier, 1884) pp. 381–2, 305–7, 345–7.

84. Miniature portrait (1831) of Nicolò Paganini (1782–1840, Italian violinist and composer), on ivory, 15.5 × 15.2 cm; exhibited at the Royal Academy, London, 1832 (no. 910). Paganini was in Dublin 29 Aug–*c.* 18 Sep and 6 Oct 1831.

85. *Rory O'More: A National Romance* (London: Bentley and Sons, 1837). For *Handy Andy* see note 4 above.

86. His ballad 'Rory O'More' dates from 1826, the three-act play from 1837, and the novel from 1842.

87. *The Kerry Post on St Valentine's Day* was exhibited at the Royal Academy, London in 1862 (no. 593) and at the Royal Hibernian Academy, Dublin in 1863. Although that was his last painting exhibited at the Royal Academy, he continued to paint and to exhibit. His last exhibited paintings were two views of Pevensey Castle, near Eastbourne, Sussex; they were shown at the Exhibition of Works of Living Artists, Glasgow Institute of Fine Arts, 1866 (nos. 274 and 313): *Remains of the North Curtain and Great Nor'-West Tower of William the Conqueror's Castle of Pevensey* (1865?) and *Ruins of the Barbican and Ivy Tower of Pevensey Castle* (1865?). In 1867, the year before his death, he painted *Mont Orgueil Castle*, the castle being located near his house in Jersey. See Samuel Lover to Arthur James Symington, 6 Jan 1867, quoted in Andrew James Symington, *Samuel Lover: A Biographical Sketch* (New York: Harper, 1880) p. 206.

88. Maginn, under the pseudonym 'O. P.', first contributed to *Blackwood's Edinburgh Magazine* 'Chevy Chase; a Poem – Idem Latinae Redditum' (6 [Nov 1819] 199–201) and 'Chevy Chase, Fitte the Second; Idem Latinae Redditum' (7 [June 1829] 323–9).

89. Jeremiah (or James) Joseph Callanan (1795–1829) collected and translated old ballads and legends during 1823–7.

90. In 1828 Maginn became assistant editor of the *Standard*, an ultra-Tory evening newspaper. In the autumn of 1829 he was the founding editor of *Fraser's Magazine*.

91. William Maginn, *Homeric Ballads, with Translations and Notes* (London: Parker, 1850); they had been published in periodicals beginning in January 1838. Matthew Arnold's comment is in 'On Translating Homer' (1860), in *On the Classical Tradition*, ed. R. H. Super (Ann Arbor: University of Michigan Press, 1960) p. 131: '. . . poems in their own way'.

92. Quoted in Alfred Webb, *A Compendium of Irish Biography* (Dublin: Gill, 1878) p. 323: '. . . talked on Seneca. . . .'

93. Maginn was a friend of William Makepeace Thackeray, whose novel *Pendennis* (1848–50) is largely autobiographical.

94. For the authorship of the anonymously published story 'Father Tom and the Pope: or, A Night at the Vatican', see note 10 above. In April 1827 Father Tom Maguire (1792–1847), parish priest of the village of Ballinamore, Co. Leitrim, and the Rev. Richard T. P. Pope, a noted evangelical controversialist, held a six-day debate at Dublin on points of

religion. Their debate, which drew wide public attention, was chaired by Daniel O'Connell (1775–1847) and, on the Protestant side, by Admiral Robert D. Oliver (1766–1850); it was published in *The Authentic Report of the Discussion, which Took Place at the Lecture-room of the Dublin Institution* (New York: Sadlier, 1827).

95. John Wilson Croker (1780–1857), Irish politician and essayist, drew the wrath of Thomas Babington Macaulay (1800–59) in a lengthy review, in the *Edinburgh Review*, 54 (Sep 1831) 1–38, of Croker's annotated edition of James Boswell's *The Life of Samuel Johnson* (London: Murray, 1831). Macaulay attacked 'the ignorance or carelessness of Mr. Croker, with respect to facts and dates' (p. 1) and filled the next fifteen pages with examples. Eighteen years later Croker returned the favour with a blistering and notorious review, in the *Quarterly Review*, 84 (Mar 1849) 549–630, of the first two volumes of Macaulay's *The History of England from the Accession of James II*.

96. *Fairy Legends and Traditions of the South of Ireland* [1st ser.] (London: Murray, 1825) and 2nd ser., 2 vols in 1 (London: Murray, 1828). The 1825 volume, which was anonymous, included folk-tales written by Croker's Irish friends after he had lost his manuscript. These unacknowledged contributors were Joseph Humphreys, Thomas Keightley, R. Adolphus Lynch, Maginn (whose 'Daniel O'Rourke' is usually judged the best story in the book) and Richard Pigot.

97. 'The Confessions of Tom Bourke', from *Fairy Legends* (1825) pp. 105–33. 'Keetings' is an error for Thomas Keightley, an Irish writer and journalist in London who befriended Croker in 1824. Keightley's books include *Fairy Mythology* (1828) and *Tales and Popular Fictions* (1834).

98. Alfred John Webb, *A Compendium of Irish Biography* (Dublin: Gill, 1878) p. 105. Sir Walter Scott's journal, 20 Oct 1826, reads: '. . . hawk, and of very prepossessing manners. Something . . .' – *The Journal of Sir Walter Scott* (New York: Harper, 1891) I, 278, and rev. edn (Edinburgh: Oliver and Boyd, 1950) p. 251.

99. This play, which Griffin began writing in 1821, was never produced or published; it is now lost.

100. Gerald Griffin, 'The Knight of the Sheep', in *Holland Tide, The Aylmers and Bally-Aylmer, The Hand and Word, The Barber of Bantry, &c.* (Dublin: Duffy, 1857) pp. 325–42.

101. *Tales of the Munster Festivals* (London: Saunders and Otley, 1826–7).

102. *The Collegians; or, The Colleen Bawn:* see note 28 above. Dion Boucicault's play *The Colleen Bawn* was written in 1860 and first performed in 1861.

103. *The Wonders* is an error for Griffin's historical novel *The Invasion* (London: Saunders and Otley, 1832), which is set in the eighth century. 'Foster' may be a mistake for John Forster (1812–76), English biographer, editor and historian. Forster had met Griffin as a classmate at University College, London in 1828 and, after Griffin's death, helped to arrange the production of *Gisippus*; see note 104 below. Forster, in his theatrical reviews in *The Examiner*, praised Griffin's play and regretted that Griffin had been neglected during life ('Theatrical Examiner: Drury Lane', 26 Feb 1842, pp. 133–4, and 26 Mar 1842, p. 197).

104. Griffin's *Gisippus* (written 1824) was produced at Drury Lane (not Covent Garden) theatre, London, on 23 Feb 1842, and in Dublin on 30 May 1842, both times with William Charles Macready. *Gisippus* was published the same year (London: Maxwell).

105. Mary Russell Mitford, *Recollections of a Literary Life; or, Books, Places, and People* (London: Bentley, 1852) III, 119.

106. William James Fitzpatrick, in *The Life of Charles Lever*, rev. edn (London: Ward, Lock, [1884]) p. 32, suggested that either the Rev. Richard Torrens Boyle or John Ottiwell could have been the model for Webber in *Charles O'Malley, the Irish Dragoon* (1840–1; Dublin: Curry, 1841).

107. Oliver Goldsmith (1728–74), Irish poet, playwright, essayist and novelist, was at Trinity College, Dublin, from 1744 to 1749; see p. 301, note 10 below, and William James Fitzpatrick, *The Life of Charles Lever* (London: Chapman and Hall, 1879) I, 38–40.

108. The Rev. Samuel Hayman to William James Fitzpatrick, 8 Mar 1876, quoted in William James Fitzpatrick, *The Life of Charles Lever* (London: Chapman and Hall, 1879) I, 54–5: '. . . stranger," said she, "is . . . people. But . . . will never see. . . . you, if. . . . tribe, that . . . away. No! no! You will. . . .'

The scene may have been the Tuscarora Indian reservation, near Niagara Falls, NY, in the spring and summer of 1829.

109. *The Confessions of Harry Lorrequer* (1837 and subsequently; Dublin: Curry, 1839).

110. *Charles O'Malley: The Irish Dragoon:* see note 106 above.

111. Isaac Butt (1813–79); the Rev. William Hamilton Maxwell (1792–1850); Joseph Sheridan Le Fanu (copy-text reads: 'Lefevre') (1814–73), who contributed to the *Dublin University Magazine* from 1864 to 1868; Samuel Ferguson (1810–86).

112. Mullinahone is six miles south-west of Callan, Co. Kilkenny. For Duffy, Davis and *The Nation*, which was founded in 1842 (not 1845), see pp. 240, note 21 and 246, note 78 above.

113. Kickham and his cousin John O'Mahoney (1815–77) supported the short-lived Young Ireland rising, July 1848, led by William Smith O'Brien (1803–64) at Ballingarry, Co. Tipperary, five miles north of Mullinahone. In 1858 O'Mahoney founded the Fenian Brotherhood in the United States.

114. The Irish Confederation was a Young Ireland association, led by William Smith O'Brien, which split from the Repeal Association of Daniel O'Connell in 1847. The Tenant League was founded in 1850; it had collapsed by 1860, when Kickham joined the Irish Republican Brotherhood (IRB), often referred to as the Fenians. Thomas Clarke Luby (1822–1901) was a founding member of the IRB but did not return to Ireland after his imprisonment (1865–71). Kickham was President of the IRB's Supreme Council from the late 1870s until his death. The Supreme Council, instituted in 1869, replaced what had formerly been one-man rule of the IRB by James Stephens. John O'Leary (1830–1907) edited the IRB paper, *The Irish People*, to which Kickham and Luby were chief contributors. He was imprisoned in 1865

and did not return to Ireland until 1885. He was President of the Supreme Council from 1885 until his death. Yeats's reference to a 'triumvirate' of O'Leary, Kickham and Luby probably was based on the 'executive document' that James Stephens gave Luby in 1864 empowering O'Leary, Kickham, and Luby to act on his behalf during his trip to America; it was used as evidence in their trials in 1865–6.

115. Blackrock is a southern suburb of Dublin.

116. Rev. Matthew Russell, Introduction (dated 27 Feb 1887) to Charles J. Kickham, *Knocknagow; or, the Homes of Tipperary*, 18th edn (1879; repr. Dublin: Duffy, 1900) p. ix: 'Children, and women. . . .' Kickham told this to the Irish poet Rose Kavanagh (1861–91); see Hester Sigerson Piatt, 'The Author of "Knocknagow": Some Personal Memories', *Irish Press*, 9 May 1933, repr. in *The Valley near Slievenamon: A Kickham Anthology*, ed. James Maher (Kilkenny: Kilkenny People, 1942) p. 25.

117. Rev. Matthew Russell, Introduction to Kickham, *Knocknagow*, p. xii: 'In the Dublin Exhibition of 1864, he had lingered long before a painting, "the Head of a Cow," by one of the Old Masters, not on account of any subtle genius he discovered in it, but "because it was so like an old cow in Mullinahone."'

118. Charles Kickham, 'St John's Eve' (dated 3 Jan 1868, Woking Prison, Surrey), in *The Valley near Slievenamon: A Kickham Anthology*, p. 67, ll. 5–8:

> Upon the lonely bridge we turn'd,
> And watch'd the roseate-russet hue,
> Till faint and fainter still it burn'd –
> As if 'twere quench'd by the falling dew.

119. For *Sally Cavanagh* see p. 242, note 29 above. *Knocknagow; or, The Homes of Tipperary* (Dublin, Duffy, 1873); *For the Old Land: A Tale of Twenty Years Ago* (Dublin: Gill, 1886).

120. Kickham's ballads 'Patrick Sheehan: A Recruitment Song' (1857) and 'The Irish Peasant Girl' (1859), which begins, 'She lived beside the Anner', are reprinted in *The Valley near Slievenamon: A Kickham Anthology*, ed. James Maher (1942) pp. 88–90, 62–3.

121. Rosa Mulholland (1841–1921) married John T. Gilbert in 1891.

IRISH FAIRY TALES

1. The summit of Benbulben (elev. 1730 ft) lies three miles north of Drumcliff Church and six miles north of Sligo.

2. Biddy Hart was the wife of Michael Hart, the source of a tale 'A Fairy Enchantment', quoted by Yeats in *Irish Fairy Tales* (pp. 49–52) and in the

'Drumcliff and Rosses' section of *The Celtic Twilight* (1893) (*Myth* 90–1);
see Mary H. Thuente, *W. B. Yeats and Irish Folklore* (Dublin: Gill and
Macmillan, 1980) pp. 121, 126–7. Yeats's great-grandfather, John Yeats
(1774–1846), was Rector of Drumcliff, Co. Sligo, from 1811 until his
death.

3. In 'Irish Witch Doctors' (1900), Yeats explained that this is 'a common
   spelll against being overheard' (*UP2* 226).

4. Collooney, Co. Sligo, six miles south of Sligo.

5. Grange, Co. Sligo, nine miles north of Sligo.

6. Rosses Point, Co. Sligo, five miles north-west of Sligo.

7. Clondalkin, Co. Dublin, is five miles west of Dublin. Just before he wrote
   this introduction Yeats had asked his friend Katharine Tynan (1861–
   1931) to send him an account of this peasant woman's vision (*CL1* 260).

8. Lady Jane Francesca Elgee Wilde, 'Seanchan the Bard and the King of
   the Cats', in *Ancient Legends, Mystic Charms, and Superstitions of Ireland*, 2 vols
   (London: Ward and Downey, 1887–8) II, 24–30.

9. Standish James O'Grady, 'Cuchulain is Knighted', in *The Heroic Period*,
   vol. I of *History of Ireland* (London: Sampson Low, Searle, Marston and
   Rivington; Dublin: Ponsonby, 1878) pp. 122–9.

10. Professor Patrick Weston Joyce (1827–1914), 'Fergus and the Air-
    Demons', in *Good and Pleasant Reading* (Dublin: Gill, 1886) [not sighted].

11. Camelot series, no. 32 (London: Walter Scott, 1888).

12. Torlough Carolan (or O'Carolan; 1670–1737), renowned Gaelic
    composer, harpist and poet.

13. In July 1891 Yeats visited his friend Charles Johnston (1867–1931) at
    Ballykilberg, Co. Down, three miles south-west of Downpatrick.

14. Yeats here gave a cross-reference to p. 79 in the anthology, where the
    term '*cohuleen druith*' appears in 'The Lady of Gollerus' (1827), by Thomas
    Crofton Croker, from *Fairy Legends and Traditions of the South of Ireland*, 2nd
    ser., 2 vols in 1 (London: Murray, 1828) I, 13.

15. Croker, 'The Soul Cages' (1827), in *Fairy Legends* (1828) I, 34, repr. by
    Yeats in *FFT* 64.

16. See p. 234, note 43 above.

17. See p. 13 above for 'one shoe maker'.

18. David Rice McAnally, Jr, *Irish Wonders: The Ghosts, Giants, Pookas,
    Demons, Leprechawns, Banshees, Fairies, Witches, Old Maids, and Other Marvels
    of the Emerald Isle: Popular Tales as Told by the People* (London: Ward, Lock,
    1888) pp. 140, 142.

19. See p. 234, note 44 above.

20. In the anthology at pp. 49–52; Yeats listed himself as 'recorder' and
    Michael Hart as 'source' (p. 49).

21. For example, Patrick Weston Joyce, *The Origin and History of Irish Names
    of Places*, 2nd edn (Dublin: McGlashan and Gill, 1870) p. 188:

    Cliodhna [Cleena] is the potent banshee that rules as queen over the
    fairies of south Munster. . . . In the Dinnsenchus there is an ancient
    poetical love story, of which Cleena is the heroine; wherein it is related

that she was a foreigner, and that she was drowned in the harbour of Glandore, near Skibbereen in Cork. In this harbour the sea at certain times, utters a very peculiar, deep, hollow, and melancholy roar among the caverns of the cliffs . . . and this surge has been from time immemorial called *Tonn-Cleena*, Cleena's Wave.

22. The distinguished Irish antiquarian scholar John O'Donovan (1809–61) is quoted from an anonymous article, 'Irish Popular Superstitions. Chapter III. Medical Superstitions, Fairy Lore, and Enchantment', *Dublin University Magazine*, 33 (June 1849) 708: '. . . Leinster, in . . . from Tonn Clenne, at Glandore, to. . . .' Drumaleague presumably refers to the hills in the parish of Dromdaleague (or Drimoleague), seven miles north of Glandore, Co. Cork. Eoghan (Owen) Mór ruled the southern half of Ireland in the second century. Yeats would not have liked to recall that O'Donovan gave a highly sceptical account of an aristocratic Irish friend's encounter in 1820 with a banshee, quoted in William G. Wood-Martin, *Traces of the Elder Faiths of Ireland: A Folklore Sketch: A Handbook of Irish Pre-Christian Traditions* (London: Longmans, Green, 1902) I, 370–1; see also I, 364.

23. On 1 December 1867 Dr Charles Carter Blake (1840–97), a Fellow and Secretary of the Anthropological Society of London, was in south-central Nicaragua, in the Chontales department, which contains La Libertad. The 1871 edition of the *Post Office London Directory* shows no no. 16 in Devonshire Street, Queen's Square. In 1884 C. Carter Blake resided at 28 East Street, Queen's Square, Yeats could have met Blake as a member of the Theosophical Society in London, 1887–90; in the 15 Mar 1889 issue of the Theosophical Society's journal *Luficer*, Blake praised *The Wanderings of Oisin and Other Poems* in an anonymous review (pp. 84–6; quoted in *CL1* 152 n. 5). The musical notation of the banshee's cry here is completely different from the longer one by Mr and Mrs S. C. Hall, which Yeats quoted in 1888 in a note to *FFT*; see pp. 16 and 235, note 49 above.

24. Untraced; for John and Michael Banim, see pp. 41–5 above. They use the term *'banshee'* in 'Crohoore of the Billhook', in *Tales, by the O'Hara Family* [1st ser.], 3 vols (London: Simpkin and Marshall, 1825) I, 122, and 'Banshee' in *The Last Baron of Crana*, in *The Denounced, or, The Last Baron of Crana*, new edn (Dublin: Duffy, 1866) p. 212.

25. Croker, 'Teigue of the Lee' (1827), in *Fairy Legends* (1828) I, 164–77; Yeats included this folk-tale in the anthology, pp. 53–68.

26. A more precise date perhaps is July or even August 1891; see the textual introduction, pp. 320–1.

27. The sources cited are as follows, in order of citation.

Thomas Crofton Croker, *Fairy Legends and Traditions of the South of Ireland* [1st ser.] (London: Murray, 1825) and 2nd ser. (1828).
Lady Wilde, *Ancient Legends* (see note 8 above).
——, *Ancient Cures, Charms, and Usages of Ireland: Contributions to Irish Lore* (London: Ward and Downey, 1890).

Sir William Robert Wilde, *Irish Popular Superstitions* (Dublin: McGlashan, 1852).

McAnally, *Irish Wonders* (see note 18 above).

Lageniensis (Father John O'Hanlan, 1821–1905), *Irish Folklore: Traditions and Superstitions of the Country; with Humorous Tales* (Glasgow: Cameron and Ferguson, [1870]).

Jeremiah Curtin (1835–1906), *Myths and Folk-Lore of Ireland* (Boston, Mass.: Little, Brown, 1890).

Douglas Hyde, *Beside the Fire: A Collection of Irish Gaelic Folk Stories* (London: Nutt, 1890).

——, *Leabhar Sgeulaigheachta* (in Irish) (Dublin: Gill, 1889).

Patrick Kennedy (1801–73), *Legendary Fictions of the Irish Celts* (London: Macmillan, 1866).

——, *The Banks of the Boro: A Chronicle of the County of Wexford* (London: Simpkin, Marshall, 1867).

——, *Evenings in the Duffrey* (Dublin, 1869).

Harry Whitney (Patrick Kennedy), *Legends of Mount Leinster: Tales and Sketches* (London: Lambert, [1855]).

The Royal Fairy Tales; Taken from the Most Polite Authors (Dublin: Cross, 1801).

The Tales of the Fairies, new edn (London: Sabine, [1800?]).

William Carleton, *Traits and Stories of the Irish Peasantry*, [1st ser.], 2 vols (Dublin: Wakeman, 1830) and 2nd ser., 3 vols (Dublin: Wakeman, 1833); new edn with autobiographical intro., 2 vols (Dublin: Curry, 1843–4).

Samuel Lover, *Legends and Stories of Ireland* (Dublin: Wakeman, 1831).

Samuel Carter Hall (1800–99) and Anna Maria Fielding Hall (1800–81), *Ireland: Its Scenery, Character, &c.* (London: How and Parsons, 1841–3).

Lady Henrietta Georgiana Marcia Lascelles (Iremonger) Chatterton (1806–76), *Rambles in the South of Ireland during the Year 1838* (London: Saunders and Otley, 1839).

Gerald Griffin, *Talis Qualis; or Tales of the Jury Room* (London: Maxwell, 1842).

——, *The Collegians; or, The Colleen Bawn: A Tale of Garryowen* (London: Saunders and Otley, 1829).

The Royal Hibernian Tales: Being a Collection of the Most Entertaining Stories Now Extant (Dublin: Warren, [1829?]). This chap-book, which Yeats had previously listed simply as '*The Hibernian Tales*' (pp. 8, 201 above) and '*Hibernian Tales*' (p. 200 above), was his source of the anonymous story 'The Jackdaw'. See Mary H. Thuente, 'A List of Sources', in *Representative Irish Tales*, ed. W. B. Yeats (Gerrards Cross, Bucks: Smythe, 1979) p. 23.

Alicia Lefanu, *Memoirs of the Life and Writings of Mrs. Frances Sheridan* [1724–66] . . . *with Remarks upon a Late Life of the Right Hon. R*[ichard] *B*[rinsley] *Sheridan* [1751–1816]; *also Criticisms and Selections from the Works of Mrs. Sheridan; and Biographical Ancedotes of her Family and*

Contemporaries (London: Whittaker, 1824) p. 32; quoted by Croker, *Fairy Legends* (1825) pp. 259–60n.

Jonah Barrington (1760–1834), *Personal Sketches of his own Times*, 3 vols (London: Colburn, 1827–30 [vols I, II]; London: Colburn and Bentley, 1833 [vol. III]).

John O'Donovan (1809–61) gives no stories in his 'Introductory Remarks' to his annotated and translated edition of the *Annals of the Kingdom, by the Four Masters, from the Earliest Period to the Year 1616* (Dublin: Hodges, Smith, 1854), but his expansive notes to the annals contain legendary stories; see, for example, the story of Balor, a leader of the Fomorians (I, 18n–21n).

Dublin and London Magazine, ed. Michael James Whitty (London, 1827 and 1829 [*sic*, it ceased publication in June 1828]). None of its issues contains 'The Fairy Greyhound'.

David Fitzgerald (1843–1916), 'Popular Tales of Ireland' and 'Early Celtic History and Mythology', *Revue celtique*, 4 (1879–80) 171–200, 268–76, and 6 (1884) 191–259.

Letitia M'Clintock (also spelled 'McClintock' and 'Maclintock'; b. 1835), 'Folk-Lore of the County Donegal', *Dublin University Magazine*, 88 (Nov 1876) 607–14 [anonymous] and 89 (Feb 1877) 241–9, and/or 'Folk Lore of Ulster', *Dublin University Magazine*, 89 (June 1877) 747–54 [anonymous], and/or 'Fairy Superstitions in Donegal', *University Magazine*, 4 (1879) 101–12, 214–20.

Dublin University Magazine, 1839.

The Folk-Lore Record (London, 1878–82), title changed to *The Folk-Lore Journal* (1833–89) and then *Folk-Lore: A Quarterly Review of Myth, Tradition, Institution and Custom* (1890).

Kilkenny Archaeological Society Transactions (1849–53), title changed to, successively, *Kilkenny and South-East of Ireland Archaeological Society Proceedings and Transactions* (1854–5), *Journal of the Kilkenny and South-East of Ireland Archaeological Society* (1856–67), *Journal of the Historical and Archaeological Society of Ireland* (1868–9), *Journal of the Royal Historical and Archaeological Association of Ireland* (1870–89), *Royal Society of Antiquaries of Ireland Proceedings and Papers* (1890) and *Journal of the Royal Society of Antiquaries of Ireland* (1891).

The Dublin Penny Journal (1832–6) and *The Irish Penny Journal* (Dublin, 1840–1).

Newry Magazine; or, Literary and Political Register, ed. James Stewart (Newry, 1815–19).

'*Duffy's Sixpenny Magazine*' perhaps refers to *Duffy's Fireside Magazine: A Monthly Miscellany containing Original Tales*, ed. James Reynolds (Dublin, 1850–4), or *Duffy's Irish Catholic Magazine: A Monthly Review* (Dublin, 1847–8).

Duffy's Hibernian Magazine: A Monthly Journal of Legends, Tales, and Stories, Irish Antiquities, Biography, Science, and Art, ed. Martin Haverty (Dublin, 1860–4); its price was sixpence.

For a listing of Yeats's folklore articles, 1889 to May 1892, in the *Scots Observer: A Record and Review* (Edinburgh, 1889–90), title changed to *National Observer: A Record and Review* (London, from 1890), see Wade 331–8.

Standish James O'Grady (1846–1928), *History of Ireland, vol.* I: *The Heroic Period* (London: Sampson Low, Searle, Marston and Rivington; Dublin: Ponsonby, 1878). Vol. II, published in 1880, is subtitled *Cuculain and his Contemporaries.*

This list of authorities is a revision of the one Yeats had published in 1888 in *FFT*. He added the newly published Croker's *Ancient Charms*, Curtin's *Myths and Folklore* (1890), Hyde's *Leabhar Sgeulaigheachta* (1889) and *Beside the Fire* (1890), and his own articles (1889–92). The older works added were Griffin's *The Collegians* (1829), Fitzgerald's articles in *Revue celtique* (1879–80 and 1883–5), and O'Grady's *History of Ireland: The Heroic Period* (1878). He added praise of Lady Wilde's *Ancient Legends*. The 'one or two' corrections were to the titles of Kennedy's *Legendary Fictions* and *Evenings in the Duffrey* (with a new error), Carleton's name, the date of the *Dublin and London Magazine* (with a new error), and the spelling of M'Clintock (from 'Maclintock'); the date of her articles was not corrected. His other changes were to delete *The Hibernian Winter Evening Tales: Being a Collection of the Most Entertaining Stories* (Dublin: Nugent, n.d.); *Transactions of the Ossianic Society* (Dublin, 1854–61); and *The Leadbeater Papers* (London: Bell and Daldy, 1862) by Mary Shackleton Leadbeater (1757–1826), author of *Cottage Dialogues among the Irish Peasantry* (London: Johnson, 1811).

WILLIAM ALLINGHAM

1. William Allingham, 'A Stormy Night: A Story of the Donegal Coast' (1887), ll. 1–2, *Irish Songs and Poems* (London: Reeves and Turner, 1887) p. 136: '. . . Town, / Where . . . Folk. . . .'

2. *Poems* (London: Chapman and Hall, 1850); *Day and Night Songs* (London: Routledge, 1854); *The Music Master: A Love Story and Two Series of Day and Night Songs* (London: Routledge, 1855).

3. These illustrations were first used in *The Music Master*: wood engravings after ink drawings by Dante Gabriel Rossetti (1828–82), *The Maids of Elfen-Mere*, facing p. 202; John Everett Millais (1829–96), *The Fireside Story* (illustrating 'Frost in the Holidays'), facing p. 216; and Arthur Hughes (1830–1915), ornaments, title-page vignette, and seven drawings (two of which, *Milly* and *Under the Abbey-wall*, are to 'The Music Master: A Love Story'). The volume was reprinted, with the illustrations, in 1860 as *Day and Night Songs*. The Rossetti drawing and another by him, *The Queen's Page*, dated 9 June 1854, were reprinted in *Flower Pieces and Other Poems*, vol. II of the collected edn (London: Reeves

and Turner, 1888), frontispiece and facing p. 189. The Millais drawing was reprinted as the frontispiece in *Life and Phantasy*, vol. III of the collected edn (London: Reeves and Turner, 1889), which also contained one of the drawings by Hughes from 1855. For Yeats's review, 12 Dec 1891, of the six-volume collected edition, see *UP1* 208–12.

4. *Laurence Bloomfield in Ireland: A Modern Poem* (London: Macmillan, 1864); *Fifty Modern Poems* (London: Bell and Daldy, 1865).

5. Patricus Walker (William Allingham), *Rambles* (London: Longmans, Green, 1873). Allingham was appointed sub-editor of *Fraser's Magazine* in 1870 and was editor from 1874 to 1877.

6. *Ashby Manor: A Play in Two Acts* (London: Stott, [1883]); *Evil May Day* (London: Stott, [1882]). Mrs Allingham contributed illustrations to Allingham's *Rhymes for the Young Folk* (London: Cassell, 1887) and a portrait and stage designs for *Thought and Word, and Ashby Manor*, vol. III of the collected edn (London: Reeves and Turner, 1890).

7. The Allinghams moved to Witley, Surrey, in June 1881.

8. The allusion to Henry John Temple, Viscount Palmerston (1784–1865), Prime Minister (1855–65), is untraced.

9. 'Four ducks on a pond' (1882), *Flower Pieces and Other Poems* (1888), p. 48 (l. 4 ends in a semicolon). The allusions are to respectively: 'The Pilot's Pretty Daughter' (1855), perhaps 'The Music Master: A Love Story' (1855) (part II, stanza xliv), 'Abbey Assaroe' (1861), 'The Winding Banks of Erne' (1861), and 'The Music Master' (part I, stanzas iv and vi).

10. 'Laurence Bloomfield in Ireland: A Modern Poem' (1864); 'The Music Master: A Love Story' (1855); 'The Lady of the Sea: A Legend of Ancient Erin', in *Irish Songs and Poems*, pp. 5–23.

11. In Blake's *Jerusalem* (1804–20?), 'hail stones stand ready to obey' the voice of Los – pl. 86, l. 36, *William Blake's Writings*, ed. G. E. Bentley, Jr, 2 vols (Oxford: Clarendon Press, 1978) p. 610. For Blakean microcosms see, for example, the opening lines of 'Auguries of Innocence' (after 1807?): '. . . a world in a grain of sand, / And heaven in a wild flower' (*WWB* III, 76; *PWB* 90: '. . . the world. . . .'; Bentley, *Blake's Writings*, p. 1312).

12. 'Twilight Voices' (1887); 'Lovely Mary Donnelly' (1854); 'The Winding Banks of Erne' (1861).

ELLEN O'LEARY

1. James Stephens (1824–1901) established the weekly newspaper *The Irish People* (Nov 1863 – Sep 1865) as a voice for the Irish Republican Brotherhood (popularly known as the Fenians), which sought armed overthrow of British rule in Ireland.

2. John Keegan Casey (1846–70), Fenian and poet, is best known for his ballad 'The Rising of the Moon' (1869). *Sally Cavanagh; or, The Untenanted Graves* (1869) was the first novel of Charles J. Kickham (1828–82), a Fenian; his ballads include 'Patrick Sheehan', 'Rory of the Hill' and 'The Irish Peasant Girl'.

3. The Young Ireland movement, founded in 1842, fostered Irish cultural nationalism; for its brief, unsuccessful rising in 1848, see p. 249, note 113 above.

4. The Irish Republican Brotherhood's plans for a rising in 1864 came to nothing. For the leadership of the IRB, see pp. 249–50, note 114 above; Stephen's title was 'Head Centre'.

5. The staff of Stephens' *The Irish People* included John O'Leary (1830–1907) as editor, Kickham, Luby and Ellen O'Leary. When the journal was suppressed in a police raid, on 15 September 1865, all the men were arrested except Stephens, who eluded capture until November and then promptly escaped from Richmond prison.

6. Algernon Sidney (or Sydney), English republican, was executed in 1683 for plotting in favour of the Protestant Duke of Monmouth to succeed Charles II. Robert Emmet was executed in 1803 after an abortive rising. This excerpt from the 6 Dec 1885 speech is slightly misquoted from John O'Leary, *Recollections of Fenians and Fenianism* (London: Downey, 1896) II, 224: '. . . treason-felony . . . hell, but . . . friends and benefactors . . . country; I . . . no benefactor. Sydney and. . . .'

7. John and Ellen O'Leary helped Yeats, Katharine Tynan, Douglas Hyde and others prepare the anthology *Poems and Ballads of Young Ireland* (1888).

8. Ellen O'Leary, *Lays of Country, Home and Friends*, ed. T. W. Rolleston (Dublin: Sealy, Bryers and Walker, 1891). Her poems in the anthology are 'To God and Ireland True', 'The Dead who Died for Ireland', 'A Legend of Tyrone' and 'Home to Carriglea: A Ballad'.

THE WORKS OF WILLIAM BLAKE

1. [Ellis and Yeats's note:] *Letter to Butts from Felpham, July 6th, 1803.*[1a]

1a. This letter from Blake to his patron Thomas Butts (1757–1845) is quoted in Alexander Gilchrist, *Life of William Blake* (London: Macmillan, 1880) I, 187: '. . . powers, while . . . understanding, is . . .'; and *William Blake's Writings*, ed. G. E. Bentley, Jr (Oxford: Clarendon Press, 1978) p. 1575: '. . . Intellectual . . . Corporeal Understanding is My Definition . . . Most Sublime Poetry'.

2. Gilchrist (*Life of William Blake*, 'Pictor Ignotus', 1st edn [London: Macmillan, 1863] I, 76) coined the term 'Prophetic Books' to describe Blake's works other than lyrics. Blake variously called them 'visions', 'prophecies', 'songs' and 'poems'; they are in loose metre or prose.

3. Algernon Charles Swinburne discussed the 'Prophetic Books' at considerable length in his *William Blake: A Critical Essay* (London: Hotten, 1868) pp. 185–304.

4. For 'the Four-fold Man' see Blake, *Jerusalem*, pl. 15, l. 6 (Bentley, *Blake's Writings*, p. 445).

   For a detailed description of the four Zoas (Urizen, Luvah, Tharmes and Urthona) see the essay 'The Symbolic System' in *WWB* I, 255–61.

Neither *WWB* (except in the photographic reproductions in its third volume) nor either edition of *PWB* includes any of the verse quotations from Blake in this preface.

5. Swinburne, who argued for Blake's sanity, called the Prophetic Books the 'strangest of all written books' but insisted that they have 'purpose as well as power, meaning as well as mystery' (*William Blake*, pp. 185–6). Gilchrist candidly admitted his 'bewilderment' as to the meaning of the poem *Jerusalem* (*Life of Blake*, I, 228). Dante Gabriel Rossetti (1828–82), who purchased Blake's notebook, assisted in the preparation of Gilchrist's posthumously published *Life of Blake*, '*Pictor Ignotus*' (London: Macmillan, 1863; 2nd edn titled *Life of William Blake*, London: Macmillan, 1880) by writing the book's last chapter from rough notes left by Gilchrist and by editing the selections of Blake's works that comprise the book's second volume. William Michael Rossetti (1829–1919) prepared a catalogue raisonné of Blake's paintings, drawings and engravings, including Blake's engraved books; it was published at the end of the second volume.

6. Edwin John Ellis (1848–1916).

7. Gilchrist, *Life of Blake* (1863) I, 186: 'Far more curious is the following song, which let who can interpret.' In the second edition (1880), the second half of the sentence was deleted (I, 231).

8. Ellis and Yeats had begun the project by 1889.

9. The unsigned biographical 'Memoir' (I, 1–232) was drafted probably by Ellis and then revised by Ellis and Yeats.

10. *Jerusalem*, pl. 11, l. 5 (Bentley, *Blake's Writings*, p. 437: 'Striving with Systems to deliver Individuals from those Systems').

11. Emanuel Swedenborg (1688–1772), Swedish scientist and mystical writer; Jacob Boehme (1575–1624), German theosophist and mystical writer.
    Blake, *The Marriage of Heaven and Hell* (1790?–3), pl. 9, para. 1 (Bentley, *Blake's Writings*, p. 76).

12. Blake, *Milton* (1804–8?), pl. e [32 in Keynes], l. 32 (Bentley, *Blake's Writings*, p. 389): 'The Imagination . . . is the Human Existence itself'.

13. Blake, *Milton*, pl. 43 [41 in Keynes], l. 7 (Bentley, *Blake's Writings*, p. 410: 'To cast aside from Poetry, all that is not Inspiration').

14. *Jerusalem*, 'To the Public', pl. 3, para. 2 (Bentley, *Blake's Writings*, p. 420: '. . . Thought, & flames . . .').

POEMS OF WILLIAM BLAKE

1. For a vigorous debunking of this supposed Irish lineage for Blake see G. E. Bentley, Jr, and Martin K. Nurmi, *A Blake Bibliography: Annotated Lists of Works, Studies, and Blakeana* (Minneapolis: University of Minnesota Press, 1964) p. 17. Yeats did not mention Dr Carter Blake in the 1893 version, where the sentence ended: '. . . a family who proudly remember the tradition of their relationship to the mystic and seer'. See a letter from

J. F. M. Blake to Yeats, 22 Apr 1906: 'I am the daughter of Dr Charles Carter Blake but I am afraid that I can give you little help as to the confirmation of the tradition you mention in your book. . . . I never heard . . . [of] any connection with the family of William Blake the poet' (NLI MS. 30, 534; SUNY-SB 24.3.59). Hugh Kenner, in *A Colder Eye: The Modern Irish Writers* (New York: Knopf, 1983) p. 162n, has pointed out that the first, brief entry for Blake in the *Encyclopaedia Britannica*, 8th edn (Boston: Little, Brown, 1854) IV, 753, reported that Blake, an 'engraver of high but wild genius', was 'born in Ireland'; the long entry by J. W. Comyns Carr in the 9th edn (New York: Hall, 1878) III, 804, corrected that error. See also Edwin John Ellis and Yeats, 'Memoir', *WWB* I, 2–4; *LTWBY* 9; and Hazard Adams, *Blake and Yeats: The Contrary Vision* (Ithaca, NY: Cornell University Press, 1955) pp. 46–7.

2. Frederick Tatham (1805–78), a young sculptor and miniature-painter who knew Blake during the last years of Blake's life, wrote a manuscript 'Life of Blake' *c*. 1832. It was first published in *The Letters of William Blake* (London: Methuen, 1906), edited by Archibald G. B. Russell, an acquaintance of Yeats's. Tatham's text is transcribed in G. E. Bentley, Jr, *Blake Records* (Oxford: Clarendon Press, 1969) p. 509.

3. The Swedish philosopher, religious writer, and scientist Emanuel Swedenborg (1688–1772) made this announcement in his *De ultimo judico, et de Babylonia destructa* (London, 1758), no. 45; English translation, *Concerning the Last Judgment*, in *A Compendium of the Theological Writings of Emanuel Swedenborg*, ed. Samuel M. Warren (1875; repr. New York: Swedenborg Foundation, 1979) p. 711.

4. This ancedote, spoken by Mrs Blake to her husband, is not in the diary of Henry Crabb Robinson (1775–1867), but is in his manuscript 'Reminiscences', written in 1852. It is quoted in the second edition of Alexander Gilchrist's *Life of William Blake* I, 385: 'He puts His head to. . . .' For Bentley's transcription of 'Reminiscences' see *Blake Records*, pp. 542–3. Yeats used the enlarged second edition (1880) extensively, so it is cited in these notes in preference to the first edition (1863); see p. 258, note 5 above.

5. Gilchrist, *Life of Blake* (1880) I, 7.

6. Tatham, 'Life of Blake', in Bentley, *Blake Records*, p. 519.

7. Blake, *The Marriage of Heaven and Hell*, pl. 9 (Bentley, *Blake's Writings*, p. 83: 'tygers').

Where Yeats quotes from Blake's poetry, I make reference to *William Blake's Writings*, ed. G. E. Bentley, Jr, 2 vols (Oxford: Clarendon Press, 1978), and Yeats's two editions of Blake, *WWB*, published in 1893, and *PWB*, published in 1893 and revised in 1905, whenever those editions print the quoted passage (other than in photo-lithographic reproductions in *WWB* III). In the explanatory notes to *PWB*, when citing Bentley I have recorded only the differences that go beyond emendation of punctuation, conventional modernisation of capitalisation, or the expansion of ampersands to 'and'.

8. John Sparrow's English translations (1645–62) of the works of Jacob Boehme (1575–1624), German mystic, were republished (4 vols, 1764–

81) with an introduction by William Law (1686–1761), the English devotional writer and ardent admirer of Boehme.

9. *Liber Paragranum*, in Franz Hartmann, *The Life of Philippus Theophrastus, Bombast of Hohenheim, Known by the Name of Parcelsus* [see p. 234, note 35b above] (London: Redway, 1887) p. 18: 'He who wants to study the . . . must wander with . . . feet over its. . . .'

10. Blake, *Jerusalem* (1804–20?), pl. 27, l. 15 (Gilchrist, *Life of Blake* [1880] I, 232, and *WWB* I, 6: 'Welling's'; Bentley, *Blake's Writings*, p. 471: 'Willans'').

11. Henry Parr; James Basire (1730–1802), to whom Blake was apprenticed 1772–9.

12. William Wynne Ryland (1732–83), engraver, was hanged for forging a cheque. Gilchrist, *Life of Blake* (1880) I, 13: '. . . man's face: it looks . . . he will live. . . .'

13. Benjamin Heath Malkin (1769–1842), *A Father's Memoirs of His Child* (1806), quoted in Gilchrist, *Life of Blake* (1880) I, 17, and in Bentley, *Blake Records*, p. 422.

14. Tatham, 'Life of Blake', in Bentley, *Blake Records*, p. 511: '. . . had it not been for the circumstance of his having frequent quarrels with his fellow apprentices, concerning matters of intellectual argument, he would perhaps never have handled the pencil & would consequently have been doomed forever to furrow upon a Copper Plate, monotonous and regular lines, placed at even distances, without Genius & without Form'.

15. Blake, 'Mary', l. 21 (*WWB* III, 82 and *PWB* 134 and Bentley, *Blake's Writings*, p. 1308: '. . . I born . . .'). Yeats's misquotation probably came from l. 22: 'Why was I not born like this envious race?'

16. Tatham, 'Life of Blake', in Bentley, *Blake Records*, p. 526: 'Upon his relating this he was asked whether he did not injure it, to which he replied with his usual fun "O I. . . ."'

17. Blake, 'Auguries of Innocence' (after 1807?), ll. 111–12 (Bentley, *Blake's Writings*, p. 1315). These lines are not part of the very brief selection given in *PWB* 90.

18. Blake, *Jerusalem*, pl. 9, l. 31 (Bentley, *Blake's Writings*, p. 435).

19. Blake, 'On Virgil' (1821?) (Bentley, *Blake's Writings*, p. 668: 'Gothic is Living Form').

20. For example, 'Contemplation' in *Poetical Sketches* (1783) (Bentley, *Blake's Writings*, p. 795: 'Clamour brawls along the streets . . . but on these plains, and in these silent woods, true joys descend: here build thy nest'). See also Blake's annotation (1801–2?, 1808–9?), *The Works of Sir Joshua Reynolds*, 2nd edn (London: T. Cadell, Jr and W. Davies, 1798) I, 48, Discourse II: 'Everything in art is definite and determinate . . . because Vision is determinate and perfect' (*WWB* II, 328; Bentley, *Blake's Writings*, p. 1468).

21. Blake, *King Edward the Third* in *Poetical Sketches* (1783) (*WWB* III, 3–20; *PWB* 17–44; Bentley, *Blake's Writings*, pp. 770–90).

22. [Thomas Chatterton (1752–70)], *Poems, Supposed to have been Written at Bristol, by Thomas Rowley, and Others, in the Fifteenth Century*, ed. Thomas Tyrwhitt (London: Payne, 1777).

23. *WWB* III, 19–20; *PWB* 42–4; Bentley, *Blake's Writings*, pp. 788–90.

The 'English metamorphosis' refers to a verse translation by Arthur Golding (1536–1606) of Ovid, *The XV Books, Entytuled Metamorphosis* (London: Seres, 1567).

24. Matthew 10:39.

25. John Flaxman (1755–1826), English sculptor and draughtsman; John Henry Fuseli (1741–1825), Swiss-born painter, illustrator, and engraver in London.

26. Gilchrist, *Life of Blake* (1880) I, 37: 'a lively little girl'. Tatham, in 'Life of Blake', gives her name as Polly Wood (Bentley, *Blake Records*, p. 517).

27. Blake, 'Never pain to tell thy love' (date unknown; Notebook [1793?–1818?] p. 115), titled 'Love's Secret' in *WWB* III, 70, and *PWB* 121; Bentley, *Blake's Writings*, p. 1000. For 'Love's Secret' see also *WWB* II, 28–9.

For the term 'Prophetic Books', see p. 257, note 2 above.

Blake, illus. to *Vala or The Four Zoas* (1796?–1807?), Night the Second, MS. p. 27 (*WWB* III, unpaged *Vala or The Four Zoas* reproductions, no. 5, and *Vala or The Four Zoas* text; Bentley, *Blake's Writings*, pp. 1113–14). Ellis and Yeats described this illustration as 'Albion seeing his softer passions outside of himself in odorous stupefaction' (II, 360); Bentley described the female figure only as 'a nude woman' and suggested that the male could be Luvah (*Blake's Writings*, p. 1113 n); Martin Butlin, *The Paintings and Drawings of William Blake* (New Haven: Yale University Press, 1981) I, 278 (no. 337.27), has added that it is 'perhaps an illustration of the afflicted Luvah's description of his sensuous love for Vala, shown in her fallen state as Rahab'.

28. Catherine Sophia Boucher (1762–1831), daughter of William Boucher (1714?–94). Tatham, 'Life of Blake', in Bentley, *Blake Records*, p. 517; Tatham misspelt the name as 'Boutcher'.

29. Tatham, 'Life of Blake', in Bentley, *Blake Records*, p. 518: '. . . she replied that she had not yet. . . .'

30. Gilchrist, *Life of Blake* (1880) I, 38: '. . . declared "She pitied him from her heart." "*Do* you pity me?" "*Yes!* I do, most sincerely." "Then I love you for that!" he replied.' The earliest report of the anecdote was in John Thomas Smith, 'Blake', in *Nollekens and his Times*, 2nd edn (1829), quoted in Bentley, *Blake Records*, p. 459.

31. Blake, *The First Book of Urizen* (1794), pl. 18, ll. 13–15, and pl. 19, l. 1 (Bentley, *Blake's Writings*, pp. 267–8).

32. Blake, *Jerusalem*, pl. 14, ll. 13–14 (Bentley, *Blake's Writings*, p. 443: 'Enitharmon is a vegetated mortal . . .').

33. The Rev. Anthony Stephen Mathew (1733–1824), a patron of Blake and of John Flaxman, resided at 27 (not 28), Rathbone Place, just north of Oxford Street. Mathew's name was misspelt as 'Matthews' here and as 'Mathews' in *WWB* (I, 25).

34. The Jew's-Harp House was a tea-garden that stood a half-mile north of the Old Farthing Pye-House Green Man, an inn near the south-east corner of Regent's Park. Blake mentioned these places in *Jerusalem*, pl. 27, l. 13 (*WWB* I, 25: '*Jews Harp House*'; Bentley, *Blake's Writings*, p. 471).

35. The poets William Cowper (1731–1800), James Thomson (1700–48), and Thomas Chatterton (1752–70).

36. Blake, 'Mad Song' (1783), l. 17 (*WWB* II, 28; *PWB* 10; Bentley, *Blake's Writings*, p. 760: '. . . fiend in . . .').

37. Blake, Introduction to *Songs of Innocence* (1789) (*WWB* III, 37; *PWB* 47; Bentley, *Blake's Writings*, p. 24: 'On a cloud I saw a child').

38. Blake, 'With happiness stretched across the hills', ll. 15–16, in a letter to Thomas Butts [22 Nov 1802] (*WWB* III, 66: '. . . one / In . . . cloud making . . .'; Bentley, *Blake's Writings*, p. 1564).

39. Blake, *King Edward the Third*, scene [2], l. 13 (*WWB* III, 5; *PWB* 20; Bentley, *Blake's Writings*, p. 773).

    Blake, *King Edward the Third*, scene [3], ll. 288–91 (*WWB* III, 14: '. . . taste and . . . sound and . . .'; *PWB* 35: '. . . taste and . . . leave them all . . .'; Bentley, *Blake's Writings*, p. 783).

40. In Blake's *Visions of the Daughters of Albion* (1793) these are English women who weep for their loss of bodily freedom; they are twelve and are variously named in *Vala or The Four Zoas* and in *Jerusalem*.

41. Blake, *Jerusalem*, pl. 69 (*WWB* III, unpaged *Jerusalem* reproductions, no. 69; Bentley, *Blake's Writings*, pp. 569n, 571 [illus.]). Ellis and Yeats described this illustration: 'A victim sacrificed on Druid rocks, – his brain cut round with flint, and his senses shrunk from imagination by the cruelties of the female, experience' (*WWB* II, 359).

42. Blake, *An Island in the Moon* (1784?) (*WWB* I, 186–201 [as *The Island in the Moon*], description and excerpts; Bentley, *Blake's Writings*, pp. 875–900). The manuscript, which is now in the Fitzwilliam Museum, Cambridge, was owned by Charles Fairfax Murray (1849–1919), English painter and collector.

43. 'When old corruption first began . . .', *An Island in the Moon*, ch. 6 (*WWB* I, 193–4; Bentley, *Blake's Writings*, pp. 883–4).

44. Blake to William Hayley, 23 Oct 1804 (Bentley, *Blake's Writings*, p. 1614: 'again enlighted with . . . and by window-shutters').

45. Blake, *The Marriage of Heaven and Hell*, pl. 2, ll. 19–20 (*PWB* 177; Bentley, *Blake's Writings*, p. 75).

46. Blake to William Hayley, 6 May 1800 (Bentley, *Blake's Writings*, p. 1532: '. . . they were apparent. . . . in my remembrance in the regions of . . . his Dictate. Forgive . . . world by it I am the companion of Angels. May. . . . Time builds Mansions . . .').

47. John Linnell (1792–1882), English painter and a patron of Blake, recorded this price in his marginalia, 1855, to anecdotes on Blake in Smith, *Nollekens and his Times*, p. 470, quoted in Bentley, *Blake Records*, p. 461 n. 1.

48. Blake, ['Vision of the Last Judgment'] (1810; Notebook, pp. 71 [part e], 72, 80–1) (*WWB* II, 393, 397 [as 'For the Year 1810. Addition to Blake's Catalogue of Pictures, &c.']: '. . . Time and Space . . .', '. . . Music, – the . . .'; Bentley, *Blake's Writings*, pp. 1009, 1017).

    Blake to George Cumberland (1754–1848), English painter and etcher, 12 Apr 1827 (Bentley, *Blake's Writings*, p. 1667: '. . . Imagination which Liveth . . .').

49. Blake, *The Marriage of Heaven and Hell*, pl. 12 (Bentley, *Blake's Writings*, p. 86).

50. The full titles are *For Children: The Gates of Paradise* (1793), *The First Book of Urizen* (1794) and *The Book of Ahania* (1795).

51. Blake, *Vala or The Four Zoas*; in *WWB* III, 19 unpaged reproductions and 176 pages of text in letterpress. For *PWB* 218–20, Yeats selected brief excerpts from *Vala or The Four Zoas*, Night the Second, MS p. 34, ll. 56–86 (as 'The Song of Enitharmon') and Night the Eighth, MS p. 110, ll. 3–28 (as 'Universal Harmony') (*WWB* III, unpaged *Vala or The Four Zoas* text, Night the Second, ll. 335–65, and Night the Eighth, ll. 550–75; Bentley, *Blake's Writings*, pp. 1125–6, 1247–8).

52. Blake, 'The Bible of Hell' (1793?), *The French Revolution* (published 1791 by J. Johnson, 72 St Paul's Churchyard), 'For Children[:] the Gates of Hell' (1793?), *Outhoun* (1793?); for Blake's lost works, see pp. 100 above and 270, note 116 below, and Bentley, *Blake's Writings*, pp. 1675–82.

53. Jacob Boehme, *Aurora; or, The Morning Redness in the Rising Sun* (1612, publ. 1634) and *Mysterium Magnum; or, An Exposition of the First Book of Moses Called Genesis* (1623).

Cornelius Agrippa (1486?–1535), German physician, theologian, and occultist, wrote *Three Books of Occult Philosophy*, tr. John French (London, 1651), and (perhaps) *Henry Cornelius Agrippa his Fourth Book of Occult Philosophy*, trs. Robert Turner (London, 1655).

For Falk, see a query and reply, both perhaps written by William Wynn Wescott, a founder of the Golden Dawn, in *Notes and Queries*, 8 Dec 1888 and 9 Feb 1889, quoted in Ellic Howe, *The Magicians of the Golden Dawn: A Documentary History of a Magical Order: 1887–1923* (London: Routledge and Kegan Paul, 1972) pp. 46–7: 'A SOCIETY OF KABBALISTS. Johann F. Falk succeeded to the directorate of a secret society of students of the Kabbalah about 1810, in London. . . . Is this society still in existence?' 'The order of mystics . . . is still at work in England. . . . The few outsiders who have heard of its existence only know of the society as "The Hermetic Students of the G. D."'

Richard Cosway (1742–1821), an eminent English miniaturist, saw spirits frequently from 1811 on; see George C. Williamson, *Richard Cosway R. A.* (London: Bell, 1905) pp. 53–61. Yeats is here more cautious than in the 'Memoir', by Ellis and Yeats, in *WWB* I, 25: '. . . Cosway, kept a house for the study and practice of magic, and left behind him at his death a considerable bundle of magical formulae.'

54. Jacob Boehme wrote, in his *Theosophical Letters*, no. 10 [1620], that his inspiration came like a shower-burst of rain (*Platzregen*) – *Sämtliche Schriften*, facsimile of 1730 edn (Stuttgart: Frommanns, 1956) IX [XXI], 40. Among the books that Yeats owned, this passage is translated by Franz Hartmann in *The Life and Doctrines of Jacob Boehme: The God-Taught Philosopher: An Introduction to the Study of his Works* (London: Kegan Paul, Trench, Trübner, 1891) p. 53: 'The inspiration comes like a shower of rain.'

55. Emanuel Swedenborg, *De Coelo et ejus mirabilibus, et de inferno, ex auditis et visis* (London, 1758); the first English translation was by William

Cookworthy (in part) and Thomas Hartley, *A Treatise concerning Heaven and Hell* (London: Phillips, 1778), with subsequent editions in 1784, 1789, 1800, etc.

James Blake (1753–1827); see Gilchrist, *Life of Blake* (1880) I, 55.

56. Blake, *The Marriage of Heaven and Hell*, pl. 3 (*PWB* 177: '. . . advent, the . . . revives. And lo! Swedenborg . . . tomb: his . . .'; Bentley, *Blake's Writings*, p. 76).

57. Blake, *The Marriage of Heaven and Hell*, pls 21–2 (Bentley, *Blake's Writings*, pp. 94–5).

58. Blake, *Milton*, pl. 20 [22 in Keynes], l. 50 (Bentley, *Blake's Writings*, p. 362).

59. Blake, *A Descriptive Catalogue* (1809), no. VIII (*WWB* II, 377: '. . . well worthy the attention of Painters and Poets. . . . foundations for grand . . .', *PWB* 253 [as 'Learning without Imagination']: '. . . well worthy the attention of . . . foundations for grand . . .'; Bentley, *Blake's Writings*, pp. 855–6: '. . . well worthy the attention of Painters and Poets . . . foundations for grand . . .').

60. Johann Kaspar Lavater (1741–1801) was a Swiss poet, mystic, theologian and physiognomist. Blake, annotation to John Caspar Lavater, *Aphorisms on Man*, tr. J. H. Fuseli (1788) p. 630 (Bentley, *Blake's Writings*, p. 1385: '. . . man for our . . .').

61. Blake, *Vala or The Four Zoas*, Night the Fourth, MS. p. 56, l. 34 (*WWB* III, unpaged *Vala or The Four Zoas* text, Night the Fourth, l. 270; Bentley, *Blake's Writings*, p. 1153).

62. See Blake, *Jerusalem*, pl. 60, ll. 56–9 (Bentley, *Blake's Writings*, p. 546: 'Babel mocks saying, there is no God nor Son of God[,] / That thou O Human Imagination, O Divine Body art all / A delusion, but I know thee O Lord . . .') and Blake's annotations (1826) to William Wordsworth, *Poems*, vol. I (1815) 374–5 (Bentley, *Blake's Writings*, p. 1513: 'Imagination is the Divine Vision not of The World nor of Man nor from Man as he is a Natural Man but only as he is a Spiritual Man[.] / Imagination has nothing to do with Memory[.]')

63. Blake, *Milton*, pl. 43 [41 in Keynes], ll. 4, 7, and pl. 35, l. 6 (Bentley, *Blake's Writings*, pp. 410, 394: To cast off the rotten rags of Memory by Inspiration[,] / . . . / To cast aside from Poetry, all that is not Inspiration'; 'The Divine Members . . .').

64. Blake, ['Laocoön'] (1820?) (Bentley, *Blake's Writings*, pp. 665–6: '. . . Israel deliverd from . . . Art deliverd from . . .').

65. Blake, *Jerusalem*, pl. 77 (Bentley, *Blake's Writings*, p. 588: '. . . before all the . . .').

See *Jerusalem*, pl. 98, ll. 18–19 (Bentley, *Blake's Writings*, p. 636: 'Circumcising the excrementitious / Husk & Covering . . . revealing the lineaments of Man').

A Descriptive Catalogue, no. XV, p. 63 (*WWB* II, 380: 'form, and determinate . . .'; Bentley, *Blake's Writings*, p. 861).

'The Little Black Boy' (1789), l. 24 (*WWB* III, 39; *PWB* 50; Bentley, *Blake's Writings*, p. 30).

Jerusalem, pl. 55, l. 62 (Bentley, *Blake's Writings*, p. 536: '. . . in minutely organized Particulars').

66. Blake, *The Marriage of Heaven and Hell*, pl. 11 (Bentley, *Blake's Writings*, p. 85: '. . . their enlarged . . .').

Jerusalem, pl. 36, l. 34 (Bentley, *Blake's Writings*, p. 493).

Milton, pl. 25, l. 59 (Bentley, *Blake's Writings*, p. 375: '. . . till the Judgement is past, till the Creation is consumed').

['Vision of the Last Judgment'] (Notebook, p. 95) (*WWB* ii, 403: 'burned up the moment men cease to behold it'; Bentley, *Blake's Writings*, p. 1027: 'Burnt up the Moment Men cease to behold it').

67. Blake, ['Vision of the Last Judgment'] (Notebook, p. 92) (*WWB* ii, 402; Bentley, *Blake's Writings*, p. 1025: '. . . the Slavery of . . .').

68. Blake, *The First Book of Urizen*, pl. 28, ll. 6–7 (Bentley, *Blake's Writings*, p. 282: 'And form'd laws of prudence . . . / The eternal laws . . .').

69. Blake, *Milton*, pl. e [32 in Keynes], ll. 19–20, 32 (Bentley, *Blake's Writings*, p. 389: '. . . Imagination: which is the Divine Vision & Fruition / In which Man . . .'; '. . . Human Existence . . .').

70. Blake, *Jerusalem*, pl. 91, ll. 55–7 (Bentley, *Blake's Writings*, p. 621: '. . . or Evil; all. . . . Go! . . .').

71. Blake, *Jerusalem*, pl. 38, ll. 12–13 (Bentley, *Blake's Writings*, p. 496).

72. The phrase is from 2 Corinthians 4:4, where St Paul uses it to describe Satan, as Blake does in *Jerusalem*, pl. 52 (Bentley, *Blake's Writings*, p. 527).

73. Blake to Thomas Butts, 25 Apr 1803 (Bentley, *Blake's Writings*, p. 1572: '. . . thus renderd Non Existent . . . seems to be the . . . all producd without . . .').

74. Blake lived at 13 Hercules Buildings, Lambeth, from autumn 1790 until September 1800.

The three large colour prints, finished in pen and watercolour, are from 1795: *Nebuchadnezzar*, 44.6 × 62.0 cm (Bindman, no. 332; Butlin, nos 301–4); *The House of Death* (also known as *The Lazar House*; illus. to *Paradise Lost*, xi.477–93), 48.5 × 61.0 cm (Bindman, no. 335; Butlin, nos 318, 320–2); and *Elohim creating Adam* (1795), 43.1 × 53.6 cm (Bindman, no. 324; Butlin, nos 289–90). For illustrations see David Bindman, *The Complete Graphic Works of William Blake* (New York: Putnam's, 1978), and Butlin, *Paintings and Drawings of Blake*.

Edward Young, *The Complaint, and the Consolation; or, Night Thoughts*, Nights i–iv (London: Edwards, 1797), 43 engraved plates; more than 500 preliminary drawings and watercolours are extant (Butlin, no. 330). For illustrations see *William Blake's Designs for Edward Young's 'Night Thoughts': A Complete Edition*, ed. John E. Grant, Edward J. Rose, Michael J. Tolley and David V. Erdman (Oxford: Clarendon Press, 1980). James Bain, 1 Haymarket, published a facsimile of one of the drawings in 1874.

75. Gilchrist, *Life of Blake* (1880) i, 125: 'When talking on . . . minds, who. . . . And it befel thus: . . . garden-door . . . scaly, speckled. . . . heels, and. . . .'

76. William Hayley (1745–1820), *The Life, and Posthumous Writings, of William Cowper, Esqr.*, 3 vols (London: Johnson, 1803–4), with six plates engraved

by Blake. Blake lived in a cottage in Felpham, Sussex, six miles east of Chichester, from September 1800 to September 1803.

77. Blake's statement reported by Allan Cunningham, *Lives of the Most Eminent British Painters, Sculptors, and Architects* (1830), quoted in Gilchrist, *Life of Blake* (1880) I, 160, and Bentley, *Blake Records*, p. 488.

78. Cunningham, *Lives of the Most Eminent British Painters*, quoted in Gilchrist, *Life of Blake* (1880) I, 160–1: ' ". . . have!" said Blake, "but. . . . creatures, of . . . songs, and then disappeared" '; and Bentley, *Blake Records*, p. 489: ' ". . . sir! . . . have," said Blake, "but . . . garden, there . . . flowers, and. . . . songs, and then disappeared." '

79. Blake, *A Descriptive Catalogue*, no. III (*WWB* II, 367; Bentley, *Blake's Writings*, p. 837).

80. This is perhaps a reference to an episode analogous to Irish fairy folk-tales of discovering a pot of gold that later disappears. Abraham de Franckenberg, in his 'The Life and Death of Jacob Behmen' (written 1651), reported that 'during the Time of his being a Herd's-Boy', Boehme found, on the summit of a hill, 'amongst the great red Stones a kind of Aperture or Entrance'. He entered it and 'there descried a large portable Vessel, or wooden Pannier, full of Money; the Sight of which set him into a Shudder'. He fled 'without taking so much as a single Piece along with him. And what is very remarkable, tho' he had frequently climbed up to the same Place afterwards, in Company of the other Herd's-Boys, yet he could never hit upon this Aperture again' – *Memoirs of the Life, Death, Burial, and Wonderful Writings of Jacob Behmen*, tr. and ed. Francis Okely (Northampton: Dicey, 1780) p. 2.

81. In Plato's *Phaedo* (259) the grasshopper or locust sings ceaselessly.

82. Blake to William Hayley, 11 Dec 1805 (Bentley, *Blake's Writings*, p. 1630: '. . . Mortal Sufferd . . .').

83. For example, *Jerusalem*, pl. 7, l. 42 (Bentley, *Blake's Writings*, p. 428: '. . . the Spectre sons of Adam, who is Scofield . . .'), and *The Marriage of Heaven and Hell*, pl. 121 (Bentley, *Blake's Writings*, p. 86).

84. Blake lived at 17 South Molton Street from autumn 1803 until 1821.

85. Crabb Robinson's diary, 18 Feb 1826, quoted in Gilchrist, *Life of Blake* (1880) I, 392: '. . . than Rousseau or Voltaire; six . . . as Homer's, and. . . . When I am commanded by the spirits, then I write; and. . . . published. The spirits. . . .'; *WWB* II, 146: '. . . Spirits, . . . Spirits . . .'; Bentley, *Blake Records*, p. 322 (diary): '. . . Rousseau – Six or Seven Epic . . . Homer and 20 Tragedies . . . write he says when . . .' and p. 547 [*Reminiscences* (1852), 19 Feb 1826]: '. . . written,["] he answered, more than Rousseau or Voltaire – Six . . . And 20 Tragedies. . . . When I am commanded by the Spirits then I write, And . . . published – The . . .').

86. Blake to William Hayley, 23 Oct 1804 (Bentley, *Blake's Writings*, pp. 1613–14: '. . . that spectrous. . . . and by window-shutters').

87. Robert Hartley Cromek (1770–1812) published in 1808 this illustrated edition of Robert Blair's poem *The Grave* (1743).

88. Blake drawings (1805) to *The Grave* (1743) by Robert Blair, engraved by Louis Schiavonetti (1771–1813), published by Robert Hartley Cromek in

The Grave: A Poem (London, 1808): [no. 12] *The Reunion of the Soul and the Body* (Bindman, no. 476); [no. 6] *The Soul hovering over the Body reluctantly parting with Life* (Bindman, no. 470); [no. 9] *The Soul exploring the recesses of the Grave* (Bindman, no. 473); [no. 8] *The Day of Judgment* (Bindman, no. 472). For illustrations see Bindman, *Graphic Works of Blake*.

89. See Blake, ['Vision of the Last Judgment'] (Notebook, pp. 68, 84) (*WWB* II, 393, 400–1; Bentley, *Blake's Writings*, pp. 1007–8, 1021).

90. Blake, ['Public Address'] (1811?) (Notebook, pp. 57, 62) (*WWB* II, 392; Bentley, *Blake's Writings*, pp. 1038, 1042). For 'firm and determinate outline', see note 65 above.

91. Thomas Stothard (1755–1834), *The Pilgrimage to Canterbury* (1806–7) oil on panel, 31.8 × 95.3 cm, Tate Gallery, London (no. 1163). Blake, *Sir Jeffrey Chaucer and the Nine and Twenty Pilgrims on their Journey to Canterbury* (or *The Canterbury Pilgrims*) (1808?), illus. to *The Canterbury Tales*, pen and tempera on canvas, 46.7 × 137 cm, Pollock House, Corporation of Glasgow; engraving publ. 1810. See Martin Butlin, *Paintings and Drawings of Blake*, no. 653 and pl. 878. For the exhibition and an illustration of Stothard's painting see Bentley, *Blake Records*, pp. 215ff.

92. Blake, 'The Land of Dreams' (after 1807?), l. 18 (*WWB* III, 76; Bentley, *Blake's Writings*, p. 1307).

Blake, *The Marriage of Heaven and Hell*, pl. 7, ll. 14, 3 (Bentley, p. 81: '. . . a year of . . .').

93. See Blake, *Vala or The Four Zoas*, Night the Eighth, MS. p. 105, l. 18 (*WWB* III, unpaged *Vala or The Four Zoas* text, Night the Eighth, l. 280; Bentley, *Blake's Writings*, p. 1235), and *Jerusalem*, pl. 49, ll. 70–5 (Bentley, *Blake's Writings*, p. 523).

94. For Blake's opinions on the artists Raphael (Raffaello Santi, 1483–1520), Michelangelo Buonarroti (1475–1564) and Albrecht Dürer (1471–1528) see *A Descriptive Catalogue*, no. III and Preface (*WWB* II, 370, 363; Bentley, *Blake's Writings*, pp. 842, 827).

95. The Pre-Raphaelite Brotherhood (1849–50), which included the artists William Holman Hunt (1827–1910), John Everett Millais (1829–96) and Dante Gabriel Rossetti (1828–82), was opposed to the highly praised art of Raphael and especially to the seventeenth-century Italian art which followed him.

96. See Blake, 'Auguries of Innocence', l. 1, and ['Vision of the Last Judgment'] (Notebook, p. 83) (*WWB* III, 76, 400; Bentley, *Blake's Writings*, pp. 1312, 1019).

97. Blake, *The First Book of Urizen*, pl. 10, l. 19 (Bentley, *Blake's Writings*, p. 254, l. [184]), and *Vala or The Four Zoas*, Night the Fourth, MS p. 54, l. 1 (*WWB* III, unpaged *Vala or The Four Zoas* text, Night the Fourth, l. 207; Bentley, *Blake's Writings*, p. 1150).

98. Blake, ['Public Address'] (Notebook, pp. 52, 24) (*WWB* II, 389, 388; Bentley, *Blake's Writings*, pp. 1031, 1052).

99. Blake to George Cumberland, 12 Apr 1827 (Bentley, *Blake's Writings*, p. 1667: 'I know too well that a great . . . Thing that does. . . . Subdivisions[;] Strait or . . . Itself & Not Intermeasurable with or by any

Thing Else[.] . . . Intermeasurable One by Another[,] Certainly . . .
Agreement . . .').

100. Robert Hartley Cromek to Blake, May 1807, publ. in *Gentleman's
Magazine*, new ser. 37 (1852) 150, quoted in Gilchrist, *Life of Blake*
(1880) I, 227: 'on half a guinea a week', and Bentley, *Blake Records*, p.
186: 'on half-a-guinea a week'.

101. John Varley (1778–1842), English landscape painter and art teacher,
was a founder of the Royal Society of Painters in Water Colours. The
quoted phrase is from Gilchrist, *Life of Blake* (1880) I, 34–5: 'father of
modern Water Colour'.

102. Blake, *The Head of the Ghost of a Flea* (1819), pencil, 15.3 × 17.9 cm, Tate
Gallery, London (no. 5184) (Butlin, no. 692.98); an engraved composite
version of the drawing is illustrated in Gilchrist, *Life of Blake* (1880) I,
303); there is also a painting, *The Ghost of a Flea* (*c*. 1819–20), 21.4 × 16.2
cm, Tate Gallery, London (no. 5889) (Butlin, no. 750 and pl. 960).

Blake, *The Man who built the Pyramids* (1819) (Butlin, no. 692.102);
replica perhaps by John Linnell, pencil, 29.8 × 21.6 cm, Tate Gallery,
London (no. 5185) (Butlin, no. 752 and pl. 979), illus. in Gilchrist, *Life
of Blake* (1880) I, facing 300.

In 1805–10 Blake had made a set of 21 pen and watercolour
illustrations to *The Book of Job* for Thomas Butts (Butlin, no. 550, pls
697–717); in 1821 he made another set of 21 for John Linnell, also in pen
and watercolour (Butlin, no. 551, pls 733–53) and based on the earlier
set; in 1825 he made 21 engravings after the second set and published
them, together with a title-page, in 1826 (Bindman, nos 625–46). For
illustrations of the engravings see Bindman, *Graphic Works of Blake*.

103. Blake completed only three in this set of pen and watercolour
illustrations to Milton's *Paradise Lost* (Butlin, no. 537); each was made in
1822 and was based on an 1808 set (Butlin, nos 536.4, 536.8, 536.11)
commissioned by Thomas Butts: *Satan Watching the Endearments of Adam
and Eve* (illus. to IV.325–535), 51.8 × 39.7 cm, National Gallery of
Victoria, Melbourne (Butlin, no. 537.1 and pl. 657); *The Creation of Eve*
(illus. to VIII.452–77), 50.5 × 40.7 cm, National Gallery of Victoria,
Melbourne (Butlin, no. 537.2 and pl. 658); and *The Archangel Michael
Foretelling the Crucifixion* illus. to XII.411–19, 427–31), 50.2 × 38.5 cm,
Fitzwilliam Museum, Cambridge (no. PD49-1950) (Butlin, no. 537.3
and pl. 659).

104. From 1824 until his death in 1827 Blake produced seven unfinished
engravings, 102 watercolour drawings, and additional sketches
illustrating the *Divine Comedy* of Dante. They were commissioned by
John Linnell, who published the engravings in 1838. Francesca da
Rimini and her lover Paolo (*Inferno*, v.25–45, 127–42) are the subject of
the first engraving, *The Circle of the Lustful* (labelled *The Whirlwind of
Lovers*), 24.3 × 33.8 cm (Bindman, no. 647). The Linnells gave Yeats a
copy of this engraving, *c*. 1892. For illustrations see Milton Klonsky,
Blake's Dante: The Complete Illustrations to the Divine Comedy (New York:
Harmony Books, 1980); for the seven engravings see Bindman, *Graphic*

Works of Blake, nos 647–53; for the drawings see Butlin, *Paintings and Drawings of Blake*, nos 812–26 and pls 1051–78.

105. Blake, 'To the Queen' (dedication to the illustrations to Blair's *Grave*) (1808), l. 10 (*PWB* 139 [as 'Dedication to the Designs to Blair's "Grave." To Queen Charlotte.']; Bentley, *Blake's Writings*, p. 819).
  For the white Rose see Dante, *Paradiso*, XXXI.

106. Blake to George Cumberland, 12 Apr 1827 (Bentley, *Blake's Writings*, pp. 1167–8: '. . . I am stronger. . . . must All soon . . . the Delusive Goddess . . . all Laws of the Members into. . . . God send it so on . . .').

107. Smith, *Nollekens and his Times* (see note 30 above), quoted in Gilchrist, *Life of Blake* (1880) I, 405: '. . . composed and uttered songs . . . Catherine that. . . . said, "My . . . mine!"', and Bentley, *Blake Records*, p. 475: '. . . composed and uttered songs . . . "My beloved, they are not mine – no – they are not mine."'

108. George Richmond to Samuel Palmer, 15 Aug 1827, quoted in Gilchrist, *Life of Blake* (1880) I, 406: 'He said. . . . brightened, and . . ."', and Bentley, *Blake Records*, p. 347: '. . . eyes brighten'd and . . . out in Singing . . .').

109. Probably based on Tatham, 'Life of Blake', in Bentley, *Blake Records*, p. 528: 'The Walls rang & resounded with the beatific Symphony'.

110. Yeats apparently conflated this from two adjacent passages in Gilchrist, *Life of Blake* (1880) I, 405–6: 'A humble feeble neighbour, her [i.e. Mrs Blake's] only other companion, said afterwards: "I have been at the death, not of a man, but of a blessed angel"' (I, 405); and George Richmond to Samuel Palmer, 15 Aug 1827, quoted in Gilchrist, *Life of Blake* (1880) I, 406: 'In truth he died like a saint, as a person who was standing by him observed' (Bentley, *Blake Records*, p. 347). Bentley has suggested (p. 342, n. 1) that Gilchrist's first passage could simply be a paraphrase from the second passage.

111. Blake died on 12 Aug 1827. Gilchrist, *Life of Blake* (1880), correctly records that Mrs Blake survived 'her husband only four years' (I, 409) and that she died 'on or about the 18th of October, 1831' (I, 411).

112. Blake, marginalia to John Caspar Lavater, *Aphorisms on Man*, tr. J. H. Fuseli (1788), no. 533, p. 181 (Bentley, *Blake's Writings*, p. 1377: 'a phantom of . . . & of the water').

113. Cunningham, *Lives of the Most Eminent British Painters* (see note 77 above), quoted in Bentley, *Blake Records*, pp. 506–7.
  'Irvingite' refers to the Catholic Apostolic Church, which is based on the teachings of Edward Irving (1792–1834), who styled himself a prophet and enjoyed great popularity in London during 1823. The Church, founded in 1832, announced the second coming of Christ and 'the restoration of the primitive Church' – *Corpus Dictionary of Western Churches*, ed. T. C. O'Brien (Washington, DC: Corpus, 1970) p. 136. It gave the title of 'angel' to the chief officer of a local church; see Plato Ernest Shaw, *The Catholic Apostolic Church, sometimes Called Irvingite: A Historical Study* (Morningside Heights, NY: King's Crown Press, 1946) pp. 171–2.

114. Blake, *The Marriage of Heaven and Hell*, pl. 21 (Bentley, *Blake's Writings*, p. 95).
115. Tatham, 'Life of Blake', in Bentley, *Blake Records*, pp. 528, 530: '. . . noble from his eccentric & elastic Mind'; 'A bad cause requires a long Book.'
116. Crabb Robinson's diary, 18 Feb 1826, quoted in *WWB* I, 146, and Bentley, *Blake Records*, p. 322 (diary): '. . . Visionary. . . .' Blake mentioned 'the Book of Moonlight' in ['Public Address'] (Notebook, p. 46); for this and the other lost works, including 'A Work on Art' (1809?) and *Outhoun* (1793?), see note 52 above, and Bentley, *Blake's Writings*, pp. 1037 and 1679–82.
117. Blake, 'The Caverns of the Grave Ive seen' (1793?–1818?; Notebook, p. 87) ll. 13–20 (*WWB* II, 75: '. . . prime, / . . . remain; / . . . rage, but . . . vain; / . . .; *PWB* 140: '. . . prime, / . . . remain; / . . . rage, but . . . vain; / . . . they hid eternally'; Bentley, *Blake's Writings*, p. 963: 'Reengravd Time . . . above Times troubled . . .').

MODERN IRISH POETRY

1. The wording of this proverbial expression varied in earlier versions of the introduction: 'Contention [1895; 'Strife' 1900] is better than loneliness.'
2. Seán Ua Tuama an Ghrinn (John O'Tuomy the Gay [or Wit], 1706/8–75), Gaelic poet and publican in Mungret Street, Limerick. Eoghan Ruadh Ó Súilleabháin (Owen Roe O'Sullivan, O'Sullivan the Red, 1748–84), Gaelic poet of Co. Kerry. Tadhg Gaedhealach Ó Súilleabháin (Timothy O'Sullivan the Gael, d. 1795/1800), Gaelic poet of Co. Cork. William O'Heffernan (called William Dall [the Blind], *c.* 1700–60), Gaelic poet of Co. Tipperary; see Yeats to Douglas Hyde, 15 Dec [1888] (*CL1* 115–16 and 116 n. 5). In 'Popular Ballad Poetry of Ireland' (1889), Yeats mentioned most of these Gaelic poets and he quoted the quatrain of invitation written by O'Tuomy (*UP1* 148). English victories at the Boyne (1690) and Aughrim (1691) effectively ended the Irish Jacobite resistance.
3. The anthology includes two poems by Oliver Goldsmith (1728–74), but none by Jonathan Swift (1667–1745) or the dramatist William Congreve (1670–1729), who published only occasional verse. Yeats also omitted Thomas Parnell (1679–1718), a member of the Scriblerus Club; Sir John Denham (1615–69), whose best-known poem, 'Cooper's Hill', describes English landscape; and Wentworth Dillon, 4th Earl of Roscommon (1633?–85), who translated the *Ars Poetica* of Horace into blank verse. Arthur James Balfour (1848–1930), who was Chief Secretary for Ireland from 1887 to 1891 and Prime Minister from 1902 to 1905, described Swift as 'an Irishman by the visitation of Heaven' ('Bishop Berkeley's Life and Letters' [1883] in *Essays and Addresses* [Edinburgh: Douglas, 1893], p. 100).
4. Thomas Moore (1779–1852), in *Irish Melodies* (10 vols, 1808–34), set his

poems to Irish folk airs. The two lyrics mentioned here are the only ones included in *BIV*.

Matthew Arnold, 'On the Study of Celtic Literature' (1866), in *Lectures and Essays in Criticism*, ed. R. H. Super (Ann Arbor: University of Michigan Press, 1962) p. 371.

5. Irish translations by Jeremiah (or James) Joseph Callanan (1795–1829) include 'The Convict of Clonmell', 'The Lament of O'Gnive', 'O Say, My Brown Drimin' and 'The Avenger', collected in *The Ballad Poetry of Ireland*, ed. Charles Gavan Duffy (Dublin: Duffy, 1845) pp. 117–18, 121–2, 131–2, 150–1; and 'The White Cockade' and 'The Girl I Love', collected in *The Songs of Ireland*, ed. Michael Joseph Barry (Dublin: Duffy, 1845) pp. 168–9, 189.

'Shule Aroon' is an anonymous ballad (early 18th c.), collected in Duffy, *Ballad Poetry of Ireland*, pp. 130–1.

'Kathleen O'More' is an anonymous song collected in Barry, *The Songs of Ireland*, p. 67.

6. Thomas Davis (1814–45) and James Clarence Mangan (1803–49) were the principal poets of the Young Ireland movement, founded in 1842, which fostered Irish cultural nationalism; see also p. 240, note 21 above. Sir Walter Scott (1771–1832), Scottish poet, novelist, and compiler of *Minstrelsy of the Scottish Border* (3 vols, 1802–3); Thomas Babington Macaulay (1800–59), English writer and statesman, author of *The History of England from the Accession of James II* (5 vols, 1849–61); Thomas Campbell (1777–1844), Scottish poet, chiefly remembered for his stirring ballads. Yeats had expressed the same opinion in 'The Literary Movement in Ireland' (1899; slightly rev. in *Ideals in Ireland*, ed. Lady Gregory [London: Unicorn Press, 1901] p. 88; *UP2* 185).

7. Untraced. Davis could praise 'the strength, the fortitude, the patience, the bravery of . . . the enrichers of the country', in comparison 'with the meanness in mind and courage of those who are opposed to them', but he never forgot their crushing poverty: 'Where else in Europe is the peasant ragged, fed on roots, in a wigwam, without education?' ('Ireland's People, Lords, Gentry, Commonalty' and 'Conciliation', in *Thomas Davis: Selections from his Prose and Poetry* [London: Gresham, n.d.] pp. 193, 277).

8. Thomas Davis, 'Tipperary', *National and Historical Ballads, Songs, and Poems*, rev. edn (Dublin: Duffy, [*c.* 1870]) p. 33, ll. 9–12: '. . . could stand / The . . . Tipperary!'

9. Thomas Davis, 'Oh! The Marriage' (air: 'The Swaggering Jig'), 'A Plea for Love', 'Mary Bhan Astór' ('Máire Bhán a Stóir: 'Fair Mary, my Treasure'), *BIV* 138–43; Davis, *National and Historical Ballads*, pp. 77–81. Thomas Davis, 'The Boatman of Kinsale' (air: 'An Cota Caol'), *National and Historical Ballads*, pp. 82–3.

10. 'Irish National Hymn' (1848) and 'Soul and Country' (1849), *Poems of James Clarence Mangan*, ed. D. J. O'Donogue (Dublin: O'Donoghue, 1903) pp. 105–7, 91–2.

11. 'O'Hussey's Ode to the Maguire', tr. Mangan (from the Irish of O'Hussey [fl. 1630], the last hereditary bard of the sept of Maguire), ll.

13–16, *BIV* 51 and *The Ballads of Ireland*, ed. Edward Hayes (Boston: Donahoe, 1857) I, 187 ('. . . bear he').

12. *BIV* includes two poems by Edward Walsh (1805–50) and two of his translations of Irish folk poems. The only poem by Michael Doheny (1805–63) included in the anthology is 'A Cuisle Geal mo Chroidhe' ('Bright Vein of my Heart'), which Yeats had singled out for praise in 1889 and 1895 (*UP1* 161, 347); Yeats explained that Doheny had written the song while in hiding, after the unsuccessful Young Ireland rising in July 1848, near Ballingarry, Co. Tipperary.

13. Sir Samuel Ferguson (1810–86); William Allingham (1824–89); Aubrey Thomas de Vere (1814–1902).

14. Samuel Ferguson, *Congal: A Poem in Five Books* (Dublin: Ponsonby, 1872) p. 53, l. 22 (book III, l. 122).

15. William Blake, ['Public Address'] (Notebook, p. 62) (*WWB* II, 383; *PWB* 253; *William Blake's Writings*, ed. G. E. Bentley, Jr, 2 vols [Oxford: Clarendon Press, 1978] p. 1042).

16. 'The Winding Banks of Erne; or the Emigrant's Adieu to Ballyshannon' (1861); Allingham was born in the coastal town Ballyshannon, Co. Donegal, on the River Erne, twenty miles north of Sligo.

17. For the Fenian movement and its 'triumvirate', see pp. 249–50, note 114 above. Charles J. Kickham (1828–82) is known more for his novels than his poems; *BIV* contains two of his poems and one by Ellen O'Leary (1831–89), but none by John Keegan Casey, whose poetry had enjoyed popular success; see Appendix 9 above for Yeats's explanation of the omission of Casey. Yeats's devotion to Irish nationalism owed much to John O'Leary (1830–1907), a Fenian journalist.

18. *BIV* omits both Frances Isabel 'Fanny' Parnell (1854–82) and Timothy Daniel Sullivan (1827–1914). Fanny Parnell's brother was the politician Charles Stewart Parnell, with whom Sullivan was associated in the Land League and in Parliament.

19. In *BIV*, at the equivalent of this passage, Yeats had supplied the following note, which refers to Charles J. Kickham (1828–82), *The Nation* (1842–91), *Catholic Opinion* (*c.* 1860?–76), and (perhaps) the *Illustrated Dublin Journal* (1861–2): 'A well-known poet of the Fenian times has made the curious boast – "Talking of work – since Sunday, two cols. notes, two cols. London gossip, and a leader one col., and one col. of verse for the *Nation*. For *Catholic Opinion*, two pages of notes and a leader. For *Illustrated Magazine*, three poems and a five-col. story."'

20. This reference to Genesis 6:14 was even more explicit in the 1895 text: '. . . an ark of gopherwood, the deluge. . . .'

21. For the heavily revised first published version (1895) of this paragraph and the next one, see Appendix 6 above.

22. Lionel Pigot Johnson (1867–1902) and Katharine Tynan Hinkson (1861–1931) were Yeats's friends. Johnson converted to Catholicism in 1891; for Johnson's claim to be Irish, see p. 274, note 9 below.

23. For Nora Hopper (later Mrs Chesson, 1871–1906) and George William Russell ('AE', 1867–1935), respectively, see pp. 116–17 and 113–15 above.

24. John 13:17.

25. Frederic Herbert Trench (1865–1923) was born in Ireland, but spent little time there; he was not included in either edition of *BIV*. His short lyric 'To Arolila: 5. Come, let us make Love deathless' is collected in *Selected Poems of Herbert Trench* (London: Cape, 1924) p. 120.

   'Ceann Dubh Deelish' ('Dear Black Head') (1894) by Dora Sigerson Shorter (1866–1918) is her only poem in *BIV* (as 'Can Doov Deelish'); it is not a translation of the anonymous seventeenth- or eighteenth-century Irish poem by that title. See 'Ceann Duv Dilis', tr. George Sigerson, in *Bards of the Gael and Gall: Examples of the Poetic Literature of Erinn* (1897), 3rd edn (Dublin: Talbot Press, 1925) p. 295.

26. Agnes Nesta Shakespeare Higginson (Mrs Skrine, 'Moira O'Neill'; b. *c.* 1870) was not included in either edition of *BIV*; Yeats's reference here is to her popular *Songs of the Glens of Antrim* (Edinburgh: Blackwood, Feb 1900).

27. Diarmad O'Curnain (1740–*c.* 1810), 'Love's Despair', tr. George Sigerson, in *Bards of the Gael and Gall*, pp. 349–50; l. 30 (p. 350) reads: 'Lost all – but the great love-gift of sorrow.' George Sigerson (1836–1925), under the pseudonym 'Erionnach', translated the second series of *The Poets and Poetry of Munster: A Selection of Songs*, collected by John O'Daly (Dublin: O'Daly, 1860). For Douglas Hyde's *The Love Songs of Connacht: Being the Fourth Chapter of the Songs of Connacht* (Dublin: Gill, 1893), of which the English portion was reprinted by the Cuala Press in 1904 with a preface by Yeats, see p. 135 above. Lady Gregory collected and translated Irish poetry and anecdotes in *Poets and Dreamers: Studies and Translations from the Irish* (Dublin: Hodges, Figgis, 1903).

28. Edward Dowden (1843–1913), Professor of English Literature at Trinity College, Dublin, was not included in either edition of *BIV*. He had published a 212-page volume of poems: *Poems* (London: King, 1876; 2nd edn 1877).

29. The first published version of the introduction was dated 5 Aug 1894. For a summary of the revisions, see the textual introduction, pp. 323–4 below.

30. John Francis Taylor (1850–1902), a Dublin barrister famed as an orator, took issue with Yeats's poor regard for the 'blazing rhetoric' of the poetry of the Young Ireland movement, as collected in the popular anthology edited by Thomas Davis, *The Spirit of the Nation* (Dublin: Duffy, 1843) (*UP2* 34). Yeats describes his quarrels with Taylor in *Mem* 52–3, 64–6, 68.

LIONEL JOHNSON

1. Rudyard Kipling (1865–1936), as in *Barrack-Room Ballads* (1892); William Watson (1858–1935), as in the political convictions of *The Purple East* (1896) and *The Years of Shame* (1896); John Davidson (1857–1909), as in *Fleet Street Eclogues* (1893, 1896); Arthur Symons (1865–1945), as in *London Nights* (1895) and *Amoris Victima* (1897).

2. Francis Thompson (1859–1907), as in 'The Hound of Heaven' (1893); Coventry Patmore (1823–96).

3. For these names of Irish other-worlds, see p. 237, note 57 above, in which Yeats quotes Douglas Hyde on the Country of the Young; *The Voyage of Bran*, tr. Kuno Meyer, commentary by Alfred Nutt, 2 vols (London: Nutt, 1895–7); Douglas Hyde, *A Literary History of Ireland: From Earliest Times to the Present Day* (London: Unwin, 1899) pp. 96–104; and Lady Gregory, *Gods and Fighting Men: The Story of the Tuatha de Danaan and of the Fianna of Ireland* (London: Murray, 1904) pp. 124, 136.

4. Visionary poems in *Homeward: Songs by the Way* (1894) and *The Earth Breath* (1897) by George William Russell ('AE'); see pp. 113–15 above and 275, note 2 below.

5. Nora Hopper (later Mrs Chesson), 'The Dark Man', in *Under Quicken Boughs* (London: Lane, 1896) p. 66, l. 23: 'While their lives' red ashes the gossips stir'. See pp. 117 above and 276, note 7 below.

6. Katharine Tynan Hinkson (1861–1931), as in *Louise de la Vallière* (1885), *Shamrocks* (1887), *Ballads and Lyrics* (1891), *Cuckoo Songs* (1894) and *A Lover's Breast-Knot* (1896).

7. In *The Death of Synge* (1904–14, publ. 1928) Yeats recalled that in the 1890s 'in Paris Synge once said to me, "We should unite stoicism, asceticism and ecstasy. Two of them have often come together, but the three never"' (*Au* 509). In a draft of a 1910 lecture, Yeats quoted Lionel Johnson's poem 'Te Martyrum Candidatus' (1895) as evidence of Johnson having written 'noble verse – the most stoical . . . of our time' ('Yeats's Lecture Notes for "Friends of My Youth"', ed. Joseph Ronsley, in *Yeats and The Theatre*, ed. Robert O'Driscoll and Lorna Reynolds [Toronto: Macmillan, 1975] p. 68).

8. Count Villiers de l'Isle-Adam, *Axël* (1890) iv.ii. This translation, which Yeats used again in *The Trembling of the Veil* (1922) and in his preface to *Axel*, tr. H. P. R. Finberg (1925) (p. 156 above), is from Arthur Symons, 'Villiers de L'Isle-Adam', in *The Symbolist Movement in Literature* (London: Heinemann, 1899) p. 56.

9. Johnson converted to Catholicism in 1891. He was active in the Irish Literary Society in London during the mid 1890s, supported Irish nationalism, and – despite an absence of Irish parents – sometimes called himself 'Irish' (for example, in a letter to Edmund Gosse, 29 Dec 1893, quoted in Raymond Roseliep, 'Some Letters of Lionel Johnson' [diss., Notre Dame University, Indiana, 1953] p. 142).

10. Quintus Sertorius (d. 72 BC), Roman general and statesman: 'Sertorius' (written 1889), in *Poems* (London: Mathews, 1895) pp. 112–14. Lucretius (96?–55 BC), Roman philosophical poet: 'Lucretius' (written 1887–90), in *Poems*, pp. 73–5. Charles Stewart Parnell (1846–91), Irish nationalist leader: 'Parnell' (written 1893), in *Poems*, pp. 31–3. On 'Ireland's dead': 'Ireland's Dead' (written 1893), in *Poems*, pp. 51–2. On the Rising of 1798: 'Ninety-Eight' (written 1894) and 'To the Dead of '98' (written 1897) in *Ireland: With other Poems* (London: Mathews, 1897) pp. 67, 79. St Columba (or Columcille; 543–915): 'Saint Columba' (written 1894), in *Poems*, pp. 114–15. Pope Leo XIII (1810–1903, Pope

from 1878): 'To Leo XIII' (written 1892), in *Poems*, p. 81.

11. Lionel Johnson, 'The Church of a Dream' (written 1890), in *Poems* (1895) pp. 84, l. 7; 85, l. 9.

12. George William Russell ('AE').

AE

1. Charles Johnson (1867–1931) founded the Hermetic Society in Dublin in June 1885; Yeats was its chairman. Their friend George William Russell ('AE', 1867–1935) did not join but was closely associated with them, especially in their study of Theosophy. Yeats moved to London at the end of 1886. From 1891 to 1897 AE lived at the Theosophical Household in Upper Ely Place, Dublin, where Yeats and William Kirkpatrick Magee ('John Eglinton', 1868–1961) were frequent visitors.

2. (William Kirkpatrick Magee), *Two Essays on the Remnant* (Dublin: Whaley, 1894); AE, *Homeward: Songs by the Way* (Dublin: Whaley, 1894) and *The Earth Breath and Other Poems* (New York and London: Lane, 1897).

3. Plotinus (*c.* 205–70) frequently emphasised the distinction between the body and the soul, which is immortal and incorruptible; see, for example, *Enneads*, iii.vi.1, iv.iii.24 and iv.vii.10, each of which is included in *Select Works of Plotinus*, tr. Thomas Taylor (1817), ed. G. R. S. Mead (London: Bell, 1895) pp. 80–1, 240–1 and 154–6. This particular quotation, which Yeats also used in a review of AE's *The Earth Breath and Other Poems* in April 1898 (*UP2* 112), is untraced. Yeats's friend Arthur Symons used the same quotation in his Conclusion to *The Symbolist Movement in Literature* (London: Heinemann, 1899; dedicated to Yeats) pp. 174–5: '. . . earth as . . . phantom scenes appear.'

4. 'Star Teachers', *The Earth Breath and Other Poems*, p. 89, ll. 15–16: 'For every star and every deep they fill / Are stars and deep within.'

5. 'Echoes', *Homeward: Songs by the Way*, p. 17, ll. 10–12: '. . . being seem; / We kiss, because . . . sought / Within a. . . .'

6. 'Symbolism', *Homeward: Songs by the Way*, p. 48, ll. 15–16.

7. 'Sung on a By-way', *Homeward: Songs by the Way*, p. 23: 'dream shaft' (l. 3); 'drink,' (l. 7).

8. 'A Vision of Beauty', *The Earth Breath and Other Poems*, pp. 15–16, ll. 20–9: '. . . shaken . . . kindled. . . . the Ages draws . . . away / Through. . . .'

9. 'The Fountain of Shadowy Beauty: A Dream', *The Earth Breath and Other Poems*, p. 39, ll. 116–19, 127: '. . . high Ancestral Self.'

NORA HOPPER

1. Northern French medieval poets, e.g. Chrétien de Troyes (12th c.).

2. Nora Hopper (later Mrs Chesson, 1871–1906), *Ballads in Prose* (stories

and poems) (London: Lane, 1894) and *Under Quicken Boughs* (poems) (London: Lane, 1896).
3. Pseudonym of William Sharp (1855–1905).
4. Untitled poem in her story 'Daluan', *Ballads in Prose*, p. 97: ' "All away to ... / ... son." / "The ... / ... gain – the ... son – / He ... ever when ... done – / He. ... .'
5. 'Daluan', *Ballads in Prose*, p. 101. 'Monday' and 'Tuesday' in Irish are *Luan* and *Máirt*.
6. *Ballads in Prose*, pp. 83–7, 125–44, 151–60 and 167–77. See also Patrick Kennedy, *Legendary Fictions of the Irish Celts* (London: Macmillan, 1866) p. 101.
7. *Under Quicken Boughs*, pp. 149 and 65–6 ('The Dark Man' opens each of its six stanzas with 'Rose o' the world').

ALTHEA GYLES

1. 'Sympathy', the only poem by Althea Gyles (1868–1949) in the anthology, had first appeared in the December 1898 issue of *The Dome* (new ser. 1, 239), together with Yeats's essay on her, 'A Symbolic Artist and the Coming of Symbolic Art' (233–7; repr. *UP2* 133–7). Ian Fletcher, who printed 'Sympathy' in his comprehensive study 'Poet and Designer: W. B. Yeats and Althea Gyles' (*Yeats Studies*, 1 [1971] 68), found only one earlier published poem by her.
2. She designed the covers for Yeats's *The Secret Rose* (1897), *Poems* (1899 and subsequent edns to 1927), *The Wind among the Reeds* (1899) and *The Shadowy Waters* (1900). The spine decoration of *The Secret Rose* (1897) was reused for *The Celtic Twilight*, 2nd edn (1902).

THOUGHTS ON LADY GREGORY'S TRANSLATIONS

1. *Imbas forosnai* ('palm-knowledge of enlightening'), one of the three ceremonies for attaining prophetic dreams, was among the requirements for a *filé*, the highest rank of the ancient Irish poets. See Yeats, 'Irish Witch Doctors' (1900), *UP2* 230; Eugene O'Curry, *On the Manners and Customs of the Ancient Irish: A Series of Lectures*, ed. W. K. Sullivan (London: Williams and Norgate, 1873) ii, 135, 208–12; and Patrick Weston Joyce, *A Social History of Ancient Ireland* (London: Longmans, Green, 1903) i, 242–5.
2. See Lady Gregory, *Gods and Fighting Men: The Story of the Tuatha de Danaan and of the Fianna of Ireland* (London: Murray, 1904) p. 444 ('Oisin in Patrick's House').

3. Yeats was twenty years old when he met William Morris (1834–96), the English poet, artist and socialist, at a meeting of the Contemporary Club during Morris's visit to Dublin, 9–14 Apr 1886, for lectures at the Dublin branch of the Social Democratic Federation. Yeats published this anecdote, but without naming Morris, in November 1886 in 'The Poetry of Sir Samuel Ferguson' (*UP1* 89). For an Irish account of the Battle of Clontarf, Dublin (23 Apr 1014), see *Cogadh Gaedhil re Gallaibh: The War of the Gaedhil with the Gaill; or, The Invasions of Ireland by the Danes and other Norsemen* (written *c*. 1016), ed. and tr. James Henthorn Todd (London: Longmans, 1867) pp. 151–217; for a Norse account see *Njál's Saga*, ch. 157.

4. For Murchadh refusing Aoibheall of Carrick-lea, a Leannan Sidhe, see *Gods and Fighting Men*, p. 87 ('Aoibhell') and Nicholas O'Kearney, *Feis Tighe Chonain Chinn-Shleibhe; or, The Festivities at the House of Conan of Ceann-Sleibhe, in the Country of Clare*, Transactions of the Ossianic Society, 2 (1854 [publ. 1855]) 101–2.

5. William Paton Ker, *Epic and Romance: Essays on Medieval Literature* (London: Macmillan, 1897).

6. See Yeats's discussion of Tír-na-nÓg in *FFT*, pp. 20–1 above.

7. Cuchulain, heroic warrior of Irish legend.

8. The Morrigu, a Tuatha de Danaan queen and goddess of battle; see Lady Gregory, *Cuchulain of Muirthemne: The Story of the Men of the Red Branch of Ulster* (London: Murray, 1902) pp. 211–12 ('The War for the Bull of Cuailgne').

9. Ferdiad, a foster-brother of Cuchulain, was persuaded by Queen Maeve to fight Cuchulain in single combat; see *Cuchulain of Muirthemne*, pp. 233, 235 ('The War for the Bull of Cuailgne').

10. See *Cuchulain of Muirthemne*, pp. 305–6 ('Battle of Rosnaree').

11. See p. 262, note 46 above.

12. See *Cuchulain of Muirthemne*, pp. 265–7, 199–200 ('The Awakening of Ulster', 'The War for the Bull of Cualigne').

13. Manannan the sea-god.

14. See *Gods and Fighting Men*, p. 191 ('The Lad of the Skins').

15. The Morrigu; see note 8 above and *Cuchulain of Muirthemne*, p. 212 ('The War for the Bull of Cuailgne').

16. In 'the Country of the Young. . . . the trees are stooping down with fruit and with leaves and with blossom' (*Gods and Fighting Men*, p. 432 ['The Call of Oisin']).

17. In the Icelandic *Grettis Saga*, ch. 45, part 15, these are the last words of Alti Ásmundarson, who was slain treacherously at his front door. See *The Story of Grettir the Strong*, tr. Eiríkr Magnússon and William Morris (London: Ellis, 1869; repr. London: Longmans, Green, 1900) p. 133: 'Broad spears are about now.' See also *Grettir's Saga*, tr. Denton Fox and Hermann Pálsson (Toronto: University of Toronto Press, 1974) p. 95: 'Broad spears are becoming fashionable nowadays.'

18. Untraced. In an earlier use of this remark, Yeats acknowledged an unnamed scholar as his immediate source (1901; *E&I* 107). James Olney has suggested that this doctrine is Heraclitan and, to some extent, also

Platonic – *The Rhizome and the Flower: The Perennial Philosophy – Yeats and Jung* (Berkeley and Los Angeles: University of California Press, 1980) pp. 119, 212.

19. See *Cuchulain of Muirthemne*, pp. 175–244 ('The War for the Brown Bull of Cuailgne').

20. The brown bull of Cuailgne and the white-horned bull of Cruachan Ai; see *Cuchulain of Muirthemne*, pp. 268–75 ('The Two Bulls').

21. The *Mabinogion*, a collection of Welsh heroic tales, was compiled in the fourteenth and fifteenth centuries; the *Morte d'Arthur* is a fourteenth-century selection of Arthurian legends.

22. See *Cuchulain of Muirthemne*, pp. 121–2, 130–1 ('Fate of the Sons of Usnach').

23. The 'beautiful, pale, long-faced' Maeve (or Medb), queen of Connacht, separately promised her beautiful daughter Findabair 'to every one of the twelve kings of Munster' as a reward for participating in the war for the bull of Cuailgne. When Findabair learned this and that 'seven hundred men had got their death on account of her . . . her heart broke with the shame and the pity that came on her, and she fell dead' (*Cuchulain of Muirthemne*, pp. 247, 251 ['The Awakening of Ulster']).

24. Deirdre, the beautiful woman whom King Conchubar intended as his bride, laments the murder of her lover Naoise, one of Conchubar's men. See *Cuchulain of Muirthemne*, pp. 134–9 ('Fate of the Sons of Usnach').

25. For these three incidents in the life of Cuchulain's wife, Emer, see *Cuchulain of Muirthemne*, pp. 54–61, 282, 327–8 ('Bricriu's Feast', 'The Only Jealousy of Emer' and 'The Great Gathering at Muirthemne').

26. Iseult, of Arthurian legend; Brunnhilda, a queen in the German *Nibelungenlied*.

27. From *Cuchulain of Muirthemne*, pp. 346, 349 ('Death of Cuchulain'): ' ". . . love," she . . .'; '. . . Conall . . . to-day: and. . . .'

28. Cruachan, the seat of the kings and queens of Connacht, is thirty-five miles south of Sligo, near Tulsk, Co. Roscommon.

29. The Hill of Allen (elev. 672 ft) is five miles north of Kildare, Co. Kildare. *Gods and Fighting Men* refers to it as 'wide Almhuin' and 'Almhuin of Leinster' ('Oisin's Children' and 'The Coming of Finn', pp. 315, 168).

30. Seat of the High King of Ireland, five miles south-east of Navan, Co. Meath.

31. For example, Sadbh, wife of Finn, in *Gods and Fighting Men*, p. 174 ('Oisin's Mother').

32. Tigearnach the Annalist (d. 1088) wrote that Finn was killed in AD 283. Douglas Hyde, in *A Literary History of Ireland: From Earliest Times to the Present Day* (London: Unwin, 1899) pp. 382–3, accepted the likely historical reality of Finn as the chief captain of King Cormac mac Art (reigned AD 254–77) at Tara (Teamhair) and of Grania as the daughter of Cormac mac Art, but Hyde noted it was an 'accident that the creative imagination of the later Gaels happened to seize upon' Finn 'and make him and his contemporaries the nucleus of a vast literature instead of some earlier or later group of perhaps equally deserving champions. Finn has long since become to all ears a pan-Gaelic champion just as Arthur

has become a Brythonic one.' See also Eugene O'Curry, *Lectures on the Manuscript Materials of Ancient Irish History: Delivered at the Catholic University of Ireland, during the Sessions of 1855 and 1856*, 2nd edn (Dublin: Hinch, Traynor, 1878) pp. 303–4 (lecture xiv); and Joyce, *A Social History of Ancient Ireland* (1903) i, 87.

33. The Annals of the Four Masters records that the reign of Eochaidh Feidhleach began 142 BC (AM 5058); his daughter was Maeve, who instigated the war for the bull of Cuailgne, in which Cuchulain was a champion (*Annals of the Kingdom of Ireland, by the Four Masters, from the Earliest Period to the Year 1616*, ed. John O'Donovan, 2nd edn [Dublin: Hodges, Smith, 1856] i, 87); O'Donovan remarked that 'no competent scholar can doubt' that the chronology of the earliest periods in the annals 'is arbitrary and uncertain' (i, xlii). The Annals of Tigernach, which mentions Cuchulain's birth, gives the date of his death as AD 2 ('The Annals of Tigernach', ed. Whitley Stokes, *Revue celtique*, 16 [1895] 404, 407).

34. Cromlech (or dolmen): a prehistoric tomb of erect stones supporting a flat stone. For the lovers Diarmuid and Grania, see note 61 below and *Gods and Fighting Men*, pp. 343–99 ('Diarmuid and Grania').

35. *Gods and Fighting Men*, pp. 450–1 ('The Arguments'): '. . . of the ducks from the lake . . . Berries. The whistle . . . Victories, or . . . ridge by the . . . Druim-re-Coir.'

36. *Gods and Fighting Men*, p. 245 ('Credhe's Lament'): 'Credhe, wife of Cael, came . . . others, and. . . . searching, she . . . fox that her nestlings. . . .'

37. For Bodb Dearg, a Tuatha de Danaan, see note 61 below. *Gods and Fighting Men*, p. 216 ('The Help of the Men of Dea'): '. . . prince or . . . Ireland without. . . .'

38. The old hunter is thought to be Orion. The Greeks hid at Tenedos during the ploy of the wooden horse at Troy. Robert Browning, 'Pauline' (1833), ll. 323–5: '. . . gods, or . . . Tenedos' (*The Poetical Works of Robert Browning*, ed. Ian Jack and Margaret Smith [Oxford: Clarendon Press, 1983] i, 47 [1888 text]).

39. *Cuchulain of Muirthemne*, pp. 175–244, 320–33.

40. *Gods and Fighting Men*, pp. 343–99 ('Diarmuid and Grania'); *Cuchulain of Muirthemne*, pp. 104–42 ('Fate of the Children of Usnach').

41. Untraced. Jacob Boehme, in *Forty Questions of the Soul* (iv.7) and *The Three Principles* (x.17), follows the biblical account (Genesis 2:19–20) of Adam naming the creatures; those passages from Boehme are quoted in Franz Hartmann, *The Life and Doctrines of Jacob Boehme: The God-Taught Philosopher: An Introduction to the Study of his Works* (1891), repr. as *Personal Christianity: A Science: The Doctrines of Jacob Boehme: The God-Taught Philosopher* (New York: Macoy, 1919) p. 152. See also Boehme, *The Aurora* (1634) tr. John Sparrow (1656), ed. C. J. Barker and D. S. Hehner (London: Watkins, 1914) p. 507 (xix.92).

42. In 'The Pursuit of the Gilla Dacker and his Horse', Feradach, a king's son, magically makes a ship for Finn from a wooden stick, with only three blows of a joiner's axe. See *Old Celtic Romances*, tr. Patrick Weston Joyce 3rd edn (London: Longmans, Green, 1907) pp. 240–2, and 'Pursuit of the

Gilla decair', tr. Standish Hayes O'Grady, *Silva Gadelica I.–XXXI.* (London: Williams and Norgate, 1892) II, 299.

43. *Gods and Fighting Men*, p. 431 ('Death of Bran').
44. See *Gods and Fighting Men*, pp. 110–15 ('His Call to Bran').
45. *Gods and Fighting Men*, p. 428 ('The Battle of Gabhra'): 'The way you would like me to be.'
46. *Gods and Fighting Men*, pp. 423–4 ('Death of Goll'): ' ". . . And O sweet-voiced . . . me; and remember. . . . And do . . . said; "but . . . lover, Aodh, the son . . . came out from . . . fought at Corcar-an-Deirg; and . . . is in want of a. . . ." '
47. The Men of Dea are also known as the Tuatha de Danaan. See *Gods and Fighting Men*, pp. 51–62, 217, 267–8 ('The Great Battle of Magh Tuireadh', 'The Help of the Men of Dea', and 'Cat-Heads and Dog-Heads').
48. *Gods and Fighting Men*, p. 96 ('Midhir and Etain'): '. . . warm, sweet streams . . . and of wine . . . care and now. . . .'
49. Untraced. See the 1902–3 draft of Yeats's unfinished novel *The Speckled Bird* (*SB* 227): 'He may even claim with the Druids that mankind created the world.'
50. *Gods and Fighting Men*, p. 456 ('The Arguments'); see also p. 162 above.
51. The glove and shoes are untraced; Yeats's source may have been an Aran Islands love song (*Au* 322). Beara made a coat for Eoghan from a salmon; see *Gods and Fighting Men*, pp. 310–11 ('Oisin's Children').
52. This saying by the Greek tragic dramatist Aeschylus (525–456 BC) is reported in the *Deipnosophists* of Athenaeus, a Greek scholar (fl. *c.* AD 200) in Egypt: '. . . the saying of the noble and glorious Aeschylus, who declared that this tragedies were large cuts taken from Homer's mighty dinners' (VIII.347e) (tr. Charles B. Gulick, Loeb Classics [Cambridge, Mass.: Harvard University Press, 1957] IV, 75). Gilbert Murray's translation is 'slices from the great banquets of Homer' (*Aeschylus: The Creator of Tragedy* [Oxford: Clarendon Press, 1940] p. 160).
53. See *Gods and Fighting Men*, p. 312 ('Oisin's Children'), and, for a richly elaborated version, pp. 286–7 ('The Wedding at Ceann Slieve').
54. The 'Fenian' (Irish Republican Brotherhood) rising of 1867.
55. Anonymous ballads that begin, 'Come all ye. . . .'
56. For the Jerusalem wager by Thomas ('Buck' or 'Jerusalem') Whaley, see John Edward Walsh's anonymously published *Sketches of Ireland Sixty Years Ago* (Dublin: McGlashan, 1847) p. 16; Yeats, "A Reckless Century: Irish Rakes and Duellists" (1891), *UP1* 202; and Robert Lynd, 'The Irish Theatre: An Interview with Mr W. B. Yeats', 6 June 1910, quoted by Donald T. Torchiana, *W. B. Yeats and Georgian Ireland* (Evanston, Ill.: Northwestern University Press, 1966) p. 19. Colonel Richard Martin (1754–1834) gave away 'two kegs of gold' on the streets of Galway in 1791; Yeats used the anecdote in a lecture in 1910 (reported in the Dublin *Evening Telegraph*, 4 Mar 1910; repr. Richard Ellmann, *The Identity of Yeats*, 2nd edn [London: Faber, 1964] pp. 205–6) and in his ballad 'Colonel Martin' (1937) (*P* 314–16).
57. Daniel O'Connell (1775–1847), Irish nationalist leader, killed Capt.

J. N. D'Esterre in a duel, 1 Feb 1815. 'The memory of the duel haunted him for the remainder of his life. He never went to Communion afterwards without wearing a white glove on his right hand as a sign of penance' – Denis Gwynn, *Daniel O'Connell*, 2nd edn (Cork: Cork University Press, 1947) p. 126.

58. This anecdote about Alexander the Great (356–323 BC) is untraced. Yeats perhaps here mistakenly inverted the tradition of Alexander urging his troops onward while in a forest in Kashmir; see the accounts, from the first and second centuries, of Quintus Curtius, *History of Alexander the Great of Macedon*, 9.1.9–10 ('forests'), 9.2.12–34, and Arrian, *Anabasis of Alexander*, 5.25ff.

59. *Gods and Fighting Men*, p. 429 ('The Battle of Gabhra'): '. . . iron. But . . . fighting men, and. . . .'

60. Yeats mentioned a 'Seaghan the fool, / That never did a hand's turn', in the 1906 version of *The Shadowy Waters*, ll. 129–30 (*VP* 228).

61. Slieve-na-Mon (elev. 2,368 ft), a mountain in south-eastern Co. Tipperary; as Sidhe Femen it was the home of Bodb Dearg, a Tuatha de Danaan; see *Gods and Fighting Men*, pp. 73–4 ('Bodb Dearg'). For the Hill of Allen, see p. 278, note 29 above. Benbulben (see p. 250, note 1 above) was the scene of the boar hunt in which Grania's lover, Diarmuid, died; see *Gods and Fighting Men*, pp. 389–97 ('The Boar of Beinn Gulbain').

62. Dundealgan (Dun Delga), Cuchulain's home, Dundalk, Co. Louth. Emain Macha, King Conchubar's capital, Navan Fort (or Hill), two miles west of Armagh, Co. Armagh. Muirthemne, a plain along the north coast of Co. Louth between the River Boyne and Dundalk.

LOVE SONGS OF CONNACHT

1. The first three 'chapters' were 'Songs of Carolan and his Contemporaries', 'Songs in Praise of Women' and 'Drinking Songs'. They were published during 1890 in Hyde's column in the weekly newspaper *The Nation*. The fifth 'chapter' was *Songs Ascribed to Raftery* (Dublin: Gill, 1903); the sixth and seventh were *The Religious Songs of Connacht: A Collection of Poems, Stories, Prayers, Satires, Ranns, Charms, etc.*, 2 vols (Dublin: Gill; London: Unwin, 1905–6).

2. Untraced; in a draft version the quoted phrase was 'sap and savour'.

JOHNSON: POETRY AND PATRIOTISM

1. Lionel Johnson (1867–1902), English poet, delivered the lecture 'Poetry and Patriotism' in Dublin, 26 Apr 1894.

2. Johnson's alcoholism increasingly afflicted him during the 1890s and led to his death, at the age of thirty-five, in 1902.

3. Lionel Johnson, 'Mystic and Cavalier' (1889, publ. 1894), in *Poems* (London: Mathews, 1895) p. 30, ll. 1–12: '. . . company? Before. . . . //. . . . // . . . eyes? / Is . . . depths? The. . . .'

SYNGE: DEIRDRE OF THE SORROWS

1. The successive drafts of *Deirdre of the Sorrows* reached letter 'O' and totalled some 1000 pages. See J. M. Synge, *Works*, iv: *Plays*, book ii, ed. Ann Saddlemyer (London: Oxford University Press, 1968) pp. xxx, 368–9; also pp. xxxii–xxxiii.
2. Synge had finished draft 'B' of the play in November 1907 and was to deliver the play to the Cuala Press in spring 1908 but did not finish it. He died 24 March 1909. See Yeats to John Quinn, 27 April 1908, *L* 510.
3. For Owen see Saddlemyer, in Synge, *Plays*, book ii, pp. 382–93, and Yeats's diary entry for 5 March 1909 in *Mem* 177 (rev. 1926 in *Au* 487).
4. Owen, who does not appear in Act i, commits suicide using his own knife in Act ii (Synge, *Plays*, book ii, p. 235).

SELECTIONS FROM THE WRITINGS OF LORD DUNSANY

1. Thomas Davis, the principal poet of the Young Ireland movement and a founder of its journal *The Nation*, died at the age of thirty-one. His funeral procession in Dublin, 18 Sep 1845, included nearly eighty carriages. Lady Jane Francesca Elgee Wilde (1824–96) contributed fervently nationalistic poems to *The Nation*, under the pseudonym of 'Sperzana'; she first submitted poems to *The Nation* in 1844. See *Irish Literature* (Philadelphia: Morris, 1904) ix, 3556.
2. The Cuala Press, Dundrum, Co. Dublin. The Library of Ireland series, published in Dublin by Charles Gavan Duffy (1816–1903), a leader of the Young Ireland movement, contained the following eight histories and three collections of ballads: Thomas Mac Nevin, *The History of the Volunteers of 1782* (1845); Duffy, *The Ballad Poetry of Ireland* (1845); Michael Joseph Barry, *The Songs of Ireland* (1845); John Mitchel, *The Life and Times of Aodh O'Neill, Prince of Ulster; Called by the English, Hugh, Earl of Tyrone* (1846); Thomas Mac Nevin, *The Confiscation of Ulster, in the Reign of James the First, Commonly Called the Ulster Plantation* (1846); Michael Doheny, *The History of the American Revolution* (1846); Denis Florence McCarthy, *The Book of Irish Ballads* (1846); Charles Patrick Meehan, *The Confederation of Kilkenny* [1642–8]: *The Rise and Fall of the Family of the Geraldines* (1846); and Thomas Darcy Magee, *The Lives of the Irish Writers of the Seventeenth Century; and the Life and Reign of Art M'Murrogh, King of Leinster*, 2 vols in 1 (1847).

3. For a list of some Dun Emer Press and Cuala Press books see note 14 below. 'Mary of the Nation' was a pseudonym of the Irish poet Ellen Mary Patrick Downing (1828–69); her remark is untraced.

4. Daniel O'Connell (1775–1847), Irish nationalist campaigner for Roman Catholic civil rights, was famed for his addresses to huge outdoor public meetings. The 'lonely and haughty person' was Charles Stewart Parnell (1846–91), leader of the Irish Parliamentary Party until his downfall in 1890.

5. Lady Gregory, *Cuchulain of Muirthemne: The Story of the Men of the Red Branch of Ulster* (London: Murray, 1902) pp. 281–2 ('The Awakening of Ulster').

   James Stephens (1882–1950), perhaps 'Where the Demons Grin', *A Broadside*, 1, no. 6 (Nov 1908) sig. [1ᵛ], ll. 1–3: 'The hill was low, but stretched away / A straggling mile or so to where / The sea was stamping, tossing gray'.

   Yeats included Charles J. Kickham's ballad 'The Irish Peasant Girl' (1859) in *BIV* 180–1; ll. 1 and 4 read: 'She lived beside the Anner . . . With mild eyes like the dawn'.

   Samuel Ferguson's ballad 'The Pretty Girl of Loch Dan', published Sep 1836 in the *Dublin University Magazine*, was collected in Duffy, *Ballad Poetry of Ireland*, pp. 54–6.

   For the novels of Charles J. Lever (1806–72), see pp. 54–6 above.

6. Ercole I d'Este (1431–1505), Duke of Ferrara, Modena and Reggio, planned in 1490, with the assistance of the architect Biagio Rossetti, an ambitious extension of Ferrara. The Via degli Angeli (now Corso Vittorio Emanuele) is the most splendid street of this 'Addizione Erculea'. The Italian poet Giosue Carducci (1835–1907) praised that street in the opening of his ode 'Alla città di Ferrara' (1895), *Rime e Ritmi* (1899), ed. M. Valgimigli and G. Salinari (Bologna: Zanichelli, 1964) p. 126.

7. A fictional city in the short story 'Idle Days on the Yann', *Selections from the Writings of Lord Dunsany* (Dundrum: Cuala Press, 1912) p. 79: 'Perdóndaris, that. . . .'

8. Untraced.

9. In 1909, when Yeats encouraged Lord Dunsany (Edward J. M. D. Plunkett, 18th Baron Dunsany, 1878–1957), a conservative opponent of Irish nationalism, to write a one-act play for the Abbey Theatre, Dunsany had published three volumes of fantasy stories set in imaginary Eastern lands.

10. Slieve-na-Mon (see p. 281, note 61 above) is numbered among Yeats's 'old sacred places' (*Mem* 124) as the site of a house of Irish gods; as Sidhe Femen it was the home of Bodb Dearg, a Tuatha de Danaan king; see Lady Gregory, *Gods and Fighting Men: The Story of the Tuatha de Danaan and of the Fianna of Ireland* (London: Murray, 1904) pp. 73–4.

    Slieve Fua (Fuad or Fuait) is an elevated region now called the Fews, in southern Co. Armagh; its highest point is Slieve Gullion (G-Cullain or Cuilinn; elev. 1880 ft), five miles south-west of Newry. It has extensive legendary associations with Cuchulain, the *Táin*, Naoise and Deirdre, and Finn. Yeats mentioned it in a note to *The Wind among the Reeds* (1899; *VP* 802) and later named it as a 'holy mountain' in *The Herne's Egg*, scene v, ll. 92–3; *VPl* 1033).

11. From Edmund Campion (1540–81) in *A Historie of Ireland* (written 1571), reported in John Edward Walsh's anonymously published *Sketches of Ireland Sixty Years Ago* (Dublin: McGlashan, 1847) p. 66:

> The intense passion of the Irish for gambling has often been observed. Campion, writing nearly three hundred years ago, mentions it, and notices a class, called Carrowes, whose only occupation, all year long, was playing at cards. He describes them as gambling away their mantles and all their clothes, and then lying down in their bare skins in straw by the road-side, to invite passers by to play with them for their glibbes [i.e. forelocks of hair], their nails. . . .

For the text of Campion see *The Ancient Irish Histories of Spencer, Campion, Hanmer, and Marleburrough*, ed. James Ware (1803; repr. Dublin: Hibernia Press, 1809) ii, 27–8.

12. 'Kubla Khan' (publ. 1816) by Samuel Taylor Coleridge mentions Mount Abora (l. 41), which is usually accepted as an allusion to 'Mount Amara', an earthly paradise in Ethiopia, mentioned by Milton in *Paradise Lost*, iv.281.

The poetry and paintings by George Russell ('AE') often incorporate his visionary encounters with gods and spirits in the Irish countryside. Yeats's one-act play *The Land of Heart's Desire*, based on Irish fairy lore, was first produced in 1894.

13. Peg Inerney is a character in *Maeve* (1900), a play by Edward Martyn (1859–1923).

14. These Dun Emer and Cuala Press books were: Douglas Hyde, *The Love Songs of Connacht* (1904); Lady Gregory, *A Book of Saints and Wonders* (1906); George Russell ('AE'), *The Nuts of Knowledge* (1903) and *By Still Waters: Lyrical Poems* (1906); John Synge, *Poems and Translations* (1909) and *Deirdre of the Sorrows* (1910); and Yeats, *In the Seven Woods* (1903), *Stories of Red Hanrahan* (1905), *Discoveries* (1907), *Poetry and Ireland* (1908), *The Green Helmet and Other Poems* (1910) and *Synge and the Ireland of his Time* (1911).

15. The play *Pelléas et Mélisande* (1892; perf. 1893), by the Belgian poet, dramatist and essayist Maurice Maeterlinck (1862–1949), was taken as a subject by several leading composers: Claude Debussy scored it as an opera (1893–5, 1901; perf. 1902); Gabriel Fauré wrote incidental music for it (perf. London, 1898), as did Jean Sibelius (1905); and Arnold Schoenberg wrote a tone poem based on it (1902–3; perf. 1905).

Alexandre Dumas (known as Dumas *fils*, 1824–95), French playwright and novelist.

16. The French poet Charles Pierre Baudelaire (1821–67) admired Edgar Allen Poe (1809–49), American poet, story-writer and essayist. Through Baudelaire's essays on Poe (1852–7) and translations of Poe (1848–65),

Poe influenced a number of other French poets, such as Stéphane Mallarmé (1842–98) and Arthur Rimbaud (1854–91).

17. Dunsany's short stories, 'The Fall of Babbulkund', from *The Sword of Welleran and Other Stories* (London: Allen, 1908), and 'Idle Days on the Yann', from *A Dreamer's Tale* (London: Allen, 1910), are included in *Selections from Dunsany*, pp. 45–67 and 69–95.

18. Alexander Gilchrist, *Life of William Blake*, 2nd edn (London: Macmillan, 1880) I, 7: 'One day, a traveller was telling bright wonders of some foreign city. "Do you call *that* splendid?" broke in young Blake; "I should call a city splendid in which the houses were of gold, the pavement of silver, the gates ornamented with precious stones."'

19. Thomas De Quincey (1795–1859), author of *Confessions of an English Opium Eater* (1821). The pseudonym 'Sir John Mandeville' was used by the anonymous compiler and inventor of a French book of travels to the East, translated as *The Voiage and Travaile of Sir John Maundeville* (*c.* 1357–71).

20. 'Idle Days on the Yann', *Selections from Dunsany*, p. 75 (which follows the text of *A Dreamer's Tales*, p. 66): '. . . danced, but . . . the ways of . . . exile dance, in . . . gypsies, for . . . for a fragment. . . .'

21. 'The Fall of Babbulkund', *Selections from Dunsany*, p. 49 (which follows the text of *The Sword of Welleran and Other Stories*, pp. 46–7); Yeats dropped four commas from Dunsany's text: '. . . things, softly . . . whisper, but. . . . again, and. . . . desert, and. . . .'

22. 'Idle Days on the Yann', *Selections from Dunsany*, p. 87.

23. 'Idle Days on the Yann', *Selections from Dunsany*, pp. 84–5.

24. 'Idle Days on the Yann', *Selections from Dunsany*, p. 92.

25. *The Gods of the Mountain* (1911), Act III, in *Selections from Dunsany*, p. 27.

26. Iseult Gonne (1894–1954), the daughter of Maud Gonne, at whose Normandy country house Yeats wrote his introduction in August 1912.

27. 'Idle Days on the Yann', *Selections from Dunsany*, pp. 91, 73.

TAGORE: THE POST OFFICE

1. 10–12 July 1913, at the Court Theatre, during the Abbey Theatre company's London tour; the first production had been 17 May 1913, at the Abbey Theatre, Dublin.

2. In the play, the Headman is a village bully; the curdseller (the Dairyman) and the Gaffer (old man) are generous and kind to the dying boy, who yearns to be outside and to travel, but who has been ordered by his doctor to remain indoors.

3. [Yeats's note:] *Sādhanā*, pp. 162, 163.[3a]

3a. Rabindranath Tagore, 'The Realisation of the Infinite' in *Sādhanā: The Realisation of Life* (London: Macmillan, 1913) pp. 162, 163: '". . . me across to the other shore!"' (p. 162).

COLLECTED PLAYS OF SYNGE

1. The request presumably came from the translator, Mineko Matsumura; his translation of *The Playboy of the Western World* had been published in 1917. See Shotaro Oshima, 'Synge in Japan', in *Sunshine and the Moon's Delight: A Centenary Tribute to John Millington Synge, 1871–1909*, ed. Suheil Bushrui (Gerrards Cross, Bucks: Smythe; Beirut: American University of Beirut, 1972) p. 257.

2. Arthur Waley (1889–1966), *Japanese Poetry: The Uta* (1919), gives line-by-line translations from the earliest anthology of Japanese poetry (*c.* 759) and from early imperial anthologies (*c.* 905 and later). Other translators were Basil Hall Chamberlain, *Classical Poetry of the Japanese* (1880) and Clara A. Walsh, *The Master-Singers of Japan* (1910).

3. Presumably 'The Sarashina Diary' (1009–59), 'The Diary of Murasaki Shikibu' (1007–10), or 'The Diary of Izumi Shikibu' (1002–03), in *Diaries of Court Ladies of Old Japan*, tr. Annie Shepley Omori and Kochi Doi (Boston: Houghton Mifflin, 1920; London: Constable, [1921]); Murasaki Shikibu is famed as the author of *The Tale of Genji*.

4. *The Aran Islands* (1901, publ. 1907), a prose description of Synge's journeys to these rugged islands off the west coast of Ireland, at Galway Bay; *The Well of the Saints* (1905); *Riders to the Sea* (1903), set in the Aran Islands.

5. An English translation, by Ernest Fenollosa and Ezra Pound, of the Japanese Noh play *Nishikigi* by Motokiyo (1363–1443) is included in *Certain Noble Plays of Japan*, ed. Ezra Pound (Dundrum, Co. Dublin: Cuala Press, 1916) pp. xx–xxi, 1–16. Lady Gregory had collected a similar story in Aran, of lovers who came after death to the priest for marriage; see Yeats, 'Swedenborg, Mediums, and the Desolate Places' (dated 1914), in Lady Gregory, *Visions and Beliefs in the West of Ireland* (New York: Putnam's, 1920) II, 337 (Coole edn, p. 335; *Ex* 68). See also Yeats's introduction (1916) to *Certain Noble Plays of Japan* (*E&I* 232). F. A. C. Wilson has pointed out that Yeats's play *The Dreaming of the Bones* (1917, publ. 1919), which portrays the twelfth-century Diarmuid and Dervorgilla in a 1916 setting, is modelled on *Nishikigi* (Wilson, *Yeats's Iconography* [New York: Macmillan, 1960] pp. 213–23).

6. John Synge died in 1909 at the age of thirty-seven. Yeats, with Lady Gregory and Molly Allgood, edited the three-act tragedy *Deirdre of the Sorrows* and arranged its posthumous production and publication in 1910.

7. No such production of *The Playboy of the Western World* is recorded, but *In the Shadow of the Glen* was performed twice in Prague in August 1907, and a one-act version *The Well of the Saints* was produced in Munich in August 1908. See Maurice Bourgeois, *John Millington Synge and the Irish Theatre* (London: Constable, 1913) pp. 146, 306, 310; John Synge to Max Meyerfeld, 17 Aug 1908, in 'Letters to John Millington Synge', *Yale Review*, 13 (May 1924) 709; and John Synge to Lady Gregory, 28 Aug 1908, *TB* 291.

WILDE: THE HAPPY PRINCE

1. Yeats lectured in Boston, 21 Sep–10 Oct 1911, during an American tour by the Abbey Theatre Company. Wilde had been translated into Hebrew (London and New York, 1907–10), but I have not traced an Arabic translation. Oscar Wilde's first collection of stories, *The Happy Prince and Other Tales* (London: Nutt, 1888) contained the title story and four others, including 'The Selfish Giant' and 'The Remarkable Rocket', which are mentioned later in this introduction. Wilde's essay 'The Soul of Man under Socialism' was published in February 1891 in the *Fortnightly Review* (new ser. 49, 292–319). The 'Young China party' could perhaps be a reference to the Youth Association, a revolutionary nationalist group founded in 1902 by radical Chinese students studying at Wasada University in Japan. This short-lived pioneering group was modelled on Young Italy. See Mary Backus Rankin, *Early Chinese Revolutionaries: Radical Intellectuals in Shanghai and Chekiang, 1902–1911* (Cambridge, Mass.: Harvard Unversity Press, 1971) pp. 22 and 248 n. 14. Ch'en Tu-hsiu (1879–1942), who later helped to establish the Chinese Communist Party, was influenced by Western socialist writings during his residence in Paris, from 1907 to 1910; his influential review *Youth* (later *New Youth*) was not begun until 1915. The present-day Young China Party was not founded until 1923.

2. Yeats arrived in London at the end of 1886; *The Wanderings of Oisin and Other Poems* was published in January 1889.

3. Reviewers often attacked Wilde for lacking originality. A *Pall Mall Gazette* (12 May 1891) review of Wilde's volume of essays *Intentions* alluded to Walter Horatio Pater (1839–94), the English scholar and writer, in labelling Wilde as capable of becoming 'a popular Pater'. Reviews of Wilde's *Poems* in the *Athenaeum* and the *Saturday Review* (both 23 July 1881) noted that Wilde's manner imitated several nineteenth-century English poets, including Algernon Charles Swinburne (1837–1909) and the poet and artist Dante Gabriel Rossetti (1828–82); see *Oscar Wilde: The Critical Heritage*, ed. Karl Beckson (New York: Barnes and Noble, 1970) pp. 91, 36, 37.

4. Samarkand (ancient name Maracanda), in eastern Uzbekistan, USSR.

5. During the early 1890s Yeats contributed to magazines edited by the English poet William Ernest Henley (1849–1903) and was a regular visitor at his home in Bedford Park, London. Yeats met Oscar Wilde in September 1888; for Yeats's description of a dinner at Wilde's home in Chelsea, see *Mem* 21–3.

6. Gustave Flaubert (1821–80), French novelist.

7. Yeats's friend Oliver St John Gogarty (1878–1957), Irish physician, wit, author, and later an Irish Free State senator, had purchased Renvyle House in 1917 as a summer house, on the Atlantic coast, forty-five miles north-west of Galway; it was burnt 29 Feb 1923. The priest might have been the Most Rev. Dr Michael Fogarty (1859–1955), Professor of Theology at Maynooth and then Bishop of Killaloe (1904–53).

8. The five stories in Wilde's second collection, *A House of Pomegranates* (London: McIlvaine, 1891), include 'The Fisherman and his Soul' (1891) and 'The Birthday of the Infanta' (1889), which are mentioned later in this introduction.

9. Yeats's account in *Mem* 79–80 is more precise. During May 1895 he returned from a half-year in Ireland and tried unsuccessfully to visit Wilde, who was free on bail, 7–20 May, between his two trials for homosexual acts. On 25 May, Wilde was sentenced to prison for two years.

10. Two (not three) of Wilde's plays, *An Ideal Husband* and *The Importance of Being Earnest*, were running simultaneously in London from 14 Feb to 27 Apr 1895.

11. 'The Doer of Good' (1894), in 'Poems in Prose', *Essays and Lectures* (London: Methuen, 1909) pp. 230–2.

12. James Abbott McNeill Whistler (1834–1904), expatriate American artist. Edward Coley Burne-Jones (1833–98), English artist. Wilde was born in Dublin and did not settle in London until the age of twenty-five.

13. The playwrights Oliver Goldsmith (1728–74) and Richard Brinsley Sheridan (1751–1816) were Irish-born; the socialist playwright George Bernard Shaw (1856–1950) was from Dublin.

YEATS: EARLY MEMORIES

1. Mrs Jeanne Robert Foster (1879–1970), an American journalist and poet, was a friend of John Butler Yeats (JBY) in New York. From 1921 she was the companion of John Quinn (1870–1924), an American lawyer and patron. Both she and Quinn were tireless supporters of JBY. She reported JBY's words, spoken to her on the evening of 1 Feb 1922, in a letter to W. B. Yeats dated 5 Feb: 'You'll surely come to sit in the morning, won't you?' (*LTWBY* 407). JBY died on the morning of 3 Feb; see William M. Murphy, *Prodigal Father: The Life of John Butler Yeats (1839–1922)* (Ithaca, NY: Cornell University Press, 1978) pp. 537–8.

2. JBY and his elder daughter, Susan Mary 'Lily' Yeats (1866–1949), arrived 29 Dec 1907 in New York, where she represented the Dun Emer Industries at the Irish Exhibition, Madison Square Garden, in January 1908; she left for Ireland on 6 June 1908. Her younger sister, Elizabeth Corbet 'Lollie' Yeats (1868–1940), had attended the Irish Exhibition in 1906.

3. The quotation from JBY is untraced. He lived at the Petitpas restaurant and boarding house, 317 West 29th Street.

4. Oil on canvas, 153 × 102 cm, in the collection of Michael Yeats; for a colour reproduction see Murphy, *Prodigal Father*, frontispiece. John Quinn gave the portrait to W. B. Yeats in 1922, but it did not arrive in

Ireland until 1923; see W. B. Yeats to John Quinn, 3 Nov 1923, excerpted
in B. L. Reid, *The Man from New York: John Quinn and his Friends* (New
York: Oxford University Press, 1968) p. 584.
5. The quotation from a letter by JBY is untraced. W. B. Yeats first
proposed this project to JBY in a letter of 21 Nov 1912, *L* 571.
6. Michael Butler Yeats was born 22 Aug 1921; JBY was born 16 Mar 1839.

GOGARTY: AN OFFERING OF SWANS

1. Oliver St John Gogarty, who was an Irish Free State senator from 1922 to
1936, had been abducted from his Dublin house by Republicans on 12
Jan 1923 and escaped that same evening, near the Salmon Pool in
Islandbridge, across the River Liffey from Phoenix Park. On 29 Feb
1923, Republicans burned his Connemara country house, Renvyle.
Security measures during the Irish Civil War so disrupted his Dublin
medical practice that he was forced to move to London from May 1923
until February 1924, although he returned frequently for Senate
meetings. Yeats attended the ceremony at which Gogarty presented the
swans to the River Liffey on 26 Apr 1924. See also p. 287, note 7 above.
2. Helicon, a mountain fifty miles west of Athens, was sacred to the Muses.
3. James F. Carens has explained the aptness of the rhythms, diction and
wit of 'Begone, Sweet Ghost' as an example of Gogarty's resemblance to
the English poet Robert Herrick (1591–1674) (and to the playwright
John Fletcher, 1579–1625) – Carens, *Surpassing Wit: Oliver St John Gogarty,
his Poetry and his Prose* (New York: Columbia University Press, 1979) p. 57.
All three poems that Yeats mentions are in *An Offering of Swans*, but 'Non
Dolet', the first poem in the volume, was the only one of these three that
Yeats chose for *OBMV*.

VILLIERS DE L'ISLE-ADAM: AXEL

1. Yeats attended a production of *Axël* (publ. 1890) at the Théâtre de la
Gaîté, Paris, 26 Feb 1894.
2. Lionel Pigot Johnson (1867–1902); see p. 112 above.
3. In *Axël*, IV.ii ('The Supreme Choice'), Axel tells Sara, 'Live? Our
servants will do that for us!' (*Axel*, tr. Finberg, p. 284). In III.i ('Ordeal by
Love and Gold'), Sara tempts Axel by saying to him, 'Cover yourself with
my hair and inhale the ghosts of perished roses!' (p. 260). The translation
of the first passage came from Arthur Symons (see p. 274, note 8 above).
The translation of the second passage was used in Yeats's review of *Axël*,
in *The Bookman* (London), 6 (Apr 1894) 15: 'Oh, to . . . hair, where. . . .'

Of the symbols mentioned by Yeats here, the forest cattle is the setting for parts II, III and IV: 'A very ancient stronghold, the castle of the Counts of Auersperg, isolated in the midst of the Black Forest' (p. 31). For the treasure of jewels and gold, see IV.i (pp. 251–3); for the lamp, see III.i ('On the Threshold') (p. 218).

4. The English occultist Samuel Liddell MacGregor Mathers (1854–1918) was a founder, in 1888, of the Hermetic Order of the Golden Dawn, which made extensive use of Rosicrucian doctrine and imagery. He moved to Paris in 1892. The Sâr (Joséphin) Péladan (1858–1918), a French writer, founded in Paris *c.* 1890 an Ordre de la Rose-Croix du Temple et du Graal which split from the Ordre Kabbalistique de la Rose-Croix and was specifically allied with Roman Catholic symbolism.

5. The French writer Remy de Gourmont (1858–1915), who championed Villiers, wrote this of him in *Le Livre des masques: portraits symbolistes* (Paris: Mercure de France, 1896) p. 91: 'C'est qu'il a rouvert les portes de l'au-delà closes avec quel fracas, on s'en souvint, et par ces portes toute une génération s'est ruée vers l'infini.'

6. Yeats met the French poet Paul Verlaine (1844–96) in Paris in 'the spring of 1894' and recounted this opinion about Villiers in an article for the *Savoy*, Apr 1896 (*UP1* 399).

7. The Russian woman was Tola Dorian (*née* Malzov) (1850–1918), who, by 1894, had published (in French) two volumes of poetry, a novel, and translations of Shelley. The play's production cost 30,000 francs; all the proceeds were shared between Villiers' widow and a nursery school. See E. Drougard, 'L'"Axel" de Villiers de l'Isle-Adam', *Revue d'histoire littéraire de la France*, 42 (1925) 533–5; and Paul Larochelle, *Trois hommes de théâtre: les trois Larochelle (1782–1930)* (Paris: Editions du Centre, [1960 or 1961]) pp. 192, 201.

    The social realism of plays written by the Norwegian dramatist Henrik Ibsen (1828–1906) was considered extreme by his contemporary audiences.

8. Pierre Félix Fix-Masseau (1869–1937), French sculptor and painter, modelled a conventionally realistic portrait bust, *Paul Larochelle in the Role of 'Axel'* (illus. in Larochelle, *Trois hommes de théâtre*, p. 197); in this bust, the actor's expression has an intensity that is perhaps reminiscent of the work of the French painter Gustave Moreau (1826–98), whose elaborately symbolic art corresponds to that of Villiers in *Axël*. Yeats admired Moreau's work. The French actor Paul Larochelle (b. 1870) played the title role in his own production of *Axël*, 26 and 27 Feb and 19 Apr 1894, at the Théâtre de la Gaîté.

9. Untraced. Moreau's symbolic art was ideologically allied with the religious idealism favoured by the French Rosicrucian Sâr Péladan.

10. The amusing anecdote about Mme Tola Dorian is mistaken. Her first husband, Prince Merchtcherski, had died while she was still young; she then married Charles-Louis Dorian (1852–1902), a French explorer and politician, and remained his wife until he died in 1902.

11. W. B. Yeats, 'A Symbolical Drama in Paris', *The Bookman*, 6 (Apr 1894) 14–16. Yeats quotes extensively below from pp. 15–16 of that article: '... returned by the path of symbolism. ... the "Axel" of ... De L'isle Adam. ... symbols and. ... of "Axel," and ... and that they have called. ... critic who sat near me, so soon as the ... Rosy-Cross, who is the chief person of the third act, began. ... opinions which everybody ... feelings which everybody ... understands? and yet in spite of all we have done, they ... De L'isle Adam. ... interesting, to ... man, with. ... man, with. ... acts. Even. ...'

12. Maurice Maeterlinck (1862–1949), Belgian symbolist playwright and poet, wrote three plays for marionettes during the 1880s and early 1890s: *Alladine et Palomides, Intérieur* ('Interior', perf. 1895), and *La Mort de Tintagiles* ('The Death of Tintagiles').

13. Untraced. A large number of critics attended the two performances at the Théâtre de la Gaîté. Larochelle gives excerpts from some eighteen reviews from French newspapers and journals, and he lists another fourteen reports in the foreign press (*Trois hommes de théâtre*, pp. 203–34).

14. Yeats's friend and fellow occultist, the English actress Florence Farr (Mrs Emery, 1869–1917), leased the Avenue Theatre, London, for the first productions of George Bernard Shaw's *Arms and the Man*, which opened 21 Apr 1894, and Yeats's one-act play *The Land of Heart's Desire*, which had opened 29 Mar 1894. The English playwright Henry Arthur Jones (1851–1929) enjoyed popular success beginning with the melodrama *The Silver King* in 1882; his *The Masqueraders* in 1894 was a 'new drama' like *The Second Mrs Tanqueray* by Arthur Wing Pinero (1855–1934), which had been the hit of the 1893 London season.

MERRIMAN: THE MIDNIGHT COURT

1. 'Cúirt an Mheadhóin Oidche' ('The Midnight Court', 1780–1, publ. 1850), a long Irish poem by Brian Merriman (d. 1808), had been published in an English translation only once before (tr. Michael C. O'Shea [Boston: no publisher, 1897]). The excerpt of the translation by Arland Ussher (1899–1980), published in an Irish magazine, is untraced.
   Wilbraham F. Trench (1873–1939) was appointed Professor of English Literature at Trinity College, Dublin, in 1913, the year he published *Shakespeare's Hamlet: A New Commentary with a Chapter on First Principles*; Yeats's name had been mentioned briefly for that chair. Professor Trench's previous book, *Mirror for Magistrates: Its Origin and Influence* (1898), had led to a chair at Queen's College, Galway.

2. [Yeats's note:] Mr Robin Flower pointed this out to me.[2a] 'Cadenus and Vanessa', which has the precision of fine prose, is the chief authority for the first meeting of Swift and Esther Vanhomrigh.[2b] I think it was Sir Walter Scott who first suggested 'a constitutional infirmity' to account for Swift's emotional entanglement,[2c] but this suggestion is not supported

by Irish tradition. Some years ago a one-act play was submitted to the Abbey Theatre reading committee which showed Swift saved from English soldiers at the time of the *Drapier Letters*† by a young harlot he was accustomed to visit.[2d] The author claimed that though the actual incident was his invention, his view of Swift was traditional, and inquiry proved him right. I had always known that stories of Swift and his serving man were folklore all over Ireland and now I learned from country friends why the man was once dismissed. Swift sent him out to fetch a woman and when Swift woke in the morning he found that she was a negress.[2e]

2a. Robin Flower (1881–1946), Celtic scholar, translator and poet. In 1925 the Cuala Press had published his *Love's Bitter-Sweet: Translations from the Irish Poets of the Sixteenth and Seventeenth Centuries.*

2b. 'Cadenus and Vanessa' (1713, publ. 1726), by Jonathan Swift (1667–1745), is a mock classical narrative about the relations of Swift ('Cadenus') with Esther Vanhomrigh ('Vanessa', 1690–1723).

2c. Sir Walter Scott, 'Memoirs of Jonathan Swift' (1814) in *The Works of Jonathan Swift*, ed. Sir Walter Scott, 2nd edn (London: Bickers, 1883) I, 225–6:

> There remains a conjecture which can only be intimated, but which, if correct, will explain much of Swift's peculiar conduct in his intercourse with the female sex. During that period of life when the passions are most violent, Swift boasts of his 'cold temper.' Since that time, the continual recurrence of a distressing vertigo was gradually undermining his health. It seems, in these circumstances, probable, that the continence which he observed, may have been owing to physical, as well as moral causes.

2d. Arthur R. Power's one-act play *The Drapier Letters* had been rejected by the Abbey Theatre, but was later accepted when, on the strength of this published remark, Power resubmitted it. The first production was on 22 Aug 1927, at the Abbey Theatre. In the play a character announces that Swift 'has an awful name for night-jaunting' (*The Drapier Letters and Her Ladyship – The Poet – and the Dog: Two One-Act Plays* [Dublin: Talbot Press, 1927] p. 8).

2e. This (apocryphal) anecdote is one of several recorded by Mackie L. Jarrell, '"Jack and the Dane": Swift Traditions in Ireland', *Journal of American Folklore*, 77 (1964) 102–3.

3. Jonathan Swift, 'Cadenus and Vanessa', *Works*, ed. Thomas Sheridan (London: Bathurst *et al.*, 1784) VII, 98, ll. 4–8 ('. . . charg'd, / On . . . enlarg'd; / That . . . / . . . dart; –'); 99, l. 36; and 100, l. 60 ('Fools, fops, and rakes').

4. Books of love poems: the Roman poet Tibullus (*c.* 60–19 BC) was contemporary with Virgil; Abraham Cowley (1618–67) and Edmund Waller (1606–87) wrote poems celebrating love.

5. Eevell of Craglee (Aoibheall of Craig Liath), queen of the Munster fairies. Yeats used a variety of names for her elsewhere in his works:

'Aoibhell of the Grey Rock', in 'The Crucifixion of the Outcast' (1894; *Myth* 152, *SR* 12); 'Aoibhill of the Grey Rock', in the preface (1902) to Lady Gregory, *Cuchulain of Muirthemne* (p. 120 above); 'Aoibhinn of Craig Liath', in his dairy, 7 Jan 1910 (*Mem* 241); and 'Aoife' in 'The Grey Rock' (1913; *P* 105).

6. The dream allegories 'The Romaunt of the Rose' and 'The Book of the Duchess' (1369) are from Chaucer's early period. W. W. Skeat's edition of Chaucer (1894–7) was the first modern collected edition from which 'Chaucer's Dream' and 'The Complaint of the Black Knight' were excluded.

7. 'The Romaunt of the Rose', ll. 49–53. The quotation varies slightly from the text of Yeats's copies of *The Works of Geoffrey Chaucer*, ed. F. S. Ellis (Hammersmith: Kelmscott Press, 1892) p. 242, and *The Poetical Works of Geoffrey Chaucer*, ed. W. W. Skeat, The World's Classics, I (London: Richards, 1903) 4, both of which read: '. . . May me . . .' (49) and '. . . dremed me, / . . . jolitee, / That al thing . . .' (51–3).

8. For the playful leaping through the flames of a St John's Eve (23 June, Midsummer's Eve) fire and the sprinkling of its ashes on fields, as echoes of pagan fertility rites, see Douglas Hyde, *A Literary History of Ireland: From Earliest Times to the Present Day* (London: Unwin, 1899) p. 91 n. 4 (24 June); and Ethel L. Urlin, *Festivals, Holy Days, and Saints' Days: A Study in Origins and Survivals in Church Ceremonies and Secular Customs* (London: Simpkin, Marshall, Hamilton, Kent, 1915) p. 142 (23 June).

9. The penal laws, an intricate series of severe restrictions on the education, ownership of property, and political activity of Catholics in Ireland, were instituted 1695–1727. Enforcement eased during the second half of the eighteenth century, and the laws were slowly rescinded by a series of relief acts in 1782, 1793 and 1829. Merriman wrote 'The Midnight Court' in 1780–1. The Jacobite rising had ended in 1691 and, to all intents and purposes, the last Stuart claims died with the pretender 'James III' in 1766.

10. Brian Merriman, *The Midnight Court*, tr. Ussher, pp. 18 [part 1, l. 74] ('. . . her laws decayed,'), 19 [ll. 76–7, 79], [97] ('. . . your lads . . .'), 23 [ll. 181–2] ('hairless crown/And snotty . . .'), 26 [l. 243] and 27 [ll. 272–3].

11. *The Midnight Court*, pp. 40–1 [part 2, ll. 205, 209–17] ('. . . clergy . . . / . . . power; / For . . . law/And . . . flaw, / And . . . / . . . the bridal bed'). The three lines (part 2, ll. 206–8) that in the poem come between the first and second lines of this excerpt were omitted, perhaps deliberately, in the first published version (1926) and in the typescript [1937] for Scribner's never-published 'Dublin' collected edition. The three lines were added, probably by the Macmillan editor Thomas Mark or by Mrs Yeats, in *Ex* 285:

> Before candid nature can give one caress?
> Why lay the banquet and why pay the band
> To blow their bassoons and their cheeks to expand?

The manuscript (NLI MS. 30,373; SUNY-SB 21.7.98) here reads only 'quote' and does not give any of the lines; neither the copy of the poem that Yeats used when writing the manuscript nor his copy of the published book is extant.

12. Edmund in *King Lear*, I.ii.1–22. Oisin rails at St Patrick in the final lines of Yeats's *The Wandering of Oisin* (1889; *P* 385–6); see also p. 131 above.

13. Robert Burns, 'A Poet's Welcome to his love-begotten Daughter' (1785); William Blake, *The Marriage of Heaven and Hell* (1790?–3).

14. Standish Hayes O'Grady, Introduction to *Toruigheacht Dhiarmuda agus Ghrainne; or The Pursuit after Diarmuid O'Duibhne, and Grainne the Daughter of Cormac Mac Airt, King of Ireland in the Third Century*, ed. O'Grady, Transactions of the Ossianic Society, 3 (1855) (publ. Dublin: O'Daly, for the Ossianic Society, 1857) 36: 'In poetry, perhaps the most tasteful piece in the language is, with all its defects, "Cuirt an mheadhoin oidhche," or the Midnight Court, written in 1781 by Bryan Merryman, a country schoolmaster of Clare, who had evidently some general acquaintance with literature'. Yeats's source was probably Douglas Hyde, who quoted O'Grady's praise in *Literary History of Ireland*, p. 602.

15. The second poem in Ussher's volume is a rambling comedy, 'The Adventures of a Luckless Fellow' (or 'The Mock Aeneid') by Donagh Rua Macnamara (Donnchadh Ruadh mac Conmara, d. *c.* 1814). That poem's second part is a dream vision which begins with Eevell of Craglee taking the poet to the River Styx.

BLAKE: SONGS OF INNOCENCE

1. In a Senate speech, 3 Apr 1924, Yeats had praised the stained glass of Harry Clarke (1889–1931) as among the best in the world (*SS* 65). The young artist was Jacynth Parsons, daughter of an English stained-glass art teacher, Karl Parsons (1884–1934), whom Clarke had known since 1913. Clarke had brought her to Dublin to introduce her to Yeats, with a view to having Yeats write this introduction (Margaret Parsons to Nicola Gordon Bowe, 2 Feb 1976, letter in the possession of Nicola Gordon Bowe). This Monday evening 'at-home' was on 29 Aug 1927. Jacynth Parsons later illustrated W. H. Davies, *Forty-nine Poems* (London: Medici Society, 1928); Karl Parsons, *Ann's Book* (London: Medici Society, 1929); John Masefield, *South and East* (London: Medici Society, 1929); and James Ching, *Let's Play the Piano: The First Music Book for Children of all Ages* (London: Mitre Press, 1936).

2. The Free State officer might have been General Richard James Mulcahy (1886–1971), Minister for Local Government (June 1927 – March 1932); he had been Minister for Defence until March 1924, when he resigned over the Army mutiny. The distinguished dramatist could have been Lennox Robinson (1886–1958), playwright and manager of the Abbey Theatre. The country gentleman might perhaps have been Lt.-Col. Sir William Hutchenson Poë (1848–1934), who maintained residences in

Co. Laois (1500 acres) and Co. Tyrone (10,000 acres). Like Yeats, he had served as an Irish Free State senator (1922–5) and was a member of the Board of Governors and Guardians of the National Gallery of Ireland (from 1904). He had lost his right leg in the Nile campaign in 1885.

3. Jacob and Wilhelm Grimm, *Kinder und Haus-Märchen* (1819–22) (English translation, as *German Popular Stories*, 1823–6); Robert Louis Stevenson, *Treasure Island* (1883).

4. The Irish Civil War lasted from June 1922 until May 1923; General Mulcahy directed the Government's military action throughout this period. Yeats had lived at 82 Merrion Square since September 1922; he first mentioned having two bullet holes in his windows on 4 Jan 1924 (Yeats to Robert Bridges, *L* 696).

   In the general election of 15 Sep 1927, which had been announced on 25 Aug, William Cosgrave's party, Cumann na nGaedheal, retained its narrow margin over the Republican Eamon de Valera's party, Fianna Fáil, which had made a strong showing in the general election of June 1927 and which eventually came to power in 1932.

5. These illustrations are: [*Boy sitting on the limb of a tree, with two squirrels*] (1927), watercolour frontispiece (colour), and perhaps *The Nurse's Song* (which also includes a squirrel) (1926), watercolour, facing p. 34 (colour); [*Full-length rear view of a female angel with long, flowing hair*], ink, illus. (probably) to 'The Chimney Sweeper'; *The Little Boy Found* (1926), watercolour belonging to W. B. Yeats (in Dec 1927), facing p. 19 (colour); and *The Little Black Boy* (1926), watercolour, facing p. 10 (colour) (the mother and little boy are African rather than Indian). (See Plate 1 for *The Little Black Boy*.)

6. Blake, 'The Little Boy Found' and 'On Anothers Sorrow', in *Songs of Innocence* (1789), pls 14 and 27 (*WWB* III, 41, 46, and *PWB* 52–3, 61–2 [as 'On Another's Sorrow']; *William Blake's Writings*, ed. G. E. Bentley, Jr [Oxford: Clarendon Press, 1978] pp. 35, 50–1). Yeats owned Jacynth Parsons' colour illustration to 'The Little Boy Found' (facing p. 19) and loaned it to the 'Exhibition of the Works of Miss Jacynth Parsons from the Age of 3–16', City of Birmingham Museum and Art Gallery, 1–15 Dec 1927 (no. 100).

7. A cancelled passage in the holograph manuscript (NLI; SUNY-SB 22.6.138) here reads 'a translation of "Axel"'. Yeats's Preface to the play by Villiers de l'Isle-Adam is given on pp. 156–8 above. Two-fifths of that preface, dated 20 Sep 1924 and published in May 1925, is merely an excerpt from a review that Yeats had published thirty years earlier, and about which he disparagingly remarked, in the 1924 preface, 'I find sentence after sentence of revivalist thoughts that leave me a little ashamed' (p. 157).

THE COINAGE OF SAORSTÁT ÉIREANN

1. See Plate 2 for the photographs of four ancient coins: Larissa (Thessaly) – horse; Thurii, a Greek city in Lucinia (Southern Italy) – bull; Carthage – horse; and Messana (modern Messina, Sicily) – hare. The invited artists were Jerome Connor; Edmund Dulac (1882–1953), a French-born English artist and a close friend of Yeats's; James Earle Fraser; Ivan Meštrović; Paul Manship; Carl Milles; Publio Morbiducci; Albert Power; Charles Shannon; and Oliver Sheppard. See section IV and notes 5–12 below for details about the artists besides Edmund Dulac.

   The five members of the committee were the chairman, Senator Yeats; Thomas Bodkin (1887–1961), Director (June 1927 to 1935) of the National Gallery of Ireland and previously a member of its Board of Governors and Guardians; Barry M. Egan, member of the Dáil Éireann and head of a firm of goldsmiths and jewellers in Cork; Dermod O'Brien (1865–1945), artist and President of the Royal Hibernian Academy; and Lucius O'Callaghan (1878–1954), architect and Director (until June 1927) of the National Gallery of Ireland. Leo T. MacCauley, a junior administrative officer in the Department of Finance, was secretary to the committee.

2. The tall, slender Irish round towers (8th–12th c.) were used as bell towers and as strongholds. According to tradition, the Treaty of Limerick (1691) was signed on the 'Treaty Stone', Thomond Bridge, Limerick. For the report of the Royal Society of Antiquaries of Ireland, see Leo T. MacCauley, 'Summary of the Proceedings of the Committee', in *Coinage of Saorstát Éireann*, p. 28; repr. in Cleeve, *W. B. Yeats and the Designing of Ireland's Coinage*, p. 34.

3. The Executive Council, centre of executive authority for the Irish Free State, was comprised of William T. Cosgrave (1880–1965) as President (1922–32) and six senior government ministers, including the Minister of Finance, Ernest Blythe, but not the Minister for Lands and Agriculture, Patrick Hogan. Three provisional decisions of the Minister of Finance were given to Yeats's committee at its first meeting, 17 June 1926: use a harp on one side of most or all the coins, use inscriptions only in Irish, and use no effigies of modern persons ('Proceedings', in *Coinage of Saorstát Éireann*, p. 20; repr. in Cleeve, *W. B. Yeats and the Designing of Ireland's Coinage*, pp. 26–7).

   St Brigid (435–523), a patron saint of Ireland; Brian Boru (926–1014), King of Ireland.

4. The Swedish two-kronor silver coin was issued in 1921 to commemorate the 400th anniversary of the war of liberation led by Gustavus Vasa (1496–1560), the founder of the Vasa dynasty. It is illustrated in Richard S. Yeoman, *A Catalog of Modern World Coins: 1850–1964*, ed. Holland Wallace, 12th edn (Racine, Wis.: Western, 1978) p. 449 (no. 58); and in Chester L. Krause and Clifford Mishler, *Standard Catalog of World Coins*, 8th edn (Iola, Wis.: Krause, 1982) p. 1631 (no. 58). The bronze medal of Vasa was designed by Carl Milles (1875–1955). The two famous plays

are August Strindberg's *Master Olof* (1872; perf. 1881 [prose] and 1890 [verse]) and *Gustav Vasa* (1899). Master Olof (Olaus Petri, *c.* 1493–1552) led the Lutheran reformation of the Swedish Church during the reign of Gustavus Vasa. For more information on Milles, see note 7 below.

5. Charles Shannon (1863–1937), English painter, long a friend of Yeats; the Kings Inn designs are untraced. In a Senate speech, 22 July 1926, Yeats unsuccessfully advocated rejecting the robes and wigs of judges of the Irish Free State High Court and Supreme Court; he praised, as 'more dignified and more simple' the Irish District Court robes designed – at Yeats's invitation – 'by a celebrated Irish artist, Sir [*sic*] Charles Shannon', and a flat velvet cap designed at the Dun Emer workshop (*SS* 125–6, 129, 132); see Joseph Hone, *W. B. Yeats: 1865–1939*, 2nd edn (London: Macmillan, 1962) p. 381.

Albert Power (1883–1945), Irish sculptor; Oliver Sheppard (1865–1941), Irish sculptor; Jerome Connor (1876–1943), Irish-American sculptor.

6. These coins were the Italian five-centesimi copper piece showing a wheat-ear, minted 1919 to 1937; the Italian two-lire piece (in nickel rather than silver) showing a fasces, minted 1923 to 1937; the Swedish two-kronor coin described in note 4 above; and the United States 'buffalo' or 'Indian head' five-cent piece in nickel, designed by James Earle Fraser (1876–1953), minted 1913 to 1938.

7. Yeats saw works by the Swedish sculptor Carl Milles (1875–1955) in Stockholm in December 1923; Yeats, together with Milles and George Bernard Shaw, attended a performance of Shaw's *Major Barbara* at the Chelsea Palace theatre, London, on 4 or 5 Nov 1926. The Serbian sculptor Ivan Meštrović (1883–1963) had impressed Yeats in 1915, when his works were exhibited at the Victoria and Albert Museum, London. Yeats applauded Meštrović's use of folk legend and his powerful style. Twelve Irish coinage designs by Milles and one by Meštrović are illustrated in Plates 3 and 4.

8. A noteworthy example of the architectural sculpture of the American sculptor James Earle Fraser is the pediment of the Constitution Avenue face of the National Archives Building, Washington, DC; for his 'buffalo' nickel, see note 6 above.

9. Publio Morbiducci (1889–1963), Italian sculptor and medallist; for his two-lire coin see note 6 above.

10. [Yeats's note:] We had written to a wrong address and our letter took some time reaching him. He made one magnificent design and, on discovering that the date had passed, gave it to the Irish Free State with great generosity.

11. Paul Manship (1885–1955), American sculptor. *Diana* (1921 [model], 1924 [gilded bronze group, 2.21 m high, Brookgreen Gardens, Georgetown, SC], 1925 [five copies, bronze with green patina, 1.22 m high, Art Gallery of Toronto, etc.]) shows Diana with a bow and one dog; a companion piece shows Actaeon being attacked by two dogs. For illustrations see *Paul Manship*, American Sculptors series (New York:

Norton, 1947) pp. 17 and 16 (*Diana* and *Actaeon*, 1924, Brookgreen Gardens); and Edwin Murtha, *Paul Manship* (New York: Macmillan, 1957) pls 26 and 27 (*Diana* and *Actaeon*, 1925).

12. Charles Ricketts (1866–1931), English artist, designer and connoisseur, long a friend of Yeats.

   Sydney William Carline (1888–1929), English painter and medallist, served as a lieutenant in the First World War. He made a commemorative medal for the Battle of Jutland (1917), but there is no record that he made one for the Zeebrugge raid, 22 Apr 1918. His portrait medallion (1923) of William Matthew Flinders Petrie (1853–1942), English Egyptologist, is illustrated in *The Studio*, 90 (1925) 247; the British Museum has a probably complete collection of his coins and medals, given by the artist's brother.

   The Director of the British School at Rome (1925–8), Bernard Ashmole (1894–), had been Assistant Curator of Coins at the Ashmolean Museum, Oxford (1923–5).

   Percy Metcalfe (1895–1970), English medallist and portrait sculptor.

13. The seal of the National Gallery of Ireland was designed in 1919 by Oswald Reeves (1870–1967), an English-born artist and craftsman who taught at the Metropolitan School of Art, Dublin, 1904–37.

14. See p. 96 above.

15. See Plate 5.

16. Illustrated in *Coinage of Saorstát Éireann*, pls iii, vi; repr. in Cleeve, *W. B. Yeats and the Designing of Ireland's Coinage*, p. 15 (partial).

17. See Plate 3.

18. Oliver Sheppard, *John O'Leary (1830–1907)*, bronze bust, Hugh Lane Municipal Gallery of Modern Art, Dublin (1908 catalogue, no. 294), illus. in *The Studio*, 91 (April 1926) 211.

   Albert Power, *Thomas Kettle (1880–1916)* (1919), plaster study, 13 cm high, National Gallery of Ireland, no. 8010, for a monument in St Stephen's Green, Dublin.

   Jerome Connor, *Robert Emmet* (1917), full-length, bronze, 2.54 m high, National Gallery, Washington DC, illus. in Máirín Allen, 'Jerome Connor – [Part] Two', *Capuchin Annual* (Dublin), 31 (1964) 363.

19. William Orpen (1878–1931), Irish painter; he taught part-time at the Metropolitan School of Art, Dublin, from 1902 to 1913.

20. The nineteen column statues which flank the three doors on the west front (Portail Royal) (*c*. 1150) of Chartres Cathedral represent 'the Ancestors of Christ, men and women mostly in royal attire' (Wilhelm Vöge, *The Beginnings of the Monumental Style in the Middle Ages* [1894], tr. Alice Fischer and Gertrude Steuer in *Chartres Cathedral*, ed. Robert Branner [New York: Norton, 1969] p. 127).

21. Untraced.

22. See Plates 5 and 6 for the original designs and the minted versions of Metcalfe's horse, bull and pig.

   On 17 April 1926 Metcalfe paid a call on the Secretary to the Department of Finance and chanced to meet the Minister for Lands and Agriculture, Patrick Hogan, who was then shown the coinage designs.

After Hogan complained to the Executive Council about some details of
the animal designs, the Minister of Finance, without consulting Yeats's
committee, submitted the designs to the Chief Inspector of Livestock,
Daniel Twomey, who presented his expert criticisms of the hunter, bull
and pig at the committee's next meeting, 8 June. Metcalfe revised his
designs using examples provided by Daniel Twomey and others.
Eventually a compromise was reached, but not until Yeats and three of
the four other members protested by submitting letters of resignation to
the Minister of Finance after the Committee's next meeting, 14 October.

23. See Appendix 12 for an omitted final section.

GOGARTY: WILD APPLES

1. Oliver St John Gogarty, *An Offering of Swans and Other Poems* (Dublin:
   Cuala Press, 1923); for its preface by Yeats see pp. 154–5 above. That
   1923 volume contained twenty-three poems, selected by Yeats; none of
   those is among the thirty-three poems, again selected by Yeats, in *Wild
   Apples* (Dublin: Cuala Press, Apr 1930). In 1928 the Cuala Press had
   published another collection of Gogarty's poems with the same title as
   the 1930 collection, *Wild Apples*, but with no preface; only nine of its
   twenty-seven poems were reprinted in *Wild Apples* (1930).

2. Gogarty was a friend of the British artist Augustus John (1878–1961).
   Yeats, who sat for portraits by John in 1907 and 1930 (three months after
   the publication of this preface), respected John's talent but considered
   him flawed by an anti-idealising exaggeration of ugliness, and perhaps by
   the artist's flamboyantly bohemian life.

3. Thomas Edward Lawrence, *Revolt in the Desert* (New York: Doran, 1927),
   pp. 193, 197 (ch. 22: 'Return to the World'): '. . . without family'.

4. For example, William Wordsworth, 'Ode to Duty' (1804, publ. 1807),
   and Samuel Taylor Coleridge, 'To William Wordsworth' (1807, publ.
   1817), ll. 43–5. In 1909 Yeats recorded in his journal: 'Wordsworth is
   often flat and heavy, partly because his moral sense . . . is an obedience to
   a discipline which he has not created' (*Au* 470).

5. George Chapman (1559?–1634), English poet, dramatist and translator;
   Walter Savage Landor (1775–1864), English poet and prose writer.

6. Gogarty, 'The Crab Tree' (1928), l. 10, *Wild Apples* (1930) p. 1.

7. 'Another Portrait' (1928), ll. 2–4, *Wild Apples* (1930) p. 8; titled 'Portrait:
   Jane . . . . .' in *Wild Apples* (1928).

8. Gogarty, 'Portrait with Background' (1928), ll. 11–20, *Wild Apples* (1930)
   p. 6; the poem's first stanza reads:

   > Devorgilla's [*sic*] supremely lovely daughter,
   > Recalling him, of all the Leinstermen Ri,
   > Him whose love and hate brought o'er the water,
   > Strongbow and Henry,

9. The writers living at Boar's Hill, near Oxford, included Yeats's friends Robert Bridges (1844–1930) and John Masefield (1878–1967).

10. At the start of the final act of George Bernard Shaw's *Heartbreak House* (1919), there is 'a sort of splendid drumming in the sky' (*Collected Plays with Their Prefaces* [London: Bodley Head, 1974; New York: Dodd, Mead, 1975] v, 159). Then, at the play's closing moment, after several explosions have been heard and after the police have told the characters to put out the lights in the house, Hector Hushabye instead turns the lights up; Nurse Guinness says, 'It's Mr Hushabye turning on all the lights in the house and tearing down the curtains' (pp. 178–9).

11. John M. Synge, 'Prelude' (1890s, rev. 1907, publ. 1909), l. 7: 'And did but half remember human words' (Synge, *Collected Works*, vol. I: *Poems*, ed. Robin Skelton [London: Oxford University Press, 1962] p. 32).

12. Gogarty, 'Aphorism (After reading Tolstoi)' (1928), ll. 19–22, *Wild Apples* (1930) p. 13 (with a comma after 'unsoilable'); titled 'Ringsend: After reading Tolstoi' in *Selected Poems* (New York: Macmillan, 1933) and later editions. Ringsend, one of Dublin's less attractive districts, is on the south side of the River Liffey, near its mouth.

13. Abdulla el Nahabi (the Robber), who was recommended to T. E. Lawrence by Ambassador Abdulla ibn Dakhil. See Lawrence, *Revolt in the Desert* (New York: Doran, 1927), p. 195 (ch. 22: 'Return to the World').

ANGLO-IRISH BALLADS

1. Frederick Robert Higgins (1896–1941), Irish poet, editor, and director at the Abbey Theatre.

2. The Battle of the Boyne, 1690; see p. 270, note 2 above.

3. Anonymous, 'The Colleen Rue', *A Broadside*, new ser., no. 11 (Nov 1935) sigs [2ʳ–2ᵛ]. For hedge schoolmasters, see pp. 24 and 46 above.

4. 'Shuile Agra', *A Broadside*, 7, no. 5 (Oct 1914) sig. [1ʳ], ll. 13–16.

5. Anonymous, 'The Boys of Mullabaun' (18th c.?), *A Broadside*, 5, no. 9 (Feb 1913) sig. [1ʳ], ll. 13–16: '. . . lamentation, I . . . consternation,/ No . . . recreation, until . . . hesitation, we're. . . .'

6. Oliver Goldsmith, 'Happiness, In a great Measure, Dependent on Constitution', *The Bee* (London), no. 2 (13 Oct 1759) 51–2: 'The music of Matei is dissonance to what I felt when our old dairymaid sung me into tears with Johnny Armstrong's Last Good Night, or the Cruelty of Barbara Allen.' Goldsmith later revised that reference to Signora Colomba Mattei, a popular Italian opera singer, to read 'the finest singer' (*Collected Works of Oliver Goldsmith*, ed. Arthur Friedman [Oxford: Clarendon Press, 1966] I, 385). The Scottish ballad 'Barbara Allen's Cruelty' was printed in Thomas Percy's *Reliques of Ancient English Poetry* (London: Dodsley, 1765) III, 125–8; see Francis James Child (ed.), *The English and Scottish Popular Ballads* (Boston: Houghton, Mifflin, 1886) II, 277–8 (no. 84B). For 'Johnny Armstrongs last Good-Night' see Child, III, 368–9 (no. 169B). Goldsmith probably was referring to Lissoy, Co.

Westmeath, in the Irish Midlands region; see his letter to Daniel Hodson, 27 Dec 1757: 'If I go to the Opera where Signora Colomba pours out all the melody; I sit and sigh for Lishoy fireside, and Johnny armstrong's last good night from Peggy Golden' (*The Collected Letters of Oliver Goldsmith*, ed. Katharine C. Balderston [Cambridge: Cambridge University Press, 1928] pp. 29–30). Yeats's immediate source could have been Patrick Weston Joyce's introductory comments on 'Barbara Allen' and a variant Irish air in *Ancient Irish Music*, 2nd edn (London: Longmans, Green; Dublin: Gill, 1906) p. 79 (no. 78).

7. Untraced. For 'Barbara Allen,' see note 6 above.

8. Clatter-bones: two pieces of bone or slate used similarly to castanets. See the illustration by Jack B. Yeats to 'Song for the Clatter Bones' by F. R. Higgins, *A Broadside*, new ser., no. 6 (June 1935) sig. [1^r].

9. These are anonymous Irish street ballads.

   'Johnny, I hardly Knew Ye' (early 19th c.), *A Broadside*, new ser., no. 9 (Sep 1935) sigs [1^v–2^v]. The first publication of the full version was in *Irish Minstrelsy: Being a Selection of Irish Songs, Lyrics, and Ballads*, ed. H. Halliday Sparling (London: Scott, 1888) pp. 491–3, 512. Yeats had included it in *BIV* 238–41.

   'Luke Caffrey's Kilmainham Minit' or 'The Kilmainham Minuet (or Minut)' (1788?), printed in John Edward Walsh's anonymously printed *Sketches of Ireland Sixty Years Ago* (Dublin: McGlashan, 1847) pp. 86–9; for words and music see Donal O'Sullivan, 'Dublin Slang Songs, with Music', *Dublin Historical Record*, 1 (1938–9) 78–80. Kilmainham Jail, Dublin, was built in 1787.

   'The Night before Larry was Stretched' (late 1780s), *A Broadside*, 4, no. 9 (Feb 1912) sigs [1^r–1^v]. This song once was attributed to Robert Burrowes, who was a fellow of Trinity College, Dublin, in 1787 and afterwards became Dean of Cork. H. Halliday Sparling in *Irish Minstrelsy* (p. 514) ascribed it to William ('Hurlfoot Bill') Maher; Sparling was the first to collect all nine verses of this song (pp. 475–7), from chap-books and ballad-sheets. For words and music see O'Sullivan, 'Dublin Slang Songs, with Music', *Dublin Historical Record*, 1, 84–6.

10. Oliver Goldsmith, as a student at Trinity College, Dublin, from 1744 to 1749, frequently wrote street ballads for five shillings each, which were published anonymously at a shop in Mountrath Street; see James Prior, *The Life of Oliver Goldsmith* (London: Murray, 1837) i, 75.

11. The Coombe is a street that has given its name to a working-class district in the ancient 'Liberties' section of Dublin, near St Patrick's Cathedral, of which Jonathan Swift was Dean from 1713 and where he was buried in 1745. Sir Walter Scott (1771–1832) was told during a luncheon at the Deanery of St Patrick's in 1825 that Swift's 'memory was as fresh as ever among the common people about – they still sing his ballads' (John Gibson Lockhart, *The Life of Sir Walter Scott* [Edinburgh: Jack, 1902] viii, 18).

12. Untraced.

13. Charles Lever (1806–72), Irish novelist, was at Trinity College, Dublin, from 1822 to 1827; see p. 54 above.

14. Anonymous Irish street ballad, 'The Croppy Boy' (late 18th c. or perhaps early 19th c.), *A Broadside*, new ser., no. 10 (Oct 1935) sigs [1ʳ–1ᵛ]. This is a variant of the ballad printed in Sparling, *Irish Minstrelsy*, pp. 46–7, 511; it is not the ballad of the same name by Carroll Malone (William McBurney, b. Co. Down, emigrated to America in 1845, d. *c.* 1892) in *The Ballad Poetry of Ireland*, ed. Charles Gavan Duffy (Dublin: Duffy, 1845), pp. 156–7.

    Anonymous Irish street ballad, 'The Shan Van Vocht' ('The Poor Old Woman', 1797), *BIV* 232–5.

    Anonymous Irish ballad, 'The Wearing of the Green' (late 18th c.), *BIV* 235–6; for the version by Henry Grattan Curran (1800–76) see Sparling, *Irish Minstrelsy*, pp. 13–14.

15. Boer war (1899–1902).

    John MacHale (1791–1881), Archbishop of Tuam, supported Daniel O'Connell, who called him 'the Lion of the Tribe of Judah'; MacHale was an ardent advocate of the peasantry during the Great Famine.

    The Irish National Land League led a violent struggle on behalf of tenant farmers against landlords from 1879 to 1882 and helped to force passage of the Land Act of 1881.

    The Phoenix Park murders were the brutal assassinations of the Chief Secretary and Under Secretary to the Lord Lieutenant of Ireland, in Phoenix Park, Dublin, on 6 May 1882, by a Fenian group called the Invincibles.

    Charles Stewart Parnell (1846–91), the Home Rule leader in Parliament, was born at Avondale, Co. Wicklow. As President of the Land League he made an extremely successful fund-raising tour of America in 1879–80. His arrest and imprisonment, 1881–2, occasioned many broadside ballads. This one is untraced, but see 'The Blackbird of Avondale, or the Arrest of Parnell' (1881), in Georges-Denis Zimmermann, *Songs of Irish Rebellion: Political Street Ballads and Rebel Songs 1780–1900* (Hatboro, Penn.: Folklore Associates, 1967) pp. 277–8 (no. 81).

16. Yeats had often visited Rosses Point, Co. Sligo, five miles north-west of Sligo. The quatrain is from 'The Dancer' (ll. 17–20) by the Irish poet Joseph Campbell (1879–1944), in *Irishry* (Dublin: Maunsel, 1913) p. 10: '. . . dead: Clay . . .'. Yeats included the poem in *OBMV* 192–3 (no. 183): '. . . dead: / Clay . . . tread!'.

    For the air 'The Rocky Road to Dublin', a slip jig, see *O'Neill's Music of Ireland*, ed. Francis O'Neill (Chicago: Lyon and Healy, 1903) p. 211 (no. 1116). For the words and music of 'Rocky Road to Dublin' in a later adaptation, see *The Irish Songbook*, ed. Pat Clancy, Tom Clancy, Liam Clancy and Tommy Maken (New York: Macmillan, 1969) pp. 54–5.

17. Richard Alfred Milliken, 'The Groves of Blarney' (1798 or 1799), *BIV* 6: 'Being banked with posies / That spontaneous grow there' (ll. 5–6); that is the text as printed from the author's manuscript in Thomas Crofton Croker, *The Popular Songs of Ireland* (London: Colburn, 1839) pp. 141–9, and repr. in *The Songs of Ireland*, ed. Michael Joseph Barry (Dublin: Duffy, 1845) pp. 112–16. Pairs of the original short lines were combined in the

version printed in the 1886 edition of Croker's *Popular Songs of Ireland*
(London: Routledge) p. 142, and in Sparling, *Irish Minstrelsy*, pp. 437–8,
so that the original's ll. 5 and 6 are l. 3: 'Being banked with posies that
spontaneous grow there.' Yeats used another version in *A Broadside*, new
ser., no. 2 (Feb 1935) sigs [1ᵛ–2ᵛ], in which l. 3 reads, 'All decked by
posies that spontaneous grow there'; a note on sig. [2ᵛ] explains:

> Different versions of 'The Groves of Blarney' are extant. The ballad
> was written originally by Richard Alfred Milliken (1767–1815) though
> it does not appear in the collected works, published after his death.
> Later versions were attributed to Father Prout [Frances Sylvester
> Mahony (1804–66)] and others. Indeed, the version published on this
> Broadside shows the touch of a more modern hand.

18. For the experiments with Florence Farr (1860–1917) chanting verse to
    the accompaniment of a zither-like psaltery, see Yeats's essay 'Speaking
    to the Psaltery' (1902), *E&I* 13–27.
19. Thomas Moore, 'At the Mid Hour of Night' (ll. 1–2), in *BIV* 11: 'At the
    . . . night, when stars . . . weeping, I. . . .'
20. John Andrew Stevenson (1760?–1833), English composer.
21. 'The Young May Moon', *Moore's Irish Melodies . . . with Accompaniments of
    Sir John Stevenson* (London: London Printing and Publishing, [1879]) p.
    270: 'The young May moon is beaming, love' (l. 1).
22. This remark by William Morris (1834–96), English poet and artist, is
    untraced.
23. The series of English comic operas (1875–96) with libretti by William S.
    Gilbert (1836–1911) and music by Arthur S. Sullivan (1842–1900). Mutt
    and Jeff animated cartoon films, begun in 1916 by artist Raoul Barré,
    were very popular in the 1920s and were briefly revived by Walter Lanz
    in the early 1930s.
24. For the nationalist Young Ireland movement of the 1840s, see pp. 240,
    note 21 and 271, note 6 above. Alfred Perceval Graves (1846–1931), the
    father of Robert Graves; Francis Arthur Fahy (1854–1935), the author of
    songs such as 'Little Mary Cassidy', 'The Ould Plaid Shawl', 'Galway
    Bay' and 'The Donovans'; Joseph Campbell (1879–1944), and Padraic
    Colum (1881–1972).
25. In the one-act play *A Deuce o' Jacks* by F. R. Higgins, first performed 16
    Sep 1935 at the Abbey Theatre, Dublin, the character Golden Maggie
    sings the comic song 'Pharao's Daughter' by Michael Moran (known as
    Zozimus; *c.* 1794–1846), a blind Dublin ballad-maker. The on-stage
    crowd of Dublin rabble joins in for the last line, 'Tare an' ages, girls,
    which o' yees owns th' ch – ild' – *The Dublin Magazine*, new ser. 11, no. 2
    (Apr–June 1936) 39–40. The version of 'Pharao's Daughter' printed in *A
    Broadside*, new ser., no. 8 (Aug 1935) sigs [2ʳ–2ᵛ], ends: ' "Tare-an-ages,
    girls, which o' yees own the child?" ' Yeats discussed Moran in 'The Last
    Gleeman' (1893), in *The Celtic Twilight* (*Myth* 47–53).
26. Yeats changed l. 3 of his poem 'The Rose Tree' (1920) from 'Maybe a

breath of politic words' to 'Some politicians idle words' when it was republished, with music by Arthur Duff, in *A Broadside*, new ser., no. 5 (May 1935). Ronald Schuchard points out that Yeats reverted to the earlier wording when the poem was recited, without music, in a BBC broadcast, 3 July 1937.

27. Compare a note by F. R. Higgins in a volume of his poems, *The Dark Breed* (London: Macmillan, 1927) p. 66: 'The younger [contemporary Irish] poets generally express themselves through idioms taken from Gaelic speech; they impose on English verse the rhythm of a gapped music, and through their music we hear echoes of secret harmonies and the sweet twists still turning to-day through many a quaint Connacht song.' For the gapped musical scape see the next note.

28. Many Irish airs were originally composed in a 'gapped' or pentatonic scale, which omits the two semi-tones of the usual modern diatonic scale. See the extended discussion in W. K. Sullivan's introduction to Eugene O'Curry, *On the Manners and Customs of the Ancient Irish: A Series of Lectures* (London: Williams and Norgate, 1873) I, dlxx–dcxviii.

29. This anecdote probably was based on Timotheus (446–357 BC), a Greek musician who was banished from Sparta for adding four strings to the traditional seven-string lyre, thereby, as the Spartan edict stated, showing that he despised 'the ancient music' and corrupted 'the ears of our youth' – Boethius, *De Musica*, MS, quoted in Edward Bunting, 'An Historical and Critical Dissertation on the Harp', *A General Collection of the Ancient Music of Ireland* (London: Clementi, 1809) pp. 11, 12n. According to Bunting and to recent authorities, the Greek lyre began with three or four strings and had reached a standard of seven strings by the fifth century BC.

30. Frederic W. H. Myers (1843–1901), *Human Personality and its Survival of Bodily Death* (1903; repr. New York: Longmans, Green, 1954) I, 102.

31. Irish folk-song is an important element in the poetry of F. R. Higgins. In the 'Music for Lyrics' section that Yeats appended in 1908 to an earlier essay, 'Speaking to the Psaltery' (1902), Yeats candidly admitted knowing 'nothing of music' (*The Countess Cathleen. The Land of Heart's Desire. The Unicorn from the Stars*, vol. III of *The Collected Works in Verse and Prose of William Butler Yeats* [London: Chapman and Hall, 1908] pp. 234–5). The tunes printed there that are ascribed to Yeats are for 'The Song of Wandering Aengus' (1893?, publ. 1897) and 'The Song of the Old Mother' (1894) (*P* 59–60). Arnold Dolmetsch (1858–1940), English musician, was a renowned authority on ancient musical instruments; Laurence Binyon (1869–1943), English poet and art historian, was an acquaintance of Yeats's; Arthur Henry Bullen (1857–1920), English man of letters, printed Yeats's collected edition of 1908. The immediate reference is to *Essays* (London: Macmillan, 1924); the music is reprinted in *E&I* 23–7.

32. George Malcolm Young (1882–1959), English historian, in 'Tunes Ancient and Modern', *Life and Letters*, 11 (Feb 1935) 546: 'singsong of speech'.

33. Louis MacNeice, 'Train to Dublin', ll. 1–3, *New Verse* (London), no. 13 (Feb 1935); collected in *Poems* (London: Faber, Sep 1935) p. 32.

34. Untraced.

35. Walter James Turner, *The Seven Days of the Sun: A Dramatic Poem* (London: Chatto and Windus, 1925) p. 25 ('Thursday', ll. 1–15). Yeats quoted this passage in *OBMV* 304 (no. 270).

SELECTIONS FROM DOROTHY WELLESLEY

1. In May 1935, while recovering from congestion of the lungs, Yeats made his selections for *OBMV*. The anthology by J. C. Squire is *Younger Poets of To-day* (London: Secker, 1932; repr. 1934 as *Third Selections from Modern Poets*), which includes 'Walled Garden' and 'Horses', the two poems that Yeats mentions below, by Dorothy Violet Wellesley (*née* Ashton), Duchess of Wellington.

2. 'Walled Garden', ll. 31–5, in *Third Selections from Modern Poets*, p. 486.

3. 'Horses', ll. 1–9, in *Third Selection from Modern Poets*, p. 481.

4. Untraced.

5. Edith Sitwell, English poet (1887–1964). The boldly stylised designs of Léon Bakst contributed to the vogue for Diaghilev's Russian Ballet (1909 ff.). The drawings that Aubrey Beardsley (1872–98) made for *Salome* (1894) are characteristic of his late style. Yeats made the same point in his introduction to *OBMV*, p. xix (section VIII).

6. These were Yeats's three selections from the fifty short poems in the 'Verses for the Middle-Aged' section of *Poems of Ten Years: 1924–1934* (London: Macmillan, 1934). In that volume's prefatory note, dated May 1934, Dorothy Wellesley explained that the poems of that section 'have been included, after some hesitation, because they represent the genuine belief or inventions of a young child, not the subsequent inventions of an adult, and as such may be of some interest or amusement' (p. v).

   'Great Grandma' opens:

   > Great Grandmama wore drawers of lace,
   > She drank her wine at tea,
   > She put on all her clothes, then went
   > And sat down in the sea.
   >
   >   (p. 295, ll. 1–4)

   In 'Sheep' she observes, 'They stand upon their breakfast, they / Lie down upon their dinner', to which she comments, 'This would not seem so strange to us . . . / If we had floors of marmalade / And beds of buttered eggs' (p. 279, ll. 3–5, 7–8). In 'England' she announces that the country's shape, on a map, resembles a 'donkey / Sitting on the sea' (p. 268, ll. 3–4). She reprinted these poems in 1954 as *Rhymes for Middle Years*.

7. 'Deserted House: Poem Sequence' (1930), part I, 'The Lost Forest', section II:

For into these woods the green water came at my will,
To flood the forest, between the tree trunks flowing;
. . .
Here the deep-sea conger himself nosed a wild daffodil;
. . .
And a flight of fishes perched on a cherry bough.
                              (*Poems of Ten Years*, p. 214, ll. 7–8, 12, 14)

8. The booksellers John and Edward Bumpus Ltd, in Oxford Street, London.

9. *Selections from Wellesley* includes most of nineteen (from the original twenty-one) sections from 'Matrix' (1928). For Herbert Read (1893–1968), 'Mutations of the Pheonix' (1923), and Walter James Turner (1889–1946), *Seven Days of the Sun* (1925), see Yeats's introduction to *OBMV*, pp. xxxi (section XIII) and xxviii–xxx (section XII).

10. Vedanta is an orthodox system of Hindu philosophy in which, as in the Neoplatonic philosopher Plotinus (*c.* 203–62), material existence is considered illusory.

11. See Dorothy Wellesley, 'Matrix': 'He knew all before he was born. // How shall he recapture that knowledge, / Slipped over edge, out of sight?' The dead '. . . like the living, can never forget / They were born' (sections XV [XIII in *Selections from Wellesley*], ll. 8–10; XVII [XV], ll. 5–6 in *Poems of Ten Years*, pp. 320–1.

    'Matrix', section XIX [XVII in *Selections from Wellesley*], l. 11, in *Poems of Ten Years*, p. 323: 'Reiteration of birth'.

12. 'Matrix', section XXI [XIX in *Selections from Wellesley*], in *Poems of Ten Years*, p. [324]: 'same, / As'; 'console, / The'.

13. Gustave Flaubert (1821–80) outlined but did not write a novel to be called 'La Spirale' ('The Spiral'), which he mentioned in letters during 1852 and 1853. In 1905 the outline was shown to E. W. Fischer, who published a description of it in 1908: 'La Spirale, plan inédit de Gustave Flaubert', tr. François D'Aiguy, *Études sur Flaubert inédit* (Leipzig: Zeitler, 1908); see esp. pp. 123–7. The outline itself was not published until 1958: 'Un inédit de Gustave Flaubert: La spirale', *La Table ronde: revue mensuelle*, no. 124 (Apr 1958) 96–8. Yeats had mentioned 'La Spirale' in *V(A)* 128 (rev. *V[B]* 70). Yeats's source was perhaps Arthur Symons or T. Sturge Moore, although they do not mention 'La Spirale' in their studies of Flaubert: Symons, 'Flaubert' (1919), *The Symbolist Movement in Literature*, 3rd edn (New York: Dutton, 1919) and Moore, *Art and Life* (London: Methuen, 1910).

14. In 'A Prince of Bohemia' (1840), Honoré de Balzac praised the vitality of imagination to be found among young Bohemians; Balzac had spent 1819–20 living in a garret on a meagre allowance from his parents.

15. [Yeats's note:] 'Ode to Georgiana, Duchess of Devonshire, on the Twenty-fourth Stanza† in her "Passage over Mount Gothard"'.[15a]

15a. Samuel Taylor Coleridge, written in 1799, ll. 6, 24, 51 ('Whence learnt . . .'), in *The Poetical Works of Samuel Taylor Coleridge*, ed. James Dykes Campbell (1893; repr. London: Macmillan, 1925) p. 149. Yeats's copy of that edition of Coleridge has the page corner turned down to mark the poem.

RUDDOCK: THE LEMON TREE

1. *C.* 12 May 1936. Margot Collis was the stage name of Mrs Margot Ruddock Lovell (1907–51).
2. She was interested in poetic drama and had met Yeats in October 1934. Two months later she and Yeats, together with T. S. Eliot, the artist Edmund Dulac, and the producers Rupert Doone and E. Martin Browne, had joined the playwright and manager Ashley Dukes (1885–1959) in plans for a season of 'Plays by Poets' at Dukes's small Mercury Theatre, Notting Hill Gate, London.
3. In 1932 she had married Raymond Lovell, who ran a theatrical company at the Little Theatre, Leeds, and was producer and leading man at Bradford, 1932–3. Later in 1933 he had a repertory company at the Theatre Royal, Bournemouth, and the Grand Theatre, Southampton.
4. Frederick Ashton, dancer and choreographer. He was appointed choreographer at Sadler's Wells in September 1935.
5. In October and November 1934 Yeats and Margot Ruddock worked on plans for her to read and sing Yeats's poems from the stage at the Mercury Theatre. Those readings never took place, but she read and chanted his poems in his last three BBC broadcasts, in 1937. For the 3 July 1937 broadcast, she was replaced as a singer by Olive Grove at the insistence of the BBC producer, George Barnes – to the delight of Edmund Dulac, who considered Ruddock's singing to be amateurish. See George Whalley, 'Yeats and Broadcasting', in Wade 472–4, and Colin White, *Edmund Dulac* (London: Studio Vista, 1976) p. 175.
6. A production of *The Player Queen* (first perf. 1919) was planned for the Mercury Theatre 'Plays by Poets' series of spring 1935. Edmund Dulac resigned from the project after a disagreement with Margot Ruddock over plans for this play, and Ashby Dukes postponed the production until September 1935. By August Yeats had abandoned hope for it. Then, as part of the celebration of Yeats's seventieth birthday, the People's National Theatre, headed by Nancy Price, produced *The Player Queen* at the Little Theatre, London, on Sunday evening, 27 Oct 1935, with matinees on 28, 29 and 31 Oct. Yeats was disappointed that Margot Ruddock was given only the supporting role of the real Queen, but a review in *The Times* (28 Oct 1935, p. 12, col. c) had high praise for Joan Maude in the title role of Decima and for Robert Newton as the dramatist and poet Septimus, while finding that 'the remainder of the long cast played conscientiously, but not without some weak spots'. William Rothenstein, after attending a matinee, agreed with *The Times* (William Rothenstein, *Since Fifty: Men and Memories, 1922–1938* [New York: Macmillan, 1940] p. 246). Soon after Yeats wrote this part of the introduction, his insistence that the leading role in *The Player Queen* be

given to Margot Ruddock led the Abbey Theatre directors Frank O'Connor and Hugh Hunt to substitute *Deirdre* for a proposed production of *The Player Queen*, with Jean Forbes-Robertson and Micheál MacLiammóir in the leading roles, 10–15 Aug 1936.

7. Yeats included seven of her poems in *OBMV*.

8. Yeats to Margot Ruddock [early Apr 1936], *LMR* 81.

9. The quotations which follow (pp. 187–9) are from her typescript 'Moments. Snatchings – and Probings' (10pp.; *LMR* 127, 129–30).

10. *C.* 15 May 1936.

11. Yeats revised her narrative [NLI MS. 30,141 and 30,388; SUNY-SB 1.11.102–9), titled 'The Catastrophe'; the published version is titled 'Almost I Tasted Ecstacy' (*The Lemon Tree*, pp. 1–9; *LMR* 91–8).

12. Untraced. A preliminary typescript version reads: 'I remember reading – I have forgotten where, except that it was in some Indian book . . .' (NLI MS. 30,321; SUNY-SB 21.4.127).

13. Untraced. The story was not carried by *The Times* or the *Irish Times*.

14. *Iliad*, x.150: 'Now on the eager razor's edge for life or death we stand' (tr. George Chapman [1559–1634], in *Chapman's Homer*, vol. ii: *The Iliad*, ed. Allardyce Nicoll [New York: Pantheon Books, 1956] p. 204).

MUSIC AND POETRY

1. Dorothy Violet Wellesley (*née* Ashton), Duchess of Wellington (1889–1956), English poet.

2. The passage echoes, but confuses, Mozart's letter to his father, Leopold Mozart, 8 Nov 1777: 'I cannot write in verse, for I am no poet. I cannot arrange the parts of speech with such art as to produce effects of light and shade, for I am no painter. . . . But I can do so by means of sounds, for I am a musician' (*The Letters of Mozart and his Family*, tr. Emily Anderson [London: Macmillan, 1938] p. 532). Yeats or perhaps Dorothy Wellesley might have misremembered a remark of Walter James Turner, who wrote a biography of Mozart that is quoted below; see note 6 below.

3. Untraced. See perhaps Mozart's letter to his father, 13 Oct 1781: 'In an opera the poetry must be altogether the obedient daughter of the music. . . . An opera is sure of success when the plot is well worked out, the words written solely for the music and not shoved in here and there to suit some miserable rhyme (which, God knows, never enhances the value of any theatrical performance, be it what it may, but rather detracts from it) . . .' (*The Letters of Mozart and his Family*, pp. 1150–1).

4. The Greek lyric poets Sappho (fl. 600 BC) and Pindar (522?–443 BC) set their poetry to their own musical accompaniment.

5. The German composer Christoph Glück's first major opera, *Orfeo ed Euridice*, came in 1762. The English composer Henry Purcell's *Dido and Aeneas* (1689?) had replaced spoken dialogue with recitative. Purcell wrote the music for John Dryden's opera *King Arthur; or, The British*

Worthy (1691). Inigo Jones (1573–1652), English architect, designed scenery for court masques. The operas of Richard Wagner (1813–83), who wrote his own libretti, date from 1841 to 1882.

6. Walter James Turner (1889–1946), in his biography of Mozart, observed that Mozart 'remained incomprehensible to the Italian opera public practically ever since' 1792, the first production in Italy of *La Nozze di Figaro* (1786), but Turner thought the reason was the musical sophistication of Mozart's operas. See Turner, *Mozart: The Man and his Works* (London: Gollancz, 1938) p. 336.

7. The German poem is untraced.

8. Yeats may have attended a concert by the Prague Philharmonic Orchestra, in London, 29 October 1937. The programme consisted of Czech music, including the popular *Slavonic Dances* (1878, 1887) by Anton Dvořák (1841–1904), and *Taras Bulba* (1915–18, 1927), an exciting orchestral rhapsody by the Czech composer Leoš Janáček (1854–1928); however, *Taras Bulba* has no vocal parts. Reports of this concert and of the Prague Philharmonic Orchestra's only other London concert, 13 October, do not mention any choral works. The reference might be to Janáček's vernacular *Glagolitic Mass* (1926), a brilliant, festive orchestral and vocal work that has extensive repetition of sung phrases, especially in the Kyrie and Angus Dei movements; it repeats 'Amin' ('Amen') at the end of the Gloria and at the opening and closing of the Credo movements. Dvořák wrote many choral works, including masses.

9. The Tetragrammaton (four Hebrew letters representing the name of God) and Agla (an acrostic of four Hebrew words meaning 'Thou are powerful and eternal, Lord') are extensively used in Cabbalism and in ritual magic, for example in S. L. MacGregor Mathers' introduction and translation, *The Kabbalah Unveiled* (1887; repr. London: Routledge and Kegan Paul, 1968) pp. 9 *et passim* (for Tetragrammaton) and 31 (for Agla). Hebrew letters are consonants rather than vowels.

10. The first of Yeats's Noh-style plays, or 'plays for dancers', was *At the Hawk's Well* (perf. 1916, publ. 1917).

11. Giotto (1276?–1337?), Florentine painter and architect.

12. Vallathol K. Narayana Menon (1878–1958) published his autobiographical poem 'Badhira Vilapam' ('A Deaf Man's Lament') in 1910, in Malayalam, the regional language of Kerala state, on the south-western coast of India. The Indian *Dictionary of National Biography*, ed. S. P. Sen (Calcutta: Institute of Historical Studies, 1974) III, 102, praises him as 'the foremost poet of nationalism in South India'.

13. The quotation from Rabindranath Tagore (1861–1941), Indian poet, is untraced.

14. Aristotle (384–322 BC) in *The Art of Rhetoric*, book III, recommended appropriate diction, but Yeats's specific reference is untraced; he often reported that the passage was a favourite of Lady Gregory's. See Introduction to *Fighting the Waves* (1934), *VP1* 567; *Au* 395 (1934); and Preface to *The Ten Principal Upanishads* (London: Faber, 1937) p. 8.

15. [Yeats's note:] Above all no accompaniment on a keyed instrument, because by that the public ear is nailed to the mathematician's desk.

Bach's diatonic scale rose with the dome of St Paul's, after the Great Fire, and satisfied the same need.[15a]

15a. The establishment of standardised keyboards in the fifteenth century produced a corresponding standardisation of musical scales. Johann Sebastian Bach (1685–1750) in *The Well-Tempered Clavier* (1722) used the extended sets of twelve major and minor diatonic scales that are now conventional. St Paul's Cathedral was destroyed in the Great Fire of London in 1666; the new cathedral, designed by Christopher Wren, was completed in 1708. Edwin J. Ellis and Yeats, in their edition of Blake in 1893, point out that Blake considered the dome of St Paul's an example of 'intellectual error', as opposed to the inspiration that characterises Gothic architecture (*WWB* I, 38).

16. At the bottom of the page, below the signatures of Yeats and Dorothy Wellesley, but above their footnote, are two excerpts from the Irish poet Thomas Moore's Preface to *Irish Melodies* (1st collected edn, 1821), as follows:

Tom Moore's Advice to a Singer

'It has always been a subject of some mortification to me that my songs, as they are set, give such a very imperfect notion of the manner in which I wish them to be performed.'

'There is but one instruction I should venture to give any person desirous of doing justice to the character of these ballads, and that is, to attend as little as possible to the rhythm, or time in singing them. The time, indeed, should always be made to wait upon the feeling, but particularly in this style of musical recitation, where the words ought to be as nearly *spoken* as is consistent with the swell and sweetness of intonation, and where a strict and mechanical observation of time completely destroys all those pauses, lingerings and abruptnesses, which the expression of passion and tenderness requires.'[16a]

16a. Thomas Moore, Preface to *Irish Melodies* (1821), repr. in *The Works of Thomas Moore, Esqr.: Complete in Six Volumes* (New York: Smith, 1825) IV, iii, vi: '. . . me, that . . .'; '. . . should *always* be . . . lingerings, and. . . .'

APPENDIX 1

1. Thomas Crofton Croker, *Fairy Legends* (1825), p. 34.
2. Croker, 'The Song of the Little Bird: A Legend of the South of Ireland. With some Remarks on Irish Holy Wells', *The Amulet of Christian and Literary Remembrancer* (London), 2 (1827) 356: 'An old woman had concluded her prayers and was about to depart, when I entered into conversation with her, and I have written the very words in which she related to me the legend of the Song of the Little Bird.'

3. For Yeats's updated version of this list in *Irish Fairy Tales* (1891), see pp. 66–7. I have here left unemended the several minor errors in book titles; for details, see p. 252, note 27 above.

APPENDIX 2

1. For this passage from Lady Jane Francesca Elgee Wilde, *Ancient Legends, Mystic Charms, and Superstitions of Ireland*, 2 vols (London: Ward and Downey, 1887–8) I, 191–2, and a subsequent sentence from *FFT* 147, see pp. 18–19 and 237, note 54 above.

APPENDIX 4

1. Edwin John Ellis (1848–1916) had made a transcription of Blake's 'Notebook' (1793?–1818?; BL Add. MS 49460, previously owned by D. G. Rossetti from 1847 to 1882 and by William Augustus White, Brooklyn, New York, from 1887 to 1927); for descriptions of the 'Notebook' see Bentley, *Blake's Writings*, pp. 1704–20, and David V. Erdman (ed.), *The Notebook of William Blake: A Photographic and Typographic Facsimile* (Oxford: Clarendon Press, 1973).
2. For Charles Fairfax Murray, see p. 262, note 42 above and Yeats to Murray [Feb 1893] (*CL1* 347); for Dr Carter Blake, see p. 258, note 1 and p. 252, note 23 above.

APPENDIX 5

1. *The Poetical Works of William Blake, Lyrical and Miscellaneous*, ed. William Michael Rossetti, Aldine edn of the British Poets (London: Bell, 1874; repr. 1890, 1891, 1893, etc.).
2. Notebook, p. 113; Bentley, *Blake's Writings*, p. 994: '. . . with holy look / In . . . .' Yeats used the 'book, (?look)' query in all editions.
3. Notebook, p. 4; see Bentley, *Blake's Writings*, p. 925, n. 1.
4. *The Poems of William Blake, Comprising Songs of Innocence and of Experience together with Poetical Sketches and some copyright not in any other Edition*, ed. Richard Herne Shepherd (London: Pickering, 1874; repr. 1887).
5. 'Fayette . . .' (Notebook, p. 98).
6. 'To my Friend Butts I write', in Blake to Thomas Butts, 2 Oct 1800 (Bentley, *Blake's Writings*, pp. 1546–7).
7. 'To my dear Friend Mrs. Anna Flaxman', in Blake to Mrs Flaxman, 14 September 1800 (Bentley, *Blake's Writings*, pp. 1538–9).
8. 'Auguries of Innocence', ll. 5–132, in the Pickering (or Ballad) MS.
9. 'I rose up at dawn of day' (Notebook, p. 89).

10. 'Since all the Riches of this World' (Notebook, p. 73) and 'Riches' (Notebook, p. 103).
11. 'Why was Cupid a Boy' (Notebook, p. 56).
12. 'My Spectre around me night & day' (Notebook, pp. 3, 2).
13. 'With happiness stretched across the hills', in Blake to Thomas Butts [22 November 1802] (Bentley, *Blake's Writings*, pp. 1563–6).

APPENDIX 6

1. 'Iris Olkyrn' was the pseudonym of Alice Milligan (1866–1953), Irish poet, novelist, and dramatist.
2. The first volume of poems by Thomas William Hazen Rolleston (1857–1920) was published in 1909: *Sea Spray: Verses and Translations* (Dublin: Maunsel).
3. For Yeats's favourable reviews of Katharine Tynan's books of poems *Shamrocks* (London: Kegan Paul, 1887) and *Ballads and Lyrics* (London: Kegan Paul, 1891), see *UP1* 119–22 and *UP2* 511–14. Her two other books of poems had been *Louise de la Vallière and Other Poems* (London: Kegan Paul, 1885), which Yeats found 'too full of English influences . . . and too laden with garish colour' (*UP2* 511–12), and *Cuckoo Songs* (London: Mathews and Lane, 1894). Yeats included her 'The Children of Lir' in both the 1895 and the 1900 editions of *BIV* (1895, pp. 207–10; 1900, pp. 207–11); 'In Iona' was in the 1895 edition (pp. 215–16), but Yeats excluded it from the 1900 edition.
4. Charles Alexandre Weekes (1867–1946) dedicated his first book of poems, *Reflections and Refractions* (London: Unwin, 1893), to his friend AE. In only the 1900 version this sentence went on to mention William Kirkpatrick Magee ('John Eglinton', 1868–1961) and his 1894 volume of transcendental essays, *Two Essays on the Remnant* (Dublin: Whaley): '. . . book, and Mr John Eglinton, who is best known for the orchestral harmonies of the *Two Essays on the Remnant*, and certain younger writers. . . .'
5. AE, 'Sung on a By-way', ll. 1–12 (of 16), *Homeward: Songs by the Way* (Dublin: Whaley, June 1894) p. 23: 'dream shaft' (l. 3). In the 1900 edition of *BIV*, this poem (p. 222) was among seven poems by AE that Yeats added; at the same time he dropped 'The Place of Rest', one of the two poems by AE that had appeared in the 1895 edition.

APPENDIX 7

1. When Co. Meath and Co. Westmeath became part of Leinster, the number of provinces was reduced to the present four.
2. Applotment: apportionment; division into plots.

3. *The Genealogies, Tribes, and Customs of Hy-Fiachrach, Commonly Called 'O'Dowda's Country*, tr. and ed. John O'Donovan (Dublin: Irish Archaeological Society, 1844) p. 455 (Appendix N: 'Cathal Dubh O'Dubhda' from *Historia familiae De Burgo* [MS., Trinity College, Dublin]): '. . . every Mac William is entitled to a tribute of five marks yearly out of the country of O'Dowd, and that the then O'Dowd, namely, Cathal Dubh, consented to the payment of this tribute, which is called a *cios cosanta*, i.e. tribute for protection'.
4. Yeats himself made this claim (p. 79 above).

APPENDIX 8

1. The 1895 edition had omitted the entire second half (ll. 41–80) of Katharine Tynan's 'The Children of Lir'.

APPENDIX 9

1. In the 1895 edition these references to the popular Fenian poet John Keegan Casey and to *Stories of Wicklow* (London: Longmans, 1886) by George Francis Savage-Armstrong (1845–1906) began: 'Two worthy writers are excluded – Casey . . .' (p. xxviii). In the 1900 edition Yeats added the phrase 'when interesting' later in that sentence, but he did not correct his perhaps deliberately generic reference, 'Songs of Wicklow', rather than *Stories of Wicklow*, the misleading title of that book of poems.

APPENDIX 10

1. [Yeats's note:] This version, though Dr Hyde went some way with it, has never been published. I do not know why. – W. B. Y., *March, 1908*.
2. The German epic *Nibelungenlied* (*c.* 1190–1210).
3. Nine of the twenty-two short stories that Yeats wrote between 1887 and 1897 have settings that could be called 'mediaeval'. In 1903, with Lady Gregory's considerable assistance, Yeats revised and in some cases recast his six stories about Red Hanrahan, putting them into the Kiltartan dialect mentioned later in the paragraph.
4. William Morris, *The Well at the World's End* (1896).
5. Lady Gregory called this the Kiltartan dialect, after the Kiltartan barony, which includes her estate, Coole Park. Robert Burns (1759–96) wrote his most successful poems and songs in the Scots dialect.
6. See *Cuchulain of Muirthemne*, pp. 82–103 ('The High King of Ireland').

APPENDIX 11

1. The final three paragraphs of this endnote to Lady Gregory, *Cuchulain of Muirthemne* (1902) were first published, under the title 'An Ancient Conversation', in the *All Ireland Review*, 3, no. 6 (12 Apr 1902) 87, as an introduction to excerpts from the forthcoming *Cuchulain of Muirthemne*. The excerpts continued in nos 6 and 7; (19 Apr 1902) 103, and (26 Apr 1902) 123.

2. For Cormac mac Art, see p. 278, note 32 above. The verse is from a literal translation in Eugene O'Curry, *Lectures on the Manuscript Materials of Ancient Irish History: Delivered at the Catholic University of Ireland, during the Sessions of 1855 and 1856*, 2nd edn (Dublin: Hinch, Traynor, 1878) p. 477: '. . . apple-tree . . . Ailinn, / . . . Yew . . . Bailé . . . / . . . into lays, / Ignorant people. . . .' O'Curry has another, more distant version at p. 466:

> The apple tree of noble *Aillinn*,
> The yew of Bailé, – small inheritance, –
> Although they are introduced into poems,
> They are not understood by unlearned people.

'*Ibar Cinn Tracta*, the yew at the head of Baile's strand', is mentioned in *Cuchulain of Muirthemne*, p. 289 ('The Only Jealousy of Emer'), which was one of Yeats's sources for his play *The Only Jealousy of Emer* (publ. 1919, perf. 1922).

3. *Gods and Fighting Men*, p. 41 ('The Sons of Tuireann'): '"'. . . poem," said the king, "but . . . understand why my own spear is brought into it, O Man of Poetry from Ireland."'

4. Untraced. Kuno Meyer (1858–1919), German scholar of Celtic languages, held posts at the University of Liverpool, the University of Glasgow, the Royal Irish Academy and the School of Irish Learning, Dublin. He later held the Chair of Celtic Philology at the University of Berlin.

5. The *Poetic* (or *Elder*) *Edda* and the *Prose* (or *Younger*) *Edda* are from twelfth- or thirteenth-century Iceland. The *Poetic Edda* is a compilation of mythological and heroic poems that date probably from the ninth to eleventh centuries. The *Prose Edda* is a textbook on poetics, supplemented by a history of the Norse gods.

6. Frederick York Powell (1850–1904), Regius Professor of History, Oxford, was a friend of John Butler Yeats and maintained a home in Bedford Park, London. Powell translated and edited Icelandic poetry, notably *Corpus Poeticum Boreale: The Poetry of the Old Northern Tongue, from the Earliest Times to the Thirteenth Century*, ed. Gudbrand Vigfusson and Frederick York Powell, vol. I: *Epic Poetry*, vol. II: *Court Poetry* (Oxford: Clarendon Press, 1883).

7. Untraced.

8. Thomas Nashe's satirical masque *Summer's Last Will and Testament* (1592, publ. 1600), ll. 1590–3, in *A Select Collection of Old Plays*, ed. John Payne

Collier (London: Prowett, 1825) IX, 67: '. . . air;/Queens . . . fair./ Dust. . . .' For an old-spelling edition see *The Works of Thomas Nashe*, ed. R. B. McKerrow (Oxford: Blackwell, 1958) III, 283.

9. The scalds (skalds), early Icelandic court poets, used elaborate, riddle-like kennings and circumlocutions.

10. The constellation 'Berenice's Hair' (*Coma Berenices*) takes its name from Berenice II of Cyrene (d. 216? BC), who offered her hair to the gods in exchange for the safe return from war of her husband Ptolemy III (282?–221 BC), King of Egypt. The quotation is untraced. Catullus, LXVI, has several references to her flaming hair in heaven, but no phrase directly equivalent to 'Berenice's ever burning hair'. Yeats later used this phrase as the last line of his poem 'Her Dream' (1929, publ. 1930; *P* 280).

11. The Tuatha de Danann, led by Nuada, conquered the Firbolg in the second battle of Magh Tuireadh (or Moy Tura, the Plain of Towers or Columns), just north of Lough Arrow, Co. Sligo. See Yeats's note to 'The Valley of the Black Pig' (1899, cut 1924; *VP* 810), and *Gods and Fighting Men*, pp. 6–7, 51–62 ('The Fight with the Firbolgs', 'The Great Battle of Magh Tuireadh'). Another semi-mythological battle of the same name had been fought twenty-seven years earlier, near Cong, Co. Mayo.

12. William C. Borlase, *The Dolmens of Ireland* (London: Chapman and Hall, 1897) [II], 867–8. See Whitley Stokes (tr.), 'The Prose Tales in the Rennes "Dindshenchas" [No. 70]: Mag Mucraime', *Revue celtique*, 15 (1894) 470, and 'The Battle of Mag Mucrime' *Revue celtique*, 13 (1892) 449, 451.

13. Beryl, a pale green crystal, was once considered magical.

APPENDIX 13

1. For *Selections from Wellesley*, Yeats chose twenty-four from the 126 poems in *Poems for Ten Years*. The only new poem, 'Fire', was his opening selection. For a study of the revisions made for *Selections from Wellesley*, see Edward O'Shea, 'Yeats as Editor: Dorothy Wellesley's *Selections*', *English Language Notes*, 11 (Dec 1973) 112–18.

APPENDIX 15

1. Professor In-sŏb Zŏng (also transliterated as Chŏng) first became interested in Yeats in 1936 as a student at Waseda University, Tokyo. He taught at the Chosen Christian School, Seoul, from 1929 to 1945, and then at the Central University and the National University, Seoul. The foreword to his anthology gives an account of his brief call on Yeats:

And I put here the words of William Butler Yeats, the world famous Irish poet, as a kind of frontispiece, which were spoken by the poet himself to me, whom I called at his sick bed in the suburb of Dublin in 1936. He sat up half way in his bed, read my manuscripts of translation Part I, which I included in this book, and spoke these words in calm and soft voice, and Mrs. Yeats typewrote them by his side, their son listening to them. (p. 11)

The poems in part I (pp. 1–165)

had been selected by the poets themselves by my request for translation. And they were translated by me till Spring 1936, and several of them were introduced through the English magazine 'The Poetry Review', published in London, when I travelled Europe for the purpose of attending the 4th International Congress of Linguists held at Copenhagen. (p. 5)

2. 'A Secret' (pp. 158 [in English] and 159 [in Korean]):

> My rumpled hair
> Combing neatly,
> I put on the little comb
> You sent to me.
>
> My weed-stained fingers,
> Washing neatly,
> I put on the little ring
> You sent to me.
>
> While little comb
> And ring I wear,
> In the glass I gaze at myself
> Reflected there.
>
> On my hand
> And in my hair,
> Is hidden a secret
> That none can share.

Professor Zŏng included three more of his own poems: 'The Ravens and the Science Hall' (116 lines), 'Mountain Climbing' (72 lines), and 'The Canna' (12 lines).

TEXTUAL
INTRODUCTIONS

Introduction and headnotes to *Fairy and Folk Tales of the Irish Peasantry*, ed.
W. B. Yeats (1888)

Yeats was commissioned to edit this anthology in the Camelot Classics series,
published by Walter Scott, London. In the summer of 1888 he selected the
contents and wrote the general introduction, section introductions, and
notes. A year before, soon after Yeats arrived in London, he had befriended
Ernest Rhys (1859–1946), who was editor of this series of one-shilling
volumes and who later was a founder of the Rhymers' Club. In a letter to
Katharine Tynan [?22–8 Sep 1888], Yeats described his work on the book,
which took three months and for which was paid £14:

> The notes to folk lore book were done quickly and they are bad or at any
> rate not good. Introduction is better. Douglas Hyde gave me much help
> with footnotes etc. . . . I have had a great deal of trouble over the folk lore
> the publishers first making me strike out 100 pages on the ground that the
> book was too long and then when two thirds was in print add as many pages
> of fresh matter because they had made a wrong calculation and I set to
> work copying out and looking over material again as the pages struck out
> had to do with the section already in type. (*CL1* 95, 97)

Fairy and Folk Tales of the Irish Peasantry was published in September 1888 by
Walter Scott, London, with co-publishers Thomas Whittaker in New York
and W. J. Gage in Toronto; a copy in the British Library is date-stamped 27
Sep 1888. An errata sheet to the 1888 edition gave ten corrections. Yeats did
not subsequently revise the introductions or notes. The 1888 edition, with
errata, is the copy-text.

In the copy that Yeats inscribed to Katharine Tynan on 21 July 1889
(Berg, NYPL), he entered eleven local corrections in ink, only five of which
were among the ten corrections listed on the errata sheet that was issued by
the publisher. Five of the six unadopted corrections are to Yeats's
introductions, and thus are of interest here. One is to a straightforward
spelling error in a proper name ('*Dallahan*', p. 14, l. 32), and I have cited
Yeats's correction as a collateral authority there. The four other corrections
that he made to his introductions, but that, for one reason or another, he
and/or the publisher did not include in the errata sheet or in any subsequent
edition, may be briefly noted here.

P. 4, l. 38. Insert 'their' before 'faces against wakes'.
P. 8, l. 33. Change 'their doorstep' to 'the doorstep'.

P. 8, l. 38. Delete 'to' before 'the words of Socrates'.
P. 14, ll. 9–11. Delete: 'They dress with all unfairy homeliness, and are, indeed, most sluttish, slouching, jeering, mischievous phantoms.'

The book was no. 32 in the Camelot Classics series, the name of which was changed first to the Camelot series and then, in 1892, to the Scott Library, in which it was no. 37. The publisher's errata were incorporated in the text of the 1892 Scott Library edition.

An illustrated edition was issued by Walter Scott, London, in October 1893, with thirteen illustrations by James Torrance, and was reissued in 1895 by Charles Scribner's Sons, New York, and Walter Scott, London. In 1902 A. L. Burt Company, a New York reprint house, added six stories ('The Fate of the Children of Lir', pp. 1–9; 'The Black Horse', pp. 57–64; 'Morraha', pp. 80–93; 'The Greek Princess and the Young Gardner', pp. 113–23; 'Smallhead and the King's Sons', pp. 194–210; and 'The Leeching of Kayn's Leg', pp. 301–32) and eighteen ink drawings (one signed H. J. Ford) for those stories. This probably unauthorised book was published as *Irish Fairy and Folk Tales*; it dropped Yeats's dedication and eight of the sixteen endnotes; the remaining notes were changed to footnotes within the text ('Gods of the Earth', p. 11n; 'Stolen Child', p. 77n; 'Solitary Fairies', p. 125n; 'Omens', p. 155n; 'A Witch Trial', pp. 211–12n; 'Father John O'Hart', p. 292n; 'Demon Cat', p. 322n; and 'A Legend of Knockmany', pp. 361–2n.). This A. L. Burt version used American spelling conventions, but less extensively than did another American edition, also titled *Irish Fairy and Folk Tales*, that was published by Boni and Liveright, New York, in 1918, as no. 44 of the Modern Library of the World's Best Books series; in 1925 the Modern Library series was transferred to Random House, New York. Four later editions were *Irish Folk Stories and Fairy Tales*, no. 21 in Grosset's Universal Library, published by Grosset and Dunlap, New York, in 1957, with American spellings; *Fairy and Folk Tales of Ireland* (which also included Yeats's anthology *Irish Fairy Tales*), published by Colin Smythe, Gerrards Cross, Bucks, and Macmillan, New York, 1973; *Irish Folk Tales*, with twelve illustrations by Rowel Friers, published by the Limited Editions Club, Avon, Conn., in 1973; and a photographic reprint of the 1918 Boni and Liveright edition, from AMS Press, New York, in 1979.

The notes written by Yeats and/or Douglas Hyde to items other than Yeats's introduction and headnotes are given in Appendix 1. I have omitted the following categories of footnotes to material that was not written by Yeats:

(1) footnotes that Yeats adopted directly from the sources of the items in the collection (1888 pp. 6, 33, 37, 155, 160, 176 [2nd, 3rd and 4th notes], 180, 181, 191, 199, 203, 268);

(2) simple bibliographical notes (1888 pp. 16, 105, 134, 151 [Yeats invented the title 'A Queen's County Witch' for this excerpt from 'Legends and Tales of the Queen's County Peasantry, No. ii – The Bewitched Butter', *Dublin University Magazine*, 14 (October 1839) 492–4], 155, 165, 168, 201, 206, 215, 229, 231, 232, 260, 280, 286 [with the title] with erratum, 290 with erratum, 294, 296, 299, 306; and

(3) simple glossary notes that probably were prepared or revised by Yeats, sometimes with the assistance of Douglas Hyde (1888 pp. 31, 51, 69 [revised by Yeats], 70 [revised by Yeats], 74, 81, 84, 106, 111, 133, 167, 169, 170, 176 [1st note], 185, 187, 193, 208, 210, 211, 231, 306 [revised by Yeats], 311).

'William Carleton', in *Stories from Carleton*, ed. W. B. Yeats (1889)

Yeats wrote the introduction, titled 'William Carleton', and selected the stories and excerpts for *Stories from Carleton*. It was published in August 1889, as no. 43 in the one-shilling Camelot series, by Walter Scott, London, with co-publisher W. J. Gage, New York and Toronto. In 1892 the series, edited by Ernest Rhys, was renamed the Scott Library, with *Stories from Carleton* as no. 48. All the notes to the stories in *Stories from Carleton* were taken directly from Carleton's *Traits and Stories of the Irish Peasantry*, new edn, 2 vols (Dublin: Curry, 1843–4), without any editorial revisions, deletions, or additions. When Yeats was writing this introduction he told Father Matthew Russell, 'I have to finish Carleton in a hurry to try and get the editor of the series out of a scrape' ([after 15 July 1889?], *CL1* 174). Soon after the book was published he further explained, again to Father Russell, 'The introduction was done very hastily to get Rhys out of a difficulty made by some one or other not being up to date' ([? week of 2 Sep 1889], *CL1* 186).

Yeats did not revise or collect the introduction. A photographic reprint of the 1889 edition was published in 1977 by Lemma, New York. The introduction was included as an appendix to *Representative Irish Tales*, ed. W. B. Yeats, foreword by Mary Helen Thuente (Gerrards Cross, Bucks: Colin Smythe; Atlantic Highlands, NJ: Humanities Press, 1979) pp. 359–64.

Introduction and headnotes (1890) to *Representative Irish Tales*, ed. W. B. Yeats (1891)

Yeats began work on this anthology of Irish fiction in the summer of 1889. He described the still tentative arrangements with the publisher, G. P. Putnam's Sons, New York, in a letter to Father Matthew Russell [? week of 2 Sep 1889]: 'I am up to the ears in Irish novelists making up the subject with view of a probable two volume selection of short stories of Irish peasant life for Puttenham's [*sic*] *Knickerbocker Nuggat* [*sic*] series. . . . The thing may not come off however I am dayly [*sic*] expecting a final clinching of the matter. The stories I am giving range from 20 to 80 pages (in a few cases of important people)' (*CL1* 186–7). By December 1889 he had broadened the criteria to make 'all the stories illustrative of some phase of Irish life' and, in a letter to Father Matthew Russell, described the collection as 'mainly tales that contain some special kind of Irish humour or tragedy' (*CL1* 198–9). The selections were to be limited to works for which the American publisher would not have to pay, primarily works that were no longer in copyright. Yeats was to submit the list of contents by 5 January 1890. He wrote the introductions to individual authors during the first two months of 1890 and then wrote the general introduction during 4–16 March 1890. He had first proofs for the book in November 1890, and it was published, in two volumes, in March 1891, as no. 28 in the Knickerbocker Nuggets series, G. P. Putnam's Sons, New York and London. Because he did not revise the work for any subsequent reissues, the copy-text is the 1891 edition.

In December 1904 Putnam's redistributed most of the contents of the two-volume 1891 edition and produced, still using the original printing plates, three separate books that were issued as nos 77–9 in the Ariel Booklets series. In listings of the series, these three volumes were collectively titled *Representative Irish Tales*, but the volumes were sold separately. The individual volumes were titled *Irish Tales, by William Carleton: Wildgoose Lodge, Condy Cullen, The Curse, Battle of the Factions* (set from the plates of I, 191–339 in the 1891 edition); *Irish Tales, by Maria Edgeworth and John and Michael Banim: Castle Rackrent, The Stolen Sheep, The Mayor of Wind-gap* (from plates of I, 1–190); and *Irish Tales, by Samuel Lover and Charles Lever: Barney O'Reirdon, Paddy the Piper, Trinity College* (from plates of II, 1–90, 205–41). I have not sighted a copy of the third volume. The selections from William Maginn, T. Crofton Croker, Gerald Griffin, Charles Kickham and Rosa Mulholland were omitted. The full contents of the 1891 edition were reprinted in 1979, with a foreword by Mary H. Thuente and additional materials, as *Representative Irish Tales* (Gerrards Cross, Bucks: Colin Smythe; and Atlantic Highlands, NJ: Humanities Press).

The four footnotes written by Yeats to works in the anthology are given in Appendix 2. I have omitted the following categories of footnotes to material that was not written by Yeats: (1) footnotes that Yeats adopted directly from the works in the anthology, (2) simple bibliographical notes (1891 II, 197, 249, 259, 339), and (3) a simple glossary footnote (1891 I, 86).

Introduction, acknowledgement note, 'The Classification of Irish Fairies' and 'Authorities on Irish Folklore' (1891) to *Irish Fairy Tales*, ed. W. B. Yeats (1892)

Yeats prepared this anthology of Irish fairy tales in the summer of 1891 for the Children's Library series published by T. Fisher Unwin, London. An appended essay titled 'Classification of Irish Fairies' is dated 'Co. Down, June 1891', and the introduction is dated 'Clondalkin, July 1891'. 'Co. Down' refers to the house of his friend Charles Johnston (1867–1931), at Ballykilbeg, Co. Down, three miles south-west of Downpatrick; 'Clondalkin' refers to Whitehall, the farm of Katharine Tynan's family near Clondalkin, Co. Dublin. Those dates supplied by Yeats are, however, only approximate, for he was in London until mid July, stopping briefly with the Tynans on his way to Ballykilbeg, where he arrived on 23 July for a stay of two weeks. He spent a second brief visit with the Tynans in Clondalkin in August and planned to return to Johnston's in Co. Down for an additional week. His first extant mention of the book, in an undated letter, suggests that in July 1891 he had not yet started the project; another undated letter suggests that the project had been nearly completed by probably 4 August (*CL1* 256, 261). Thus late

July or early August 1891 is a more likely dating for 'Classification of Irish Fairies' than the 'June 1891' date that was printed. Another appended item, 'Authorities on Irish Folklore', which is undated, contains no works published subsequent to July 1891. His own contribution to the fairy tales in the anthology, 'A Fairy Enchantment' told by Michael Hart and recorded by Yeats, is undated. His prefatory poem, 'Where My Books Go' (*P* 529), is dated 'London, January 1892'.

Irish Fairy Tales was published in 1892, probably in May, as stated in the *English Catalogue of Books*, in the Children's Library series of T. Fisher Unwin, London, with two illustrations by Jack B. Yeats; this is the copy-text. The English sheets were issued in New York with the title page of Cassell Publishing Company, also in 1892. An unrevised second impression of the 1892 plates was issued in October 1900 by T. Fisher Unwin, London. In 1973 *Irish Folk Tales* was incorporated in a reprint titled *Fairy and Folk Tales of Ireland*, published by Colin Smythe, Gerrards Cross, Bucks, and Macmillan, New York.

The present edition gives Yeats's introduction (titled 'An Irish Story-teller'), an acknowledgements note, and both of the items that the book included as appendixes, 'Classification of Irish Fairies' and 'Authorities on Irish Folklore'. Appendix 3 gives the footnotes to works by other authors, except for (1) the numerous footnotes that Yeats adopted directly from the works in the anthology and (2) brief glossary footnotes (1892 pp. 16n, 45n, 69n, 79n, 151n, 153n, 172n, 175nn, 185n). I have not sighted the originals of two of the items collected in the anthology and thus I have included in Appendix 3 two footnotes that may have been adopted directly from those works: p. 70n (to 'The Fairy Greyhound') and p. 115n (to Patrick Weston Joyce, 'Fergus O'Mara and the Air-Demons', from *Good and Pleasant Reading for Boys and Girls: Tales, Sketches, and Poems* [London: Simpkin, 1885; Dublin: Gill, 1886]). Yeats's poem 'Where My Books Go' (*P* 529) and his one brief contribution to the fairy tales in the anthology, 'A Fairy Enchantment', told by Michael Hart and recorded by Yeats (1892 pp. 49–52), are outside the scope of this volume.

'William Allingham 1824–1889' (1891) and 'Ellen O'Leary 1831–1889' (1891), in *The Poets and the Poetry of the Century*, ed. Alfred H. Miles (1892)

In 1891 Yeats wrote these brief introductions and chose the poems for the William Allingham and Ellen O'Leary sections in a ten-volume collection, *The Poets and the Poetry of the Century*, ed. Alfred H. Miles (London: Hutchinson, Oct 1892) v, 209–12 (Allingham), and vii, 449–52 (O'Leary). See Yeats to Katharine Tynan [24 July 1891] and Yeats to Susan Mary Yeats [11 Oct 1891] (*CL1* 258, 265). The introductions were reprinted, without revision, in the second, expanded edition of twelve volumes, *The Poets and Poetry of the Nineteenth Century* (London: Routledge and Sons; New York, Dutton, July 1905) v, 241–4 (Allingham), and ix, 55–8 (O'Leary). Both introductions were included in *UP1*: pp. 259–61 (Allingham) (259, l. 21: 'verse' rather than 'verses'; 260, l. 20: 'tears.' rather than 'tears!') and 256–8 (O'Leary).

Preface (*c.* 1892) to *The Works of William Blake: Poetic, Symbolic, and Critical*, ed. Edwin J. Ellis and W. B. Yeats, 3 vols (1893)

This preface to the three-volume edition *The Works of William Blake: Poetic, Symbolic, and Critical* (London: Quaritch, Feb 1893) I, vii–xiii, was signed by both Edwin John Ellis and Yeats; I have found no evidence for determining their individual contributions to it. No manuscripts or proofs of the preface are extant. The lengthy biographical memoir, later in volume I of *The Works of William Blake*, was printed probably in November 1891, so the preface might perhaps have been written as early as 1891. In an undated letter [*c.* 19 Jan 1892], Yeats had told D. J. O'Donoghue that *The Works of William Blake* probably would be published in April 1892 (*CL1* 282); in another undated letter, to John O'Leary [? week of 9 Jan 1893], Yeats announced, 'The Blake book will be ready some time next week' (*CL1* 344; see 344 n. 4).

All four corrections given on an errata sheet pasted in facing p. xvi have been adopted in this edition, but two of those errata have been also mentioned in the list of emendations because of a possible ambiguity in the directions for one and an unambiguous error in the directions for the other. Neither the preface nor the edition itself was reprinted during Yeats's lifetime. A photographic reprint of *The Works of William Blake* was published in 1973 by the AMS Press, New York.

Introduction to *Poems of William Blake*, ed. W. B. Yeats ([1893], rev. 1905)

Yeats edited and wrote an introduction and notes for *The Poems of William Blake* in the Muses' Library series, published by Lawrence and Bullen, London, and issued in New York by Charles Scribner's Sons, New York. The first mention of the edition is in an undated letter [? week of 9 Jan 1893] (*CL1* 344). The book was published probably in November 1893. A copy in the British Library is date-stamped 12 Jan 1894. The series editor was Arthur Henry Bullen (1857–1920). Yeats's personal copy of a large paper edition from Lawrence and Bullen, 1893, has three corrections to the introduction (p. xxii, l. 18: 'great cathedral may' changed to 'great Abbey may'; p. xxvi, in margin at l. 9 next to '51, Leicester Fields': '? Green St'; p. xlvii, l. 3: 'the Florentine and' changed to 'the Venetian and') (pp. 83, 85, 97 above).

Only the first two of those corrections were among the many changes Yeats adopted for the second edition, which was titled *Poems of William Blake*, published June 1905 by George Routledge and Sons, London, and issued in New York by E. P. Dutton. The second edition is the copy-text. The Muses' Library series had been transferred to George Routledge and Sons in 1904, and in 1910 that publisher issued the second edition in a new series, 'Books that marked Epochs', no. 2. The text of the 1910 issue was identical with the 1905 version except that the signature letters in the bottom margins were deleted; the title was *Mr. William Butler Yeats introduces the Poetical Works of William Blake, born in 1757, died in 1827*. In 1920 Boni and Liveright, New York, issued a completely reset version titled *Poems of William Blake*, in the Modern Library of the World's Best Books series. It introduced six typographical errors, but corrected seven from the 1905 edition and one (p. 92, l. 6 above), present both in the 1893 edition and in the 1905 edition. The Modern Library series, which in 1925 was transferred to Random House, New York, kept the book in print until about 1932. The Muses' Library second edition (1905) was reissued by Routledge in 1969 and 1979; the Harvard University Press was co-publisher for the 1969 reissue.

A brief paragraph of acknowledgements that followed the introduction, on a separate page, is given in Appendix 4 above. Yeats probably wrote all of the extensive notes, which supplement and explain the poems in the collection; none of the notes is to Yeats's introduction. The complete notes are given in Appendix 5 above. Corrected galley proofs of the notes to the 1893 edition are extant (NLI MS. 30, 289; SUNY-SB 23.10.4–25).

'Modern Irish Poetry' (1894; rev. 1899, *c.* 1903, 1908), repr. from *A Book of Irish Verse Selected from Modern Writers*, ed. W. B. Yeats (1895, rev. 1900)

Yeats first mentioned, in an undated letter written in July 1891, that he was to edit 'in all likelihood [*sic*] a book of Irish Poems' (*CL1* 256). Three years later, on 26 June 1894, he reported that his Irish anthology was 'nearly finished' (*CL1* 391); he dated the introduction 5 August 1894. Methuen and Company, London, published *A Book of Irish Verse Selected from Modern Writers with an Introduction and Notes by W. B. Yeats* in March 1895. One of his notes is to his introduction and thus has been placed with the present edition's notes to the introduction. All of his other notes are to poems in the anthology and are given in Appendix 7 above; I have excluded the one that Yeats quoted directly from James Clarence Mangan and three from Samuel Ferguson. As was also true for Yeats's earlier anthologies, he received assistance on some of the notes, perhaps from Douglas Hyde.

In 1899, for a revised edition that was published by Methuen in London in January 1900, Yeats added a short preface, rewrote the introduction (retitled 'Modern Irish Poetry'), slightly revised the acknowledgements, and changed the selection of poems by some contemporary poets. Briefly, in the introduction, titled 'Modern Irish Poetry', to the second edition, Yeats trimmed the discussion of Douglas Hyde, dropped T. W. Rolleston, added specific references for Katharine Tynan Hinkson, added Nora Hopper, added a brief mention of John Eglinton (pseudonym for William Kirkpatrick Magee), and dropped a quotation from a poem by AE that was added to the poems in the anthology itself. For a discussion of the revisions, see Phillip L. Marcus, *Yeats and the Beginning of the Irish Renaissance* (Ithaca, NY: Cornell University Press, 1970) pp. 221–2. In the preface, dated 15 August 1899, Yeats commented at some length on the revisions:

> I have not found it possible to revise this book as completely as I should have wished. I have corrected a bad mistake of a copyist, and added a few pages of new verses towards the end, and softened some phrases in the introduction which seemed a little petulant in form, and written in a few

more to describe writers who have appeared during the last four years, and that is about all.

That preface is given in Appendix 8 above. The portion of the 1895 introduction in which he had discussed the contemporary poets whose selections were changed for the second edition of the anthology is given as Appendix 6 above. An interestingly revised excerpt from the acknowledgements to the second edition is given as Appendix 9 above.

The 1900 edition reused, without change or correction, the 1895 plates for the poems on pp. 1–208 and 225–49 and for the notes, which are on pp. 250–7. An error was left uncorrected in each of the two opening works, excerpts from Oliver Goldsmith's 'The Deserted Village' (l. 3: 'later' rather than 'latest'; and last line: 'He' rather than 'His'). John P. Frayne has pointed out (*UPI* 38 n. 8) a serious error that was left uncorrected in Thomas Moore's 'The Light of Other Days' (l. 10: 'The cheerful homes now broken!' rather than 'The cheerful hearts now broken!'). Similarly, errors in the notes on pp. 255 and 257 were left uncorrected (p. 221, l. 18: 'executioners' rather than 'executioner'; p. 223, l. 2: "woman, is" rather than "woman', is"). Signature 'P' from the 1895 edition (pp. 209–24) was reset and a new signature 'P2', paginated 225A–32A, was inserted to accommodate the changes that Yeats made in the selection of contemporary poets. Those changes begin with addition of the missing last five stanzas of Katharine Tynan's 'The Children of Lir'; that had been the 'bad mistake of a copyist' – perhaps Yeats himself – mentioned in the new preface.

Methuen reissued the second edition, without changes, in September 1911, January 1912, and 1920, labelled as third, fourth, and fifth editions. These reissues ignored the important changes, to be described below, that Yeats made to the introduction for separate publication in 1904 and 1908. The only American production of *A Book of Modern Irish Verse* was a photographic reprint, of the 1900 Methuen edition, in 1978 by the AMS Press, New York.

Probably in 1903, Yeats revised the introduction, 'Modern Irish Poetry', for *Irish Literature* (III, vii–xv), published in 1904 in Philadelphia by John Morris. The associated editors of that ten-volume anthology included Douglas Hyde and Lady Gregory; its editor-in-chief was Justin McCarthy. Yeats made verbal changes throughout the essay and deleted the mentions of Charles Weekes and William Kirkpatrick Magee ('John Eglinton'). He added a paragraph on Frederic Herbert Trench, Dora Sigerson Shorter, and Agnes Nesta Shakespeare Higginson (Mrs Skrine, 'Moira O'Neill').

The final changes came in 1908, when 'Modern Irish Poetry' was included in Yeats's collected works, volume VIII, *Discoveries. Edmund Spenser. Poetry and Tradition; and Other Essays* (pp. 115–30). Yeats added a postscript dated April 1908, but the only other changes were minor. That 1908 version, published December 1908 by Bullen at Stratford-on-Avon, is the copy-text.

'Lionel Johnson' (1898, rev. 1900, 1908), 'AE' (1898, rev. 1900), 'Nora Hopper' (1898, rev. 1900) and 'Althea Gyles' (1900), in *A Treasury of Irish Poetry in the English Tongue*, ed. Stopford A. Brooke and T. W. Rolleston (1900)

These four essays were used as introductions to selections in the anthology *A Treasury of Irish Poetry in the English Tongue*, ed. Stopford A Brooke and T. W. Rolleston (London: Smith, Elder, Dec 1900) pp. 465–7 (Johnson), 485–7 ('AE'), 471–3 (Hopper) and 475 (Gyles). The first three essays were slightly revised and lengthened from their first publication in the Dublin *Daily Express* (as 'Mr. Lionel Johnson and certain Irish Poets', 27 Aug 1898; 'The Poetry of A. E.', 3 Sep 1898; and 'The Poems and Stories of Miss Nora Hopper', 24 Sep 1898). Those newspaper versions have been reprinted in *UP2* 115–18 (Johnson), 121–4 (AE), and 124–8 (Hopper). 'Althea Gyles' was written *c.* 1900, specifically for *A Treasury of Irish Poetry in the English Tongue* (Dec 1900), and has not been previously collected. Yeats's single, rapid draft of the paragraph on Gyles is extant in the Lady Gregory papers at the Berg Collection, New York Public Library (folder 64B5456). The American edition of *A Treasury of Irish Poetry in the English Tongue* (New York: Macmillan, Dec 1900) used the London text. A second edition of the anthology in March 1905 (New York: Macmillan; London: Smith, Elder) kept Yeats's text unchanged; a separate, short biographical note furnished by the editors, and not written by Yeats, was revised to include a reference to Johnson's death. The essays were unchanged in all reprintings of the second edition of *A Treasury of Irish Poetry in the English Tongue* (May 1905, Mar 1910, July 1915, 1923, and Feb 1932).

In April 1908 Yeats considered 'AE' and 'Lionel Johnson' for his collected works (WBY to Lady Gregory, 17 April 1908), but chose only the latter, which he revised for *Discoveries. Edmund Spenser. Poetry and Tradition; and Other Essays* (Bullen: Stratford-upon-Avon, Dec 1908) pp. 185–8. That is the copy-text. In the collected edition, 'Lionel Johnson' is mistakenly dated 1899 rather than 1898. Yeats did not include any of these essays in his later collections.

'Thoughts on Lady Gregory's Translations': Prefaces (1902 and 1903; rev. 1905, 1908, 1912), repr. from Lady Gregory, *Cuchulain of Muirthemne* (1902) and *Gods and Fighting Men* (1904)

Yeats compiled 'Thoughts on Lady Gregory's Translations' from his prefaces to Lady Gregory's *Cuchulain of Muirthemne* and *Gods and Fighting Men*. The first of those prefaces is dated March 1902 and was published in April 1902, together with an endnote titled 'Note by W. B. Yeats on the Conversation of Cuchulain and Emer', in Lady Gregory's *Cuchulain of Muirthemne: The Story of the Men of the Red Branch of Ulster* (London: John Murray) pp. vii–xvii and 351–3. Yeats's heavily revised manuscript draft of 'The Conversation of Cuchulain and Emer', signed but undated, is extant in the Lady Gregory papers at the Berg Collection, New York Public Library (folder 64B5976). The preface was set from a typescript (Berg, NYPL, folder 64B5972) on which Yeats made corrections and extensive revisions prior to a few further corrections made by Lady Gregory and then a few more by the publisher or printer. The last half of the endnote had been used, earlier in that same month, as an introduction to several extracts from the forthcoming book;

those extracts were published anonymously, under the title 'An Ancient Conversation', in the *All Ireland Review*, 3, no. 6 (12 Apr 1902) 87, col. a; the continuations on 19 and 26 April carried a subtitle, 'From Lady Gregory's forthcoming book' (pp. 103, 123–4). The preface and the endnote were left unrevised in frequent reprintings of *Cuchulain of Muirthemne* by the London publisher, John Murray, as late as April 1934, and by the New York publisher, Charles Scribner's Sons, who imported bound copies from England and issued them in October 1903.

The other portion of 'Thoughts on Lady Gregory's Translations' is Yeats's preface, written in 1903, to Lady Gregory's *Gods and Fighting Men: The Story of the Tuatha de Danaan and of the Fianna of Ireland*. His signed, undated manuscript draft is extant in the Lady Gregory papers at the Berg Collection (folder 64B5967). The galley proofs of that preface, date-stamped 20 October 1903, were corrected, prior to 26 October, by Yeats and probably Lady Gregory (Woodruff Library, Emory University, Atlanta, Special Collections PB 1421 / G7 / 1903, vol. i). In the page proofs the preface section is date-stamped 5 November 1903, when Yeats was at sea, *en route* to New York for a lecture tour. Lady Gregory corrected those page proofs and then must have given one set to the printer and mailed one set to Yeats in America, for on 9 March 1904 Yeats presented a set of these page proofs, corrected in Lady Gregory's hand, to John Quinn in New York, with the inscription 'I had this copy about with me for lecturing and have given it to Quinn the morning of sailing' (Berg, NYPL).

Gods and Fighting Men was published in London by John Murray in January 1904, with Yeats's preface on pp. ix–xxiv. The New York publisher, Charles Scribner's Sons, imported bound copies from England and issued them in March 1904. John Murray published, in December 1905, a slightly revised version, which over-corrected a mis-set comma (p. ix, l. 22), introduced two new typographical errors (p. xiii, l. 31: 'nigh-crested' rather than 'high-crested'; and l. 32: missing punctuation after 'Tenedos'), deleted two commas (p. xvi, ll. 31, 32), changed 'dishes' to 'fragments' (p. xx, l. 17), and shifted the pronoun 'one' to 'we' and 'our' (p. xxi, ll. 9–15) except for 'one goes one's' (l. 14). Those plates were reused without further correction in subsequent reprintings by John Murray in 1910, 1913, 1919 and 1926.

Yeats made some local revisions in each of the prefaces when he prepared them for his collected works, volume VIII, *Discoveries. Edmund Spenser. Poetry and Tradition; and Other Essays*, where they were published in December 1908 as 'Lady Gregory's "Cuchulain of Muirthemne"' (pp. 131–46) and 'Lady Gregory's "Gods and Fighting Men"' (pp. 147–69), respectively. Then, for his collection *The Cutting of an Agate*, published 13 November 1912 by Macmillan, New York, he deleted the opening two sections of his preface to Lady Gregory's *Cuchulain of Muirthemne*. He drafted those changes in pencil in his copies of *Cuchulain of Muirthemne* (London: Murray, 1907) and the 1904 first edition of *Gods and Fighting Men* (in the possession of Anne Yeats; see Edward O'Shea, *A Descriptive Catalog of W. B. Yeats's Library* [New York: Garland, 1985] pp. 110–12, nos 792 and 795). The 1912 version, in the Macmillan, New York, edition of *The Cutting of an Agate* (pp. 1–11, 12–35) is the last to be revised by Yeats, and thus is the copy-text.

Yeats dropped both prefaces completely in the London edition of *The*

Cutting of an Agate, published 8 April 1919 by Macmillan. Both prefaces remained excluded from collections of his essays and were not mentioned in the lists of proposed contents for Scribner's never-published 'Dublin' collected edition or the never-published Macmillan collected 'Edition de Luxe' / 'Coole Edition'. Both prefaces were subsequently reprinted in *Explorations* in 1962, with extensive copy-editing by Macmillan's editor, Thomas Mark, perhaps in consulation with Mrs Yeats. The *Explorations* version was mistakenly based on the John Murray, London, uncorrected first editions of 1902 (*Cuchulain of Muirthemne*) and 1904 (*Gods and Fighting Men*), except that a group of four pronouns (*Ex* 26, ll. 10, 14, 16) use the 1905 (and following) reading. Thomas Mark and perhaps Mrs Yeats presumably were not aware of the relatively extensive changes and deletions that Yeats had made for the 1908 and 1912 versions, and so mistakenly turned to the easily available editions of Lady Gregory's books. Because Yeats had made those changes for the 1912 edition in his personal copies of *Cuchulain of Muirthemne* (1907) and *Gods and Fighting Men* (1904), both of which are extant in his library, the posthumous copy-editing by Thomas Mark and perhaps Mrs Yeats lacks textual authority. The *Explorations* version of the prefaces was used for the volumes published by Colin Smythe in 1970 and by the Oxford University Press, New York; those volumes are *Cuchulain of Muirthemne: The Story of the Men of the Red Branch of Ulster* (Gerrards Cross, Bucks: Colin Smythe; New York: Oxford University Press, 1970) pp. 11–17 ('Preface': omits a question mark at p. 16, l. 32, and adds a signature at the end) and 264–6 ('Note . . . on the Conversation . . .': corrects typographical error [quotation marks] at p. 265, l. 21, and omits a comma at p. 266, l. 4), and *Gods and Fighting Men: The Story of the Tuathe de Danaan and of the Fianna of Ireland* (Gerrards Cross, Bucks: Colin Smythe, 1970; New York: Oxford University Press, 1971) pp. 11–20 ('Preface', dated 1904: adds double quotation marks at p. 13, ll. 39 and 41, capitalises 'And' at p. 16, l. 4, and deletes 'of mind' after 'habit' at p. 18, l. 27).

Preface to *The Love Songs of Connacht: Being the Fourth Chapter of the Songs of Connacht*, collected and tr. Douglas Hyde (1904)

This brief preface to the Dun Emer Press edition of *The Love Songs of Connacht: Being the Fourth Chapter of the Songs of Connacht*, collected and translated by Douglas Hyde, was published 4 July 1904; the colophon states that the book was finished on 16 April 1904. Yeats's pencilled first draft is extant in the Lady Gregory papers at the Berg Collection, New York Public Library (folder 64B5983).

Yeats did not revise or collect this preface. A facsimile of the book was published in 1972 by the Irish University Press.

Untitled preface to Lionel Johnson, 'Poetry and Patriotism', in *Poetry and Ireland: Essays by W. B. Yeats and Lionel Johnson* (1908)

This brief, untitled preface to Lionel Johnson's lecture 'Poetry and Patriotism' in the Cuala Press edition *Poetry and Ireland: Essays by W. B. Yeats*

and Lionel Johnson was published on 1 December 1908; the colophon states that
the book was finished on 8 October 1908.

Yeats did not revise or collect this preface. A facsimile of the book was
published in 1970 by the Irish University Press.

Preface to John M. Synge, *Deirdre of the Sorrows: A Play* (1910)

Yeats wrote this brief preface, dated April 1910, for the first publication of
John Synge's unfinished play *Deirdre of the Sorrows*. That Caula Press edition,
according to its colophon, was finished on 30 April and was published on 5
July 1910, but Ann Saddlemyer has cited a letter in which Elizabeth Yeats, of
the Cuala Press, told a subscriber that the 'first proofs were just being
corrected on 28 July 1910' (J. M. Synge, *Collected Works*, vol. IV: *Plays*, book II,
ed. Ann Saddlemyer [London: Oxford University Press, 1968] p. 367). The
Caula Press edition is the copy-text.

Also in 1910, John Quinn prepared a private American edition, *Deirdre of
the Sorrows: A Play*, which used the Cuala preface (pp. v–vi), unchanged
except for adding a comma, which I have adopted and have cited in the list of
authorities for emendations to the copy-text, and one, probably mistaken,
emendation ('this knife' changed to 'his knife' at the end of the fourth
sentence). Quinn was dissatisfied with the accuracy of the Cuala Press text of
the play, and so withheld his first edition, which had followed the Cuala Press
text of the play, and issued a second edition, probably using the gatherings
prepared for his earlier edition, but with the addition, at the end of the book,
of nine pages of corrections to the text of the play. Page proofs of Quinn's
edition, with no markings on the preface pages, are extant in the Berg
Collection, New York Public Library. Identical page proofs, also unmarked
on the preface pages, and date-stamped 27 October [1910], are in the
collection of the Harry Ransom Humanities Research Center, University of
Texas at Austin. The preface from the Cuala Press edition was reprinted in
1968 by Ann Saddlemyer as an appendix to her standard edition of the play,
in J. M. Synge, *Collected Works*, IV, 179–80. For detailed discussions of the
Quinn editions, see Saddlemyer (ed.), pp. 179n and 367, and Colin Smythe's
forthcoming revision of *A Bibliography of the Writings of W. B. Yeats*, by Allan
Wade.

Introduction to *Selections from the Writings of Lord Dunsany* (1912)

This introduction, dated 1912, to the Cuala Press edition *Selections from the
Writings of Lord Dunsany* was published in October 1912; the colophon states
that the book was finished on Lady Day, which in Irish usage here refers to
the Feast of the Assumption, 15 August. The holograph manuscript is extant
(NLI MS. 30, 272; SUNY-SB 21.2.66–75). The Cuala Press edition is the
copy-text.

Yeats did not revise or collect this introduction. A facsimile of the book was
published in 1971 by the Irish University Press.

Preface to Rabindranath Tagore, *The Post Office*, tr. Devabrata Mukerjea (1914)

Rabindranath Tagore's short play *The Post Office*, in an English translation by Devabrata Mukerjea, was first published, without Yeats's preface, in *Forum* (New York), 51 (Mar 1914) 455–71. Yeats's holograph manuscript of the preface is extant (NLI MS. 30, 292; SUNY-SB 23.1.56–7). The preface was first published in Rabindranath Tagore, *The Post Office* (London: Macmillan, Mar 1914) pp. v–vi. The timing of this edition departed from Yeats's usual practice, in that the Macmillan edition was published prior to the Cuala Press edition, Rabindranath Tagore, *The Post Office: A Play* (Dundrum, Co. Dublin: Cuala Press, finished on 24 June and published on 27 July 1914); preface sig. A4ᵛ. The Macmillan edition is the copy-text. The preface remained unchanged in the Cuala Press edition and in the frequent reprintings of the Macmillan edition, the first of which was in April 1917.

Untitled preface (1921) to J. M. Synge, *Shingu Gikyoku Zenshu* ('Collected Plays of Synge'), tr. Mineko Matsumura (1923)

The text of Yeats's holograph manuscript (NLI; SUNY-SB 3.10.175–6) of this preface was freely edited, especially in its punctuation, for publication in *Shingu Gikyoku Zenshu* ('Collected Plays of Synge'), tr. Mineko Matsumura (Tokyo: Shincho-Sha, 1923), preface unpaginated. From those emendations, which are in the printed copy-text but which were made presumably by a Japanese editor, I have accepted five commas, one semi-colon, two full points (where the manuscript shows sentence division by spacing and capitalisation), one sentence division (p. 145, l. 21), and the deletion of an erroneous 'and' (p. 145, l. 28); each of those items is listed below:

Page.Line	MS Reading
145.13	end I
145.18	yesterday I
145.21	living how
145.22	quality to
145.28	last play and his
145.30	dialect and
145.32	it He
146.1	England and
146.3	him but
146.5	pleasure W. B. Yeats

Yeats did not revise or collect this preface, so the Tokyo edition is the copy-text. In 1972 the preface was reprinted as a note to Shotaro Oshima's article 'Synge in Japan', in *Sunshine and the Moon's Delight: A Centenary Tribute to*

John Millington Synge, 1871–1909, ed. Suheil Bushrui (Gerrards Cross, Bucks: Colin Smythe; Beirut: American University of Beirut, 1972) pp. 262–3 n. 14.

Introduction to Oscar Wilde, *The Happy Prince and other Fairy Tales* (1923)

This introduction to *The Happy Prince and other Fairy Tales*, volume III of *The Complete Works of Oscar Wilde*, Patron's Edition de Luxe in twelve volumes, was first published in Garden City, NY, by Doubleday, Page in 1923 (pp. ix–xvi). Padraic Colum (1881–1972), John Drinkwater (1882–1937), Richard Le Gallienne (1866–1947), and Arthur Symons (1865–1945) contributed introductions to other volumes in the edition. Yeats's holograph manuscript of the opening one-third of the introduction is extant (NLI MS. 30, 489; SUNY-SB 22.6.102–3), as is a complete typescript, corrected by Yeats (NLI MS. 30, 158; SUNY-SB 12.1.90–5). In 1925 the edition was reissued as *The Writings of Oscar Wilde* in New York by Gabriel Wells after three errors in the introduction had been corrected, either by an editor or by Yeats. That is the copy-text. Those three corrections were the insertion of a missing question mark (p. 149, l. 33) and the correction of two spelling errors: 'calcedony' changed to 'chalcedony' (p. 150, l. 21) and 'Ernest' changed to 'Earnest' (p. 150, l. 36). The plates of this subscription edition of 575 numbered copies were reused in 1927 for the Connoisseur's Edition, published in New York by William H. Wise.

Yeats did not collect this introduction. It was reprinted in 1955 in a limited edition of *The Happy Prince*, published in New York by Kurt H. Volk (48 pages, not sighted).

Preface to John Butler Yeats, *Early Memories: Some Chapters of Autobiography* (1923)

W. B. Yeats first proposed this project to his father, John Butler Yeats, in a letter of 21 November 1912. According to William M. Murphy's detailed account, John Butler Yeats did not start writing until the beginning of 1917, when his daughter Elizabeth Corbet 'Lollie' Yeats had convinced him to allow the Cuala Press to publish his memoirs. He continued work on the two handwritten notebooks and an unknown amount of typescript in 1917, 1918, 1919 and perhaps beyond. At his death, on 3 February 1922, the unfinished autobiography was sent to Ireland, where presumably W. B. Yeats selected and edited the portion that was published by the Cuala Press. No manuscript of the printed version of the autobiography or of the preface is extant. On 5 June 1922 Yeats received the first proofs from the Cuala Press *Early Memories*, and, in a letter to John Quinn, described his father's memoirs as 'not quite all that he wrote but all that he finished' (*L* 684). For additional background see *L* 653; William M. Murphy, *Prodigal Father: The Life of John Butler Yeats (1839–1922)* (Ithaca, NY: Cornell University Press, 1978) pp. 472–3, 544 and 637 n. 63; and *J. B. Yeats Letters to his Son W. B. Yeats and Others: 1869–1922* (London: Faber, 1944) p. 263. Production of *Early Memories* was completed during the last week of July 1923, and the book was published in September 1923 by the Cuala Press, Dundrum, Co. Dublin. That is the copy-text. Yeats did not subsequently revise or collect the preface. The Irish University Press published a facsimile of the book in 1971.

Preface (1923, rev. 1924) to Oliver St John Gogarty, *An Offering of Swans and Other Poems* (1924)

This preface, dated 30 August 1923, for a collection of poems by Yeats's friend Oliver St John Gogarty, first appeared in Oliver St John Gogarty, *An Offering of Swans*, published by the Cuala Press, Dublin, in January 1924, sigs B2^r–B2^v; its colophon reports that the book was finished on 20 October 1923 and published in 1923. Two spelling errors were corrected and the punctuation was improved for the preface's next printing, which is the copy-text: Oliver St John Gogarty, *An Offering of Swans and Other Poems* (London: Eyre and Spottiswoode, Aug 1924) pp. 3–4. Yeats proably was responsible at least for the exclamation mark, which replaced a full point, at the close of the preface, although the other, more minor emendations could well have originated with the publisher. The second page of a two-page typescript with revisions in Yeats's hand is extant (NLI MS. 30, 299; SUNY-SB 21.2.107).

Preface (1924) to Jean Marie Matthias Philippe Auguste Count de Villiers de l'Isle-Adam, *Axel*, tr. H. P. R. Finberg (1925)

Yeats agreed, in May 1924, to write this preface for H. P. R. Finberg's then only half-completed translation (Finberg to Yeats, 30 May 1924, NLI; SUNY-SB 1.2.97). Yeats's undated holograph manuscript is extant (NLI MS. 30, 285; SUNY-SB 21.2.33–7).

The preface (dated 20 Sep 1924) to the drama *Axël*, by Jean Marie Matthias Philippe Auguste Count de Villiers de l'Isle-Adam, translated by H. P. R. Finberg and illustrated by T. Sturge Moore, was published in London by Jarrolds Publishers in May 1925, pp. 7–11; this is the copy text. The preface includes excerpts from Yeats's essay 'A Symbolical Drama in Paris', *The Bookman* (London), 6 (Apr 1894) 14–16.

Yeats did not subsequently revise or collect the 1924 preface. It was reprinted in 1970 in a translation of *Axël* by Marilyn Gaddis Rose (Dublin: Dolmen Press) pp. xiii–xv.

Introduction to Brian Merriman and Donagh Rua Macnamara, *The Midnight Court and The Adventures of a Luckless Fellow*, tr. Percy Arland Ussher (1926)

Yeats's undated holograph manuscript (NLI MS. 30, 373; SUNY-SB 21.7.77–99) of this introduction to Percy Arland Ussher's translation of 'The Midnight Court' by Brian Merriman is in a loose-leaf notebook with prose and working notes from *c.* 1925. The introduction was published in Brian Merriman and Denis Macnamara, *The Midnight Court and The Adventures of a Luckless Fellow*, tr. Percy Arland Ussher (London: Cape, Sep 1926) pp. 5–12. The American edition (New York: Boni and Liveright, 1926) used the English sheets.

The copy-text is the typescript (HRC, Scribner's Archive, box v) that Yeats submitted in 1937 for Scribner's 'Dublin' edition, volume xi. This typescript is an exact transcription of the published text of 1926 except for one probable typing error (TS. p. 1, last line, 'poems' rather than 'poem' [p. 159, l. 23]) and the replacement of the author's signature with a date. The typescript has two hand-written corrections, the first of which is definitely not in Yeats's hand ('be' changed to 'by' [TS. p. 3, l. 11] and 'her' changed to 'he' [TS. p. 7, l. 4]); its title-page is Yeats's holograph.

In 1939, shortly after Yeats's death, the introduction was typeset in Macmillan's never-published collected 'Edition de Luxe'/'Coole Edition', volume xi, which was to be titled *Essays and Introductions*. Mrs Yeats corrected that volume's extant page proofs (BL Add. MS.55895), which are date-stamped 19 July 1939, but the pages for this introduction (pp. 306–10) are part of a missing group of sixteen pages.

The introduction was reprinted in *Explorations*, published 23 July 1962, with numerous corrections that resemble those made throughout *Explorations* by the Macmillan editor Thomas Mark and perhaps by Mrs Yeats. Its emendations that go beyond the textual principles of this edition and thus have not been adopted are the addition of three lines of verse that Yeats had perhaps deliberately omitted from within a quoted passage (see p. 293, n. 11 above); spelling or word changes at p. 159, l. 31 ('blunts' rather than 'blunt'), p. 160, l. 4 ('fools, fops, and' rather than 'fops and fools and'), p. 161, l. 12 ('laws' rather than 'law'), p. 161, l. 15 ('investigate – "your lads' rather than 'investigate – "the lads') and p. 292 n. 2, l. 5 ('enquiry' rather than 'inquiry'); and the hyphenation of 'serving man' and 'folklore' at p. 292 n. 2, ll. 6–7.

Prefatory letter to the Medici Society, in William Blake, *Songs of Innocence*, illus. Jacynth Parsons (1927)

Yeats wrote this preface, which adopts an epistolary format, in September or October 1927. An undated holograph manuscript of all except the opening three sentences is extant (NLI; SUNY-SB 26.6.138–42). The preface describes events that took place on 29 August 1927. It was published in November 1927 by the Medici Society, London, in an edition of Blake's *Songs of Innocence*, illustrated by Jacynth Parsons. See p. 294, note 1 above for information on the circumstances leading to this preface. The preface was not subsequently revised or collected. The copy-text is the Medici Society edition.

'Introduction to *The Coinage of Saorstát Éireann*' (1928)

Yeats wrote this essay as chairman of the Committee Appointed to Advise the Government on Coinage Design. The corrected typescript (NLI MS. 30, 866) suggests that the printer was responsible for the spelling of names, for example, changing 'Evan Mestrovich' to 'Ivan Meštrović' and changing 'McAuley' to 'McCauley' [*sic*], an improvement but still a misspelling of 'MacCauley'. The new coinage was issued 12 December 1928. The essay was published in December 1928 or January 1929, in *Coinage of Saorstát Éireann 1928* (Dublin: Stationery Office) pp. 1–7, with the title 'What We Did or Tried to Do'. The other contents of the book were a foreword by Ernest Blythe, Minister of Finance; a list (written by Yeats, NLI MS. 30, 893) of the six members of the Committee; 'Irish Coinage – Past and Present' by J. J. McElligott, Secretary to the Department of Finance; 'Summary of the Proceedings of the Committee' by Leo T. MacCauley, Secretary to the Committee; 'Biographies of the Artists' by Dermod O'Brien, President of the Royal Hibernian Academy; and a postscript by Thomas Bodkin, Director of the National Gallery of Ireland. Illustrations were the Irish Free State coins, designs submitted by the artists, and photographs supplied to the artists. Appendixes contained the letter of instruction and conditions sent to the competing artists, comments by the Deputy Master of the Royal Mint, and the text of the Coinage Act of 1926.

The typescript (HRC, Scribner's Archive, box v) that Yeats submitted, probably in 1937, for the Scribner's 'Dublin' edition, volume xi, is a transcription of the published text of 1928. The typescript corresponds to the Stationery Office published text except for some typing errors, one instance of word-division at p. 170, l. 5 ('today' rather than 'to-day') and one instance of more precise diction, in describing the doors of Chartres Cathedral at p. 170, l. 24 ('doors' rather than 'door'). Yeats emended the title on the typescript by adding, in pen and ink, 'Introduction to The' in front of the typewritten 'Coinage of Saorstat Eireann'; one straightforward typing error of word-division was corrected in an unknown hand.

In 1939, shortly after Yeats's death, Mrs Yeats sent an unmarked carbon copy of that 1937 typescript to Macmillan, where it received some light copy-editing, presumably by Thomas Mark (Macmillan Archive, Basingstoke). The essay was typeset in Macmillan's never-published collected 'Edition de Luxe'/'Coole Edition', volume xi, which was to be titled *Essays and Introductions*. Mrs Yeats corrected those page proofs, which are date-stamped 19 July 1939 (BL Add. MS. 55895, pp. 349–56). My list of emendations mentions the instances where my emendations match those made in the Macmillan copy-editing and/or on the proofs. The few posthumous emendations that go beyond the textual principles of this edition and thus have not been adopted for this edition are the change of a comma after 'have' (p. 166, l. 9) to a semi-colon in the copy-editing and then to a colon in the proofs, expansion of 'St.' (p. 167, l. 11) to 'Saint', the erroneous addition of a hacek to the letter 'c' in 'Mestrovic' (p. 168, ll. 12 and 19), and the hyphenation of 'stamp paper' (pp. 169, l. 13).

The essay was reprinted in *SS* 161–7 (Appendix iii, and also in Brian

Cleeve (ed.), *W. B. Yeats and the Designing of Ireland's Coinage* by W. B. Yeats, J. J. McElligott, Leo T. McCauley [*sic*], Thomas Bodkin, Arthur E. J. Went and Brian Cleeve, New Yeats Papers, 3 (Dublin: Dolmen Press, 1972) pp. 9–20 (p. 10, l. 19: 'Patrick' rather than 'Brigid'); the Dolmen Press edition usefully incorporates illustations.

Preface (1929) to Oliver St John Gogarty, *Wild Apples* (1930)

The Cuala Press had printed a private edition (50 copies) of Oliver St John Gogarty's volume of poems *Wild Apples* in 1928, with an introduction by George Russell ('AE'). That introduction was also used in a 1929 edition of *Wild Apples* published in New York by Cape and Smith.

Yeats wrote his preface to *Wild Apples* in November 1929 (Gogarty to Yeats, 13 Nov 1929 [NLI: SUNY-SB 3.10.20]) for a second Cuala Press edition published in April 1930; the colophon states that the book was finished 22–8 February 1930. Yeats's holograph manuscript is extant (NLI; SUNY-SB 29.7.273–5).

He did not revise or collect the preface. The Cuala Press edition is the copy-text. A facsimile of the 1930 Cuala Press edition was published in 1971 by the Irish University Press.

'Anglo-Irish Ballads', by F. R. Higgins and W. B. Yeats, in *Broadsides: A Collection of Old and New Songs* (1935)

This introduction for the collection of monthly broadsides published during 1935 by the Cuala Press is signed by F. R. Higgins and Yeats. I have found no specific evidence about the extent to which Higgins contributed to the writing of the introduction. The prose style suggests that Yeats was sole author, but Higgins probably contributed, even if indirectly, much of the technical information about Irish music, such as the remarks about the 'gapped' scale. No manuscript is extant. All three preliminary typescripts have revisions in Yeats's hand, and the two pages of manuscript supplements to the earliest typescript are in Yeats's hand (NLI MS. 30, 804). The final typescript (NLI MS. 30, 279; SUNY-SB 21.3.183–91) has holograph corrections and revisions in at least two separate hands, one of which may be Yeats's. The signatures of Higgins and Yeats at the end of the typescript are in the same hand as some of the revisions on the typescript; it is definitely not Yeats's hand. The corrected final typescript corresponds exactly to the text published by the Cuala Press in December 1935, which is the copy-text. This introduction was not subsequently revised or collected. A facsimile reprint was issued by the Irish University Press in 1971.

Introduction (1935) to *Selections from the Poems of Dorothy Wellesley* (1936)

Yeats, after having met Dorothy Wellesley a few months earlier, suggested in

August 1935 that she select some of her poems for publication in book form. He began writing an introduction, of which a fragmentary first draft manuscript is extant in the Berg Collection, New York Public Library (folder 61B7697). On 8 September he sent her a full draft, which has been published in *Letters on Poetry from W. B. Yeats to Dorothy Wellesley* (London, New York, Toronto: Oxford University Press, 1940) pp. 25–9. The book was declined by Faber and Faber in October 1935, and was then published by Macmillan, London, in June 1936 as *Selections from the Poems of Dorothy Wellesley*. Yeats's introduction (pp. vii–xv), dated 1935, incorporated extensive local changes and a few additions to the draft version in his letter of 8 September 1935. Probably in the summer or autumn of 1937 Yeats had a typewritten copy of the introduction prepared for submission to Scribner's, New York, for the 'Dublin' edition of his works (HRC, Scribner's Archive, box v). He kept a carbon copy (NLI MS. 30, 151; SUNY-SB 12.5.224–230) and submitted the typescript, perhaps via his agent, A. P. Watt in London, to Scribner's in New York, probably in November or December 1937. The typescript, which is the copy-text for this edition, was not copy-edited by Scribner's, except for the pencilled notations at the top of the title page, 'Yeats Vol XI' and '14', and page numbering (399–405). The typescript version dropped a prefatory paragraph from the 1936 edition (p. vii); that paragraph is given in Appendix 13 above. Yeats presumably did not proof-read the typescript, since each of its four typing errors of single characters was left uncorrected in the typescript ('blook' rather than 'bloom', 'slid' rather than 'wild', 'thin' rather than 'think', and 'soman's' rather than 'woman's'), as was the probably unintended omission of the word 'the' (p. 184, l. 23; see list of emendations). Scribner's 'Dublin' edition was never published.

In 1939, shortly after Yeats's death, Mrs Yeats sent an unmarked carbon copy of that 1937 typescript to Macmillan, where it received some light copy-editing, presumably by Thomas Mark (Macmillan Archive, Basingstoke). My list of emendations mentions the instances where my emendations match those made in the Macmillan copy-editing. The three posthumous emendations that go beyond the textual principles of this edition and thus have not been adopted for this edition are the capitalisation of 'black country' (p. 183, l. 14), changing 'Nature' (p. 183, l. 36) to lower-case, and correction of the Coleridge quotation's 'Where' (p. 185, l. 11) to 'Whence' (see p. 306, note 15 above).

The introduction was typeset in Macmillan's never-published collected 'Edition de Luxe'/'Coole Edition', volume XI, which was to be titled *Essays and Introductions*. Mrs Yeats corrected that volume's extant page proofs (BL Add. MS. 55895), which are date-stamped 19 July 1939, but the pages for this introduction (pp. 312–16) are part of a missing group of sixteen pages.

Most of the 1936 edition of *Selections from the Poems of Dorothy Wellesley* was destroyed by fire during the Second World War. Yeats's introduction was reused in Dorothy Wellesley, *The Poets and Other Poems*, Penns in the Rocks series, no. 1 (Tunbridge Wells, Kent: Baldwin, 1943) pp. 3–6, with the old prefatory paragraph and with the addition of a headnote that explained the loss of the 1936 edition. All of this was titled 'Foreword', with a row of asterisks to separate the 1943 headnote from the 1936 materials. All of that material was reprinted, with some minor emendations, in Dorothy Wellesley (Duchess of Wellington), *Selected Poems* (London: Williams and Norgate, 1949) pp. vii–xi. The headnote, in its 1943 version, is given in Appendix 14 above.

———————

Introduction (1936) to Margot Ruddock, *The Lemon Tree* (1937)

The first section of this introduction had been published as 'Prefatory Notes on the Author', dated June 1936, with six short poems by Margot Ruddock, in the *London Mercury*, 34 (July 1936) 206–8 (prefatory notes), 208–10 (poems). The holograph manuscripts of that section are undated (NLI MS. 30, 388; SUNY-SB 1.11.110–12, 22.5.187–9). Later that year, Yeats made extensive local revisions and added the second section, dated December 1936. Two successive typescript versions of the new section, with holograph revisions, are extant (NLI MS. 30, 321; SUNY-SB 21.4.127–8, 125–6). The expanded version was published as the introduction to a collection of Ruddock's poems, *The Lemon Tree* (London: Dent, May 1937), pp. ix–xiv, which is the copy-text. The first section, as originally published in the *London Mercury*, was reprinted in 1975 in *UP2* 501–5 (verse fragments set in italic and with varying indentations).

———————

'Music and Poetry', by W. B. Yeats and Dorothy Wellesley, in *Broadsides: A Collection of New Irish and English Songs* (1937)

This introduction for the collection of monthly broadsides published during 1937 by the Cuala Press is signed by Yeats and Dorothy Wellesley, but was written solely by Yeats. In a letter to Dorothy Wellesley on 16 November 1936 he asked her,

> Will you sign the new introduction with me? . . . It need not be written for several months; it can be written by me and signed by both, written by you and signed by both, written by both and signed by both. We can get a hold of Turner and incorporate his musical learning and pretend it is our own. Please send me a wire to say if you will consent to sign (autograph) it with me. (*Letters on Poetry from W. B. Yeats to Dorothy Wellesley* [London: Oxford University Press, 1940] pp. 114–15)

Then on 20 November [1936] he wrote to ask again, 'Will you sign with me the preface to the new bound up Broadsides?' (*Letters on Poetry*, p. 116). The heavily revised holograph manuscript of the introduction is entirely in Yeats's hand (NLI MS. 30, 396; SUNY-SB 21.1.121–30 and 21.4.122–4), as are the corrections and revisions on the typescript that was used by the printer (NLI MS. 30, 792). In a letter written while staying at Dorothy Wellesley's house in Sussex, 15 July 1937, Yeats told Edmund Dulac, presumably referring to this introduction, 'My "manifesto" says some of the things you say in your notes' about music and poetry (*L* 893). After its publication by the Cuala Press in December 1937, this introduction was not revised or collected by Yeats. A facsimile reprint was issued by the Irish University Press in 1971.

APPENDIX 15   Letter from Yeats to In-sŏb Jung [Zŏng], 8 Sep 1936, published as front matter to *An Anthology of Modern Poems in Korea: (100 Poets and 100 Poems)*, ed. and tr. In[-]sob Zŏng (1948)

Yeats dictated this brief letter during a visit by In-sŏb Zŏng, a Korean teacher, translator and poet, on 8 September 1936 at Riversdale, Rathfarnham. Twelve years later, after the Second World War had ended, Professor Zŏng published the letter as front matter to *An Anthology of Modern Poems in Korea: (100 Poets and 100 Poems)*, ed. and tr. In[-]sob Zŏng (Seoul: Mun Hwa Dang, 15 Aug 1948) p. 3. Because there is no evidence that Yeats meant the letter to do more than help Professor Zŏng find a publisher, I have relegated the letter to an appendix.

COPY-TEXTS USED
FOR THIS EDITION

In the following summary, copy-texts for appendixes are listed after the corresponding main item. The copy-texts for Yeats's notes printed in the explanatory notes (pp. 229–316 above) are as specified for the main item or appendix to which they refer.

Fairy and Folk Tales of the Irish Peasantry, ed. W. B. Yeats, Camelot Classics series, no. 32 (London: Scott; New York: Whittaker; Toronto: W. J. Gage, Sep 1888) pp. ix–xviii (introduction); errata slip; 1–3, 47, 61, 80, 94, 108, 128–9, 146–9, 200, 214, 260 (headnotes); and xii n., xvi n., 319, 321–3 (notes to introduction and headnotes).

APPENDIX 1 *Fairy and Folk Tales of the Irish Peasantry*, ed. W. B. Yeats, Camelot Classics series, no. 32 (London: Scott; New York: Whittaker; Toronto: Gage, Sep 1888) notes on pp. 38, 131, 150, 160, 161, 168, 207, 213, 220–2, 295, 299, 309, 320–1, 323–6. (See textual introduction, pp. 318–19 above, for a list of exclusions.)

'William Carleton', in *Stories from Carleton*, ed. W. B. Yeats, Camelot Series, no. 43 (London: Scott, Aug 1889) pp. ix–xvii.

Representative Irish Tales, ed. W. B. Yeats, Knickerbocker Nuggets, no. 28, 2 vols (New York: Putnam's, Mar 1891), I, 1–17 ('Introduction'), 19–24 ('Maria Edgeworth'), 141–50 ('John and Michael Banim'), 191–6 ('William Carleton'); II, 1–3 ('Samuel Lover'), 91–2 ('William Maginn'), 129–30 ('T. Crofton Croker'), 161–4 ('Gerald Griffin'), 205–9 ('Charles Lever'), 243–5 ('Charles Kickham'), 281 ('Miss Rosa Mulholland').

APPENDIX 2 *Representative Irish Tales*, ed. W. B. Yeats, Knickerbocker Nuggets, no. 28, 2 vols (New York: Putnam's, Mar 1891) notes on I, 178, 190; II, 157–9 (endnote), 331 (bibliographical headnote). (See textual introduction, p. 320 above, for a list of exclusions.)

Irish Fairy Tales, ed. W. B. Yeats, illus. Jack B. Yeats, The Children's Library (London: Unwin, May 1892) pp. 1–7 ('Introduction', dated July 1891), 8–9 ('Note'), 223–33 ('Classification of Irish Fairies', dated June 1891), 234–6 ('Authorities on Irish Folklore').

APPENDIX 3 *Irish Fairy Tales*, ed. W. B. Yeats, illus. Jack B. Yeats, The Children's Library (London: Unwin, May 1892), notes on pp. 70, 115, 153, 190. (See textual introduction, p. 321 above, for a list of exclusions.)

'William Allingham 1824–1889', in *Charles Kingsley to James Thomson*, vol. v of *The Poets and the Poetry of the Century*, ed. Alfred H. Miles (London: Hutchinson, Oct 1892) pp. 209–12.

'Ellen O'Leary 1831–1889', in *Joanna Baillie to Mathilde Blind*, vol. vii of *The Poets and the Poetry of the Century*, ed. Alfred H. Miles (London: Hutchinson, Oct 1892) pp. 449–52.

Edwin John Ellis and W. B. Yeats, Preface to *The Works of William Blake: Poetic, Symbolic, and Critical*, ed. Ellis and Yeats (London: Quaritch, Feb 1893) i, vii-xiii and errata sheet pasted in facing p. xvi.

Introduction to *Poems of William Blake*, ed. W. B. Yeats, 2nd edn, The Muses' Library (London: Routledge, June 1905) pp. xi–xlix.

APPENDIX 4 Acknowledgements, in *Poems of William Blake*, ed. W. B. Yeats, 2nd edn, The Muses' Library (London: Routledge, June 1905) p. 1.

APPENDIX 5 *Poems of William Blake*, ed. W. B. Yeats, 2nd edn, The Muses' Library (London: Routledge, June 1905) notes on pp. 261–77.

'Modern Irish Poetry' (with a postscript dated Apr 1908), *Discoveries. Edmund Spenser. Poetry and Tradition; and Other Essays*, vol. viii of *The Collected Works in Verse and Prose of William Butler Yeats* (Stratford-on-Avon: Bullen, Dec 1908) pp. 115–30.

APPENDIX 6 *A Book of Irish Verse Selected from Modern Writers*, ed. W. B. Yeats, 1st edn (London: Methuen, Mar 1895) pp. xxiii–xxiv.

APPENDIX 7 *A Book of Irish Verse Selected from Modern Writers*, ed. W. B. Yeats, 1st edn (London: Methuen, Mar 1895) notes on pp. 250–7.

APPENDIX 8 Preface (dated 15 Aug 1899), in *A Book of Irish Verse Selected from Modern Writers*, ed. W. B. Yeats, 2nd edn (London: Methuen, Jan 1900) pp. xiii–xv.

APPENDIX 9 Excerpt from acknowledgements, in *A Book of Irish Verse Selected from Modern Writers*, ed. W. B. Yeats, 2nd edn (London: Methuen, Jan 1900) p. xxvii.

'Lionel Johnson', in *Discoveries. Edmund Spenser. Poetry and Tradition; and Other Essays*, vol. viii of *The Collected Works in Verse and Prose of William Butler Yeats* (Stratford-on-Avon: Bullen, Dec 1908) pp. 185–8.

'A. E.', in *A Treasury of Irish Poetry in the English Tongue*, ed. Stopford A. Brooke and T. W. Rolleston (London: Smith, Elder, Dec 1900) pp. 485–7.

'Nora Hopper', in *A Treasury of Irish Poetry in the English Tongue*, ed. Stopford A. Brooke and T. W. Rolleston (London: Smith, Elder, Dec 1900) pp. 471–3.

'Althea Gyles', in *A Treasury of Irish Poetry in the English Tongue*, ed. Stopford A. Brooke and T. W. Rolleston (London: Smith, Elder, Dec 1900), p. 475.

'Thoughts on Lady Gregory's Translations', in *The Cutting of an Agate* (New York: Macmillan, Nov 1912) pp. 1–35.

APPENDIX 10 'Lady Gregory's *Cuchulain of Muirthemne*', in *Discoveries. Edmund Spenser. Poetry and Tradition; and Other Essays*, vol. VIII of *The Collected Works in Verse and Prose of William Butler Yeats* (Stratford-on-Avon: Bullen, Dec 1908) pp. 133–6 (sections I and II).

APPENDIX 11 Endnote, titled 'Note by W. B. Yeats on the Conversation of Cuchulain and Emer (Page 23)', to p. 23 ('The Courting of Emer: Cuchulain's Riddles'), in Lady Gregory, *Cuchulain of Muirthemne: The Story of the Men of the Red Branch of Ulster* (London: Murray, Apr 1902) pp. 351–3.

Preface to *The Love Songs of Connacht: Being the Fourth Chapter of the Songs of Connacht*, collected and tr. Douglas Hyde LL.D., 'An Craoibhín Aoibhinn', President of the Gaelic League (Dundrum, Co. Dublin: Dun Emer Press, 4 July 1904) sig. [A2^r].

Untitled preface to Lionel Johnson, 'Poetry and Patriotism', in *Poetry and Ireland: Essays by W. B. Yeats and Lionel Johnson* (Dundrum, Co. Dublin: Cuala Press, 1 Dec 1908) pp. 19–20.

Preface to John M. Synge, *Deirdre of the Sorrows: A Play* (Dundrum, Co. Dublin: Cuala Press, 1910) sigs A3^r–A3^v.

Introduction to *Selections from the Writings of Lord Dunsany* (Dundrum, Co. Dublin: Cuala Press, Oct 1912), sigs B2^r–B6^r.

Preface to Rabindranath Tagore, *The Post Office*, tr. Devabrata Mukerjea (London: Macmillan, Mar 1914) pp. v–vi.

Untitled preface to *Shingu Gikyoku Zenshu* ('Collected Plays of Synge'), tr. Mineko Matsumura (Tokyo: Shincho-Sha, 1923), unpaginated.

Introduction to Oscar Wilde, *The Happy Prince and other Fairy Tales*, vol. III of *The Writings of Oscar Wilde*, 2nd edn (New York: Wells, 1925) pp. ix–xvi.

Preface to John Butler Yeats, *Early Memories: Some Chapters of Autobiography* (Dundrum, Co. Dublin: Cuala Press, Sep 1923) sigs A2^r–A3^r.

Preface to Oliver St John Gogarty, *An Offering of Swans and Other Poems* (London: Eyre and Spottiswoode, Aug 1924) pp. 3–4.

Preface (dated 20 Sep 1924) to Jean Marie Matthias Philippe Auguste Count de Villiers de l'Isle-Adam, *Axel*, tr. H. P. R. Finberg, illus. T. Sturge Moore (London: Jarrolds, May 1925) pp. 7–11.

'*Introduction to "The Midnight Court"*', TS with corrections probably not in Yeats's hand and a title-page in Yeats's hand [1937], submitted for Scribner's 'Dublin' edition, vol. xi (HRC, Scribner's Archive, box v).

Prefatory letter to the Medici Society, in William Blake, *Songs of Innocence*, illus. Jacynth Parsons (London: Medici Society, Nov 1927) pp. vii–viii.

'*Introduction to THE COINAGE OF SAORSTAT EIREANN*', TS with title revised in Yeats's hand and one correction in an unidentified hand but otherwise uncorrected [1937], submitted for Scribner's 'Dublin' edition, vol. xi (HRC, Scribner's Archive, box v).

APPENDIX 12   Section viii of 'What We Did or Tried to Do', in *Coinage of Saorstát Éireann 1928* (Dublin: Stationery Office, 1928 [or Jan 1929]) pp. 6–7.

Preface to Oliver St John Gogarty, *Wild Apples* (Dublin: Cuala Press, Apr 1930) sigs B2^r–B3^v.

Frederick Robert Higgins and W. B. Yeats, 'Anglo-Irish Ballads', in *Broadsides: A Collection of Old and New Songs* (Dublin: Cuala Press, Dec 1935) sigs [C1^r–C2^v].

'*Introduction to* Selections from the Poems of Dorothy Wellesley.' uncorrected TS. [1937], submitted for Scribner's 'Dublin' edition, vol. xi (HRC, Scribner's Archive, box v).

APPENDIX 13   Introduction (prefatory paragraph) to *Selections from the Poems of Dorothy Wellesley* (London: Macmillan, June 1936) p. vii.

APPENDIX 14   Anonymous headnote to the untitled introduction to Dorothy Wellesley, *The Poets and Other Poems*, Penns in the Rocks series, no. 1 (Tunbridge Wells, Kent: Baldwin, 1943) p. 3.

Introduction (dated June 1936, Dec 1936) to Margot Ruddock, *The Lemon Tree* (London: Dent, May 1937) pp. ix–xiv.

W. B. Yeats and Dorothy Wellesley, 'Music and Poetry', in *Broadsides: A Collection of New Irish and English Songs* (Dublin: Cuala Press, Dec 1937) sigs [C1^r–C1^v].

APPENDIX 15 Letter from Yeats to Mr Jung [Zŏng], 8 Sep 1936, in *An Anthology of Modern Poems in Korea: (100 Poets and 100 Poems)*, ed. and tr. In[-]sob Zŏng (Seoul: Mun Hwa Dang, 15 Aug 1948) p. 3 (with a reproduction of the typed letter) (Korean translation, p. 4).

EMENDATIONS TO
THE COPY-TEXTS

In addition to the abbreviations listed above on pp. xviii–xx, the following special abbreviations are used in the list of emendations printed following.

1891   *Representative Irish Tales*, ed. W. B. Yeats, 2 vols (New York: Putnam's, 1891)

1902   Preface to Lady Gregory, *Cuchulain Muirthemne: The Story of the Men of the Red Branch of Ulster* (London: Murray, 1902) pp. vii–xvii.

1904   Preface to Lady Gregory, *Gods and Fighting Men: The Story of the Tuatha de Danaan and of the Fianna of Ireland* (London: Murray, 1904) pp. ix–xxiv

1908   'Lady Gregory's *Cuchulain of Muirthemne*', in *Discoveries. Edmund Spenser. Poetry and Tradition; and Other Essays*, vol. VIII of *The Collected Works in Verse and Prose of William Butler Yeats* (Stratford-on-Avon: Bullen, Dec 1908) pp. 133–46.

1912   Introduction to *Selections from the Writings of Lord Dunsany* (Dundrum, Co. Dublin: Cuala Press, Oct 1912) sigs B2^r–B6^r

1920   *Poems of William Blake*, ed. W. B. Yeats, The Modern Library of the World's Best Books (New York: [Random House], 1920)

1923/4   Preface to Oliver St John Gogarty, *An Offering of Swans* (Dublin: Cuala Press, 1923 [Jan 1924]) sigs B2^r–B2^v

1926   Introduction to Brian Merriman, *The Midnight Court and The Adventures of a Luckless Fellow*, tr. Percy Arland Ussher (London: Cape, Sep 1926) pp. 5–12.

1928   'What We Did or Tried to Do', in *Coinage of Saorstát Éireann 1928* (Dublin: Stationery Office, 1928) pp. 1–7

1936   Introduction to *Selections from the Poems of Dorothy Wellesley* (London: Macmillan, 1936) pp. vii–xv.

1939c   Copy-edited TS. for Macmillan's never-published collected 'Edition de Luxe' / 'Coole Edition', vol. XI, Macmillan Archive, Basingstoke.

1939p   Corrected page proofs, date-stamped 19 July 1939, for Macmillan's never-published collected 'Edition de Luxe'/ 'Coole Edition', vol. XI, BL Add. MS. 55895.

Bentley   *William Blake's Writings*, ed. G. E. Bentley, Jr, 2 vols (Oxford: Clarendon Press, 1978)

Carleton (1843)	William Carleton, Introduction to *Traits and Stories of the Irish Peasantry*, new edn (Dublin: Curry, 1843).
Cuchulain	Lady Gregory, *Cuchulain of Muirthemne: The Story of the Men of the Red Branch of Ulster* (London: Murray, 1902)
Gods	Lady Gregory, *Gods and Fighting Men: The Story of the Tuatha de Danaan and of the Fianna of Ireland* (London: Murray, 1904)
Mercury	'Prefatory Notes on the Author' (dated June 1936), *The London Mercury*, 34 (July 1936) 206–8.

Page.Line	Copy-text Reading	Authority for Emendation

FAIRY AND FOLK TALES

5.4	Dierdre	Proper name
7.1	À'Kempis	Proper name
10.10	Fergusson's	Proper name
10.16	[Yeats printed this word in square brackets]	
10.17	[Yeats printed this phrase in square brackets]	
10.29	*Tuath De Danān*	Proper name; *FFT* 1, l. 10
10.30	[Yeats printed this phrase in square brackets]	
10.34	conscience – consistency	None
11.13	hoards	None (homophone)
12.13	milking	None
14.32	*Dallahan*	Proper name; correction on copy in Berg, NYPL, inscribed 21 July 1889
15.13	Shakespere's	Proper name
15.26	[Yeats printed this word in square brackets]	
16.4	[Yeats printed this headnote and the parenthetical Irish words in square brackets]	
18.8	fairies' love	None
18.12	[Yeats printed this word in square brackets]	
19.12	know [line division] ledge	Quoted text
20.33	[Yeats printed this headnote in square brackets]	
20.37	Oisen	Proper name; *FFT* 146, l. 17
21.13	M. De La Boullage Le Cong, who	Proper name
22.18	*Tuath-De-Danān*	Proper name; *FFT* 1, l. 9

WILLIAM CARLETON

24.19	Fryne	Carleton (1843) I, xi
24.23	Fryne	Carleton (1843) I, xi
26.20	Calderon	Proper name
26.38	Fardarougha	Title of work
27.18	Go-easy	Title of work

REPRESENTATIVE IRISH TALES

Page.Line	Copy-text reading	Authority for emendation
30.33	Barry	Title of work
31.40	school-master	None; [see p. 24, ll. 9, 18 above]
32.5	excepts "The Traits and Stories,"	Title of work
34.6	*Teer-nan-oge*	Proper name
34.25	McClutchy	Title of work
35.4	Nolans	Title of work
35.10	"The Mayor of Windgap"	As 1891, ɪ, 149, ll. 12–13 (p. 45, ll. 17–18 above)
35.12	said "the	None
35.24	Nolans	Title of work
36.19	Kavanagh	Title of work
36.27	Kavanagh	Title of work
36.27	Knocnagow	Title of work
37.23	seas	None; [compare the same phrase in another probable reference by Yeats to the four provinces of Ireland, in his 'Some Recent Books by Irish Writers', *The Boston Pilot*, 18 Apr 1891: 'the four sees of Ireland'; LNI 131 silently emended 'sees' to 'seas'.]
37.31	Hack	Place name
38.34	"A plea for the education of Women"	Not title of work
37.35	Parents	Title of work
37.37	"Frank and Rosamond,"	Two works, not one
39.32	Colambry	Character name
40.8	"Harry," "Lucy,"	One work, not two
40.9	Orlando	Title of work
40.19	De	Proper name
41.27	years'	None
41.36	Nolans	Title of work
43.21	Celts'	Title of work
43.22	*Teer-nan Oge*	Proper name
44.6	Nolan	Character name
44.7	Nolans	Title of work
44.15	essays, – "The	None
44.24	Crohors	Title of work
44.24	Nellhook	Title of work
44.28	Nolans	Title of work

Page.Line	Copy-text reading	Authority for emendation
45.3	*The*	Not part of title here
45.29	Nolans	Title of work
46.6	town land	None
46.30	Fryne	Character name
47.20	Calderon	Proper name
48.7	Ahadara	Title of work
48.8	Valatine McClutchy	Title of work
48.10	the "Young	None
48.16	Go Easy	Title of work
50.10	*Blackwood*	Title of periodical
50.16	*Blackwood*	Title of periodical
50.19	*Blackwood*	Title of periodical
50.37	well known	As 1891, ɪɪ, 1, l. 5; 2, l. 26; 205, l. 4 (p. 49, ll. 4, 35; p. 54, l. 4 above)
52.32	Holland Tide	Title of work
53.11	joined "The Christian Brothers," where	None
53.14	the "North Monastery," Cork,	None
53.16	Gessipus	Title of work
53.31	Gessipus	Title of work
55.21	*The*	Title of periodical
55.21	*Review*	Title of periodical
55.28	*The*	Title of periodical
55.32	Lefevre	Proper name
56.17	Mullenahone	Place name
56.25	Mullenahone	Place name
57.7	Mullenahone	Place name
57.16	Salley Kavanagh	Title of work
57.16	Knocnagow	Title of work
57.18	Salley Kavanagh	Title of work
57.25	Sheehan," and	None
57.26	Anner," will	None

IRISH FAIRY TALES

58.10	spinning-jinnies	None
60.36	Cuculain'	Title of work
61.15	fairy,') and	None
65.9	1st December	None
65.15	5th February	None
66.9	Curtins's	Proper name
66.12	*on*	Title of work
66.17	Griffen's	Proper name
66.28	*Review*	Title of periodical

Page.Line	Copy-text Reading	Authority for Emendation

WILLIAM ALLINGHAM

69.7	*Frazer*	Title of periodical
69.18	Whitby	Place name

ELLEN O'LEARY

71.16	Kavanagh	Title of work

THE WORKS OF WILLIAM BLAKE

77.4	Boehmen	Proper name
78.16	The prophets and apostles, priests and missionaries, prophets [end of l. 6/start of l. 7] and apostles	Errata sheet (possibly ambiguous): 'Preface, page xiii, line 6 and 7, *omit* "Prophets and Apostles."'
78.25	whenever	Errata sheet, though it wrongly gives the line no. as 10 (instead of 16)

POEMS OF WILLIAM BLAKE

80.18	Crab	Proper name
81.8	Wellings'	Gilchrist, *Life of Blake* (1880); WWB; see also p. 260 n. 10 above for text in Blake's poem: 'Willan's'
83.14	Wellings'	Gilchrist, *Life of Blake* (1880); WWB; see also p. 260 n. 10 above for text in Blake's poem: 'Willan's'
84.11	now' too,	*PWB* (1893), 1920
86.4	*Poetic*	Title of work
86.7	Matthew's	Proper name
86.10	*Green Man*	Text of poem
86.18	Thompson	Proper name
87.4	*The*	Title of work
87.8	Matthews	Proper name
87.20	"The	Title of work
87.33	do	None
87.34	The	Title of work
87.34	of	Title of work
88.28	"The	Title of work
88.38	"The	Title of work
88.40	but 'open	*PWB* (1893), 1920

Page.Line	Copy-text Reading	Authority for Emendation
89.18	"The	Title of work
89.19	"The	Title of work
89.32	Othoon	Title of lost work [Bentley, *Blake's Writings*, p. 1679]
90.33	The	Title of work
91.31	and the	*PWB* (1893)
92.6	judgment "passes	1920
92.28	Jerusalem; "all	None
93.27	thoughts	*PWB* (1893)
93.32	water colour	*PWB* (1893)
94.38	epigram	None
97.12	bring	None
97.32	Durer	Proper name
99.8	"Dante"	None
99.36	"My . . . mine."	Quotation within a quotation; copy-text mistakenly has double quotation marks for both sets
99.38	he	None
100.28	phrase, "made a bad book – we	None
100.31	Crab	Proper name
100.33	Othoon	Title of lost work [Bentley, *Blake's Writings*, p. 1679]
100.35	MS.	None

MODERN IRISH POETRY

108.27	'A.E.'	Pseudonym's usual style

LIONEL JOHNSON

111.22	'A.E.'	Pseudonym's usual style
112.18	XIII., it	None
112.35	1899.	This essay was first published in 1898

AE

113.1	'A.E.'	Pseudonym's usual style
113.16	'A.E.'	Pseudonym's usual style
113.25	'A.E.'	Pseudonym's usual style

NORA HOPPER

Page.Line	Copy-text Reading	Authority for Emendation
116.17	Trouveres	Proper name
117.13	Bahalaun	Title of work
117.15	Aonan-nan Righ	Title of work

THOUGHTS ON LADY GREGORY'S TRANSLATIONS

Page.Line	Copy-text Reading	Authority for Emendation
120.18	[No section division]	1902, 1908
121.4	Tir-nan-og	Proper name
121.6	nearness, cherished	1908
121.17	*Tir-nan-og*	Proper name
121.23	anything, that	1908
121.23	handle, to	1908
121.33	Mananan	Proper name
121.36	terror and	1902, 1908
122.18	[No section division]	1902, 1908
122.34	Conal	Proper name; *Cuchulain*, pp. 130–1, 349
123.11	bird, or	None
123.25	Conal	Proper name; *Cuchulain*, pp. 130–1, 349
123.32	[No section division]	1902, 1908
124.7	[No date]	1902, 1908
125.1	[No section division]	1904, 1908
126.24	[No section division]	1904, 1908
126.35	Mananan	1904
127.25	[No section division]	1904, 1908
128.7	[No section division]	1904, 1908
129.37	refuses. 'It. . . . man.'	1904, copy-text lacks enclosing quotation marks for quotations within quotation
130.7	[No section division]	1904, 1908
130.23	Country Under-Wave	*Gods*, pp. 104, 324, 337
131.7	[No section division]	1904, 1908
131.35	of	1904, 1908
132.25	[No section division]	1904, 1908
133.32	complained as	None
133.33	dying of	1904
133.38	'No . . . me.'	Copy-text lacks enclosing quotation marks for quotations within quotation
134.6	[No section division]	1904, 1908
134.17	Slieve-na-man	Proper name

Page.Line	Copy-text Reading	Authority for Emendation
134.20	Cuchulain of Muirthemne [title set in Roman and without quotation marks]	Title of work

SYNGE: DEIRDRE OF THE SORROWS

137.7	more always	None; [page proofs for a never-published revised version of John Quinn's 1910 private edition (HRC)]

SELECTIONS FROM THE WRITINGS OF LORD DUNSANY

139.21	of the 'Pretty	Title of work
140.30	AE.	Pseudonym's usual style
141.4	AE.	Pseudonym's usual style
141.14	Allen	Proper name
141.36	Allen	Proper name

COLLECTED PLAYS OF SYNGE

145.9	me, now	MS. (NLI; SUNY-SB 3.10.175)
145.9	Whaley	Proper name
145.12	middle ages	None
145.16	wind swept	None
145.16	plays, or	MS. (NLI; SUNY-SB 3.10.175)
145.17	courtladies	MS. (NLI; SUNY-SB 3.10.175)
145.18	attitude	MS. (NLI; SUNY-SB 3.10.175)
145.21	is in	MS. (NLI; SUNY-SB 3.10.176)
145.21	story, or	MS. (NLI; SUNY-SB 3.10.176)
145.23	Islands, or	MS. (NLI; SUNY-SB 3.10.176)
145.24	Sea' or	MS. (NLI; SUNY-SB 3.10.176)
145.26	anecdote which	MS. (NLI; SUNY-SB 3.10.176)

Page.Line	Copy-text Reading	Authority for Emendation
145.28	peasant-plays	MS. (NLI; SUNY-SB 3.10.176)
146.3	translations	MS. (NLI; SUNY-SB 3.10.176)

WILDE: THE HAPPY PRINCE

149.35	said 'Why	None
150.3	plain" "purple	None
150.37	rigourous	None

J. B. YEATS: EARLY MEMORIES

152.5	eighty second	None
152.5	hours	None
152.10	Foster 'Remember	None
152.15	last' he said 'I	None
152.30	vaccillation	None
153.6	known he	None
153.25	say 'Though	None

GOGARTY: AN OFFERING OF SWANS

154.18	successes	1923/4
155.13	[No date]	1923/4

MERRIMAN: THE MIDNIGHT COURT

159.1	*Introduction to "The Midnight Court"*	None
159.22	poems	MS. (NLI MS. 30,373; SUNY-SB 21.7.80), 1926; [*Ex*]
160.15	Spirits	MS. (NLI MS. 30,373; SUNY-SB 21.7.83); [*Ex*]
161.26	still. 'After	None
162.15	Cuchullain's	Proper name; [*Ex*]
162.20	daughter	Title of work
162.27	Eewell	1926, proper name; [*Ex*]
162.28	judgement	1926; [*Ex*]
162.35	the	Title of work
162.35	"Mid-night	Title of work
162.38	that Giolla	Proper name; [*Ex*]
163.2	MacConmara	1926; [*Ex*]

Page.Line	Copy-text Reading	Authority for Emendation

BLAKE: SONGS OF INNOCENCE

165.5	Blake – would	None

THE COINAGE OF SAORSTÁT ÉIREANN

166.1	*Introduction to The COINAGE OF SAORSTAT EIREANN*	None
167.32	inn	1926; [1939c, 1939p]
168.12	sculpton	1926; [1939p]
168.12	Mestrovic	Proper name, 1928
168.13	sculpton	1928; [1939c, 1939p]
168.14	thythmical	1928; [1939c, 1939p]
168.16	designed	1928; [1939c, 1939p]
168.19	Mestrovic	Proper name, 1928
168.20	sculpton	1928; [1939c, 1939p]
168.23	sculpton	1928; [1939c, 1939p]
169.16	it	1928; [1939c, 1939p]
171.8	pig's made	1928; [1939c, 1939p]

GOGARTY: WILD APPLES

173.7	Devorguilla's	Text of poem (1928 Cuala edition), proper name
173.11	affrontery	Text of poem
173.21	replied 'We	None
173.29	overhead 'Turn	None
174.8	end And	None

ANGLO-IRISH BALLADS

178.24	the	None
178.33	bright' 'Moore	None
178.34	'Moore' William	None
178.34	once 'is	None
180.2	Frederick	Proper name
181.3	hedge-schoolmasters	Yeats's usual spelling

SELECTIONS FROM DOROTHY WELLESLEY

182.2	*Introduction to* Selection from the Poems of Dorothy Wellesley.	None

Page.Line	Copy-text Reading	Authority for Emendation
182.18	spring	1936, text of poem in all editions; [1939c]
182.21	blook	1936, text of poem in all editions; [1939c]
182.22	sild". Three	1936, text of poem in all editions; [1939c]
182.25	thin	1936, text of poem in all editions; [1939c]
183.2	War-horse	1936, text of poem in all editions; [1939c]
184.4	*Sun* a	1936
184.23	there 'reiteration	1936; [1939c]
184.34	soman's	1936
185.4	'L'Aspirail'	Title of work; *V(A)* 128 *V(B)* 70; [1939c]

RUDDOCK: THE LEMON TREE

186.5	arrived. A	None
186.22	can do do upon	*London Mercury*
186.32	of the 'Player Queen'	MS. (NLI MS. 30,388; SUNY-SB 22.5.187): of The Player Queen
187.12	Bronte's	Proper name
187.23	'The Upanishads'	None
187.32	go' . . . 'Shape	*London Mercury*
188.1	me!' . . . . 'Good	*London Mercury*
189.19	though in in every	TS (NLI MS. 30,321; SUNY-SB 21.4.125)

APPENDIX 1

194.18	[Yeats printed this in square brackets]
195.3	[Yeats printed this in square brackets]
195.12	[Yeats printed this in square brackets and with no italics]
195.29	[Yeats printed this endnote in square brackets]
196.32	[GEAN-CANACH] None
197.11	*gean-canach's* None
197.31	[Yeats printed this in square brackets]
198.14	[Yeats printed this in square brackets]
198.15	[Yeats printed this in square brackets]
200.3	Carlton's Proper name

APPENDIX 3

202.3	Griffen	Proper name

Page.Line	Copy-text Reading	Authority for Emendation

APPENDIX 4

202.13	introduction: Mr.	*PWB* (1893)
202.14	from "The Island of the	Title of work

APPENDIX 5

204.14	*The Songs*	Title of work
204.19	narrative "The Island of the	Title of work
204.19	"The	Title of work
204.20	"The Cloud and	*PWB* (1893)
204.20	Love", "The Poison	Title of work
204.27.	"The Songs of Innocence" and "The Song of	Titles of works
204.28	"The	Title of work
204.28	and Experience, showing	Title of work
204.30	"motto	Title of work
204.30	Innocence and Experience	Title of work
206.10	"The	Title of section in *PWB* (1893), *PWB* and 1920
206.17	church, and	*PWB* (1893)
206.28	sooth	*PWB* (1893), Blake text Notebook, p. 113; Bentley, *Blake's Writings* p. 994
207.9	head. *A Cradle*	Title of work
207.10	"The	Title of work
207.10	to "A Cradle	Title of work
207.11	"The	Title of work
207.13	book. *Tirzah*	Title of work
207.16	"The	Title of work
207.17	"the	None
207.18	"The	Title of work
207.23	"The	Title of work
207.23	and Experience	Title of work
207.24	"The	Title of work
207.27	"The	Title of work
207.28	it have	*PWB* (1893)
207.33	or Miscellaneous	*PWB* (1893), 1920
207.36	discovered "Island of the	Title of work
208.21	combine, but	*PWB* (1893), 1920
208.35	from "The Island of the	Title of work
209.1	"The	Title of section in *PWB* (1893), *PWB* and 1920
213.13	*Nobodady*	Title of work
214.14	"the	None

Page.Line	Copy-text Reading	Authority for Emendation
214.16	"I . . . West"	Copy-text mistakenly uses double quotation marks both for this quotation within a quotation and for the larger quoted passage
214.33	Swedenborg [no full point]	*PWB* (1893), 1920
214.37	1795 There	*PWB* (1893), 1920
215.1	Blake, It	*PWB* (1893), 1920

APPENDIX 6

217.1	'A.E.'	Pseudonym's usual style

APPENDIX 7

221.18	executioners	None
221.25	*Entertainment*	Title of work
222.2	little	Text of poem
222.11	['your]	None
223.2	woman, is	None

APPENDIX 8

223.37	A.E.. with	Pseudonym's usual style None (for expected comma instead of extra full point)

APPENDIX 12

228.5	McCauley	Proper name

NOTES

233n35.1	Elephas	Proper name
233n35.3	Elephas	Proper name
236n53.3	"1711,	Quotation within a quotation
237n57.4	*Tir-na-hóige*; the	None
292n2.3	letters	Title of work
306n15.2	stanza	Title of work

INDEX